COBWEB EMPIRE
(Cobweb Bride Trilogy: Book Two)
Vera Nazarian

Cover Art Details:
"Mysteriarch" by Sir George Frampton, 1892; "Corinthe, a Seated Female Nude" by Jean-Leon Gerome (1824-1904); "Palazzo Labia Venice" by Antonietta Brandeis (1949-); "Main Street in Samarkand from the Top of the Citadel, Early Morning" by Vasily Vereshchagin, 1869-70; "Swinton Park Tree by Night" by Andy Beecroft (geograph.org.uk), January 14, 2007; "Tree silhouetted in radiation fog" by Andy Waddington (geograph.org.uk), November 22, 2005; "Star-Forming Region LH 95 in the Large Magellanic Cloud," Credit: NASA, ESA, and the Hubble Heritage Team (STScI/AURA)-ESA/Hubble Collaboration, Acknowledgment: D. Gouliermis (Max Planck Institute for Astronomy, Heidelberg).

Interior Illustration:
"Map of the Realm and the Domain," Copyright © 2013 by Vera Nazarian.

Cover Design Copyright © 2013 by Vera Nazarian

ISBN-13: 978-1-60762-122-5
ISBN-10: 1-60762-122-3

Trade Paperback Edition

September 25, 2013

A Publication of
Norilana Books
P. O. Box 209
Highgate Center, VT 05459-0209
www.norilana.com

Printed in the United States of America

Cobweb Empire

Cobweb Bride Trilogy: Book Two

Leda

an imprint of

Norilana Books

www.norilana.com

Acknowledgements

There are so many of you whose unwavering,
loving support made this book happen—
My gratitude is boundless, and I thank you
with all my heart.

First, my dear friends and fantastic first readers:
Anastasia Rudman, F.R.R. Mallory, and Susan Franzblau.

Indiegogo Acknowledgements

And all the generous and wonderful **Indiegogo backers**, you who are amazing friends, colleagues, supporters, readers, fans, and one-time strangers who are now friends:

Benefactor

Anonymous (two)
Anastasia Rudman
Brook and Julia West
Cheryl Martin
E. Hareth
Jean Mornard
Joseph Hoopman
Melanie Duncan
Nicole Platania
R-Laurraine Tutihasi
Susan Franzblau

Patron

Anonymous (two)
Bridget McKenna
Elyn Selu
EL Fox
Kris Marchu
Lisa Moore
Stephanie Piro

Supporter

Anonymous (two)
bdculp
Joan Marie Verba
Robert L. Slater

My deepest thanks to all for your support!

Map of the Realm and the Domain

For all those who have gone before . . .

Drink once, and forget everything you know,
Drink twice, remember everything you knew,
Drink for the third time and you die.

Cobweb
EMPIRE

Cobweb Bride Trilogy
Book Two

vera nazarian

Chapter 1

Before the night was over, everyone in the village of Oarclaven knew that Percy Ayren had killed her grandmother.

It was more than just the sin of murder that had them in an uproar. Rather, in a world suspended—a world where death had stopped and no one could die—it was a terrible *miracle*.

First, in the early evening twilight, the neighbors heard the sound of many horses approaching, the crunching snow, and the dull ringing of plate armor and chain mail. Metal parts scraped and clanged as a knight and his men-at-arms, followed by a freight cart, came to a halt before the decrepit Ayren house, of all places. Someone went up their porch—a poor excuse for one, just a few snow-dusted wooden planks raised up to create a step barrier and keep the weather out. The door opened and closed a few times. Next came a lengthy pause of about a quarter of an hour, while the nearest neighbors continued to stare through slits in shutters, overwhelmed with curiosity at such an unheard-of sight.

And then there was a sudden anguished female cry—no doubt Niobea, the Ayren wife was wailing—followed by more shouts and commotion. The men-at-arms waiting outside stirred, but no one made any move to enter. Not even the great knight himself—he who was clad in black armor and seated atop the largest soot-black warhorse the villagers had ever seen. He merely observed, his helmed head barely turned in the direction of the house with the poorly thatched roof.

At last the door flew open and out came Percy—yes, the neighbors were certain it was she, the middle daughter of the house, as the hearth-light from within revealed her face and stocky figure. Percy came tearing down the porch, followed by her mother, Niobea, clutching a woolen shawl and screaming after her. In their wake came Alann, her father, and the other two daughters, everyone speaking all at once, and the two girls starting to bawl outright.

"Get out! *Get out!* Begone from this house, you who are of the devil, and no daughter of mine!" Niobea screamed, between bouts of weeping, like a madwoman.

"Wait!" Alann interjected, his own face stricken. "Stop this instant, silence, goddamit, woman! Persephone, come back! You listen here—"

"Murderer!" ranted Niobea.

In that moment Percy stopped a few steps from the porch, breathing hard, and turned around to look at her mother. The girl was bareheaded in the cold, her poor coat unlaced, her feet hastily shod in the wraparound woolen shoes that had not even had a chance to dry off. And the gawking neighbors realized that she had just returned home from having gone to be a Cobweb Bride together with half the young women of the Kingdom and the Realm.

She had returned, but obviously, something terrible had happened.

"Daughter, wait!" Alann spoke, looking at her. "You don't have to go, not if I say so."

"I am sorry, father—mother," Percy said loudly, and none of her family or the neighbors had ever heard her speak this way. Her voice was strong and resonant and cold like the evening air, and it seemed to cut like a knife . . . until it broke momentarily as Percy choked on a sob. "I am so sorry. But it had to be done. Gran was suffering. I could not have her suffer any more. Not like that. . . . And neither could you—you *know* it is so!"

"Is that why you came back?" Patty, her youngest sister sniffled and wiped her nose and cheeks with the back of her hand. "To help Gran move on? How—how did you do it?"

At that point most of the neighbors started to come out of their houses, no longer concerned with the soldiers in the street, only with the possibility of a miracle. . . .

And the black knight, who had been watching silently up to that point, spoke in a soft but powerful baritone. "What has happened, girl? Has anyone harmed you in there?"

"Harmed her?" Niobea shrilled, holding on to the doorway and barely standing upright. She was a tall woman, ordinarily rather stiff and proud, and it was strange for anyone who knew her to see her thus, broken and shuddering, overwhelmed by a complex mixture of terror and grief. It had to be this onslaught of emotion that somehow made her forget herself and carry on like a shameless madwoman before a knight of the Realm. "She came back and brought *death* with her! She did—whatever ungodly witchcraft she did, to her poor ill grandmother—and it has *killed* her!"

"What?" the knight said, while a multitude of troubled voices swelled all around, in flutters of fear and breath curling with vapor on the icy wind. "How is that possible? Or do you mean to say she has dealt this grandmother of hers a mortal blow?"

"I will not ask who you are, My Lord, or what is happening that you come to be here," spoke up Alann Ayren—somewhat more in control of himself than Niobea, and thus cautious—and fully aware of the strange honor paid to his impoverished family and hovel by the presence and company of the grand knight. "But my mother lies *dead* in my house, right now. Not dying, not in that terrible halfway place between mortal illness and actual death, but *gone* entirely. Bethesia Ayren is dead and gone in the old way, the way it used to be before death stopped."

Waves of voices fluttered around them, growing louder, moving from house to house. Across the street Uncle Roald, their neighbor, thunderously cleared his throat and milled on his own porch, while his wife whispered and looked over his shoulder from their opened door.

"Percy?" said the knight. "Is this true?"

There were many stares then, as Alann, Niobea, the two other Ayren girls, and indeed the entire neighborhood, took in the unbelievable notion that the lofty knight not only *knew* of the existence of Percy Ayren, but he called her by her given name.

"Yes." Percy replied quietly in a steady voice, not looking at him, but continuing to stare at the doorway where her parents stood.

"But how? What happened?"

"I—don't know. I touched her and then—"

"And then you killed her!" Niobea cried.

"Enough, woman!" Alann exclaimed. "If you do not shut your mouth now, I will—"

"You will do what, husband? Your daughter has brought evil to this house! Your mother is *dead!*"

"Yes, and *blessed be!*" Alann looked at his wife. And his eyes—oh, his eyes were terrible and resigned and triumphant.

Niobea saw his expression, and her legs nearly buckled underneath her. She now held on to the doorway with both trembling hands, dropping the shawl from the crook of her arm to the flimsy old wooden planks that constituted their porch, covered with a fine layer of fresh snow. "What? You mean that you approve of this deviltry underneath your own roof, Alann Ayren?"

Alann took a deep breath of ice air. "Call it what you will," he said. "But my mother is at peace now, and suffers no longer. If that is deviltry, then so be it."

"What? At peace, you say?" Niobea took a deep breath also, and began loudly. "And how in blessed Heaven do you know that she's at peace? For all we know, she may now be condemned to eternal damnation, all because of our daughter's tainted hands, a girl who's been touched by death—"

"Why not have the priest come over and judge for himself if there is indeed ungodly taint here, woman!"

"And so he should! Blessed is your mother that she had at least received the Last Rites some days ago, else it would be unbearable for her poor soul, likely burning in the flames, and her poor body, to wait thus in the unholy darkness. You will go for Father Dibue, first thing in the morrow, while she lies thus with us, growing cold in the night—"

"And you think, wife, I don't know that—"

"Obviously you don't know what *your* daughter has done, else you would not be so calm about it—"

"She is *your* daughter too, as much as she is mine! She is our child, and this thing that happened is a miracle—"

They could have gone on in this manner for endless painful moments, but Percy herself interrupted. "I am leaving," she said, and everyone heard her, and again the street was plunged into silence. It was true dark now, and except for the faint lights coming from parted window shutters and doorways, there was no illumination. The moon had not risen yet, and no one along the street dared to bring out and light a torch. Their faces were plunged in deep shadow, silhouettes backlit by hearth fires. Eyes glittered. . . .

"Did you hear me, mother? No need to speak of me at all, I had only come back for a moment, not to stay, but to see you all, and to say goodbye. It is true, I hoped to stay overnight, but—I am going now. Going south, and not coming back again . . . at least not for a long time."

Alann turned to her, his face twisting with pain. "Child! What are you saying? Do not let your mother's muddled anger drive you away! This is your home, always! You know that! And whatever you did to Gran, it is for the best! Not an unholy thing, I say, but rather the opposite! She was indeed suffering, and she wanted, needed to pass on—"

"I know," Percy said gently. "But I have to go, Pa. There is something I must do." And then she looked at the knight and his men, and back at her parents. "It is getting late, and if it is all right with you, my father, I will sleep in the barn, for this night only. Don't worry, mother, I will not enter the house. But you must offer proper hospitality to this knight, the Lord Beltain Chidair—"

At the mention of the name, everyone erupted. Chidair was the surname of the enemy; the Dukedom of Chidair bordered on the Dukedom of Goraque, which was where Oarclaven was situated, and the two were chronically at war. And furthermore, only a few days ago—indeed, on the very day that death had stopped—they had just had a great skirmish, their forces meeting, battling it out on the frozen surface of Lake Merlait, the two Dukes and their armies, Ian Chidair and Vitalio Goraque. So, what was a high-ranking Chidair knight doing here in Goraque lands? Wasn't there a truce between them, at least for the duration of the unnatural cessation of death?

"No need. I will not impose on your hospitality," the knight spoke loudly, over the tumult. "I am here with no intent to harm, merely passing through this village, bound by common truce with your own Duke. And your daughter, Percy, is traveling with me. She is hereby under my protection."

"My Lord," Alann spoke, taking in this astounding information with an unreadable face, and barely inclining his head, while Niobea bowed her head more deeply. "Of course you are welcome to this house and my own bed. Forgive me, but we do not have much in the way of comfort that you might be accustomed to, nor regular visitors."

"Comfort is a luxury. We have our own supplies and will

make camp here. The barn looks to be adequate for our needs, considering we were planning to spend the night under the stars."

Niobea must have finally found reason. "Oh! My—My Lord," she began to stammer. "If I can serve you in any way—"

But from thereon the knight ignored the Ayrens, master and mistress both, and signaled his men-at-arms. They started dismounting, and there was much industry, and unpacking of items, while horses were led off the road and toward the back of the small Ayren property, and nearer to the roomy but somewhat drafty barn, occupied at present by the single Ayren horse.

Soon, the only thing remaining on the street in front of the house was a large cart. It was hitched to an oversized, pale draft horse, and there were several people, mostly girls, huddled inside. Percy made her way toward it, and, as her family stared in surprise, she spryly got up on the driver's seat and then with a sure hand untied the reins and lightly snapped them, accompanied with a "Whoa, Betsy!"

Next thing they knew, the cart and its occupants turned into the Ayren backyard, and Percy fearlessly guided the very large animal past their small picket fencing, and to the back, near the old elm tree.

Alann turned to Niobea, with a look of stunned loss as to what to do next. Niobea's face was no less befuddled. The good thing was, she seemed to have forgotten for the moment what unnatural thing her daughter Persephone had done. Forgotten that her mother-in-law was lying dead indoors; that there was no more rhythmic endless sound of a death rattle filling the house. . . .

"Ma?" the youngest Ayren daughter Patty said. "Should I heat up some water for tea? I dunno if we have enough tea for so many people, but I think we might need to use the really big kettle—"

Percy was cold. It was more than the normal chill of evening, but a cold that had come from her own *self*, had risen in the pit of her belly and seeped into her bones from the inside out, immobilizing her, and making her sluggish.

Even now she moved mechanically and did things as though she were not piloting her own body, but someone else—*someone else* was pulling Betsy's reins, and maneuvering the cart, and then coming to a full stop near the barn where the soldiers had already started to make camp.

Someone else got down from the driver's seat; someone else adjusted her listless hair falling around her bare forehead, where in moments sweat had turned to ice. . . . Where was that woolen shawl now?

Oh, it was back in the house. She had come in through the front door and had taken it off carefully and proudly, and handed it back to her mother. Then, she—no, someone else—went to her grandmother's bedside, and did something—

No!

Percy shuddered, coming "awake" inside her own head, slammed into the present reality, the hardness of the moment. And here she was, drained of all life, drained dry and made empty like a hollow cornhusk.

She took a big breath, and it all came back momentarily, full force—the fullness of power, the cathedral ringing in her mind. It was an overflowing sound of deep bells, and she had been *tolling on the inside* with the rich darkness, even long moments after it was all over—after she had touched death's *shadow* at the foot of her grandmother's bed, held their hands and pulled the two together—death and the old woman.

To do it, she had reached deep into herself where a tiny bit of death's heart was lodged like a splinter. It was she, and not someone else.

She did it.

Gran was dead.

She knew it. And she had named herself.

Death's Champion.

"Percy!"

Someone had spoken behind her. Percy recognized the voice of the only man in the cart, and turned around to look. Vlau Fiomarre, the young dark-haired Marquis, was asking her something, his voice barely raised above a whisper. He was dressed as a shabby servant, nondescript. His once-handsome face was bruised. And his eyes were dark as midnight and almost lifeless with many days of exhaustion.

Percy was immediately reminded of who was in the cart right beside him.

The dead girl.

Claere Liguon, the very Royal and very dead Infanta of the Realm, Grand Princess and daughter of the Emperor, sat on the other side of Vlau Fiomarre. She was like a neatly folded, weightless thing of snow, drained of all blood, brittle and delicate and frozen like spun sugar, covered with the poor disguise of a cheap woolen cloak once belonging to a palace servant. No one but her closest travel companions knew her identity, not even the ordinary ranking soldiers in the knight's retinue.

"Percy," repeated Vlau, his eyes glittering in the near dark. "Remember, it is as we had discussed earlier. You will not speak anything of her. We will downplay her presence as much as possible. Please, not a word to your family."

"Yes, I know."

And then he added. "What—what has happened in there? Is it but mistaken nonsense, or did you really somehow cause your grandmother to *pass on?*"

"I—" Percy began.

"*How* did you do it?" the Grand Princess herself uttered the question, in a laboring voice that was like soft mechanical bellows, whistling slightly, as the breath escaped her dead, frost-filled lungs.

They were all watching her, the other girls in the cart, Emilie, Marie, Niosta, Lizabette, breaths held, all staring.

But before another word was said, there was the sound of quick footsteps from the direction of the house, and another familiar intrusion saved Percy from having to explain the impossible.

"Percy, are you there?" Her eldest sister, Belle, had come hurrying from the front porch, past her stunned parents, stepping right into the deep snow. She was carrying their fine shawl, the one that Niobea had dropped.

Belle, lovely and thin, and shivering in her rough-spun housedress, stood at the side of the cart, ignoring everyone else there, and thrust the length of quality vintage wool into her sister's hands. "Take this, Percy. It is yours now, by all right. If mother wants you never to enter the house again, then it is yours."

"I can't take this, Belle! You know it's hers, and it's the best shawl we have."

But Belle made a small stifled sound, and simply deposited the shawl in her sister's arms, then turned around and quickly ran back, wading through a tall snowdrift at some point, and returned inside the house, having done her single act of rebellion.

Percy held the shawl awkwardly and watched her turn the corner, heard her parents' voices on the front porch, and Belle's single exclamation of protest. Then, the front door banged.

Percy Ayren felt the resounding slam of that door echo in her gut. She then turned back to the denizens of the cart. "The barn is somewhat drafty but warmer than the outside. We can bed down in the hay, next to all the horses—if there's any room left after the knight and his soldiers take over. I'm sure we'll have plenty of hot water for tea, though there's never anything cold-brewed, and not much hope for foodstuff from my Ma and

Pa. Supplies are low this time of year. Oh, and of course we can always sleep here in the cart. Indeed, we may very well have to."

And then she added, "Welcome to my home."

It had turned out as Percy predicted. After the Chidair men-at-arms made themselves at home in their backyard and barn, stabling the great war charger belonging to the knight and the rest of their horses close together, next to the solitary Ayren family mare in its stall, there wasn't much room left for any people in the barn, except for one small corner. The black knight, Lord Beltain Chidair had no intention of taking the spot for himself, but Riquar, his bearded second-in-command, insisted, seeing how his Lord was still somewhat weak from the prolonged military ordeal of the past week and a half, and needed a warm place to continue his healing.

And thus, after they had the backyard campfire going, and after they had all eaten the good bread and cheese, drunk the tea from the large water kettle that Belle and Patty carried outside from the house, a few blankets were laid out on the rushes and hay in the deepest corner of the barn. Percy moved some old pails out of the way to make room.

The knight was assisted by Riquar out of his heaviest plate armor, leaving on his hauberk and woolens underneath, and lay down without much protest. In the moments that she could glimpse his lean handsome face framed by the soft wisps of dark brown hair, Percy observed his excessive pallor, the light sheen of sweat on his brow, and knew that the day had taken its toll on him, despite his showing of strength all through the ride.

"Is there anything you require, maybe from within my father's house, such as additional blankets, My Lord?" she asked, standing above the knight while Riquar pulled at some loose ties of his woolens, adjusting them for his lord's comfort.

Beltain, leaning back against a blanket-covered pile of hay, barely looked up at her, and his gaze was unfocused at first, because for some reason it now required effort to keep his eyes open. But his words, however soft and weary, were precise. "What did you say? 'My Lord,' you said. . . . This is the first time I hear you address me properly. No more 'Sir Knight' or 'you.' What happened? Have you come to your senses?"

Percy felt a rush of fire in her cheeks, followed by a wash of cold. Good thing it was so dark, with only the campfire outside casting a warm glow through the opened door of the barn. Just enough to show his pallor and glittering eyes, while her own face was backlit in silhouette.

"I don't know," she replied plainly. "I suppose, it being my father's house, and you being here and not—out there in the strange forest—"

"Come, now. Something happened. Or rather—*you* did something. And it did something to *you* in turn. Whatever impossible thing you did with your grandmother to grant her death—it's related, is it not?" He spoke softly, looking up at her. And his slate-blue eyes, their liquid gaze now intent upon her, reflected the radiance of the campfire. "Who are you, *what* are you really, Percy? Or should I now call you 'Persephone,' as you call me 'My Lord?'"

"No need," she replied. "I am not really able to—speak of what has happened, nor do I understand it, but I can tell you I am mostly the same. Not entirely, but *mostly*. Call me what you will."

She looked at him, expectant, agitated and yet somehow frozen on the outside, forgetting to draw breath, and for once not avoiding his direct gaze. And his gaze was relentless upon her, in silence.

There was a long peculiar pause.

And then at last he took a deep weary breath of his own and said: "Why don't you bring the sick girl into the barn. What is her name, Emilie? There is room enough here for a few more bodies, next to me. . . ."

"That is kind of you, Sir Kni—My Lord."

He watched her steadily, and—it occurred to her—seeing only her dark silhouette against the glow outside.

"What of—the *other* girl?" Percy said, to avoid the continuation of the strained silence, but not daring to mention the Infanta outright.

"No," he said. "Leave her be where she is. . . . Less apparent, that way. Besides, she is rather well guarded."

Percy knew he was thinking of the Marquis Vlau Fiomarre, the man ever present at the Infanta's side. Indeed, why not? Let them both stay in the cart, and call less attention to themselves, instead of being singled out.

Percy nodded then drew away from him at last. She moved past Riquar who was still arranging pieces of armor, past the many horses—including Jack, the knight's great black warhorse, and Betsy—and slipped outside. She walked in her familiar backyard, made surreal by the presence of camped out soldiers. The once-pristine covering of white snow was now trampled by many feet of men and horses, churned and beaten down into brownish sludge that had frozen into the earth. A fire pit was dug among the snowdrifts where in the spring would have been a long vegetable patch and herb garden.

The remaining girls who had gone to be Cobweb Brides with her, and were now returning home, had found spots for themselves in the yard, to eat and drink tea. She noticed how they lost most of their caution of the knight's men-at-arms. Little dark-skinned foreigner Marie and street-smart urchin Niosta were both seated near the fire, their threadbare coats pulled tight about them, talking to an older soldier, and there was soft, subdued laughter, and not a few crude snorts from Niosta. Nearby, Lizabette Crowlé, with her somewhat superior big-town airs, was snapping open a burlap blanket, and biting her lip disdainfully in the direction of the giggling sounds. Emilie Bordon, a simple swineherd's daughter, still rather ill and occasionally coughing, sat deep in the cart with her feet pulled up, a steaming mug in one hand, and a blanket over her head.

However, at the sight of Percy, everyone seemed to glance at her momentarily. Or did she imagine it? The conversations certainly did not cease. But—had they started to look at her strangely, differently, after what had happened with Gran?

Percy tried not to think, and instead touched Emilie's shoulder gently, saying, "In the barn you go, it's warm there." She then helped the girl down from the cart, past the two remaining shapes of the marquis and the Infanta, lying perfectly still next to each other.

One dead, one guarding the dead, thought Percy.

After Emilie was situated in the barn near the already fast-asleep knight and a couple of his men, Percy emerged again, and stood momentarily. She lingered, looking at the scene before her, a scene of superimposed worlds—at these people who had become her strange travel companions, who were about to spend the night in her family's backyard next to their house, while her parents hid within, and the empty husk that was the body of her grandmother lay on her old bed, in the dark corner, where her death shadow had once stood like a sentinel. . . .

Percy did not know exactly when the tears started to pour— not until her face was streaked with the icy fingers of cold, and each wet streak was like a scratch of cruel claws of winter.

In the first light of dawn, Alann Ayren left to bring Father Dibue, as Niobea had insisted.

Percy, lying huddled in the cart, was awakened from dark abysmal sleep by the sound of their front door shutting, and the creaking porch, and her father's familiar footfalls crunching against the snow, then receding down the street.

It was strange to hear it from this vantage point, lying *outside* the house as opposed to within. Percy felt a moment of disorientation, of existential vertigo, forgetting where she was, and then it all came slamming into place.

She had killed Gran.

Percy's face was cold, the tip of her nose almost frozen, as the wool shawl had come unwrapped around her face in the night, making her skin numb. She stirred in the bluish morass of receding darkness that was the dawn, feeling someone's body on the other side—it was Marie, still asleep. And beyond her lay Niosta, a small lump under a blanket. A very fine snow had sprinkled them all with a delicate sheen of powder overnight.

Behind them, closer to the back of the cart, slept the Marquis Fiomarre, and furthest in the back lay *she* whom he guarded.

Lizabette had found a spot in the barn next to Emilie, with the knight and a few of his soldiers, all taking advantage of indoors warmth which Percy herself had given up for the sake of these "houseguests." And with the other Oarclaven girls gone— they had been dropped off at their respective homes earlier—this gave them all plenty of room to stretch, at least for this night in the cart.

Tomorrow might be a different matter.

But first, there was today to reckon with.

Percy quietly pulled back her blanket, dusting off the light sprinkles of snow, and added it on top of Marie's blanket. She then crawled out of the cart and went to take care of nature's business in their familiar outhouse.

By the time she was done, struggling with the extra layers of clothing, some of the soldiers were up also. And so were some of the neighbors, as could be heard from the voices along the street, and the more than usual number of passerby at this early hour.

Come to gawk at me, thought Percy. *Gawk at the misfortunate Ayrens and their accursed daughter, and the strange soldiers in their yard.*

She allowed herself a few moments of self-pity, and stared

dully as two of the men-at-arms set to making a breakfast fire, and one of them placed a well-aged and cured baton of smoked sausage to warm on a spit. Its pungent apple-wood smoke aroma soon wafted throughout the yard. And then, as more people came awake and came out of the barn, and the hungry horses started making noises, she pushed self-pity away, and got to work. The kettle needed fresh water, and then Belle and Patty came out, dressed in their headscarves, coats, and mittens for the outdoors, to help with some of the chores in the backyard camp. Percy observed her eldest sister's beautiful wretched face, and it looked like Belle had not had any sleep, judging by the dark sunken smudges under her eyes. Meanwhile, Patty looked no better.

"Where will you go?" Belle whispered, taking a moment when no one was paying them attention.

"I don't know. . . . Letheburg. Maybe farther south."

"But what will you do there? Why must you go so far? Can't you just stay here in Oarcalven, maybe stay at someone's house temporarily until mother comes around? What can you do, so far from home?"

Percy sighed. "I've some things to do, Belle. Gotta return a horse and this cart to someone in Letheburg. And—other things to do."

"But, *what* things? What crazy nonsense is this? And you have never even *been* to Letheburg! Are you really leaving home? You can't! I don't care what happened, and our father is right, Gran is at peace now! Whatever mother says now, you know she'll come around—"

"No." Percy said. And then added, "Is—Gran—"

"She is lying still, in her bed, as she was when you left. Her face is restful and her forehead is cold, I touched her just now. . . . She is gone, Percy. Completely gone. Mother is keeping vigil in a chair next to her bed. She insisted we all touch Gran, to make sure."

"I was scared," said Patty then, also moving in to whisper with them. "I am sorry, I didn't want to touch Gran, not like this. But Ma said to do it."

"I am so sorry." Percy softly watched her youngest sister.

"I know. But, don't be." Patty was looking into her older sister's eyes with intensity. "Are you really Death's Champion, Percy? Is that like being his Bride? Did he give you magic of sorts, death magic?"

"Don't say such ungodly things, Pat!" Belle began, but Percy interrupted gently.

"I think it may be something like that. I don't know how exactly, or what it is I did to let Gran go. But Death had assigned me a task that must be done. As a Champion does his Lord's bidding, so must I do *his*. But—please don't tell Ma or Pa, all right? It will only upset them more. Because, well, thing is—I can *see* death. I could always see it, for as long as I remember. Or at least, its shadows . . . when they stand next to people, next to the dying. Before, I could only see them, but now . . . now I can also *touch* them."

And as Patty and Belle stared at her in growing awe, Percy finished. "With Gran, I think, what I did was put her *shadow* inside her. I took hold of it, and it obeyed me, like a child. . . . It is not evil at all, just a part of being. It was like a sorrowful wild thing—a thing lost."

"Oh!" Patty gasped. "So then how—"

"Percy!"

They turned at the sound of a familiar childish voice, and there was Jenna Doneil, their neighbor from a few doors down, and Percy's fellow Cobweb Bride and traveling companion of the last few days. She waved at them frantically as she ran into the Ayren yard, her poorly shod feet sinking in snowdrifts with each step. Jenna was a skinny, fair-haired child of no more than twelve, and apparently she had run here from her home down the street, bare-headed in the dawn cold, and had barely managed to pull her old coat on.

"Jen? What is it?" said Percy. "Is something wrong? Are you all right?"

"Morning, Jen," said Belle. "Now, why are you not dressed properly, child? You'll catch your death of cold in this freezing air—"

And then Belle went silent, likely realizing what she just said, "catch your death."

But Jenna grabbed Percy's arm with both her cold little hands, without mittens, and she started pulling at her. "Percy! Oh, Percy, you gotta come with me, please! Come!"

"Where, Jen? What is it? Did something happen at home? Are your parents treating you well, since we returned?"

"No!" Jenna exclaimed, then amended. "I mean, no, they are fine, Ma and Pa both. I didn't think they would be, but they were happy I returned and wasn't any kind of Cobweb Bride or anything. But—but, you gotta come, please! It's awful, I could not sleep, it's still there in the back of the house, same as it was when we left!"

"What are you talking about, Jen?" said Patty. "What is?"

"The pig!"

"Holy Lord!" Belle exclaimed, and started to cross herself.

Percy frowned, growing very cold on the inside. A wave of memory came to her, that terrible evening when the Doneil livestock butchering turned into a nightmare, and the animal would not die. . . .

And Jenna resumed pulling her arm, and crying, "Please, Percy, you have to come and help it! I know you can! What you did yesterday, my parents say it's some kind of dark unholy magic, probably, but I know they're wrong! Everyone's talking, but I know you helped your Gran, and you can help the poor pig! I beg you, *please* come!"

"Oh Lord, no!" Belle whispered. "No, Percy, oh no, you shouldn't go—"

Jenna wailed, so that heads turned in their direction. "But she's gotta!"

"Stop it, Jen!" It was young Patty who spoke up angrily, then shoved the barely younger girl lightly with one arm. "Percy has better things to do, and you are just a stupid dunce-head—"

Jenna's thin little earnest face started to contort and then she was sobbing, loudly and thickly, snot gathering at her nose with each juddering gasp.

"That's enough now, all right, I'll come." Percy looked up, meaningfully nodding to her own sisters to move away. She then took the weeping girl by the shoulders, holding her then giving her a solid but gentle shake.

"It's all right, Jen. Here, wipe your nose, now. I'm coming with you."

Chapter 2

It took them five minutes to walk down the street to the Doneil house. Belle and Patty stayed behind, following their sister only with frightened looks that seemed to have become a permanent fixture with them.

Jenna hurried, moving almost at a run, ahead of Percy, and pulling her by the arm.

But at the door to their house, on their porch, she stopped.

"It's in there, in the back . . ." she said, shivering, clutching at her dress with her fingers. "But you have to be really quiet, please. . . . Pa and Ma are still asleep upstairs, and they don't know I went to get you."

She then opened the door slowly, and it was all dark inside. No hearth light, no tallow candle, nothing.

Percy felt a sickly pang of nausea in her gut, felt her insides twisting. But she took the first step forward and then the next, finding herself in the large barn-like area that the Doneils used on the first floor for their livestock. The family raised everything from goats, geese, and chickens, to cows. And they engaged in everything from selling eggs and milk to butchering.

Percy's footfalls made a slight crunch against the brittle hay and rushes strewn on the floor, and she inhaled a metallic unpleasant scent.

There was—she could hear now—a constant shuffling

noise in the back near the wall, and Percy was suddenly infinitely grateful there was no light.

She soon realized she did not need it.

She could see *through* the dark.

The small, squat, quadruped *death shadow* of the young pig stood cowering pitifully in the corner. While next to it, in the darkness, something lurched against the wall and bumped softly, quietly, to no end. . . . It was what was left of the animal's damaged body. . . .

Percy felt a terror, the scraping finger-claws of winter slash across her own innards, petrifying her into a moment of impossible ice and immobility. Vertigo came, and she felt a pull at the top of her forehead on both temples, a sudden prickling that raised every hair on her body. . . it was as though her conscious *self* was detached and floating high overhead near the wooden beams, just to get away, screaming to be far, far away from this, all of this—

She took in a sharp cutting breath, and then advanced forward, despite herself.

The world narrowed to a focus.

Percy Ayren reached the corner of the back wall, and leaned forward, while a now-familiar ringing gathered all about her, the darkness congealed, and the grand tolling of bells echoed in her mind, as the power rose inside her, like well water surging. With one hand she reached for the small *shadow*, feeling its tangible thickness and layers, and ran her fingers gently against an ethereal hide, calming it, loving it, stroking it. . . .

With the other hand, Percy reached for something that was better left undescribed, feeling clammy cold, a slippery horror of broken flesh and bone and slick bristling hide.

Metallic smell was everywhere, rising.

And then she pulled the *shadow* and guided it into the remains of the animal—feeling the two connect, touch, blend, for one brief instant only, as a circuit of energy was completed, and she was its third point, a conduit.

The pig shuddered, in infinite relief, and then its poor body expired, falling to the floor in a lump of permanent silence.

Percy stood over it, breathing fast as though she had just run some distance. And then she turned around, and went outside, into the growing daylight.

They returned to the Ayren house, with Jenna dancing every step and exclaiming in crazed joy, "Oh, it's free! Oh, thanks be to Dear God in Heaven! Oh, Percy, you did it, I knew you would, I just *knew* it!"

Percy walked in silence, looking straight ahead, her expression grave. As they passed neighbor houses, she noted with her peripheral vision how people stared at her, oh, how they stared! From her to the happy and hollering girl they looked. And in moments, many approached to ask Jenna what had happened.

"The pig is dead! It's finally dead! Oh, it's at peace at last! Percy helped the pig pass on! She did it! Just like she helped her Gran, she helped—"

"*Hush!* That's enough, quiet already!" Percy hissed, seeing how Jenna was telling the whole neighborhood things that could be taken all kinds of bad ways, dangerous ways.

"What has Percy Ayren done?" asked old Martha Poiron, in a quavering but very loud voice, standing at her door in her usual dark brown dress and grease-splattered apron, as they passed the Poiron house. "What have you done, Percy? What in Lord's name is going on? Will someone tell me what is going on?"

Percy reluctantly came to a stop. She could not just walk by old kind Martha without a response, without at least meeting her rheumy old eyes. She stood, gathering herself for speech, while her temples still carried an echo of grand bells.

But Jenna took Percy's hand and replied first, smiling with

pride. "Percy has helped the pig die! The one that couldn't die! It's at peace now!"

"What? You mean that sorry thing that Nick Doneil had trouble with and beat to a pulp?" The speaker was Jack Rosten, a large muscular man with a scraggly wheat-colored beard, on his way to the workshop.

Jenna turned to see him there, and immediately her smile fled and she herself shrank away. Jack Rosten and her Pa had a horrid deal between them that Rosten's second son Jules was going to marry her in exchange for some livestock, as soon as spring came. Jack Rosten was hard and mean, and his sons were even worse.

"Let's go, Jenna," said Percy in reply. She then grabbed Jenna's arm and pulled her after her, saying, "Morning, Mistress Martha, it's nothing, really. . . ."

"Hold it, girl!" Jack Rosten called behind her. "That's not nothing! Hold up, I say! Did I hear that right, you did something to make the pig *die?*"

"Forget the pig! Didn't you hear? Last night, she killed her own grandmother!" This time the speaker was Rosaide Vellerin, another neighbor, and the biggest gossip in Oarclaven.

Just their rotten luck, thought Percy. Rosaide, standing with her arms folded in satisfaction, in her own front yard next to Martha's small place, also happened to have a longtime feud with Percy's mother. And she really took pleasure in putting down the Ayrens whenever possible—which was, to be honest, not that common, since the impoverished family had a reputation for decency.

Percy walked rapidly, dragging Jenna behind her, hearing Rosaide yell in her wake. "Have you no shame, Persephone Ayren?"

When they made it to the Ayren house, there was Alann Ayren, together with Father Dibue and Niobea, talking quietly on the porch, and the soldiers moving around in the backyard among the smell of wood smoke and roasting sausage.

"There she is!" said Niobea. Her face was hard and pale in the light of morning, and she looked exhausted and sleepless.

"Where have you been, Persephone, child?" Alann said, far more gently.

Father Dibue, the village priest, was a large, ruddy-faced man with straw-colored hair, a jutting chin and coarse features. The hood of his coat was as usual worn over many layers of closely wrapped grey shawls against the cold, on top of the woolen habit, since he was always on the go, and spent so much time outside, walking from house to house all day long.

"Good morning, my child," said the priest, looking at Percy, and his expression was wary but his eyes not unkind.

"Good morning, Father," said Percy, stopping before them, since she had been addressed. "And, Pa . . . and Ma."

"Your Grandmother has indeed passed on. May the Lord have Mercy on her soul, and may she rest in His Bosom and in all Heaven's Light," said Father Dibue with a tired sigh, deciding not to beat around the bush. "And I am told that somehow you had something to do with it."

"Yes," Percy said simply.

The neighbors were watching them. And the soldiers in the yard had come around to stare, some still holding chunks of bread and sausage and mugs of tea.

"Would you kindly explain to me what exactly you *did*, Persephone?" Father Dibue continued. "I realize you've been to Death's Keep, and something happened there. What does it mean exactly, now, that you're Death's Champion? Don't be afraid to speak the truth, girl."

"I am not entirely sure, Father, but it means, I think, I can help the dead pass on."

"But how? I do want to understand you better, you can imagine how unusual, how unnatural this whole thing is—I of course must make certain it is God's Hand at work here, and not the *other*—"

Percy felt her head filling with remote cold, and a wave of now familiar darkness. And then, just as quickly it receded, and she blinked.

"Well, speak up, daughter!" Niobea said loudly. "The Holy Father asked you a question, and you must answer him now!"

"I am sorry, but I don't know how to answer. I don't know what it is," Percy said softly. "I only know that it feels like the right thing to do. I see death's shadows near the dead. I bring the two together, that is all. If that is indeed God's Will—that the dying be granted peace in one way or another, even if Death Himself has stopped and cannot do his work here on earth, and if I have been given this ability, then—then I do not see how it could be wrong."

"Now, you do realize how presumptuous that sounds, child?" said Father Dibue, after a long pause. "It is presumptuous indeed for a mere child of your age to presume to know what is God's Will at any given moment. While I do understand our present difficulty—that the world is placed in very strange circumstances right now—but given such a thing, it is especially important that we carefully examine this from the proper angle of faith and righteousness—"

"There is nothing more to examine, Holy Father," came a powerful baritone from the back. It was the black knight, standing fully dressed except for his heaviest armor plate, holding a steaming mug in one hand. His head was bare and the top of his wavy brown hair shone in a soft nimbus, full of golden highlights in the morning sun. The overnight rest had done him some good, for, except for a new shadow of stubble, his face was smooth and composed, without the strain of weariness of the previous day.

"The girl tells us she has been given this ability to ease the dead," Lord Beltain went on, "and I see nothing wrong with it, considering what else is going on in the world around us."

Father Dibue bowed his head respectfully. "True enough, it is not as if the girl is going around randomly murdering anyone." And then he glanced momentarily with new alarm at Percy. "You cannot do that, can you, my child? That is, you cannot simply kill a healthy person from a distance?"

Percy frowned. She was at a complete loss as to how to respond.

"I would think," the black knight again spoke in her stead, "that being Death's Champion is an honorable circumstance, and murder is not a part of her gift."

"Percy is a good child," said her father suddenly. "She means no harm to anyone, I can promise you." And speaking thus, Alann worriedly looked back and forth from the priest to his wife to the knight. So far, the discussion had not taken a dangerous turn, but he had a bad feeling about it, considering that a minor crowd was once more beginning to gather around them, as more and more neighbors and other villagers congregated on the street. Various murmurs were heard, and Rosaide Vellerin and her big mouth were recognizable more than once above the voices of others, together with the utterances such as "shameless hussy" and "witch" and "unholy doings."

Father Dibue decided to make a quick conciliatory decision on the matter, since, to be honest, he was generally overwhelmed by the events of the past week. The priest was infinitely weary, even more generally confused, secretly frightened, and had no desire to incite a mob. All things considered, what Persephone Ayren had done was no more terrible and no more unnatural than what was the present alternative for the suffering dead.

"And so I see," said the good Father wisely. "Furthermore, I have examined the late Bethesia Ayren's mortal remains, especially her countenance, and she appears to be as godly and peaceful as possible under the circumstances. This tells me that her soul is with the Lord, and since I myself had administered the Last Rites earlier, all is as it should be. It is therefore safe to rule out any influence of witchcraft, or any other unholy means in this case—"

"But what about the pig?" Someone on the street yelled out.

"What—What's this?" the priest asked.

"She made the Doneil pig pass on, just now!"

Father Doneil's brows rose, and he looked back at Percy with newly rising concern. "Is this true?"

"Percy only helped the pig!" exclaimed Jenna Doneil, at Percy's side, meanwhile clutching at the front of her own coat and dress, as was her fretful habit. "And she didn't just do it on her own, I asked her to do it, Father!"

Percy nodded silently.

The priest exhaled in some relief, recalling the horror of that incident. "Then, it is all the same," he said. "If I remember right, that was a terrible thing that had happened. So, it is indeed God's Will that the creature is now at rest. And now, enough, I declare, I am quite satisfied that all is well here." He nervously handled the rosary in his fingers, and pulled out his mittens from a voluminous pocket. "Master Ayren, Mistress Niobea, have you all the burial arrangements in hand? Yes? Good. Let me know when you expect the funeral, and I will perform the mass. . . . Now I think we have all seen enough here, and I will be on my way—"

"Thank you, Father," said Alann Ayren, handing the priest his payment in a small pouch.

The priest took it matter-of-factly then picked up his large bag from the porch. "Wonderful! And so, I wish you all a good and blessed day, Master, Mistress, and you, of course, My Lord—"

As he came down the porch, nodding to everyone, and then walked past Percy, Father Dibue briefly placed his large meaty hand on her forehead, and gave her a loud blessing. "Fare thee well, my child, Persephone Ayren, never falter from the path of righteousness, and always do the Lord's bidding, now!"

Percy gratefully looked up in his faded watery eyes, and saw a benevolent expression there. At the same time, since the priest continued onward and down the street, the neighbors started to disperse, seeing that nothing more was going to come about.

"I think it is time we were on our way," said the black knight to Percy, without looking at her parents.

"Yes," she said. "But first, I need a bite to eat. . . ."

"You may come inside, daughter," said Niobea from the porch.

Percy looked up, meeting her mother's eyes, and saw a reluctant acceptance there. The priest had examined things, and made his decision, and apparently it was no more than Niobea could do.

"Thank you, Ma. But it's all right, I will eat in the yard."

"You—" Niobea paused, gathering herself, it seemed. "You do not have to go."

Percy stood facing her mother. "Actually, I do . . ." she replied softly. And then Percy turned away, and followed the knight into their backyard.

Niobea could only watch in silence.

They were back on the road within the hour. Percy was done eating in a hurry, stuffing her face with chunks of bread and cheese and tea, while the soldiers were packing up and readying the horses. After another tearful farewell from Jenna Doneil, hanging onto Percy's neck, and tight hugs from her sisters, Percy had Betsy once again hitched to the cart, and all the girls back in their seats, next to the Infanta and the marquis.

Betsy and the cart pulled out slowly from the Ayren yard, wheels and hooves crunching on the fresh overnight dusting of snow, flanked by Chidair soldiers, and the tall imposing knight, fully armored, and seated on his great warhorse. They turned onto the street, heading south, with Alann and Niobea and Belle and Patty watching from the porch with grave faces, and the rest of the neighbors not trying particularly hard not to stare.

They look, and yet they do not even know what it is they see, thought Percy, glancing sometimes behind her, and seeing the Infanta huddled in her poor cloak.

The familiar parts of Oarclaven were soon behind them, as the rutted road wound outside the village, and was soon framed by hedgerows on both sides, and beyond, snow-covered fields. A dark speck of a bird or two circled the sky.

Overhead, the winter morning sun shone brightly for once, and there was as yet no overcast.

The knight did not approach the cart, nor did he look back at any of them for more than a brief glance, but rode up ahead with Riquar and a few others. In general, there was silence among the men-at-arms.

After about an hour of traveling, as they were passing a few poor farm houses just off the road, Emilie stirred in her blanket and told them she was home.

"There it is." She pointed at a small thatched-roof building among a couple of others, none of them enough to comprise a settlement that was large enough to be called a village, and all of them partially buried in snow, with only one cleared path leading off the main thoroughfare.

Percy tightened Betsy's reins, and the draft horse came to a graceful stop, snorting loudly. The knight and his soldiers slowed down also, watching casually as Emilie clambered down from the cart, holding her small travel sack and blanket, and then said her farewells to everyone.

"Get well, my friend Emilie Bordon, please!" Marie spoke warmly, in her heavy accent, waving to her.

"Yeah, don't wanna hear you dropped dead, and then woke up again an undead scarecrow," said Niosta, chortling. Then, realizing what she was saying, she put her hand around her mouth in some chagrin, and glanced in the Infanta's direction.

"Thank you for everything, Percy," Emilie concluded, wiping the side of her reddened nose. "Sorry I was sick so much of the time . . . and no good to anyone. Just a dumb bedwarmer."

"Don't be a ninny-fool," said Percy. "Not your fault you got sick. And you were more useful than you can imagine, even as a bedwarmer! Can't have too many warm bodies when sleeping in the cold. Besides, you were there for all of us, the best you could. And you got lucky too, not being a Cobweb Bride."

Emilie grinned, then immediately sneezed.

"Eeow! Now, off to your own warm bed with you and your snots!" Percy said gruffly. "Hurry! And I promise, I'll see you when I come around back this way."

"You better!" Emilie smiled again, then waved one more time, and started running slowly, as well as she could, up the cleared path, nearly stumbling in the icy spots underneath the snow. They watched for a few seconds, making sure that she got inside safely, and the door of her home closed behind her.

"At last," said Lizabette, with a brief ingratiating glance in the direction of the Infanta. "More room in the cart for *our betters*, and of course now that poor creature can get some proper help for that nasty sneezing illness, in her own home."

"Whoa, Betsy," said Percy, taking up the reins, and ignoring the comment. They were moving again.

After a few moments of silence, the Infanta, Claere Liguon inhaled a deep breath of crisp air in her mechanical doll lungs, and she spoke suddenly. "I have decided," she said in a soft voice, and at first to no one in particular.

Everyone in the cart turned to look at her. And the black knight, riding a few paces ahead, gave away the fact that he was apparently paying very close attention to everything indeed, and heard every word, by turning around immediately to look.

"What is it?" Vlau Fiomarre was staring closely at her.

But Claere ignored him, and turned her head directly to

address the one driving the cart. "Percy Ayren," she said. "The next time we stop for a rest, I have one thing to ask of you. I want you to grant me my final death."

Chapter 3

The Kingdom of Tanathe reposed in the southeast region of the Domain. Its western side bordered with the Kingdom of Solemnis—which in turn connected with distant Spain in the southwest—and on its northern side was the Kingdom of Serenoa. To the east lay Italy, and directly south, the balmy seawaters of the Mediterranean.

Tanathe was a verdant sun-filled land, with orchards of succulent peaches and figs, olive trees in abundance, and great dark grapes ripening on laden vines. There was never winter here, no snow, only a brief season of crispness in the air, and a deeper chill at night.

The small southern peninsula known as the Tanathean Riviera was considered to be heaven on earth. In its heart was the city of Riviereal—land-bound and yet built upon the last outflow of the great river Eridanos as it ran all the way from the distant northern Kingdom of Serenoa, cutting through Tanathe and emptying within the peninsula—not into the great sea, but somewhere on a southern plain, into the earth itself.

Eridanos never reached the sea. And yet, legend said, it continued flowing beneath ground, through caverns and deep crevices of the land that knew no sun, until it found the Mediterranean.

Some said it continued to flow through the underworld.

The Island of San Quellenne was visible from the shore. In the cream and milk haze of the balmy delicate overcast, it looked like a large floating slice of white chocolate upon the silvery-mauve waters of the Mediterranean.

The young boy stood on the sandy beach of the Tanathean Riviera, watching the seagulls circle over the island. He was skinny, no older than seven, and wore nothing but baggy cotton pants that were rolled above his knees to keep the surf away. His olive skin was tanned to a brazen glow, and his unruly black hair curled in the breeze.

The boy blinked from the spray, and raised his hand to shield his eyes from the general glare.

In that moment the sun came out, and the haze fled. The seawaters were suddenly deep resonant blue, as though the eye could focus at last and the world achieved proper hue and contrast.

"Flavio!"

The boy did not turn at the sound of an irate female voice.

"Flavio San Quellenne! What is wrong with you? How many times must I go chasing you around the sand dunes? Mother says to come home or be spanked!"

The boy turned around and then cheerfully waved at his sister.

The girl calling his name was older, at least eighteen, and a proper young woman. She wore a long simple sleeveless dress of similar white cotton, and her hair and skin were both a rich darkened bronze. The long hair was gathered in a plait, which streamed like a dark plume of fire behind her, down her back and to her waist. She had the airs of a nobly raised maiden.

"Come! Come here, Jelavie!" he replied. "I have something funny to show you!"

"What?" The girl waded through the sand, her woven sandals sinking with each step, until she stood at the child's side on a more solid section of beach right at the water's edge, that darker stripe which had been moistened by the sea into firm consistency.

A mere stride away from the tip of her sandals, the foam rolled in.

The boy pointed to the island, its whiteness blazing in the sun.

"Look! The mountain is gone!"

"What?" The girl shook her head in frustration at her brother, but then glanced into the distance, squinting against the sun.

And then drew in her breath. . . .

"No," she said, blinking. "It cannot be. That is merely the haze, a mirage . . ."

"What's a mirage?"

"Nothing, just an illusion from the heat in the summer."

"But it's not that hot today."

"It is hot enough. . . ."

The girl continued to stare and observed only the flat whiteness of land where there would normally be a small double-headed mountain with jagged pale cliffs on the right side.

"Saga Mountain is gone!" repeated the boy.

"Silence, Flavio!" The girl's voice was troubled now, but not in the usual way. "I tell you, it is but the mist and the haze, nothing more. . . ."

"Then why can you see the sky there? Only blue sky, Jelavie! And look, a bird!"

Jelavie stood looking, perfectly quiet, forgetting to reply, as the wind whipped her plait of hair into a metallic frenzy, and set loosened curling tendrils around her temples.

"Saga Mountain! Saga Mountain is gone! It is hiding!" the boy intoned, making it into a song, and then looked away, seeming to forget, and ran to pick up a shell and some bits of turquoise sea glass.

His sister continued to stand, frozen in place, looking at the strange *changed* topography of the island, refusing to believe her own vision. She blinked repeatedly, rubbed her eyes. Long moments passed, and there was no longer any remainder of haze or morning mist upon which to blame the disappearance of something as impossible and large as a mountain.

Eventually, as the boy continued to make small happy chatter and collect treasure from the sea as it was washed upon the shore, Jelavie turned away and strode after him, throwing occasional wary, puzzled glances back at the island and the new line of the horizon in place of the missing mountain.

"Enough, let's go home, Flavio," she said at last, taking him by the hand which was clutching a greedy handful of polished rocks and shells.

"No!" The boy began to frown and pull in her grasp.

"Let's *go!*" his sister said, raising her voice to the commanding level of a high-born lady, namely the Lady San Quellenne, their mother.

But as they struggled lightly in the customary manner of siblings, and she managed at last to pull him along, Jelavie threw one glance in the direction of the sea—just one more time, as though to make sure. Just one more time. She had purposefully occupied herself with normal concerns for the last few moments, just so that she could allow herself this one secret peek . . . in case the world itself needed that time, a magical pause of sorts, long enough to conceal and reveal. And then, just maybe, she hoped the world decided to cooperate and "put things back" the way they always had been.

But it was not to be.

This time, as her gaze hungrily searched the line of the horizon, there was still no mountain.

Furthermore, the entire Island of San Quellenne was gone.

In its place there was only the sea.

Many leagues inland, at the very spot where the Kingdom of Tanathe ended, precisely at its northwestern corner, lay the Supreme Seat of the Domain, known as the Sapphire Court. Neither a true city nor an isolated citadel, it incorporated elements of both. And in its overall structure and purpose it mirrored its northern foreign counterpart, the Silver Court of the Realm.

The Sapphire Court was a jewel of civilized urban splendor, with a Palace of the Sun to rival the grandest edifices in Europe. It was said that the King of France was inspired by it to such a degree that he too became the Sun King and commenced building architectural wonders. Meanwhile, Rome took one look at the Catedral D'Oro y Mármol and was duly humbled upon comparing it with Rome's own lesser Basilica di San Pietro.

There were other wonders in the Sapphire Court, structural miracles such as the Triple Aqueduct that spiraled and ascended upon itself into a three-decked tower, which then pressurized and fed all the fountains in the city and outlying estates for miles around. The great Dome of the Stadio Soffio di Dio, or the "Breath of God," was made of polished flat pieces of mirror glass, layered and assembled into infinite reflective facets—in truth, a divine, breathtaking sight, as though a luminary cousin of the sun descended to earth and perched upon a mortal building. As a result, the entire Stadio shone so brightly in the sunlight that it was impossible to look at it directly, except on overcast days.

Other structures were similar works of art, sporting exquisite stonework, mosaics of Venetian glass, sculpted reliefs and cornices, veined marble overlaid with gold. And indeed there was so much gold in the place, that if one ascended the highest towers or took a bird's eye view, the Sapphire Court was a golden morass of light.

Why then, such a name? Why not a "Golden" Court in the south to parallel the Silver Court in the north?

The answer was ensconced within the Palace of the Sun. For inside its grandest hall stood a throne carved of a single giant gemstone, a pale blue sapphire that undoubtedly had immortal origins, and must have been a divine gift upon the first Sovereign of the Domain.

The present Sovereign, Rumanar Avalais, sat upon this impossible throne that was the color of wind, if wind had swept down from the icy north and, while still in motion, turned to solid glass, achieving an earthly hue—just a breath of color, an ethereal hint of distance, a ghost of faint blue fading into lavender.

And yet, when *she* sat upon the Sapphire Throne, no one noticed its jeweled glory. They noticed only her.

Rumanar Avalais was their greatest queen and their ultimate mystery.

The noble line of Avalais was rumored to have its roots in classical Hellenistic antiquity, hailing from the shores of the Aegean, where the gods walked in the shadow of the lofty Parnassus, in groves of olive and cypress. And as her forefathers, Rumanar Avalais was ageless.

She was youthful, of indeterminate age; at times appearing a virgin maiden, at other times a mature voluptuous matron worthy of being the mother of the Domain. It seemed, one looked upon her and always saw a different thing, fluid from moment to moment. But it was always the one ideal vision that *felt* precisely right for that particular instance of perusal.

And somehow, once the onlooker's gaze fell upon her softly leashed splendor, it never occurred to question anything of her nature—age, origins, ancestry, not even the subtleties of her will, her desire, or her intent. Nothing mattered once you saw her, and from that instant forward she merely *was*, and in her being, she fulfilled the purpose of any gathering. Her presence within a room was the most natural consequence of all lives, of all expectations.

It seemed that Rumanar Avalais had always ruled, and no one knew or could recall her not being the Sovereign. Her regal Sire was long-deceased, the oldest quavering duchesses at court informed in rheumy whispers, when prompted. Or possibly it was her mother, or grandmother, they added. In short, none could remember the precise details, only that the glorious Sovereign of the Domain appeared no older than thirty, and had been thus for as long as one could recall.

Rumanar had skin as flawless and fair as milk, painted with a rosy blush of Balmue wine. Her hair, when undisguised by powdered wig or other headdress, was gold wedded to persimmon, that rare intermediate hue of deep blonde or pale red that makes the most brilliance. Her eyes were blue, as blue as the sapphire upon which she sat, with a clear or languid look. When she stood up and walked, she was statuesque and commanding, large and overwhelming, yet pliant with a lithe grace of the wilderness. And when she smiled, or spoke in her soft articulate voice, breaths were held all around. . . .

To call the Sovereign a beauty would have been a tawdry falsehood. It was best to admit that in her perfection, she was terrifying.

On that one particular day the Sovereign sat down upon the Sapphire Throne to grant Court Audience to an agent of the King of Solemnis and a few noble others, and to hear reports from abroad as relayed from her various clandestine operatives.

The Sovereign wore a crinoline dress of crimson, threaded with black, with midnight lace at the ends of her long sleeves and around the delicate whiteness of her plunging neckline. A cabochon jewel of blood-black, filled with tiny golden embers of what appeared to be captured light, was suspended on a fine gold chain around her throat, and rested in the deep crevice between her succulent breasts. Her eyes were outlined in smoky exquisite kohl, and her lips, like ripe bronzed plums. Not a hint of other courtly paint anywhere else upon her face, its skin retaining the unblemished perfection of matte alabaster. And her own bountiful hair, free of wig or powder, was artfully twisted, wound, threaded with jewels, and sculpted into a tall, intricate headdress upon which rested the Sovereign Crown.

The grand Hall of the Sun was around her, with its gilded ceiling and embroidered brocade curtains, its molded walls and support columns of alabaster and marble, and its infinite garlands of crystal suspended from hundreds of chandeliers and sconces. At her feet was the polished floor of deep red semi-precious stone inlay.

At her side was her favorite advisor, Ebrai Fiomarre.

Ebrai was the eldest son of the traitor to the enemy Realm, the Marquis Micul Fiomarre. After having been banished, in ignominy and upon pain of death, from the Realm by the Liguon Emperor himself (each man having received a discreet, last-moment stay of execution only after the upper clergy intervened with the Emperor upon a technicality of clemency—circumstances which only a few in the Realm properly knew or understood, for it was an ugly, muddled affair, the details of which the Sovereign savored), the two Fiomarre noblemen made their home here in the Sapphire Court. And here, they generously shared their in-depth political knowledge and common hatred of their former homeland with their new Avalais liege.

The Realm and the Domain were ever at odds with each other, the Fiomarre were notorious exiles or believed to be dead by most of their former countrymen, and the Sovereign found much amusement in having them thus at her side.

After unburdening himself to the extent that he was able in the early days, spilling his personal and political bile before the Sovereign and her advisors, Micul Fiomarre soon turned into a recluse and was rarely seen at Court functions. Fortunately his son had no such desire to hide from the world. And thus Ebrai

Fiomarre became a fixture at the Sapphire Court.

"Your Brilliance, I am entirely at your service," often spoke the younger man, Ebrai, looking directly in her eyes with his steady gaze of half-concealed dark intensity. It was always there, the simmer just under the surface. . . . And the Sovereign was not entirely sure if it was a neutral passion fueled by general anger at everything, at his bittersweet lot in life (bitter for the loss of his homeland, and sweet for the gain of his place at her Court), or if it was also a secret warm passion toward herself.

This made Ebrai entirely fascinating.

"And yet—" he always concluded his opening declaration thus, with astounding bluntness—"Your Brilliance, I would not place your full extent of trust in one such as myself, or my noble father. For we have betrayed once. . . . And as such, you must know that we are both unreliable."

And in answer to such commendable rhetoric, the Sovereign merely smiled. But first she observed the dark-haired, fiercely handsome man before her with an unwavering gaze of her own. And she willed her gaze to consume him. He was either playing a remarkable game of political expediency to gain her trust by a display of frankness, or he was indeed remarkable. It mattered not; for the moment he continued to pique her curiosity.

She derived pleasure from psychological dissonance, from wondering—it was one of her few personal pleasures of the mind. And hence, the cryptic smile—a gift of puzzlement in turn, to him, every time. Her smiles, faint and rare, were more potent that words.

Today however, Rumanar Avalais wore an expression like a mask.

The Audience this morning promised a number of possible complicated pieces of news. For the moment, the Hall was empty except for the rows of her personal guards behind the throne and lining the walls, and Ebrai, clad in black velvet, standing just below the dais of the throne, at her left side.

To the right of the throne was a waist-high slim marble pedestal, and upon it sat a small exquisite statuette of a goddess wrought of pure gold, no more than two feet tall. The golden female shape—nude except for a wide collar, matching wrist bracelets, and an exotic headdress—was stilled in a seated partial-lotus position with one knee upraised vertically, and her hands folded at her feet.

It was to this antique pagan goddess that the Sovereign turned for ultimate advice and in clandestine worship, it was rumored—for why else give it such a place of prominence?—even though no one had actually seen the Sovereign engage in such activity, and even though she publicly observed the true faith of the Church and attended holy mass in the chapel.

The Sovereign did not look at either her left or her right side, and signaled with her finger to the Chamberlains at the door.

The Audience commenced.

The first to approach through those doors was the expected Duke Raulle Deotetti of Solemnis.

The Duke, in his late sixties, wore a formal powdered wig. Clad in dark olive brocade and broad black sash of honor that were the colors of Solemnis, he strode heavily the entire length of the deep red mosaic floor, and stopped before the dais with a deep weary bow. His courtly form was impeccable, and yet it strained him to maintain it for the required lengthy pause.

The Sovereign seemed to know his difficulty, that imperceptible quivering of muscles in his waist and at his knees, as he remained bent before her. And she let him remain thus, for a few breaths longer than necessary, watching his pained ordeal.

At last, she spoke.

"Welcome, my dear Raulle. Do rise. What news do you bring us? But first—how is your lovely Beatrice?"

"Your Brilliance is ever kind," replied Deotetti,

straightening his back slowly, and only the twitch in a single facial muscle reflecting his plight. "The Duchess, my wife sends her adoration and infinite regards to Your Brilliance. As for her condition, I regret to say that she is—*deceased*, if one may use such a term now. Her illness, as you might recall, was lengthy, despite her relative youth, and the disease progressed and culminated in a crisis just last week, so that her mortal flesh failed. And now she requires neither rest nor sustenance. She sits at her embroidery now, day and night."

"As your Liege, we are grieved by her death, but rejoice at her fortune of non-death." The Sovereign spoke softly. "And as a woman, I am relieved to know that she remains at your side, and can thus tend to you and to the little ones. How many are there now, four?"

"Five, Your Brilliance. A son was born just this fall."

"Ah, five. Well then, that one will be your last. Take good care of your little one—an heir, is he not?—since you will now have no more, unless you commit polygamy. Five becomes your final number. Oh, and do bring them all here to Court, the next time you visit."

The Duke inclined his head in a short, pained bow.

"Now then," she continued. "What has your King to say to me?"

Poor Duke Deotetti bowed for the third time, conforming to protocol. "His Majesty, King Frederick Ourin of Solemnis, sends His warmest regards to Your Brilliance," he began. "His Majesty also conveys that the battalions are ready to march, upon Your Brilliance's Orders."

"Good. Tell His Majesty that my Orders are hereby given. Have the battalions proceed north, by way of western Balmue, and wait along the western shores of the River Styx, but do not cross it."

"If one might suggest," Ebrai Fiomarre spoke in a soft courtly manner, and his low compelling voice had the richness of velvet, "it may be more prudent to cross the river at that point, for the battalions will then be facing the Fiomarre lands directly, at the border of Balmue and the Kingdom of Styx. Otherwise they will still have to make a far more difficult crossing farther up north, past the Domain border and within the Realm itself. If you cross the river while still in Balmue, you will have a strategic advantage. And, you will have me to guide you through the lands of Fiomarre. . . ."

Ebrai spoke reasonably, turning his elegant aquiline profile in the direction of the Duke, but gently addressing the Sovereign.

She watched him indirectly, with her peripheral vision—the impeccable lines of his jaw, the slight dimple at his jutting chin, the dark shadow of stubble just under the skin that could not be banished even by the most skilled barber's close blade. He was like a beautiful raven, with his wavy locks unmarred by a wig, and his heavy expressive brows framing dark eyes.

Such an earnest face.

"No," said the Sovereign, interrupting Ebrai, without looking in his direction, and all her attention upon the elderly Duke. "The battalions will wait along the western shores of the river, without crossing it."

"Your Brilliance's Orders will be conveyed to His Majesty exactly." Duke Deotetti confirmed, nodding his bewigged head carefully.

"That is all," said Rumanar Avalais. "You may go with my blessings. Godspeed!"

And bowing for the last time, the Duke backed away from the dais, and then hurried out of the Hall.

The Sovereign turned her face to Fiomarre. "My dear Ebrai," she said. "Do not interrupt me thus again. During an Audience, you may only observe. Make your recommendations privately, afterwards."

Ebrai's eyes were a study in leashed intensity. He inclined

his head, and whispered, "Afterwards may be too late."

But the Sovereign was once again turned away and motioning to the Chamberlains. The doors were opened to admit the next in line for an Audience.

The entrant was a spry young man with a fair complexion, short, slender and unassuming, dressed simply as a second-tier courtier, with a plain unpowdered wig. He moved quickly across the expanse of the hall, and his light footfalls made no sound along the stone floor.

"Quentin Loirre," said the Sovereign in a very different, lively tone, speaking almost playfully. "What have you for me?"

"Your Brilliance!" The young man bowed like a sleek cat, and kept a very composed countenance and unblinking eyes, but his skin betrayed him, breaking into a fierce blush. "I have a carrier bird with a message from Lethe. A certain Lady wishes to convey her news of success. The Chidair Duke has been convinced and has switched sides. Hoarfrost is now an Ally of the Domain."

"My dear boy, you always have such good news for me. Tell me more of what the Lady says."

"The Lady assures Your Brilliance that Duke Ian Chidair, known as Hoarfrost, is precisely as dead as rumored, furious at his fate, and halfway-mad. But he is otherwise sufficiently reasonable, and quite interested in your offer."

"Can he offer me arms?"

"Yes, he can. He has amassed an army of men in a similar condition to his own. It is apparently a natural selection, for the dead clamor to him, and he now commands enough rabble to storm a city, much less hunt Cobweb Brides."

"And how successful has he been in his hunting?"

Quentin paused, as though attempting to recall. "Begging all pardons, but the message did not go into sufficient detail."

"No matter. But when you write back, inquire regarding this one detail."

"It will be done as Your Brilliance Commands."

"Indeed. Do keep us well informed in that regard. And now, this is what you will write to the Lady in our confidence: tell her that Chidair, the Blue Duke, Hoarfrost—call him what you will—is to gather his army and advance south. Tell him that in due course I shall meet him halfway and unite our ranks. But first, he is to make his stand at Letheburg."

Ebrai did not blink, nor did he make any movement. But his breath seemed to have stilled somewhat.

The Sovereign was perfectly aware of the difference in her favorite advisor's breathing, as she continued to disregard him and instead watched young Quentin Loirre with her impassive gaze.

The young Loirre bowed crisply, and then was dismissed with one finger.

When the youth was gone from the Hall, the Sovereign again turned to Fiomarre. "Well?" she said. "What is your reaction now, my dear Ebrai?"

Ebrai looked at her with a stilled expression. "My reaction is a mixture of distress and relief," he said, his dark eyes meeting hers openly. "I am stirred by the fact that this long-desired military action is happening at last. And I am elated that revenge is in sight. Altogether the combination is too much for me . . . I am frankly rendered speechless. . . ."

"And yet your words are so eloquent, even now."

Ebrai Fiomarre bowed.

The Chamberlains were directed to admit the next party seeking Audience. They announced the Count Lecrant D'Arvu of Balmue and the Countess Arabella D'Arvu.

The Count was a middle-aged, vigorous man with a dark complexion and an artful powdered platinum wig, dressed in somber black of mourning. And his wife was similarly clad in a black court dress, with no embellishments except mourning lace and a black, stark, unpowdered wig. The Countess had a thin, pinched face, and eyes red from weeping. She was possibly youthful, but grief had wrung all life juices from her, and she moved at her husband's side like a shade.

"Approach, D'Arvu," the Sovereign spoke to them.

"Your Brilliance," spoke the Count and Countess, bowing and curtsying in unison.

"Yes, what news from Balmue?" The Sovereign did not bother with personal courtesies.

"It is all as planned, and Balmue stands ready to proceed at the border," the Count replied in a weary voice. "Furthermore, the Ambassador, Marquis Nuor Alfre, is newly returned from his Realm visit to see the Liguon Emperor at the Silver Court, and is at present back home in Ulpheo, at the court of His Majesty King Clavian Sestial. He says—that is—the news he brings is rather remarkable."

The Sovereign watched with softly lidded languid eyes. "Go on. What news?"

There was a tiny pause before Count D'Arvu replied. "It appears, Your Brilliance, that the Imperial House Liguon is in mourning. The Emperor's daughter, the Infanta, has suffered an assassination, on her sixteenth Birthday Feast Day, only a week or so ago. She has been struck down with a dagger through the heart, and because death no longer takes us, she is now dead, yet 'lives'—she is one of the so-called undead. And the traitor murderer, the man who struck her—this is the truly remarkable part—is none other than Vlau Fiomarre, the middle son of the Marquis Micul Fiomarre and the brother to the man who now stands at Your Brilliance's side."

At the mention of the name "Vlau Fiomare," Ebrai made a small sound that was immediately stifled.

"Oh! What a marvel indeed!" The Sovereign spoke in delight, her voice taking on a warm timbre, and she immediately turned to her favorite. "Good heavens, Ebrai! Your family never ceases to astonish! Now your younger brother has distinguished himself indeed! Naturally, I welcome him and expect him to join us here, if he is at all at liberty to do so."

"I—" said Ebrai, "I am equally astonished as Your Brilliance."

"If one might add, Your Brilliance," Count D'Arvu continued, "the news gets even stranger. It appears that the dead Infanta, Claere Liguon, had decided that she is the Cobweb Bride. She has left her father's court, perversely taking her murderer with her, in order to travel north in search of Death's Keep in the most distant portion of the Kingdom of Lethe, somewhere in the Northern Forest in the Dukedom of Chidair. Our sources tell us that she may be somewhere out there even now, traveling discreetly and in secret. She has not yet been intercepted."

"A dead Grand Princess and her murderer, traveling together? What exquisite torment for both . . ." the Sovereign said with a delicate smile.

"It is so indeed, Your Brilliance. But the result of this, of course, is that the Emperor is in agony and upheaval, and he is certain to be at his weakest now. Furthermore, with the cessation of death, and the newly proclaimed Law of the land sending all young daughters to be Cobweb Brides, the Realm itself is at its most vulnerable. The populace is distracted, grieving, forced not only to deal with the undead—as we are, here in the Domain—but in addition to give up their daughters. And since the three Kingdoms of the Realm are in turmoil, one dares assume they will not stand easily with their Kings and the Emperor who had thus surely betrayed and abandoned them."

"You speak things that bode well for our campaign. Go on. Is there anything else?"

"There is. . . ." For the first time, the Countess D'Arvu spoke, in a faint voice. And her husband threw her a nervous glance.

"My dear Countess Arabella, what is it?" The Sovereign

now glanced in the woman's direction, directing the full force of her serpent gaze and terrifying beauty upon the supplicant.

"Your Brilliance, if I may—" The Countess curtseyed deeply again. "I beg Your Brilliance's indulgence in listening, for I have come for one purpose only, and it is to beg and plead with Your Brilliance on behalf of Lady Leonora, our only daughter, who is in Your Brilliance's service, and has not been seen or heard from for the last month."

Rumanar Avalais continued to look at the Countess.

"If Your Brilliance might possibly have the means of calming a very distraught and foolish mother—that is, if there is anything that may be divulged as to our daughter's present . . . situation—"

"Whatever do you mean, my dear?" said the Sovereign, and the blue of her eyes was like the soothing blue of sky. "Could it be that Lady Leonora, that sweet forgetful child, did not remember to write you a letter? Why, she has been somewhat indisposed for the last week, and I told her to keep to her bed, and rest and regain the roses in her cheeks. I even sent my own physician to tend to her. But she is so eager to serve me, I am afraid she must have overtired herself yet again."

The Countess D'arvu's face came to sudden joyful life. "Oh, Your Brilliance!" She fell into a deep eager curtsy, this time voluntarily. "A thousand blessed thanks! We have been so terribly worried! That is, we have not heard, and had no idea! How ill is she? Might it be possible to see her?"

"Now, now, Countess, I do not recommend anyone attend the sweet girl in her quarters just yet, for I am told she might not be up to receiving visitors. It is best that we let nature's healing take its course, and in the meantime she will be sure to write as soon as she is up to it."

"I do hope," put in Count D'Arvu, courteously, "that she is not contagious?"

The Sovereign gave a gentle reassuring laugh. "Not at all, I am told. It is simply exhaustion and a bit of a stomach malady that will pass soon enough. But now, as she is one of my dearest young Ladies-in-Attendance, you must know how much I love and worry about her myself. Had there been anything in the *least* truly wrong with her, you would have had my personal carriage at your door."

The Count and Countess bowed again in grateful unison.

"Now then, I do hope it is all settled in your mind, my dears. Is there anything else you have for me?"

"Nothing more but our deepest gratitude, Your Brilliance," uttered Countess D'Arvu.

But her husband cleared his throat and said, "Oh, I had almost forgotten, Your Brilliance, there is one more thing. Though, I am unsure if it is even of any import, or relevance. But it is a bit of a curiosity, a wonder, one might say. And it just happened overnight."

"Indeed? Go on."

"I am told by one of my reliable sources who is also in Lethe, that there is an interesting rumor being passed around in the north country. Not sure where it originated, but it is said a young woman has appeared—a girl, in some tiny godforsaken village there—who has the miraculous ability to put the dead to rest, *permanently*."

"What did you say?"

The Count drew his brows together in an effort of thought. "My source places the rumor somewhere in the northernmost villages in the Dukedom of Goraque. Within hours the peasants have spread it like wildfire, as far as Letheburg. Supposedly, a day ago, an old woman has *died*—in the true way. Her body remains while her spirit has flown. *How* she died—when no one else can die—is unknown. But they say her own granddaughter is responsible."

The Sovereign moved forward slightly, her back no longer against the throne.

"This is a very interesting rumor indeed," she said, and her languid eyes opened fully, clear and sharp as glass.

"I thought it might be of some interest to Your Brilliance. Because quite a few of those villagers speak of her as though she is the Cobweb Bride, found at last. While others call her something else altogether—they call her Death's Champion."

"Could she really be this Cobweb Bride? Or is it merely superstitious country nonsense?"

"I do not know, Your Brilliance, I only know there has been much talk of this, and supposedly the girl has also similarly *killed* someone or something else—"

"I am glad you told me about this particular curiosity, Count." The Sovereign spoke without looking at him or anyone, her gaze directed at some indefinite point before her. "Now, I want you to find out more. Get me the source of these rumors, and learn everything you can about this Death's Champion. If she is real, I must know."

"Yes, Your Brilliance."

"Excellent! Now go. And oh—be sure to find out what *else* this girl can do."

The Count and Countess made their courtly obeisances and backed out of the Hall.

The Sovereign lifted her finger and proclaimed. "The Audience is over."

Was it a trick of the candlelight, but her eyes, so very blue, for a moment appeared as black as night.

Chapter 4

"I want you to grant me my final death," Claere Liguon said to Percy Ayren.

Vlau Fiomarre heard those words issuing out of the dead girl's lips, and it struck him like thunder.

"No!"

Before he could stop himself, before he even knew what force was driving him, the exclamation came forth unbidden, and he was leaning forward in the cart, staring at her with a wild expression on his face.

Percy, meanwhile, pulled hard at Betsy's reins and abruptly stopped the cart.

"What?" she said, turning around fully to stare at the Infanta.

Everyone else was staring also. Even the soldiers stopped riding, and gathered in a cluster around them. The knight rode back a few paces and paused directly at the side of the cart closest the Grand Princess. From the side of his eyes, Vlau Fiomarre momentarily noted the knight's careful attentiveness. But mostly, Vlau's attention was upon the Infanta, while a fever arose in his mind, an urgent impossible storm of . . . *grief.*

The Infanta's white, sallow face, frozen like a delicate mask, was trained upon Percy.

The other girl was looking at her with a shocked

expression, and then a gathering frown.

"I am sorry to startle any of you with such a pronouncement," said Claere, her breath coming like clockwork. "Maybe I should have waited until we were stopped, so I could speak to you alone, Percy. Maybe—but I am unsure if I might have had the requisite courage to ask. This way, at least, I ask in public, and make it more formal, more *real*."

"What—what exactly are you asking me, Your—Claere?" Percy said very quietly. She had nearly used the Imperial form of address before the unsuspecting soldiers, nearly giving the Infanta away, but stopped in time.

"You know what I ask. Do for me whatever you have done for your grandmother, Percy, and help me pass on."

It was certain that none of the soldiers had known up to that point that it was the Emperor's daughter, riding in that peasant cart. And likely, most of them had no inkling of the Infanta's undead condition. But now, everyone knew that a *dead* girl was among them. . . .

"I—" Percy clenched the reins so hard that Betsy was making unhappy snorting noises at the extreme pull on her harness.

Vlau felt his head growing so cold, so impossibly cold, and the sweat of fear was gathering on his brow. "No," he said again, this time more rationally. "You cannot take your leave of this world just yet."

The Infanta suddenly turned to him and her great smoky eyes were trained fully upon him. "What does it matter to you— Vlau?" *She too had almost said, "Marquis."*—"Why in heaven's name would you protest something you have been fighting so ardently to achieve? I thought you wanted me dead!"

At that last part, everyone looked at Fiomarre. Several girls exchanged startled, unbelieving glances of confusion.

"What had once been intended . . . no longer matters in the least," he retorted, finding that he had to speak in this somewhat

convoluted manner now, for he could not reveal *anything*—
neither his role in her death to the others, nor his present feelings
to *her*. Not a thing, to anyone! And least of all, could he admit
the extent of the cold, grieving, passionate darkness rising within
him—not yet, and possibly not ever. And thus he had to feign
indifference and practicality. "You cannot die just yet, for there
are things in this mortal world you must still do."

"What things?" The Infanta was looking at him with a
strange, indescribable expression, a combination of despair and
serenity, and *something else* hidden even deeper beyond. Vlau
could not fathom what it was, but it held him, mesmerized
him . . . and thus he steadily returned her gaze.

"He is right," said Percy. "First of all, what you ask is such
a serious thing, that I am afraid to even consider it right now."

"But you *can* do it!" The Infanta swiveled her stiff frozen
head again to look at Percy.

"Yes, I can. But—but I am not sure I *should*." It was
obvious that Percy was painfully struggling to express her
conflicted thoughts. Ever since last night, she had seemed
extremely unlike her usual steady self—the self that Vlau
Fiomarre was used to seeing—and was instead like an uncertain
child, a bundle of vulnerable indecisiveness. This request was
apparently the last straw. "I mean," she continued, stumbling in
her words, "Gran was one thing, it was what I'd set out to do all
along. And that poor pig, well, that was something else that had
to be done. But you! You are—" Here Percy sharply went silent
because, Vlau guessed, she had almost said, *"you are the
Emperor's daughter."*

The black knight must have made a similar conclusion,
because he spoke up in a loud commanding tone. "Enough. It is
clear this discussion is untimely. Let us keep moving now, and
you can continue this—whatever *this* is—when we come to our
next stop on the road."

Percy frowned and threw him one sharp glance, but did not

argue. She turned her back on the passengers in the cart, deep in thought, and took up the reins.

They resumed moving forward along the snowy road, past endless shabby hedges and fields, and occasional poverty-ridden homesteads, in the direction of Letheburg.

Vlau gathered himself, maintaining an impassive demeanor, and watched from the corner of his eye how the doll of ice and spun glass, the sculpted undead creature at his side, sat motionless in the cart, retreating into herself. She raised the hood of her coat and now even her face was obscured.

And Fiomarre, next to her, imagined her face as it had been in those moments, and the new grief ate at him slowly, softly, turning into despair.

Percy drove Betsy forward mindlessly, holding on to the reins with a fixed grip, and she thought: *the Infanta of the Realm has just asked me to kill her.*

Holy God in Heaven, what was she to do? Death's Champion, indeed! Percy was a pitiful mess. She did not know what she was doing. . . . Possibly, she was still in shock.

No, that is not true. I know exactly what I am doing. . . .

Percy exhaled a breath held far too long, then ventured to look around her—at the slowly receding sparse bushes laden with snow on both sides of the road, at the knight's men riding alongside the creaking cart, chain mail and plate armor gleaming in the occasional bursts of winter sun past the cloud mass. The black knight himself was far up ahead on his great warhorse, Riquar at his side. They did not look back even once.

At some point, long moments later, things began to lose tension, and the girls in the cart started chatting softly.

Percy threw a dazed glance backward, and saw the Infanta was motionless and hooded, while the dark young man seated next to her had an occluded expression, and seemingly watched the passing road.

"Did I somehow miss it," Lizabette spoke up suddenly, "but isn't there supposed to be a scraggly forest at this point, as we get closer to Letheburg? Why are there only tedious fields, and not a tree in sight? Are we on a different road?"

Marie and Niosta, the only other remaining girls in the cart, looked around them, and then Niosta said, "There's no other road, there's only this one. Hmm, it seem' like 'ere should be some trees now. I remember when my sis Catrine an' I were here last, headed in the other direction, there were trees, an' rotted stumps aplenty."

"Yes, that's what I remember too," said Lizabette. "Unless I am mistaken completely and we still have some ways to go."

"I don't know," Percy said, watching Betsy plod forward. "I've never been this way before, never been this close to Letheburg."

Little Marie stayed quiet and simply shrugged.

A few hours later, somewhat past noon, as the road meandered and curved around new hillocks that seemed to spring up before them out of nowhere, and it was apparent there was no forest anywhere, the black knight called a stop at the foot of one such rise next to a semi-circle clearing. They made camp in a spot that was not completely in the open, as would have been the case had they stopped earlier in the open fields.

"We'll stop here for a meal and rest," he said, after approaching the cart. He was looking at Percy directly.

She nodded, not quite meeting the gaze of his slate-blue eyes, and slowed down Betsy.

The soldiers moved all around them, horses were led off the road, and soon a fire-pit was fashioned out of bits of twigs and frozen mossy earth underneath cleared snow.

The girls scattered around the shrubbery to answer calls of nature, and there was some friendly general conversation, as the men-at-arms opened travel bags, and got out the bread and cheese and leftover sausage. There was even a small flagon of ale that started making rounds.

Percy stood fiddling with Betsy's feedbag when she heard the Infanta's measured soft voice behind her.

"When you are done with your task, I would speak with you, Percy," said Claere Liguon, with unusual dignity, standing upright with difficulty, one lily-white hand holding on to the railing of the cart. At her side stood her death-shadow—a loyal eternal sentinel, a faint human shape, billowing like a smoke-stack of quivering darkness. . . .

"Just a moment," Percy mumbled, and turned away, and continued handling the bag of grain, slowly, reluctantly, then adjusting Betsy's harness with dawdling movements.

Vlau Fiomarre approached the Infanta from behind.

"Please . . ." he said in a whisper, and reached out to place his hand on Claere's slim shoulder. His strong fingers dug into her skin, but her dead flesh was unaware of the pain that she otherwise would have been feeling. "Before you do this thing, I must speak with you. Come this way!"

The Infanta obeyed, or rather, was maneuvered a few paces away, where they stood in relative privacy near a tall hedge, while the campsite bustled around them in the rising smoke from the cook fire.

Vlau's fingers were still upon her, holding her shoulder in a vise.

"What would you have me do or not do now, Marquis?" she said, raising the gaze of her great eyes upon his own. Her expression was blank, emotionless—truly *dead* now. But her voice retained a tiny last vestige of life, as expressed through a tone of bitterness and irony.

He stared, his dark intense face leaning over her, inches away. There was a rising fury there, barely contained, as he observed this thing before him, this cold dead thing that he himself had *made*. . . .

Why did he bother with her now? What was it? Was it not over now, everything, since the events of Death's Keep? Had it not been revealed that the Infanta was not the Cobweb Bride, and hence had nothing left in the world to do, no reason to go on, no damned purpose?

She had sat down in the snow then, having given up. And they had talked to her—Percy especially, had spoken to her, words of encouragement and hope.

While he—he, the murderer who had plunged the accursed dagger into her poor fragile heart—he had no purpose remaining to him also. Neither hate nor revenge for his family's foul maltreatment at the hands of her father the present Emperor—none of it mattered any longer.

"What would you have of me?" she repeated, jerking him out of a dark madness, a momentary reverie of memory and regret.

"You cannot die!" he responded fiercely in a near-whisper. "I cannot allow it!"

Her eyes were impossible to describe.

"I am dead already, Marquis. Enough! It is too late to change it. And now, in the name of God, if there is any honor left within you, you must allow me the only possible peace I may yet have—oblivion."

"No—"

"No indeed. We are *done* speaking!"

And having uttered this, she forcefully disengaged herself from his grip, then moved away with slightly jerking movements, and retreated along the hedge in an even more secluded spot, to await Percy.

Percy was taking her time with Betsy, more than usual, and overheard some of their pointed, strange exchange.

Lord, but she did not want to face the Infanta, not for *this*. She just couldn't. . . .

Percy braced herself, and turned around, having tarried long enough. She walked through the snow, powder crunching underfoot, and stopped before the dead Grand Princess and her death-shadow.

"Your Highness . . ." Percy bit her lip.

Not far away, she noted Vlau Fiomarre still stood in place, watching them with his relentless, burning gaze. His lips were moving, whispering: *"No . . ."*

"Percy Ayren. Thank you for your courtesy. We may speak in private here. And, I would have you perform the *act* now."

"Your Highness—are you absolutely certain?" Percy felt a bone-deep cold rising inside her, a growing sense of remoteness, so that she was pulled deeper within herself, seeing the world through a thicker layer of distance. Indeed, her vision warped and doubled. First she could see the Infanta's death shadow right alongside her, then it would wink out of awareness, then reappear again as Percy struggled to focus.

"Yes . . . I am certain. Please, *do it*. Do not make me beg again, for I might not have the strength to proceed."

"But—would you not rather return to your parents at Court, and maybe say your goodbyes? Maybe you will reconsider, since there is no going back on this kind of thing—I mean—"

A pair of great beautiful eyes framed by sunken hollows watched Percy.

"Please . . ." Claere Liguon said. "That I am still here has been a miracle of additional time given me. . . . I should not be here. . . . It is wrong, and I do not belong among the living. That you have the ability to set me free is another miracle. Only, if I may ask you—afterwards, when it is all done—return my body to the Emperor, my father, to be laid to rest in our ancient family crypt, as has been the Liguon way always. . . . And now, *please proceed!"*

Percy felt her heart breaking.

The death shadow stood poised, as though realizing it was time.

Percy heard the darkness rising, the churning in her mind, the layers upon layers of morass, opening inside her like a starless night, and the tolling of bells. Meanwhile, in the real world the sun came out momentarily and shone a bleak spot of radiance upon the white receptive face of the Infanta, her soft wisps of ashen hair. Somewhere behind them, high above, a bird sped by, calling. . . .

Percy removed her mittens, stuffed them in her pocket. The crisp winter air rushed in to numb her fingers. She stepped forward and took the cold dead hand of the Grand Princess, feeling it like a shock of ice, feeling the dead girl tremble. . . .

"I am ready . . ." said Claere Liguon, closing her eyes.

And with her other hand, Percy reached out and drew her fingers toward the sentinel shadow—

All at once, from everywhere around them came a terrible crashing noise.

Percy started. The overflowing ocean of darkness in her mind instantly receded, while that *deep unspeakable place* slammed shut. With a cry of alarm she dropped the Infanta's hand, and spun about. They both stared as the campsite filled with new riders, and there were foot soldiers coming from all directions—down from the top of the hillock and around from the road—and there was the neighing of horses, battle cries and hoarse yells of men-at-arms.

The next few seconds were absolute chaos.

"Oh God!" uttered Claere Liguon, forgetting herself, forgetting everything that *almost* happened.

The Chidair soldiers had been peacefully eating when the attack came, but they were impeccably trained to react within seconds.

As three mounted knights in full armor came bearing down upon them from the top of the rise, and at least half a dozen soldiers on foot rushed in from every direction, the black knight—who had been seated near the fire and drinking from a mug with the others—sprung up like lightning, casting his mug aside, and grabbed his nearby sword from the bundle at his feet.

"To arms!" he cried, and the men-at-arms reacted swiftly, and steel was drawn from scabbards everywhere.

They clashed in seconds.

The stranger foot soldiers, dressed in poor motley rags and wearing no noticeable military colors, sought to overpower, but the Chidair soldiers struck back fiercely. And, in moments, enemy limbs were hacked off by the better-trained Chidair, while the strangers wallowed on the ground.

The first of the three knights, disguised by a dull battered helm and lowered visor, brandishing a heavy flanged mace, made directly for Lord Beltain Chidair, recognizing him as the leader—but it was a grave mistake.

Beltain leapt forward, despite his imperfect physical condition. And before the attacking knight could bring down his mace, he found himself pulled out of his saddle and onto the ground, grappled down by the black knight, while his mount ran wild. The two of them rolled, then Beltain was up first, and pounded at him from above with his gauntled fist and the flat of his great sword, then the pommel, in a thunder stroke—Percy noted in those wild instants of hyperawareness—as though even in this instance he wanted to grant a modicum of mercy.

"Surrender, or lose your limbs!" Beltain cried hoarsely.

But the knight underneath him made no answer.

And soon it became obvious something else was not quite right.

For one thing, there was no blood. . . . By this time in such a skirmish, the snow would have been painted bright red. Instead, there was nothing.

Indeed, as the Chidair men defended themselves, their enemy did not bleed, and instead, they themselves soon received gashes and cuts that discolored the snow.

The other two knights, seeing how easily their comrade was

felled, suddenly turned around, and retreated, their horses laboriously riding up the same hillock they had descended moments ago—all in silence.

The foot soldiers however were not so easily driven off.

The girls were screaming. Marie cowered near the cart while Niosta and Lizabette dove directly underneath it. The Chidair soldiers offered them some protection and stood their ground, defending the general area of the campsite and their own horses.

"A sword! Someone, give me a sword, *now!*" Vlau Fiomarre exclaimed a few feet away, as abruptly from behind the hedge another three drably clad attackers surfaced and made directly for the Infanta and Percy.

Percy whirled around, and blinked, seeing double again, just as she had minutes ago. Because instead of three man-shapes, she saw *six*.

Three men and, flanking them, their three death-shadows.

And then, as Percy glanced around the entire clearing, she realized that not a single one of their attackers was one of the living.

They were all *undead*.

"Beware! They are not alive, My Lord! *Dead!* They are all dead, all of them!" she cried in the direction of the black knight, and he paused for an instant in his struggle and glanced at her.

But Percy had turned away already, facing the grisly carved-up face of a mortally wounded dead man inches away, as he came for her with a long ugly hunting knife. Up-close, the side of his skull was split open and old clotted blood had dried like rust over his matted straw-hair. His eyes were glazed, fixed in their frozen sockets, no longer quite human.

Before Vlau Fiomarre had an instant to react, tearing off a large branch for the closest weapon at hand and running toward them, the dead man reached for her. . . .

Percy put her hand up in an involuntary defensive gesture.

But the moment her fingertips felt the pressure of the dead man's chest, the roiling darkness in her mind was back, with a snap—a churning winter storm. Without pausing to think, she reached for the shadow at his side, feeling its billowing ghostly shape attaining tangible resilience . . . and she *pulled* with her mind, fiercely, in pure furious instinct.

The shadow of death collapsed into a vapor funnel, and was sucked into the dead man's flesh.

He fell instantly, fingers losing the grip on the knife. His body was an empty shell before it hit the ground.

Percy stood above him, breathing deeply, her head ringing with the cathedral tolling of bells.

But there was no time to stop and consider.

There were two more men coming, and the Infanta was right behind her, defenseless. . . .

Vlau had reached her in two strides, and he engaged the first of the attackers, feinting with the thick branch in one hand, and then striking with his fist.

The second man was Percy's.

Rather, he did not know it yet. Because he lunged at her, with a dull roar of creaking bellows that was his voice. Instead of moving away, Percy took him in her embrace, and with her left hand she grabbed his shadow.

It took less than a second. She *pulled* the two together, and again, the man's entirely lifeless body collapsed at her feet.

Breathing harshly, Percy then turned to Vlau's attacker. And while he was distracted with the marquis, she touched the dead man from the back—lightly this time, not even requiring a close embrace—and at the same time she took his shadow of death, as though it were an obstreperous child, in one furious hand, and she jerked it into the body, shoving it *inside* and feeling it dissolve.

The third man fell with a sigh of broken bellows, growing quiet and eternal.

"Who *are* you?"

Vlau Fiomarre stood at her side, looking in dark wonder.

Percy took one side step, staggering, because in that moment she felt herself abysmally drained of all energy, and so terribly cold. "I am—" she began, then again went silent, because vertigo made the whole world spin in a carousel of winter sky and snow and black shrubbery. It occurred to her that it was such an odd thing that she could barely remain upright.

Meanwhile, Claere Liguon was in the same spot where she had been left, motionless, observing Percy's every move with her great stilled eyes. "No . . ." she whispered, the moment Percy's weary gaze rested on her. "Now that I saw you do it, I don't think I can die—just yet."

"Oh, good . . ." Percy heard herself speak through a curtain of rising white noise in her temples, the sound of rushing blood. "Because I don't think I can do it yet again now, Highness . . ." she managed to utter, then inhaled several times deeply to keep herself from fainting.

The fighting behind them in the campsite had drawn to a close. Now that they knew what they were dealing with, the Chidair soldiers had overpowered the dead, by crudely divesting them of limbs, or using netting. The few that still remained upright were tied together and questioned by the black knight.

"Who are you? Who sent you to attack us?" he spoke, looming above them like an angel of death.

A few of the dead men grinned back silently. Others stared with vacant frozen eyes.

Beltain Chidair removed the helmet from the silent fallen knight and revealed a dead man with an old head wound that had damaged his face and jaw and apparently vocal chords, which explained his inability to respond during the fight. And now the dead knight merely rolled his eyes in pointless anger and made gurgling sounds from his slit throat. He was of no use.

"Speak, or I will start cutting off your limbs one by one,"

pronounced Beltain wearily to the other prisoners. "You will spend eternity, or however much time we have left to us, as rotting stumps. *Headless* rotting stumps."

Despite her own unnatural exhaustion, Percy made her way toward them. "My Lord," she said, raising her voice for effect. "If you like, I can simply put them all to rest." She was on her last strength; she was bluffing, but no one else had to know.

Beltain glanced at her, and even in her exhaustion Percy felt an alarming inner lurch of emotion upon meeting his clear-eyed gaze.

He frowned, for a moment misunderstanding her intent, and then Vlau Fiomarre approached, and said, "Just now—Three men lie stone-dead, over there . . ."

"What? *Oh.*" And Beltain understood.

Everyone was glancing in the direction where three corpses were sprawled near the edge of the shrubbery. The Chidair soldiers knew, but their attackers had no notion of what awaited them, of what had just happened to three of their comrades.

"You," said Beltain to one of the undead. "You still have functional eyes, and you can turn your neck, can you not? Stop grinning, look yonder, and tell me what you see."

For a moment the dead man did nothing. And then he craned his head slowly.

And he *saw.*

Something terrible came over his pale lifeless face. "They are really *dead?* But—how?" he managed to say, his lungs creaking.

"How? Death has a Champion, that's how. Death himself might be a lazy bastard shirking his Duty, but apparently there is still a way for us to die in this world." Beltain drew closer, to stare at the dead man with a gaze of blue steel. "Would you like to meet your Maker now? Make your choice, man. You can either remain in this mortal world as you are, or we send you directly to Hell. Rather, *she* sends you directly to Hell while I watch. Oh, but Hell can wait—first, I'll cut off a few of your fingers and then your arms. Then, I'll go a bit lower. So, what will it be?"

The man spoke. He told them that the undead have been gathering from all parts and heading north, flamed by a rumor that the Duke of Chidair, known as Hoarfrost, was welcoming them all with open arms. It was good to ride under the banner of the Blue Duke, one of their own.

"Then why did you attack us, you fools?" Beltain said. "Did you not see our colors? We are Chidair."

"Yes, but you are still living," the dead soldier replied, his fixed eyes unblinking. "We no longer ride together with your kind."

"Why the hell not?"

In answer, the man paused, and his jaw moved in a strange unnatural rictus, neither a grin nor a baring of the teeth. "War," he said. "War is coming."

Chapter 5

Duke Ian Chidair, called Hoarfrost, strode through the long dark hallway on an upper story of the Chidair Keep, slamming his beefy fist against the antique, blackened wooden doors that he passed, until the timbers sagged under each blow, and pulling down tapestries of his ancestors.

"No son! No son of mine! I will . . . find him . . . and kill him!" he roared, taking ragged mechanical breaths between every few words, for his lungs were dead, and his heart had long since ceased beating and was frozen cold like a cut of meat.

"I have no son!" ranted Hoarfrost. "He is dead to me, and when I find his carcass, I will make him deader yet! First, I will break his neck, then dismember him for betraying me!"

The Duke was a giant of a man—or rather, he had once been a man, and now was but a giant *thing*, an undead monster shaped like a man, with a barrel chest and a wildly tangled briar-thicket of frozen dark hair and beard, covered with leaves and twigs and bits of lake sludge. All this foul matter had adhered to his body when he had fallen through the ice during the battle on top of frozen Lake Merlait, right after he had received his mortal wound.

Because it had happened on that same day when Death stopped, the Duke suffered the horror of having to die yet not die, drown yet not drown, wade underwater and then break through the ice when he reached the shore, emerging a lifeless and yet animated corpse. And the dirt and mud had since permeated him, soaked into his hair and clothing, his blood-drenched hauberk and chain mail, and the pale blue surcoat with the heraldic emblem of his house—none of which he ever removed since the day of the battle and his body's death.

It was whispered all through the Keep that the Duke was mad. None but a madman would rise up against his liege the Queen of Lethe, and ultimately the Liguon Emperor of the Realm, and take it upon himself to terrorize the countryside. He and his equally dead soldiers, fallen in the battle, rode on endless day-and-night patrols. They were out hunting all the young women who were obeying the Royal Decree of the land and traveling north in search of Death's Keep to become Cobweb Brides.

The captured girls and women of all ranks were led—and in some cases dragged—through the snow and brought back to the Chidair Keep and the surrounding town, and imprisoned all over the place. And rumor had it, they were eventually all going to end up very badly.

Those men of Chidair who were not dead, cowered in fear, and tried to keep away from direct contact with their dead Duke as much as possible, for they actively feared for their lives. They too patrolled the northern forestlands reluctantly, for they had no choice but to obey. But more and more of them secretly took up their families and households and left the Keep and the town quietly.

Even the Duke's own son, Lord Beltain Chidair, known in the countryside as the terrifying black knight, had deserted his father, riding off with a small detachment of soldiers on patrol and never returning. Apparently, when Beltain did not come home the first night after his patrol duty, it was assumed that he was simply occupied or lost, but soon enough the various scouts came back with strong rumors that he and his fellow deserters were seen on the road heading south into Goraque territory.

At first, Hoarfrost did not believe it. The first man who came to report this news, suffered a blow to the head, and was killed immediately, then picked himself and his leaking brains up from the floor, and stumbled his way out of his liege's chamber.

The next two men to confirm this in Hoarfrost's presence, were both dead already. They had elected to go in together, and even they shrank away in terror at the thunderous voice of their liege lord upraised in curses and periodically broken by breath being drawn like creaking bellows, followed by crashing metal and breaking furniture.

The only thing that seemed to have a mellowing effect on the Duke's rage was a young lady, one of the few captured high aristocrats from the Silver Court, who was cool and impassive and who was also a self-admitted spy on behalf of the Domain.

Lady Ignacia Chitain of Balmue, had been captured by Hoarfrost himself on one of his patrols, together with two of her aristocratic companions, and she immediately revealed to Hoarfrost her connection to the clandestine intrigue that he had been a part of for many days now. A number of weeks ago, Duke Chidair had received hand-delivered messages from couriers directly from the Sovereign of the Domain, offering him an alliance, and telling him to expect a visit from a secret agent of the Domain. At first he had taken it for foolery, but then, certain events vaguely hinted at by the missives had come to pass, and it all started to make sense. The last message, just before Lady Ignacia's "capture," was a promise of "an Alliance and Eternity." And with death's cessation Hoarfrost finally knew that his time on this earth, and his continued physical existence now depended on such an alliance.

Armed with this certainty, Hoarfrost reluctantly decided to listen to the young lady. She was immediately treated with honor, housed in fine quarters, and separated from her two former friends who were given much less pleasing accommodations under lock and key. The latter—Lady Amaryllis Roulle and Lord Nathan Woult—had been the most brilliant young members of the scandalous set at Court, and—together with Ignacia—the three had called themselves the League of Folly. Now, the League was broken, Ignacia revealed as a foreign spy and traitor to the Realm, and her friends were locked in a cold, crudely-furnished country chamber not worthy of Imperial serving staff, much less nobles of the Silver Court.

At present, as Hoarfrost had to somehow ingest the news of his son's betrayal, and before he destroyed the entire Keep with his fury, Lady Ignacia had taken it upon herself to pacify him.

Thus, as Hoarfrost strode through his unfortunate corridor and wrecked everything around him, a voluptuous well-dressed lady in a sage green dress, with a tiny cinched waist, with an abundance of auburn hair that was presently confined and pinned up into an artful sculptured hairdo, followed quietly in his footsteps, just a length of corridor out of sight, waiting for the best opportunity to approach him.

The Duke raged his way up another flight of well-worn circling stairs into a turret of old crumbling stone in the oldest portion of the Keep. And the lady followed, always keeping to one flight below, stepping lightly and soundlessly, and glancing with distaste at the crumbling antique ruin around her that was not merely this sorry wing but indeed could have been said of the majority of Chidair Keep. At some point, as she carefully stepped over a torn length of ancestral tapestry that possibly cost a fortune and had just been ripped off its hanger—the venerable antique depicting faded stars, fleur-de-lis, and curling vines on a verdigris and night sky background—she felt the icy gusts of winter wind above her. And thus she knew the Duke had reached the top.

She emerged behind him carefully but relentlessly, and stepped into deep virgin snow. The battlements here were deserted, and she saw only a few deep footprints sunken in the snowdrifts, before her gaze encountered the great shape of Hoarfrost. He stood just a few steps away, near the crenellated parapet wall, leaning into the wind that was whipping his hair and the tatters of his damaged surcoat.

Ignacia looked up, shivering, pulling her skirts closer about her, and regretted not bringing a shawl. But then, it would have covered the splendid cleavage that she had meant to use to its fullest advantage—all that cream-and-lilies rosy flesh bursting from the courtly neckline of her velvet dress. . . .

Overhead was a white winter sky with a faint blue haze, a scrolling dream. A faint mass of darker clouds rode low on the horizon to one side—she was unsure if she was facing north or east—and the bleak sun was just past zenith. Beyond the walls were short thatched snow-laden roofs of an impoverished town, scattered haphazardly, and farther yet, among the whiteness, the dark trees of the northern forest, surrounding them on all sides, all along the haze of the horizon.

Where Hoarfrost stood, just a few paces away, the wall rose even higher, and there was a spot where a pole was fashioned, and upon it rode an old weathered banner, snapping in the gusts and rimed with snow. It had once been pale blue, with the heraldic symbol of Chidair and an Imperial strip of black and silver, with a gold and red fringe of Allegiance to the Realm. Now the colors had faded into whiteness, and only the shape of the embroidery remained to mark the insignias, sprinkled by snow. The Imperial fringe too was no longer true gilt and red but a washed out yellow and rust, while the black and silver strip had faded to muddled grey. No one had bothered to replace it, not in decades, for the remotely situated Chidair with their crude warring ways and their godforsaken wilderness were indeed little better than savages. . . .

Lady Igancia took another step in the snow, placing her tiny foot in the already existing massive footprint made by the giant man before her. She straightened and called out to the Duke.

"Your Grace! May I join you?"

Hoarfrost turned around slowly, swiveling his barrel torso. And his tangle-haired, dirty, dead face was a garish mask of horrors, starting with the round glassy eyes, permanently open wide in a glare. "What the devil?" he hissed in unrepressed fury, then immediately stilled. "Oh it's you, little ladybird. . . . Come to watch the damned father curse his thrice-damned whelp of a son, are you? What the hell do you want now?" He ended on a far calmer note however, and his fixed eye-marbles were trained upon her, taking in the sight of her.

Ignacia smiled and gave him a deep lingering curtsy, leaning forward intentionally far more than courtly protocol dictated, so that her chest fairly strove against the velvet neckline. What a sly little thing she was, and how differently she acted now that the tedious pretence enacted for the Silver Court was over. *There* she had played the bland ninny and the ingénue, playing second fiddle to Amaryllis, her raven-haired beautiful "friend," and always fading into the background, making herself insipid and idiotic for the sake of her assignment, and patiently biding her true nature and her time.

But here, she was no longer constrained, and instead was engaging her main role and skilled function as adept seductress.

And as seductress, her gaze was direct, full of brilliance, and her eyes bore into whomever she addressed with a force of many suns.

"I want to know, Your Grace, if you have received any more new messages from the Sovereign."

"I might have, had I bothered to know about the damned things!" His voice exploded in a sudden acceleration of gears turning a great rusted piece of machinery. "My mind has been on other matters, such as a certain runt from my own litter—" and he bashed his right fist against the top of the nearest snow-capped wall—"who has gone off and left his father and abandoned his filial duty—may he be cursed for eternity—"

"My condolences," she interrupted in a steady voice, never taking her gaze off his face, as he turned about this way and that, raining his fists down upon the tops of the crenels and merlons that interspersed the walls, and scattering snow. "But it might encourage you to know that your forsworn son will meet his retribution at your hands soon enough, as Her Brilliance's plan is enacted on this side of the world. The part that you must play will be divulged shortly. Do not turn away any messenger, not even in this bitter hour of your familial . . . loss."

"Loss, you say? It is not a loss but a *calamity!* Chidair is done with! I had but one son, and now I have none! No son of mine will bear progeny, no more little whelps running around the stones here, and thus the long honorable line of Chidair comes to an end!"

He glared in strange stilled madness, a colossus of a mad god fixed in the raving moment of his highest point of passion. Hs frozen jaw drawn, his teeth bared with difficulty, he was close to bursting into an avalanche of stone.

But the living sight of her, radiating so much repressed energy, so much creamy *living* flesh, that great thick mass of up-swept fiery hair, soothed him yet again, even if for a moment.

"It may seem a calamity indeed, and yet, Chidair does not have to end," she said. "*You* are Chidair. And as a vassal of the Sovereign, you will remain Chidair for as long as this firmament stands beneath your feet."

Hoarfrost exhaled one long shuddering breath, with a hiss of broken ice and winter.

"Such pretty things you say. . . ."

He approached her, moving his legs like thick tree-trunks, and stopped, towering over her. She watched him steadily, and did not move back, not even an inch.

And her lips were set in that interim place between a smile and nothing, where the curves of her cheeks quivered into hollows at the corners of her mouth. She did not smile just yet, waiting for him to say something else.

And he did.

"Such pretty things . . ." he repeated, his monstrous face near her own. Had he been living, his panting breath might have washed over her cheeks.

"The message," she repeated. "You will receive a message with instructions to gather your forces and advance."

"Is that so, comely lady? And where should this old rotting carcass advance?"

In that moment she smiled, deeply, allowing the dimples to bloom forth and her plump lips to shape themselves into irresistible things.

"South," she said. Her gaze slithered downward demurely, and his fixed eye-marbles could not turn in their sockets, so he craned his neck down slowly, until he was staring directly at the globes of her breasts rising gently against green velvet with each breath.

She was boundless, compelling; the sight of her evoked rolling waves upon the ocean.

"I am a dead man," he said, quieter than anything he uttered all day. "Unfortunately, little bird, all I can do is advance my armies. But I see, that is what you intended to say?"

"It is all I intended to say, Your Grace. South, to Letheburg."

She continued to smile.

And the dead man recalled for a moment—through the layers of his suspended distance, past the unresponsive flesh— what it had been like to be alive.

Their room was small, perpetually dark, filthy, and unheated, complained Lady Amaryllis Roulle, a slim elegant beauty, standing in a monastic chamber of bare stone before a small arch window that had the view of nothing but peasant rooftops and a bleak sky.

The young man, Lord Nathan Woult, seated on one of the two thin cots moved against each opposite wall, raised his own pale thoughtful face that he'd been holding between his hands. "Ah, my dear," he said, "how I would kill for an herbed chicken cutlet, dressed in Burgundy and fennel sauce. . . and a goblet of rosy-gold summer wine!"

"Fie, my dear, if you could kill, I would suggest you start with something or someone else, far less delectable."

"Killing, even if one *could* manage to do it these days, requires a modicum of effort. Purportedly, one is required to lift a finger; maybe even flex a wrist. I suppose I will have to console myself instead with sipping icy water from this woeful little wooden cup—or is it a miniature horse-bucket? What would you call this thing? A trough?"

And he looked dejectedly at the floor near his feet where a pair of small plates and cups sat directly on the stone slabs lacking even the tiniest peasant comfort of strewn rushes.

The man was arrogantly handsome, and of the same high-contrast dark hair and tender pale skin combination as the lady, which made them a fitting pair to rule the faerie court. They could have been brother and sister, with their sharply chiseled, perfect features—he with lean angular lines and she with delicate polished roundness. And yet they were unrelated, and unattached, except for bonds of courtly friendship and a mutually shared sarcastic disposition. As a social threesome with Lady Ignacia Chitain, they had been the League of Folly at the Silver Court, and rained barbs of wickedness upon the entirety of *le haut monde*.

That they had been betrayed so unspeakably by one of the own, none other than the blandly complacent Ignacia—who, it must now be admitted, merely parroted them and their wit and vivacity—was a shock that still lingered between them. After Ignaica had made the revelation of her true nature and purpose before that brute Duke Hoarfrost whose "hospitality" they now enjoyed, they were forcibly separated from Amaryllis's Curricle of Doom and its team of splendid thoroughbreds. Amaryllis was limping from her sprained ankle, and Nathan assisted her in his best gentlemanly fashion, despite the gruesome undead soldiers shoving them every few steps along the iced and slippery cobblestones. They were led through a wintry sludge-covered courtyard and then indoors, then through a winding hive of corridors of the old Keep, directly up to the doors of this solitary chamber. They were shoved inside, the door locked and bolted, and then, in the twilight, they had lost all track of time.

For the first hour, Amaryllis refused to even touch her cot much less sit on it, or—God forbid—lie down, calling it "unfit for humanity" and the faded wool blanket "distasteful rags." She stood stubbornly leaning against the wall, pale and near-faint with exhaustion, yet expecting any moment to be called forth and relocated to better quarters, or in the least, expecting a personal visit from the Duke. However, no one came, and moments turned to hours. Amaryllis had to sit and rest her injured ankle, but only after Nathan first spread her burgundy winter cape on top of the servant's blanket, repeating the same with the other cot upon which he spread his own dark and expensive winter greatcoat.

Now they could at least sit, without touching the squalor, and pretend that all was well. Eventually as the room grew even colder and went fully dark with night, they lay down and wrapped themselves in their outer clothing and slept fitfully along each wall.

And now it has been at least a day and a half, possibly two or even three. Who was counting? The night had fallen at least twice and no one bothered to provide them with a proper candle or even a decent hot meal. If one stared through the miserly small window, there was only bleak sly, a few dingy roofs, and perpetual winter haze. There were occasional hurried footfalls in the corridor beyond their cell, and sometimes faintly heard speech, as servants or guards moved around the Keep.

Twice a day their door was opened, and some slovenly, harried maidservant accompanied by a silent guard would bring them two small wooden plates with bread and possibly cheese, and a pitcher of water. The food was surprisingly edible, so that even Nathan did not complain, though he did consume his portion ravenously, while Amaryllis pecked at hers and hardly ate at all.

The maid also took their chamberpot to empty, which was another horrid discomfort, since the room afforded no privacy, and Amaryllis was understandably a highborn prude. She insisted each of them turn to the wall and shut their eyes and ears when the other made use of the unmentionable item.

And thus they slept or sat around or paced the few steps, while hours ran forward without respite.

It made no difference that each time someone came to their chamber they both expressed their outrage and demanded to be let out and to see the Duke, and invoked the name of the Emperor. The guard outside the door remained impassive, and the poor maids—a different girl each time—merely curtsied painfully, and hid their faces, shaking their heads in silence or mumbling something sufficiently full of mortification.

"Really, why do you bother?" said Nathan, after Amaryllis started to stomp her foot, then recalled she had a sprained ankle, and instead nearly threw the empty plates at the latest servant.

"Because I refuse to die here!" hissed Amaryllis, turning her back to him and striding to the window with only a minor limp (her ankle was healing reasonably well during this enforced period of inactivity). Her slim shoulders, clad in now-rumpled dark red velvet, shook in fury.

"The circumstances are a bit beyond anyone's control just now. Besides, if you recall, these days there is no death, and thus neither you nor I may have the fortune to abscond from this grandiose dull torment of a mortal coil. Be glad they are feeding us at all. Think of the alternative!"

"Yes, but for how long will they continue to feed us?"

"Who knows? Really now, what does anything matter, darling girl? The world has all gone to hell and there's no chicken cutlet to be had. Soon, all that is edible will be gone and done with. Might as well make merry while we still can."

"This, in your opinion, is making merry? You disappoint me, dearest boy."

The young man yawned tiredly, mussing his once perfectly groomed hair that he had worn, without a wig, underneath a fur hat that he had long since removed and had been using for a pillow.

"Oh, I am so infernally bored . . ." he drawled. "Remind me why we bothered to come on this Cobweb Bride adventure? Good lord, whatever were we thinking?"

"If I recall, we were thinking of steak. Or was it you or *she* that had been thinking of steak?" By "she" Amaryllis of course meant Ignacia.

"Do you suppose that even then, this whole thing was planned in advance? That is—did she orchestrate a clever machination of sorts, to get us to come out here in the first place? If it had been her intention to make contact with the Duke Chidair all along, she likely used *us*, playing on our very frivolous nature, to get us to drive her here! By God, what a nasty little vixen she has turned out!"

"Well, yes, I dare say she has been playing us for a very long time," Amaryllis said softly. "I can never forgive this. *Never*. She has made us into unspeakable fools—"

"Now, why in all Heaven would you *want* to forgive her, dearest?" Nathan raised his hands up nearer to the spot of faint day-glow from the window and fiddled with his well-groomed fingernails that had in the last few days acquired a bit of dirt.

"Oh, but I *don't* want to forgive her at all," replied the dark beauty, standing before the window and looking out. "What I want is to be placed in a position where I am at my leisure to forgive her—or not. I want her to *beg*."

"That would be highly unlikely now."

"Yes, I am aware, Nathan. But you must allow me to dream. While we languish in this dungeon, a lady must have some dark passion to occupy her mind lest she lose all decorum and begin to grow soft in the head and sing ditties, or worse, prance around in a courtly dance with no partner but herself."

"Good thing about your hurt ankle then, for it prevents you from such a display."

Amaryllis was about to retort something, when there was a peculiar soft sound at their door. It was different from the usual sequence of "pair of footsteps, servant and guard," then "dull thud of the bolt and the lock being turned." This sound was careful, secretive, and there had been no other noise to signal anyone's approach, only a tiny click of metal, and then the door opened.

A messy, red-haired, freckled girl's head peeked inside. Then there was the striking of two flints together, and a tiny candle bloomed with golden radiance.

Nathan and Amaryllis both squinted, their vision overwhelmed after days away from direct light.

"Hello, Your Lordships!" sounded a vaguely familiar voice, speaking in a loud whisper. "No need to be alarmed! Tis me, Catrine! Remember me? I fixed your wheel!"

Amaryllis recognized the voice as belonging to one of the girls on the road who had helped them with reattaching the wheel of the wrecked curricle.

"Catrine, you say?" Nathan raised one brow and stared, actively thinking.

"Oh, I do remember you," Amaryllis said. "Were you not a robber's child? Something about your father robbing carriages, and so you gave us a bit of a fright. Or at least Nathan here had a bit of a fright, if I recall."

"Why, yes that's me and my sis Niosta! See, I knew you'd remember, Your Ladyship! Not that we were gonna really rob'ya or anything!" Catrine continued in the same whisper, grinning widely with her little face of crooked and missing teeth. And then she put one finger to her mouth in a "hush" gesture and softly shut the door behind her and entered the room all the way, holding the candle before her. The moving flame cast wildly flickering shadows against the walls.

"Now, Your Lordships're all probably thinkin', what is Catrine doing here?"

"Why yes, we are." Nathan continued observing her, far less bored than he had been a few moments ago. "But what interests me most is how you managed to get in here without being seen, and whether you have a key and a way to get us out."

"They grabbed me an' the other Cobweb Brides in the forest, same as you, I warrant. But they don't keep the likes of us locked up, only the fancy ladies and lords such as Yourselfs. We—they got us workin'. I'm supposed to be carryin' stuff."

"Oh, is that so?" Amaryllis stepped forward, favoring one foot. "Do they not think you can simply run away?"

Catrine snorted. "There's nowhere to run. Sure, it's the forest out there, but to get to it you have to get past them high walls, and there is no way to climb that far down. The gates are guarded. And all the girls are too scared to try anything."

"But not you," concluded Nathan.

"Hell, no, I'm scared too—beggin' Your Lordship and Ladyship's pardon for the foul language an' all—but I know better. I ain't no fool! I seen some girls try to run. Two or three of 'em take off every day, after they give 'em work to do around the Keep. But they all get caught, and the ones that do, get thrown in the dungeon—the real dungeon they got down deep below."

"You mean *this* is not a dungeon? This horrendous icy wine cellar we are being forced to endure?" said Amaryllis, only partly in jest.

"Oh, hell, no! Beggin' pardon again!" Catrine whispered then rubbed her nose with the back of her hand, while the candle in her other hand flickered lightly. "This here you got is some fine quarters! Nuttin' pretty of course, but at least it's got beds an' a dry floor."

Amaryllis shook her head.

"So how did you find us, girl?" Nathan said.

"I heard the servants talkin', and then they told some of us to bring around dinner to all the fancy 'prisoned ladies. We all know where each one of you is locked up! Cause the crazy ole' dead Duke an' his men an' his servants don't have time to feed the Cobweb Brides, so they make all of us do it."

"So what does the Duke plan to do with all of us?"

Catrine's expression immediately reflected fear. She shrugged, then after a pause, muttered, "I dunno, an' nobody knows! He just keepin' us back from Death's Keep, they say, an' then, who knows? I don't want to find out!"

"How many Cobweb Brides would you say are there?" Amaryllis said.

"Dozens, 'undreds!" Catrine's eyes widened. "The fancy ones locked up are takin' up most of this floor and there's them three more long corridors, and there's two more stories above, an' one below!"

Nathan frowned.

"So anyway—" Catrine paused momentarily, listening to the sounds outside, because there were footsteps in the hallway, but then the sound receded. "Anyway, here I am, cause I recognized they were talking about you and your fancy bit'o carriage—"

"Curricle," said Amaryllis.

"Yes, currey'cul, beggin' pardon," Catrine amended. "So

anyway, I got thinkin' that I come by here an' see what is what, maybe even help."

"A brave sentiment. But—why exactly might you bother to help?" Nathan folded his arms together, watching the little chit. "You do realize I no longer have gold coins on me, since the villains confiscated my purse? Thus, there's nothing to pay you with."

"And even if there were coins, how could you help?" Amaryllis added. "Since you say that escape is impossible."

"Aha! But I didn't say that, Your Ladyship!" Catrine's dark eyes glittered with energy, reflecting the light of the candle. "I said there was nowhere to go, not with the high walls and the guards everywhere, an' the forest out there. But now that I've been all over this Keep, carryin' stuff, I know there's a way out. It ain't easy. And I can't go alone. So, I figure, I get you out too, and we all run together. That is—both Your Lordships, an' me, an' also them two Letheburg girls, Sybil an' Regata who're down here too."

"If you have other girls to run away with, why do you need us?" Amaryllis pursued the thought. "Mind you, I am pleased to be so generously included in this adventure, but you are not telling us everything, are you?"

The candle flickered minutely in the girl's skinny, grubby hand. She wet her lips with her tongue, made a smacking noise, as if it helped her think.

"Well?"

"All right," Catrine said. "Tis true, I do need Your Lordships to come along, in order for this to work. . . ."

"For what to work?"

"The boat."

"The *what?*" Amaryllis felt the need to take a seat on her cot. "I think," she said, "you need to start from the beginning. Now, explain—and do it quickly, before someone else comes and finds you here."

"Oh, all right, I guess I must." Catrine got down in a crouch and placed the candle in its rusty metal holder on the stone floor. She then sat down on the floor herself, crossing her legs underneath her ragged skirts.

"There's only one way to escape from Chidair Keep," she said, switching again to a whisper. "You have to go directly down. And I mean, *down*. Around here, they say—they say it's down into the Underworld."

Chapter 6

The undead soldiers were left behind at the campsite, tied up and attached to each other in a great bundle of frozen human limbs, so that they were unable to cause any more harm for the moment. As the black knight's men-at-arms moved about the beaten-down snow of the clearing, hurriedly packing up their gear and readying the horses, the dead watched them with their unblinking glassy eyes.

Percy, still weakened from her actions and lightheaded, sat in the cart, drinking a mug of leftover tea that she'd poured from a cooling pot that remarkably had not been overturned during the skirmish. She was trying not to look around her, not at anyone . . . and especially not at the restrained prisoners and their roiling sea of death-shadows that massed and billowed about them like grey smoke stacks, invisible to all but herself.

It was as if they were *calling* to her.

With a strange sixth sense—an altogether new sense that she had only recently acknowledged and was beginning to understand—she could *feel* them from all the way across the clearing.

Lizabette, Niosta and Marie quietly cowered in the back of the cart next to their travel bundles, and sometimes glanced at Percy sideways. The Chidair soldiers walking about the campsite also stared briefly at her as they passed.

It was as if everyone's eyes were upon her, constantly. Percy was so unused to such attention that the sensation was stifling and overpowering.

Meanwhile, Claere Liguon lingered a few steps away, and there was a lost expression on her usually placid face.

"I am glad you have decided not to die," Vlau Fiomarre said quietly, approaching her.

Claere turned, woodenly adjusted her cloak about her pale white flesh. She spoke without looking at him. "It is only for the moment, Marquis. I know now that I cannot quit this life just yet, not after seeing how it is—how it is done. I have no strength to die like that, and yet I have no will or means to live. So—a conundrum. Things were so much easier when I thought I had no choice in the matter. But, I suppose I must gather myself for something, some purpose yet."

Fiomarre's steady unreadable gaze did not waver as he watched her. "You heard the dead man. There is a war brewing. And you are—" here he whispered—"you are Liguon."

"I am nothing . . . a mockery . . . a shadow."

In that moment, the black knight took the opportunity to approach them. He and Fiomarre exchanged a pointed glance, slate-blue eyes clashing with midnight black. And then Beltain nodded to him, and inclined his head deeper before the Infanta.

"Your Imperial Highness," said the knight, casting his baritone very softly so that his men nearby would hear nothing of substance. "Apologies for the interruption, and for the incident we just had. But—I trust that this *thing* that you had mentioned earlier—your so-called wish that you expressed to the *girl* back when we were on the road—is now no longer your desire." As he spoke the word "girl," he glanced at Percy who had just finished drinking and put down her mug, and in the same moment looked in their direction. She caught his eyes, then quickly looked away and started to rummage through the basket in the cart behind her.

"No indeed, Lord Beltain," the Infanta said. "It is indeed no longer my intention to die just yet. I thank you for your continued allegiance. We will proceed as we had originally planned. Onward, south." And then she added: "I also would thank you, knowing that, had I chosen otherwise, you would have delivered my lifeless body to my father. If something were to happen—I can count on your honor to do it."

Beltain's grave expression did not change, as he inclined his head again, and said, "Yes, always."

"Then, let us proceed," Claere finished, turning away, and made her way to the cart with slow careful movements of her fragile dead limbs. Fiomarre, after another dagger-sharp glance at the knight, followed her and assisted her inside, while Percy and the other girls made room. Lizabette fussed, whispering "Your Imperial Highness" with every breath and tried to make a proper pillow for the Infanta's back out of some plumped-up satchel and blankets.

While they were rearranging the cart, Beltain came up to Percy and spoke in the same quiet manner he had spoken to the Infanta and Vlau earlier. "You and I need to talk," he said, putting his hand, bare of gauntlet, lightly on Percy's shoulder.

She had her back to him and was removing Betsy's feedbag. At his touch she started lightly, then turned around. He caught her momentarily frightened expression, ephemeral like a fleeing bird, and then she fixed her countenance into an impassive mask. "My Lord."

"Come," he said. And letting go of Betsy she followed him, in some confusion.

They walked several paces in the packed snow, past a few Chidair soldiers, and past the huddled group of dead prisoners— *no, do not look at them, ignore their many death-shadows, ignore, ignore!*—and neared the spot close to the brush and hedges where the three truly dead corpses of men lay motionless on the ground.

Beltain stopped and looked down at the bodies pensively, then looked at Percy. "You did this?" he said softly. "Is it true? I want to be absolutely sure."

She met his gaze, and the winter sun shone bleakly at them in that moment, breaking through the overcast, so that Beltain's dark brown hair started to glimmer with a nimbus of gilded light at the edges, and the pallor of his face was emphasized.

He in turn saw her own extremely pale rounded face with its own brand of exhaustion, and the new weariness in her eyes.

"Yes," she said. "I did it, My Lord."

"I will not ask you how. But—can you do it again?"

She stared at him coldly. "What do you mean?"

His eyes observed her oh-so-closely. "I mean, if we are attacked again, how quickly can you react, and if needed, put more of the dead to rest?"

She signed, then took a big breath, then frowned, thinking.

"Well?"

"I am not completely sure . . . but, in a while, I can probably do it again."

"Good. How many do you think you can take out?"

"I—I don't know. What kind of a question is that?"

"Don't be offended, girl, it is a solid question. I need to gauge your range and strength, and whether you need to stand up-close to—"

"What am I, a musket?"

It was possibly the first time that she had seen him laugh. Not a smirk, not even a chuckle, but a full-throated handsome baritone laugh, a sound that rang through to her bones, and sent a strange shiver down her spine.

"Forgive me," he said then, quieting, and his manner was relaxed and unexpectedly open. "I am used to managing weapons and armor, not metaphysical forces such as yours. I mean no insult to you; only want to understand what it is that we have here. What it is that you *wield*."

I wield darkness and the abyss. . . .

But she only said, "I am not sure how or what it is I do, but apparently when the dead come near, I *feel* them, and I feel the pull to set them aright."

He watched her speaking, never taking his eyes off her, not for a moment, seeing the minute shadows in the hollows of her rounded cheeks and the new circles under her eyes, her stringy wisps of hair coming loose from the folds of her shawl near her temples, the vapor of her breath curling in the icy air.

"I also must thank you," he said, "for stepping forward before the prisoners with your brave words. What you said helped convince them to talk."

"I don't know what came over me. It was mostly an empty threat," she replied, having no strength for anything but honesty also. "I was tired, so tired afterwards . . . I don't think I could have ended a fly, much less another one of them."

"What matters," he said, "was that they thought otherwise. You are recovered now, I hope?"

"Yes. . . ."

"Good. Now, let us get back on the road. Oh, and do me a favor—the next time Her Imperial Highness decides she wants to die, please let me know before you do anything. Fair enough?"

"I will." Percy looked away, her gaze returning to the three lifeless bodies of the attackers lying in the snow. "Should we maybe—bury them?"

Beltain had started to turn away, and now his gaze returned upon her, like a thing tangible. "No," he said, and his manner had grown hard. "I leave them here for anyone to see. Let the dead prisoners observe and remember, and let anyone who might come upon this also know. Let them know that Death has a Champion."

They were on the road once again and by late afternoon had arrived at the outskirts of Letheburg. There had been little traffic on the thoroughfare in either direction; a few carts, occasional riders, and solitary dejected girls walking north in the opposite direction, likely to be Cobweb Brides. Everyone steered clear of the black knight and his soldiers, and similarly bypassed the creaking cart and the slow-moving cream-colored draft horse. The scenery had been the same white snow-blanketed fields and occasional brush, and not a trace of forestland. And now, houses and roadside establishments showed up more frequently, the closer they got to the main city gates.

"It really is strange! I insist, there was a small forest here before," Lizabette said, several times, as the shapes of the sprawling city grew in the haze before them. "Yes, I distinctly remember passing a stretch of trees, not too far beyond Letheburg. Sparse, to be sure, and not particularly good trees, but enough to make a wood."

"Either you misremember, or the forest uprooted itself and marched somewhere else on little knobby rooty feet," said Percy at last in frustration.

"It heard you were coming!" Marie giggled, then stilled fearfully as Lizabette gave her a schoolmarm frown.

"For once, I think ye're right, 'Bette," said Niosta from the back. "I remember the forest. Without it, this road seems much shorter!"

"It's *Lizabette*, not 'Bette," the other girl said with dignity. "And, thank you."

"Once we get to Letheburg, where do we go?" Percy mused out loud, to no one in particular. "I have directions to get to Grial's house, but that's about all I know. I expect she will want the cart back at last, and Betsy too. And then we have to take Her—*Claere* wherever—"

"We will be heading directly to the Winter Palace." It was the black knight who spoke. He had once again demonstrated an infernal ability to listen in to everything, and had fallen back to ride next to the cart.

"All right. . . ." Percy held Betsy's reins, not feeling particularly confident.

"No," said Claere, her voice as always emerging as a peculiar mechanical thing. "We will go to see Grial first. I too want to thank her for the use of this conveyance. And I think I would very much like to meet her, from all that I've heard."

The knight paused only momentarily before inclining his head in faultless courtesy. "So be it."

A quarter of an hour later, they were at the gates of Letheburg.

The city wall was the biggest structure that Percy had ever seen—greater even than Death's Keep that had been wrought of sky-flung twilight shadows. Massive slabs of pale mauve-hued granite piled on top of each other stretched in both directions without end, and rose upward for at least fifty feet in height. And beyond the crenellated tops there were small slim turrets with pennants flying, regularly spaced along the perimeter. The decoratively framed iron gates of at least two stories in height stood wide open, and the city guard barely acknowledged the Chidair knight and his men with a curt salute as they entered the city square and passed by Carriage Row with its many conveyances and drivers for hire. There was everything here, from impoverished hackneys to high-end sedan chairs and luxury carriages of polished carved wood trim and gold.

"Look!" said Niosta, pointing, "There's the Royal Winter Palace, you can just see it! All them glass windows!"

"Lordy, Lord, I see it! Must be dozens upon dozens of them!" Marie exclaimed.

Percy stared in the direction and could just make out, over the nearest red shingle rooftops dusted with snow, in the distance, a tall impressive structure with indeed a great number of windows, glittering in the bleak setting sun.

The black knight ahead of them drew up his great horse, and the Chidair men spread out to flank the cart on all sides, because the noise and foot traffic here increased considerably. Interspersed with normal passerby were also peculiar sorry-looking shapes, including elderly men, women, and a few children, who huddled in pitiful lumps near the edges of the square, and once or twice came underfoot, moving with slow stiff motion of long-frozen creaking limbs. They raised their white faces up at the riders, revealing glassy-eyed stares with little human recognition left beyond apathy, and stretched their palms out by habit, asking, by their gestures alone, for alms.

Percy did not need to see the upright sentinel shadows at their sides to know they were dead. Apparently not all the dead had abandoned their places to head north and join the massing ranks of their kind, nor were they interested in a war with the living. . . .

"Where to?" Beltain paused again next to Percy, bending slightly in his saddle to speak and be heard above the street noise.

Percy was honestly overwhelmed. She did not even know where to begin, and only muttered, "We need to find Burdon Street, and then, I think, Marriage Street, and then Rollins Way. . . ."

"You!" Beltain turned to the nearest stopped equipage driver a few steps away. "Do you know which way to Burdon Street?"

"Burdon?" The man creased his brow. "Not sure, Lordship. I think it was back there." And he pointed toward the heart of the city. And then he added, "But I wouldn't bother if I were you. It ain't there now."

"What?"

The driver shrugged, wiped his red-nosed weathered face with the back of his gloved hand. "Streets 'ave been disappearing lately."

"What do you mean?" Percy asked, stunned, and thus forgetting her place and not bothering to let Lord Beltain Chidair handle the discussion.

But the other driver did not seem to notice or care whom he was talking with. Apparently things such as rank were much more mixed up in a big city such as Letheburg. "Just as I said, Missy," he replied, nodding to her. "Streets are going missing. As in, gone completely. No longer where they have been."

"But how?" Percy continued, while the knight looked on, equally puzzled.

The carriage driver let out a long breath, rubbed his chin and then the bridge of his nose, while his bushy brows went up and down, as if assisting in his thought process.

"Well, speak on, man, explain. Because it makes no sense, what you say." Beltain's voice cut in.

"Aye, it makes no Godly sense, agreed, Lordship," said the man at last, this time raising his hat a bit in apologetic courtesy. "But it started about the same time as the other ungodly thing, which is, as you know, death stopping. Folks around town couldn't find their own home streets, an' at first it was assumed, what with all the woe and despair, the poor bastards—beggin' all pardon—had downed a few cups too many. Well, when other decent folk, including fine teetotaler women who wouldn't touch a drop, came running in tears, after looking for their homes for hours, you can be sure we all took notice."

"I still don't understand what exactly you mean," Beltain said. "Streets disappearing?"

"Aye, at first disappearing an' then coming back, usually late in the day."

"You're sure you haven't had a few cups too many yourself?"

"Oh, no, Your Lordship! I don't touch the stuff, haven't had a drop of spirits since three winters ago, not even on holidays! Got to drive this carriage properly. . . . No, what happens is—it goes like this: you gets yourself out of your house in the morning and take a walk somewhere, minding your own business. You comes back, sometimes after a long day's work, tired, and just wanting to get a bite to eat and your own bed to fall into and, well, your whole neighborhood looks *different*. Whole blocks missing! Not just houses, but whole sections of streets, even entire streets themselves. Sometimes as much as a mile disappears! So you run around looking for it, and you call the constables an' the night watch, and ask the neighbors, and usually no one can remember anything about when it happened, when things disappeared, that exact moment. It's like pouf, some kind of unholy magic!"

"This is madness."

"Well, sure it is! Imagine, Lordship, if it were you that just lost your whole residence! Now, the good news for a while was, if folks wandered around for a bit, and came back, sometimes— mind you, only *sometimes*—things returned back the way they had been, as if nothing happened. And the people who'd been in those missing places, those missing houses and blocks, claimed that they were there all along and nothing had been amiss all day. Unfortunately, in a day or so, those same places and people inside 'em, disappeared again, and this time, for the most part, they didn't come back."

"So you're saying that this Burdon Street has disappeared?"

"Aye, Lordship, just two nights ago. Together with two adjacent alleys and a portion of Bailey Square."

"What about Marriage Street?" Percy said.

"Marriage Street, Marriage Street . . . let me think now. Ah, yes, it's gone too. Same block as Admiralty and Harlows. All gone."

Percy felt a cold creeping sense of dread. "What about Rollins Way?" she tried.

But the carriage driver perked up. "Rollins Way, if I recall, was still there this morning, and even at least a couple of hours ago. You're in luck, in fact, because now with all those missing streets, it's much closer to this square than it had been before! See that red brick house?" he pointed with his driving stick. "Just make a turn into the side street behind it, and another right, then a left, and there you have it, Rollins Way."

"Oh dear," Lizabette muttered, "I do hope Grial will be there!"

"Grial, did you say?" A huge grin came to the driver's face, and he flashed his crooked teeth. "Why didn't you say you wanted Grial?"

"Jupiter's balls! You know Grial?" Niosta piped up from the back, rather impressed.

The driver snorted. "Know Grial? Why, *everybody* knows Grial! And if you're looking for her house, it's indeed on Rollins Way, the little brown building with a shingle up on top that says *'Grial's Health & Fortune Chest'* in red and black big letters, you can't miss it—"

"Thank you!" Percy said in relief.

"Don't thank me, Missy, thank the Good Lord that Rollins Way still stands, and Grial's place along with it!"

Beltain drew out a few coins and handed them to the driver. "A thanks for your help."

The man pocketed the money, smiling, and raised his hat up. "Thank ye kindly, Your Lordship, and welcome to Letheburg!"

Moments later they had ridden past the landmark brick house, and after a few turns, were on Rollins Way. The Chidair soldiers moved ahead, riding two abreast, and Percy carefully maneuvered Betsy and the cart past a sharp turn into a small street along slippery snowed-over cobblestones of the larger street and onto rutted snow-sludge dirt. This was a row of many houses whose upper floors were jutting outward and overhanging like balconies, and whose narrow windows were mostly shuttered against the winter cold.

In the shadow of one such overhang, Grial's shingle was prominent, and swung a bit crooked above a cheerful storefront window with lacy curtains on the other side, and a wooden door recently painted red.

The girls were all excited for some reason, as though they were about to meet up with a long-time friend.

And indeed, they did.

Before Percy was done fiddling with Betsy's reins, the red door flew open and out came Grial herself, wearing her usual dingy apron over a patchwork housedress, with a small kerchief band to hold back her frizzy beehive of dark kinky hair. Grial's figure was buxom and shapely, her face was youthful and handsome, and her black eyes sparkled with good cheer.

"Well, what have we here, my dears! A bunch of girls, pretty as daisies, and my darling Betsy! And my cart! And fine gentlemen too, goodness gracious!" she exclaimed, putting her hands on her hips.

"Grial!" Percy exclaimed. An involuntary grin bloomed on her face, lighting her up on the inside with instant warmth.

It suddenly felt like they had come home.

There were many echoes of "Grial! Grial!" as other girls descended from the cart, and then Vlau Fiomarre nodded politely, as he helped the Infanta down. Claere stood up like a mannequin, unsteady on her feet, and clung to the wall railing of the cart.

"And who might you be, Lordship?" Grial looked up fearlessly at the black knight in his armor and chain mail, seated atop the great black charger, and wearing ice-blue colors of Chidair.

"I'm wondering the same thing about you," he replied with bemusement. "You appear to be quite famous. Am I right to assume you are a witch woman?"

"Me? Goodness, I'm just an old bag," the frizzy-haired woman replied, and did not blink even once, meeting his steely gaze. "But I see you are a fine knight! And as such, you and your men are certainly welcome to my humble little dwelling, and I dare say although it's a very cozy little home, there will be plenty of room for all of you. Well, not exactly all of you, since I must draw the line at horses—no horses indoors, I say!—and Betsy and your own handsome Jacques will just have to share stalls in the back of the house—"

The knight visibly froze. "What did you say? *Jacques?* How did you know the original name of my horse? Especially since I never use it and call him Jack?" He threw a glance at his second-in-command Riquar at his side, and then back at Grial.

The rest of the men-at-arms all around the cart grew still also, all of them staring at Grial, and not a creak of armor or clink of metal and leather harness came from them or their own mounts, so quiet they became. . . .

And in that silence, Grial made a sound that was somewhere between a snort and a barking laugh. "Why that's not a big secret! Jacques told Betsy, and Betsy of course tells me everything. Seriously, if you want your boy to keep a better lid on it, you need to let him know! Jack indeed! He is a bona fide Frenchman, and rather proud of his roots."

The black knight shook his head in wonder.

"Now then," Grial said, throwing her hands up, then clapping them together industriously, "off yer horses, everyone! And let's get you to the back of the house, see this little alley right here, and then we settle in! Come along, pumpkin"—she turned to Percy—"and let's get Betsy and this lovely cart of ours turned around properly—"

For the next quarter of an hour, they led and unsaddled horses, carried things, and made a sludgy mess of what was left of the snow underfoot.

And then they entered Grial's house.

While the girls hugged Grial, the half a dozen soldiers filled up the small chintz-covered parlor with its brightly printed calico draperies, fringed and tasseled pillows, and a pair of sofas on curving legs that surely must have seen better days somewhere at Court.

"Gentlemen, do not sit down on *anything*, I pray!" Grial exclaimed. "I want no soggy rusty stains on any of my furniture! Off to the back kitchen with you and off with yer armor! If it jingles and jangles or clinks and clanks, it does not belong in my parlor!"

She pointed her finger at the black knight himself. "And you, sir, Lordship, you, most of all! Remove your plates at once! And I beg you not to trail snow on that rug!"

Percy bit her lip in mild terror at what Beltain's reaction to such treatment might be. But apparently the black knight too was under Grial's peculiar spell, because he smiled lightly and with a nod and a hand motion to his men, he and his soldiers exited the room.

Only the girls and Vlau Fiomarre remained.

"And you!" Grial said, looking sharply at the dark-haired nobleman and his bruised but handsome face and his impoverished servant's attire. "I see no metal bits on you, so you feel free to sit! Right there, here's a nice chair for you, young man."

Vlau paused, briefly glancing at Claere who stood shyly near the doorway, and was looking around her at all the colorful fabric decor. She had seen and known immeasurable riches and wonders at the Imperial Silver Court, but it was Grial's cheerful living room that seemed to have an effect on her, unlike anything, and possibly for the first time in her existence.

"Sit!" Grial repeated to the marquis.

And it was no different than training a hound. Fiomarre found himself in a deep chair as though his limbs had moved of their own accord.

While Lizabette perched on the sofa next to Marie and Percy, and Niosta climbed into a quilt-draped rocking chair near the window, Grial approached Claere Liguon.

Percy held her breath . . . because there came a natural moment of silence.

"Now, what and who have we here?" said Grial intently, stopping before the Infanta. With both hands she gently lowered the faded red woolen hood covering the girl's listless cobweb hair.

"I am Claere." The Infanta's soft creaking voice filled the room with a mechanized echo. "I am . . . dead," she added. A shadow of movement briefly surfaced on her lifeless doll countenance.

"And I am so truly sorry . . ." Grial replied softly, and a heart-breaking gentleness came to her eyes. "Your Imperial Highness, Claere Liguon, it is my honor to have you in my parlor."

"How did you know. . . ?"

"To be honest, I've been expecting you—all of you, in fact." And Grial looked at all of them with a single glance panning around the room. "All of you, my Cobweb Brides. And you, Percy—or should I say, Death's Champion."

"How did you—" Percy began to ask also, then shook her head as if to clear it.

"First, I am going to brew some tea and see what's edible and fit to be consumed for supper by fine gentlemen and ladies such as yourselves. Then we can chat and catch up. Because, trust me, there is *plenty* to be catching up on, and plenty that has already caught up with us, whether we like it or not. Surely you must know, dearies, that *things are going on!*"

"Grial, it is so very nice to meet you," shy little Marie spoke up all of a sudden, "but I am so confused. I am sorry, my—my language is not very good. But—*what* is going on?"

Grial took a deep breath, wiped her hands on her apron and

sat down on the sofa next to Lizabette. She then leaned forward, resting elbows on her knees, and looked around at all of them. "Well, besides the death thing, there's the rest of the world. It's the blessed world itself, sweetlings. The world all around us is *fading away*."

Chapter 7

The farthest eastern borders of the Kingdom of Balmue jutted up against the Kingdom of Serenoa in a dry-land "archipelago" which was an eternal fertile summerland known as Elysium. Meanwhile, just miles to the north began the Aepienne Mountains, a grand white-capped range that meandered true north, its sharp peaks scraping heaven. The Aepiennes held back snow and winter, which was safely contained beyond the foreign border of the Domain, so that all the icy cold and whiteness was forever on the Realm side.

Here, in Elysium, it was always summer. The region consisted of verdant grassland and farming country, and was renowned for its rolling fields of exquisite flowers of every hue.

Succulent poppies and lilies-of-the-valley sprinkled the verdigris grasses, swaying in the gentle breeze. And among them, caressed by the loving sun, arose stalks of fragrant honey-clover, periwinkle, lavender, cornflowers, primroses, forget-me-nots, pansies, violets, sweet alyssum, and infinite varieties of daisies, dandelion, heather, and baby's breath. Occasional clumps of feathered rich carnations topped rises, and hedges of honeysuckle strove to the sky.

It was a pleasure-dream to walk the fields. The local children came to play here, running and rolling among the pointillist riot of multi-colored blossoms, while young lovers came falling down together to lie in the heady cloud of fragrance permeating the rainbow land around them, and to daydream while gazing at the heavens.

The nobility from all of the Domain and the aristocrats from the Sapphire Court, made frequent pleasure excursions to the Elysian Fields, where they held picnics and played games of chase among the flowers, and picked enough blossoms to return to Court with elaborate flower garlands in their hair. The flowers here were so abundant that special harvesters were sent to provide the local towns and the Court itself, with flowers for all occasions. Even the Sovereign herself was known to visit, and her servants were regularly dispatched from Court to pluck bouquets of her favorite flower, the narcissus, together with the rare pale asphodel and delicate orchid, which was all bound in strings of gold, beribboned, and delivered to her Palace chambers.

Today had been exceedingly hot. The heavy perfumed air rippled over the fields, honeybees wallowed in sweet nectar and butterflies floated like airborne flowers, while a haze stood up all the way to the horizon on all sides, blurring the edges between land and sky. The golden sun was sinking, painting the western dome of sky with a deep orange glow and lower edges of the horizon with an echo-corona of plum violet. Not much longer than a few minutes remained before sunset.

Three young men dressed in noble finery and four similarly attired young ladies frolicked in the tall flowers. The ladies were just past their childhood years and entering the first blush of womanhood. Each was dressed in pale white or pastel dresses of satin sheaths with over-layers of gauze and delicate crepe, holding up their skirts immodestly above silk stocking-covered ankles as they ran and squealed in delight.

"Sidonie! You must stop immediately, my sweet Lady Sidonie! Or your punishment will be severe, I promise!" The blond young man in silk trousers and billowing shirt, laughed and cried out, running just behind the small quick girl who was out far in front of them all.

"Catch me if you can!" she replied, continuing to race forward, the creamy tops of her breasts bouncing in the revealing décolletage, and her once-carefully arranged hair spilling behind her in a riot of auburn waves and crushed flowers.

"If Valentio cannot catch you, then surely I will!" exclaimed another young man, with darker hair and a larger built, running very fast and gaining on them both from the back.

"Will my punishment be a mere kiss?" cried Sidonie into the wind, without looking back at any of them. "Because I have tasted Valentio's kiss before, and his lips require a soothing balm, for they are chapped and dry like fish scales!"

"You have not had my kiss, Sidonie!" cried the dark haired young man again, passing Valentio. "I promise you sweetness like this entire field!"

The three girls running in the back laughed, and then one of them shrieked in breathless wildness while the third young man took a detour and grabbed her around the waist.

A sudden gust of warm wind blew in Sidonie's face and it sent a fluttering shimmer through the grass and blossoms, a wave sweeping like a comb upon the surface.

The disk of the sun was now a sliver at the horizon. At the same time an invigorating roar of air moving powerfully against the land flooded and overwhelmed the silence.

When it receded, all things were quiet again; even the laughter of the ladies and the young men seemed to have faded away.

So quiet it was that Sidonie, panting hard and running at a breakneck pace, could not help glancing behind her at the unusual lack of voices of her friends.

She glanced, and immediately her pace broke, and she stopped with an off-balanced stagger, panting wildly, holding on to her abdomen and forgetting the bursting ache in her lungs.

Behind her, there was no sign of any of the young men or the ladies. Indeed, as her unbelieving eyes took in the sight, the *field* itself—that had only moments ago stretched for miles to the horizon—was suddenly only about fifty feet behind her, ending sharply, and behind it a clearing began, nothing but dull packed earth and a rocky incline, and then, a sharp rising hillside.

Sidonie made a sound of terrified disbelief, because she was now looking up at the foothills of the Aepienne Mountains.

The Sovereign was alone in the Hall of the Sun. After she had ended her Audience and dismissed her personal guards, the Chamberlains, and even her advisor Ebrai Fiomarre, the gilded doors shut behind them all.

She remained seated on the Sapphire Throne, motionless and engrossed in thoughtful silence. The crystal garland chandeliers with their infinity of candlelight bathed the hall in a soft warm radiance. The Sovereign herself resembled a perfect alabaster statue of a goddess, reclining somewhat to one side against the wind-colored precious stone seat, with crimson folds of fabric cascading from her courtly dress to drape the polished jewel facets of the throne.

For the duration of that solitary contemplative state, her eyes had been closed.

And then, Rumanar Avalais straightened in her seat and opened her eyes.

In that first moment of revelation, they appeared to be dark twilight shadow-places . . . and then, with a blink they were pure sky-blue.

Briefly caressing the sapphire armrests with her fingertips, the Sovereign stood up. She stepped to the right of the throne, stilling before the pedestal and its small golden effigy. She observed the old goddess, seated in her partial lotus position. And then she reached out and placed her hand upon the top of the crown headdress. For several long seconds she stood, holding the gold, feeling it warm up from the contact with her fingers, until the metal was the same temperature as her flesh. Then, with a small twist, she pushed down.

As the goddess figurine rotated ninety degrees in her fingers, there came a brief grinding noise from somewhere in the back of the throne.

Rumanar Avalais released the statuette and silently stepped down the dais and stood behind the throne, looking down at the precious inlaid floor, its mosaic having swung apart in clever interlocking geometric jigsaws. In its place was revealed a gaping square opening of darkness and a flight of stairs leading down. . . .

Having no need for illumination, the Sovereign placed her gold-slippered delicate foot upon the first stair, and then the next, and descended into the darkness.

As she sank in the passage, a soft grey glow started to seep upward from the innards below, until the stairs and floor were sufficiently illuminated to reveal a room-sized stone chamber, and beyond it, an open corridor from which came more of the same even illumination, silvery lavender in hue and coming from niches in the corridor walls.

Rumanar Avalais stepped from the last stair unto the sterile stone floor, into that chamber of nothing but monochrome grey. She walked, gliding like a swan upon the waters of a slate stone ocean, and entered the corridor.

She passed the arching wall niches with their matte glass lamp sconces obscuring hidden torches—it was the nature of the frosted glass that created the strange, homogenous silvery light permeating the place—and then the hallway curved slightly and she emerged into a large chamber, that seemed to billow with a cloud of the same anemic light.

The walls of the room were all pallor, nearly white, and here the sconce lamps were more frequent, circling the perimeter to cast cool lunar radiance upon an impossible sight. . . .

The room was filled with motionless human figures, all covered in fine, white gossamer cobwebs.

At first they seemed to be statues, shaped in different positions, most seated on chairs, a few upright, and in the very center of the chamber, upon a flat long slab of carved marble, one figure lying in repose.

They were all women. The cobwebs covered them with such a fine layer of whiteness that they appeared ageless, smooth-featured, like beautiful life-sized dolls. Every inch of their skin, the folds of their clothing, their hair and lashes and lips, everything was effaced into gossamer whiteness. And then the cobwebs stretched beyond the surfaces into empty space all around them, creating infinite garlands of translucent netting that filled the chamber, and traveled in infinite threads to bind them together into one marvelous sepulchral artwork of hell.

The women had been stilled in a variety of poses and the strangest detail was the condition of their eyes.

In every instance they were open. The eyes, liquid and *alive*, had no cobwebs to dull them on the surface. It was as if the diligent spider that had spun this infinite web somehow made a detour around each eyelid and lash and left the eyes themselves free of silken bonds.

The women, frozen eternally, continued to gaze at the cobweb empire around them. And although their eyes did not move, nor did they blink, they had in them a certain living flicker of awareness, a pooling well of intensity that spoke eloquently on their behalf.

Or maybe it was only a trick of the light. . . .

The Sovereign, Rumanar Avalais, paused only for a moment at the entrance. There was no expression on her perfect face, and she approached the first female figure, seated in a chair. This one was obviously young, and the cobwebs had not yet grown sufficiently thick upon her to obscure the rosy colors of her skin, gathered chestnut hair, and chartreuse brocade court dress, and thus make her into the same homogeneous doll of matte porcelain that had been the fate of the others.

"And how are you today, my sweet Lady Leonora? Ah, but you grow pale . . ." the Sovereign said in a voice of warm honey. As she spoke, her face took on a delightful glow and a loving motherly expression never displayed in public. She reached out with her fingertips to caress the chestnut curls of the girl with their beginning nimbus of white silk, that bare dusting of cobwebs, then stroked the maiden's delicately matted cheek.

At the Sovereign's approach, the eyes of Leonora seemed to widen just an infinitesimal degree, and her lips too appeared to almost move, poised on the living brink. Possibly, in her fixed silence, she strove to speak. . . . And all around her the other cobweb statues also seemed to strive, imbued with a wind of living *presence*, an intangible aura that almost made the cobwebs flutter as each microscopic thread grew taut with intensity and *sang* into the void of the chamber.

And yet, it was all an illusion. Every one of them remained still and frozen and lifeless, except for their liquid staring eyes.

"It is so nice to see you, my Leonora," continued the Sovereign, and then, drawing closer to the girl's ear, proceeded to whisper, in the same loving tone. She imparted news of the girl's parents and chastised her for her missed duties at Court that apparently she had been shirking. "Your mother, the Countess D'Arvu was just telling me now how much she worries for you, and how she had not heard a word from you for the entire month. How could you be so thoughtless, Leonora? What a careless, thoughtless daughter! How could you not write to your poor dear mother? Really now, I expect more of my Ladies-in-Attendance. . . ."

With another finger-stroke of the maiden's cheek, Rumanar Avalais placed a delicate kiss on top of her hair, and then left the Lady Leonora behind, and entered deeper into the cobweb morass, while motionless eyes followed her in a trick of perspective from all directions.

She visited with every one of the female statues, touching a cheek here, a forehead there, raining dewdrop kisses upon the fingers of one childlike delicate girl half-reclining on a settee and completely encased in a cocoon of whiteness. She lowered herself in a mass of crimson crinoline skirts before another maiden, seated primly on the floor itself. Kneeling, the Sovereign put her arms around her, embracing the sorrowful thing in the center of the cobwebs, so that her own dress was now covered with a dusting of sticky threads, and her sleeves edged with black lace and her alabaster neck were stained with white gossamer silk.

"Now, now, I am here, my Marie-Louise," she crooned. She then arose and spoke to a Lily here and a Beatrice there, naming them each with such heartfelt delight. As she moved among them, the Sovereign spread out her arms, stroking the cobwebs themselves, entering deeper into the center of their grouping.

In the middle, where the cobwebs were thickest, and she had to tear through them with her fingers, in order to take even a step, was the bed of marble, like an altar to some ancient god of silk and bleak shadows.

Upon the sepulchral slab lay a woman clad in pure white. Whiter than white she was, even underneath the cobwebs. And only her skin retained a hue of distant sunset, and her hair had once been the color of pure harvest gold, only a few shades lighter than the auburn ruddy gold of the Sovereign.

Rumanar Avalais approached the altar and stood looking down upon the maiden in white. Unlike the others, she did not attempt to touch or caress this one lying before her. Instead, she only looked intently, with a strange occluded gaze of profound grave thought.

And then she leaned over her, drawing very close but never touching. After a pause of immeasurable moments, the Sovereign's lips, succulent as gilded plums, with their finely outlined edges, moved silently in incantation, or possibly, prayer.

The nature of the light here, in the middle of the chamber, was different somehow. It was darker, and the glow of the lamps along the walls could not penetrate the gossamer filter enough to seep through the endless veils of cobwebs. The young woman, in all her whiteness, seemed to be also in a place of darkest shadow. And only her face with its still lovely features and dilated eyes that revealed the same sky-blue color as that of the Sovereign, had a strange spotlight illumination upon it, coming from directly overhead.

The maiden's liquid eyes reflected pinpoints of starlight—indeed, what appeared to be rainbow dots of illumination—and if one were to look up in the direction of her eternally striving gaze, the mystery of the colored stars would have been revealed.

High overhead, right above her cobweb-smothered face, was a skylight. It was made of what appeared to be tinted clear glass, and then—if one looked closely enough—the glass resolved itself into sharp sapphire facets.

Directly overhead, fixed into the chamber ceiling, was the base of the Sapphire Throne.

Chapter 8

They ate a cheerful supper around Grial's large kitchen table, a hearty meal of spicy fried potatoes and soft, spreadable blue-veined triple-crème cheese atop chunks of freshly baked crusty bread—all of it being food and grain that had been harvested or set to ripen before the Event of death's stopping, and thus, edible. But first Grial had fussed around the kitchen and hearth for half an hour, with the girls trailing, peeling old tubers, onions, and rummaging through spice racks, and pouring cinnamon-brewed apple cider into tankards for the seated men.

"Normally I'd make all you gentlemen lend a hand here," Grial said. "But I am afraid you're like elephants, big and lovable and clumsy as you please—and the ears all floppy in some cases, too—and you would stomp all over my well-organized cooking area. Therefore, do take advantage of the idle time and sit around and drink this cider! Sorry, I have no stronger stuff to offer, but the ale house is closed for the night."

The soldiers grinned at their hostess, speaking among themselves in relaxed voices, and Riquar smoothed his bushy beard in a self-conscious manner. Beltain, meanwhile, thanked her and took a tankard for himself, and the men-at-arms followed his lead.

Vlau took his own drink last, carefully watching, from the corner of his eye, the Infanta who was sat primly on a small chair that had been brought in from the parlor specifically for her and placed in the corner, away from the table. Her winter cloak had been removed indoors, and underneath she wore the plain grey servant's dress. Her ash hair lay limp around her shoulders, her thin arms at her sides, hands folded in her lap. The chair had been placed at an angle so that she could look straight ahead and observe the entire kitchen, while still being out of the way.

Knowing that the men were watching them, the girls put on aprons and bustled. Lizabette eagerly attempted to do everything herself, and ordered Marie and Niosta around, or else corrected their performance, while Grial occasionally threw them bemused glances as she stirred the hissing skillet over the flames.

Percy quietly peeled endless batches of potatoes, standing before a wooden counter with her back turned to everyone, and glanced around but occasionally, only to catch the look of Beltain's slate-blue eyes upon her. Was it simply an infernal coincidence? Yet when she turned away, did she also continue to feel the almost tangible pressure of his gaze upon her back?

After Lizabette had made yet another annoyingly instructional pronouncement, Niosta took up the large platter with the round head of perfectly aged, soft-ripened cheese fresh out of the larder, and said loudly to her: "Here, would you like to cut?"

"Of course!" Lizabette immediately took the long knife from the wood cutting board with its readied slices of bread, and she grabbed the cheese platter from Niosta. "Here is how it's done properly when you serve soft cheeses: it is best to first soak the knife blade in cold water, then dry it with an actual fluffy towel, which is to say this is not a particularly fluffy towel but it will have to do, then—" And she started to demonstrate the technique.

Marie and Niosta stared at each other, then Niosta rubbed the back of her hand against her freckled nose and pronounced dramatically, "Look, everyone, Lizabette just cut the cheese!"

And they burst into hard giggles while some of the soldiers joined them.

"Why, that is the most *childish* and horrid thing to say—" Lizabette put down the knife and whirled around, with a stormy expression and a dropped jaw, at which point Grial said, "Now, hold it right there, dearie! I want to cut the cheese myself! Here, you work the skillet, while I cut enough cheese to make this kitchen into a cheesy paradise! This is fine aromatic stuff, and I dare say, no matter how much you and I cut, we cannot cut enough!"

The meal was eventually all prepared and far more quickly consumed. When everyone finally sat down, the table was a tight squeeze, and Percy ate seated cozily between Niosta and Grial, everyone elbowing each other. Conversation was minimal, and petered out altogether after a little bit of uncomfortable and fearful speculation on the nature of the "world fading around them, and how no one precisely knew what it was that it *meant* or what was actually going on." Soon it had gotten to be dark outside, for they could see the indigo twilight through the small kitchen window.

"If you must know, the world fades in particular around *this* exact time," Grial said, pointing with her finger to the window. "It is the end of twilight, just when true evening comes. . . . That's when most people report things going missing, such as streets and houses, and occasionally, spouses."

Everyone grew a little quiet, a little more serious. They listened to the small sounds outside, the evening wind. It was as if they were all waiting for something to disappear around them.

Moments passed.

"Why twilight?" asked Marie.

"Are you not aware that twilight takes things?" Lizabette said in a superior tone, looking down over her nose at the younger girl. "You've seen it happen at Death's Keep! Why, we've all seen it, the fading shadows."

"That's absolutely right, duckie." Grial nodded. "Shadows fade both in the light and in darkness. To be precise, they escape from one and run into the other. And now that the world is *broken*, they apparently also take things along with them as they go. And twilight is the high time of shadows; it itself is one whole big *Shadow*, if you must."

"What strange, dark times we live in . . ." Beltain mused.

"True indeed, Your Lordship. But if you ask me, *every* time seems strange and dark," Grial said, "when you are living smack in the middle of it. It's only much later, afterwards, once you've lived long enough to look back, that you can start to see both the bright colors and the dark spots properly—and sometimes, you even see polka dots and clubs and diamonds and even hearts— and yes, a very common thing, you do get to see these pesky little string floaters in your eye! In any case, age is nothing more than the acquisition of Temporal Perspective! Oh, and rheumatism too, I must add."

A couple of the older soldiers nodded at that.

Afterwards, when the teakettle boiled and everyone held either a large mug or a petite china cup of the hot soothing brew back in the parlor, Grial took Percy aside quietly.

"Tell me, child," said the frizzy-haired woman with her dark, dark eyes. "What is it that you must do? I know you've met Death and certain things happened—no, don't ask me how I know. But oh, all right, if you must, rumors are faster than the wind, and everyone in the Letheburg marketplace is talking about a young woman from Oarclaven whose grandmother has been granted the ultimate release of true death. Supposedly, this young woman also freed a dying pig, and possibly a coop of chickens—or is it a herd of water buffalo, and a partridge in a pear tree? And so, what I want to know is, what comes next for you?"

"Oh, Grial, I wish I was certain," Percy whispered. "But the only thing I know is, I can *feel* it, feel the death-shadow that belongs to the Cobweb Bride. And it is pulling me south. At first I thought it might be here, in Letheburg, but it is not. It is somewhere out there, much farther. . . ."

"Then, so be it." Grial squeezed Percy's hand with her large warm one. "You will keep traveling onward, along whatever road that comes before you, together with the poor dead princess and the rest of them. But first—tomorrow morning I am going to drive you over to the Palace of Lethe, where another grandmother urgently needs your help."

In the morning, Grial was true to her word. As soon as everyone had woken up all around the very cozy house—a small house that somehow managed to have enough rooms on the inside to fit every single soldier and girl and provide a comfortable spot to sleep, either on a cot or a sofa that had seemingly materialized out of nowhere—they had a quick breakfast and got ready to depart.

Since the black knight had thought it prudent to take the Infanta to the Winter Palace of Lethe in the first place, he was in perfect agreement with Grial's plan. Lord Beltain Chidair expected to acquire additional special protection for his Imperial charge from the Crown Prince himself—royal reinforcements in the form of added guards, a closed carriage and change of horses, and anything else that might serve them for the rest of the journey to the Silver Court.

In the pale blue dawn light and chill air, with vapor curling on their breath, Grial hitched up Betsy to the familiar cart. And this time she herself got up in the driver's seat while Percy and the girls rode as passengers, with Vlau and the Infanta in the very back. The knight and his men made up the rear and advance guard, and together they navigated the meandering narrow streets of the city.

"Turn right! No, left, Your Lordship!" Grial cried out periodically to the men riding before them. "Turn on Baker

Street! Ah, no, blast it, Baker Street had flown the coop the other day, I forgot! All right, forget Baker Street, turn onto Alhambra, then Royal Way, and follow it straight to the Palace!"

In half an hour, they finally emerged from the small streets onto the large Royal Way—lined by rows of brass-decorated street lanterns, still sputtering with fading golden glow and burning the last of their oil in these early hours—which opened up into Lethe Square that surrounded the Winter Palace of Lethe.

It was still early morning, heavily overcast, even though no new snow had fallen overnight. The dome of sky sat in a tumult of silver and slate with thick storm clouds, directly over the Palace, so that it seemed that Heaven itself was pushing down upon the world below with its infinite grey cotton layers.

Their group moved past the snow-covered slippery cobblestones of the square and approached the filigree metal gates, guarded on both sides.

The black knight identified himself as Lord Chidair, and within moments they entered past the gates into a long driveway approach to the front of the Winter Palace. Here, helpful grooms and footmen were at hand, and while the Chidair men-at-arms and the girls were led into suitable servant quarters to wait, Beltain offered the Infanta his arm in a courtly gesture. Vlau followed immediately behind with a strange fiercely guarded look on his face, and they crossed the splendid doorway of the corridor to the Royal quarters. Surprisingly, Grial came right behind them. And seeing Percy linger in the small parlor with the other subdued and gawking girls, Grial motioned her with one hand to come along.

It was thus that Percy hastily came after, walking with her head lowered, genuinely afraid to take a needless step upon the exotic carpets and the polished shining floors, and even more terrified at the inconceivable splendor at eye-level and overhead—rich velvet and brocade curtains hanging over windows of remarkable clear glass, tasseled fabrics embroidered with gold and silver thread into delicate patterns, grand portraits on the walls in immense ornate frames covered in gold leaf, chandeliers hung with crystals that were no doubt shattered stars, exquisite painted ceilings, cornices and elaborate crown moldings, and everywhere servants in such fine livery that it was a hundred times fancier than anything she'd seen in her home village even on parade days. . . .

Lord in Heaven, she was in the Winter Palace!

They walked quickly along the corridor and were delivered before two ornate wooden doors covered with dark lacquer and with gilded crests upon them, bearing the formal insignias of Lethe.

The doors were opened, and Lord Beltain Chidair took one step forward, leading the Infanta within, making sure she was properly in front.

But all his fine courtly effort was wasted, because Grial came noisily from behind, and moved past them, walking directly upon the Royal Persian carpet. An impressive but severe middle-aged gentleman with grizzled temples, dressed in expensive mourning and seated at a small writing desk near the window was quietly speaking to a uniformed advisor. On the other side of him, reading in a wing chair, was the gentleman's exhausted regal spouse. Seeing them both, Grial exclaimed with a brief bow: "Your Royal Highnesses! Begging all pardons, but we are here at last, arrived with such important matters and such important people!"

Beltain did not have time to be properly surprised by the temerity of the woman, when the Infanta herself stepped forward, and pronounced, gathering air into her lungs so that her voice came out clear and strong: "I am Claere Liguon, Grand Princess of the Realm and its environs, and I seek the hospitality of the Royal House of Lethe."

The severe man with the grizzled temples was the Crown Prince Roland Osenni of Lethe, and the woman seated next to him, holding a book, was the Princess Lucia.

At the sight of the Emperor's daughter, wearing her poor servant's disguise, with her thin ashen hair lying in matted wisps on her shoulders, with her pale and bloodless skin, but holding herself up as a proper Royal, there was no doubt as to who she was. Prince Roland hastily got up from behind the desk. He gestured to his advisor to move aside and walked toward her, taking the Infanta's hands into both of his own, regardless of Royal or Imperial protocol.

"My dear child! Your Imperial Highness, you are most welcome here! But oh, what has happened to you? What abysmal horror! We have heard everything, and Lucia and I are both grief-stricken at your plight!" The Prince's voice was painfully emotional, and his countenance was weary with chronic grief.

Princess Lucia had dropped her book and was up also, coming forward to reach out with her hands for the Infanta, with a similar grave and exhausted look on her face. But something made her pause at the last instant, just before actually touching the dead girl's grey, ice-cold fingers. "Dearest Claere," she said gently, instead of touching. "Welcome indeed! Anything that you might wish for is yours. Lethe is at your disposal, and surely, a change of more suitable attire might be in order—Oh, I remember you as a much younger girl, the last time I saw you—has it really been five years ago? But oh, you likely don't remember any of it now, for we had all been at the Silver Court at such a busy time, and the Silver Hall was filled with so much other Royalty—"

"Princess Lucia, I do remember you," Claere replied. "You were so kind to me even then, and I remember your gift of the windup tumbling monkey. I still have the toy in my bedchamber—that is—" and here the Infanta's voice became more stilted, laborious, as she pulled in the air for the shaping of each word. "That is, I *had* the toy in the chamber that had been mine while I was still . . . alive."

"Oh, dearest child! What a tragedy, and oh that the villain who did this to you were to suffer a thousandfold for what he had done! He ought to be put to death—but, oh, what am I saying, of course, it is not possible now—now that no one can die—*no one*—" The Princess grew silent, and her lower lip started trembling.

While she had been speaking thus, Vlau Fiomarre, standing at the back, had grown impossibly still, and his expression was more lifeless than that of the dead Infanta.

Claere's great smoke-hued eyes, sunken in their deep hollows, however, had a momentary transcendent, almost joyful spark in them. "Oh, but he is not a villain, he who struck me down," she said unexpectedly.

And then the Infanta turned around and for the first time in days, it seemed, looked directly and openly at Vlau Fiomarre—looked at him with an intense all-seeing perusal that cut deep, far deeper than the skin, or even the heart—with a sight of wisdom and serene acceptance. "The Marquis Fiomarre has been wronged terribly, in what I believe is a misfortunate set of circumstances. In trying to revenge his family, he merely followed the true calling of his conscience. He is my companion now, and I have long forgotten what it is like to be without him at my side."

With a fragile smile, strange and impossible, she came up to him and took Vlau by the arm. Holding him thus, all the while looking up at his face, she led him a few steps forward, while everyone stared in dark unbelieving wonder.

"Please accept this man as my companion," she spoke to the room at large.

And feeling that shocking touch of her cold, faerie, lifeless fingers upon his arm, Vlau Fiomarre trembled with an emotion for which there were no words.

"What? You!" said the Prince of Lethe, training his

thunderous gaze at the marquis. "Why, *you* are the one who did this foul, treacherous deed? And you dare show up here, at Her Imperial Highness's side?"

For his part, Lord Beltain Chidair stared at Fiomarre, hard and stricken. "I was not aware—" he began.

But the Infanta raised her arm and stopped all their tumult and protests and accusations with one Imperial gesture of power.

"Enough," she said. "It is all over and done with, and I repeat, this man is not to be treated as a criminal, but as my loyal servant. He is here because it is my will. Everything is different now; the world itself is no longer as it was. Old laws do not apply, and old wounds will not be healed with old retribution."

"But my dear child—" the Prince tried again.

"No," the Infanta said loudly, and her voice rose to echo in the chamber. "I am a child no longer. And thus, I ask for your forbearance."

"Claere—Your Imperial Highness," said Princess Lucia in pliant resignation. "It will be as you wish. This man will be tolerated and treated courteously, for as long as such is your desire."

"For that I thank you!" The Infanta's countenance, fixed in death, somehow managed to hold relief and the closest thing to animation. She stood aside then, as though having accomplished all she intended, and grew silent. Fiomarre, the man at her side, dark and distraught, stepped back also. He, her one-time murderer and now her strange companion, had been silent through all this revelation, for truly there were no words, nothing that he could say either to justify or further condemn himself.

Indeed, with just a few kind words she had devastated him.

Several uncomfortable moments passed where no one said a word.

Eventually Prince Roland Osenni cleared his throat. "Now then," he said, with one serious look to his advisor who was dutifully waiting nearby. "And who else have we here? I see

Chidair colors. . . ."

The black knight stepped forward, with a curt but proper bow, and introduced himself.

"The Blue Duke's young son! Ah, I do remember you now, Lord Beltain," said the Prince. "I recall you're one hell of a jouster, and they say quite a wild thing or two about your prowess in battle. Indeed, I see some bruises on you even now."

Beltain merely inclined his head, with a somewhat darkened expression, and meanwhile could not help another hard, questioning glance in the direction of Fiomarre.

Percy, who had been standing right near the doors, in back of them all, and digesting the same impossible news about the marquis as everyone else, noticed that Vlau himself was in a truly bad state. He was hardly able to remain upright, and she noticed how his fingers were locked together in such a grip that they almost shook. He did not look at anyone except the Infanta. She alone was his anchor now. . . .

"So tell me how fares Duke Hoarfrost, your father?" Prince Osseni continued. "From what I hear these days, not too well, especially after that fateful battle last week. Might one hope that the Chidair and Goraque matter is settled for now?"

"My father is dead," replied Beltain. "And as a dead man he has been acting in a manner which does not suit a man of honor, having gone against your own Decree in regard to the Cobweb Bride. Therefore, I am forsworn, and serve the House Liguon directly."

"Hmm—does that mean that you serve the House of Lethe also? Or have things gone off completely?" There would have been a trace of bemusement in the older man's voice had he not been so exhausted.

"Indeed, I do." And the knight bowed in a genuine expression of fealty.

"Good! And I see that you have done well by Her Imperial Highness and had delivered her safely here, despite all that unfortunate Cobweb Bride business, through all that snow and ghastly bad weather, I am told, and various other obstacles, I assume—"

"That is so," Beltain said. "And now, I would ask Your Highness for a favor of an added escort, carriage and a change of horses, so that we can continue on, to return the Grand Princess to the Silver Court."

"You shall have it, naturally," said the Prince, his voice fading tiredly. He glanced around the room, at the surface of his desk, noting belatedly one of his discarded powdered wigs sitting there, and not on his head, yet again. Prince Osenni then straightened the edges of his jacket and again looked at his advisor. "And now, I seem to have a bit of other Court business that must be handled. Therefore, if Your Imperial Highness would pardon me, and I am certain, Lucia can entertain you while—"

"Ah, but first there is another important item of business, Your Royal Highness!" Grial spoke up unexpectedly. It seemed that, for the last few moments, in a very peculiar way they'd all forgotten she was there. But now that she spoke, everyone once again was aware of her overwhelming presence.

"Dear Lord! Not you, Grial!" Prince Osenni exclaimed, with an immediate frown. "How did you—*who* let you in?"

"Now, Roland, please!" Princess Lucia hastily intervened. "It is always good to see Grial here, is it not?"

"The pleasure is mine, Your Royal Highness!" Grial exclaimed, stepping up. "Now then, as I said, there's an *item* of business that cannot wait for any other items of business—if you get my drift."

The Prince and Princess both started in varied degrees of confusion. "No, as usual I don't 'get your drift,'" muttered Prince Osenni who was one of the very few people in all of Lethe who bore no love for Grial and instead found her an infernal nuisance.

"It has to do with Her Royal Majesty! Why, I assume the poor dear Queen Andrelise is still unrelieved of her suffering, is she not?"

"What?" The Prince stilled and listened, as though he had forgotten briefly and now again could hear the echo, the endless death rattle that followed him in every room of the Palace.

He could almost hear it . . . the eternal rhythmic dying *breath* of the old Queen who lay in final agony yet would not die.

"Yes, I see it is precisely as I was afraid it would be," Grial said with a sympathetic look at His Highness.

"What? What are you going on about? Yes, of course it is *all the same* as it has been!" Prince Roland exclaimed in sudden fury, as the remembered grief struck him full force.

"Oh, Grial, is there anything, *anything* that you can do?" Princess Lucia interrupted, starting to wring her hands at the sight of her husband's condition.

"Goddammit! There is nothing she can do!" he cried. "You know it; we have tried her and her witch ministrations already, and all her so-called good advice—"

"It's so very true, Your Royal Highness," Grial said in a calm voice. "There is nothing I can do. However, there is someone else here who can do a whole lot." And Grial turned to point at Percy.

"This, Your Highnesses, is Persephone Ayren, from Oarclaven, in Goraque. Step up, Percy, come forward now, yes, right here—"

Percy felt her breath catch in her throat as she obediently moved forward while everyone looked at her. Holy Lord, the Crown Prince of Lethe and his wife were staring at her!

Percy swallowed, then made the most accurate and deep curtsy since she was five and her mother had first taught her how to bend at the knees and clutch her skirts. . . .

Prince Osenni glared at her in leftover anger. "Who?

What's this?"

In that moment his advisor discreetly moved up to him and whispered something in his ear. The Prince replied also in *sotto voce*, ending with "—no, it couldn't be, is that her?"

But it was Grial, with her bright ringing voice, who clarified. "Yes, Your Royal Highness, you've heard the rumors, this is *that* girl from Oarclaven that everyone's talking about. Took 'em all of one day to spread the news here and back!"

"What. . . ?" Percy opened her eyes wide, parted her lips, probably muttered something—she was unsure what was happening. . . .

The sudden griping terror of the notion that out there, in the great big world, *everyone was talking about her*, in addition to the *other* thing—the boiling current of darkness now permanently running in the back of her mind—it made her head spin! Earlier, back at Grial's house, when the older woman first mentioned it, brought up the rumors in the marketplace, for some reason Percy did not quite register the full significance of it. She had listened to Grial's words, paid heed, but did not *understand*. But now, here before the Royals, for the first time, the meaning sank in. . . .

Prince Osenni's grim expression changed to thoughtful, and the intensity of his gaze eased somewhat. "Is this true? You are the girl? The one who supposedly did some magic mumbo-jumbo or witchcraft or other unholy nonsense and cured her grandmother?—not cured, I should say, but killed her?"

"Your . . . Royal Highness. . . ." Percy lowered her head again, took a breath and looked up into the old man's tired sorrowful eyes. And as she did thus, seeing their true nature, her own terror receded. He was not a Crown Prince, but just an aging man, grieving for his own mother, nothing more. "Yes," she said, meeting his gaze with her own clear eyes. And then added: "If there is something similar I can do here—"

"Yes!" Princess Lucia exclaimed. She rushed forward and

gripped Percy, and squeezed her arm until it hurt. "You can help Her Majesty pass on!" Then, glancing at Grial, she added: "Oh, yes, I knew you would come up with something, dear Grial, thank you! Oh, thank you—"

"Wait! No, no, this is impossible, how can we be certain she can do it, whatever it is she does, or that it would work?" The Prince frowned, suddenly indecisive when given the prospect of a real choice in the matter.

"It never hurts to try, Your Royal Highness. Nothing to lose, that hasn't been lost already," Grial said. Her so-very-dark eyes trained on him were sympathetic. And as always they made the Prince of Lethe inexplicably shiver. . . .

Prince Roland Osenni inhaled deeply, tasting this sudden new air of choice. For it was not merely grief that moved him. Oh, grief was there, proper and filial, naturally. But if things took their proper turn, he was profoundly aware that he would be King.

Percy was taken through several finely decorated corridors along luxurious runner carpets upon which she gingerly took each step with her dirty peasant footwear. While others of their party remained in the first chamber, she followed the Crown Prince, Princess Lucia, Grial, and several liveried servants, into a great opulent chamber, dimly lit and smelling of linen, rosewater, and old age.

A roaring fire was lit in the marble fireplace to keep the boudoir of the Queen comfortable, and the brocade window curtains were drawn to keep the daylight out.

In the center was a great four-poster bed with tasseled, gathered valances, and rich ancient wood that had been polished and trimmed with gold. The bedding was soft mahogany fleece and pale cream silk, imbued with layers of time and royal tradition. Generations of royalty had been lulled in it to their rest.

Several physicians were present, and half a dozen servants performed quiet useless tasks because they must.

Yet another tray of food stood cold and untouched, going to sinful waste at a time of coming universal hunger, next to a tray of elixirs, medicinal brews, and mixtures in flasks and decanters.

But the first thing, of which Percy became aware when she entered, was the regular rasping sound of the old Queen breathing.

The death rattle. . . .

It instantly reminded her of Gran. Like a flood, the memories came, of only two days ago, when she first took death's shadow by the hand and gave Gran her release.

And now, here it was, the death-shadow of Queen Andrelise, standing up like a royal sentinel at her bedside. As soon as Percy entered, the shadow focused, gathered its shape of translucent smoke and darkness . . . and it turned to her. The Queen's death-shadow regarded Percy as a hound regards its master. And the old Queen herself, a goblin creature of shrunken flesh and bones, lay, surrounded by the ocean of silken bed coverings, and her rolling eyes followed Percy's movements.

"Well. . . ." Prince Roland came up to his mother, and taking her withered hand in his own, he regarded her silently. After a few moments he started to shake and broke down, his age-lined face contorted into a disarray of grief, tears coming in big sloppy drops that turned to running streaks.

Percy stood at the foot of the bed.

"What must you do?" Princess Lucia was right next to her, whispering in her ear.

"It is not much," Percy replied. "I need to touch her, just for a moment, I think. It takes only a moment. . . ."

"Then *do* it!"

"No, wait!" The Prince raised his tear-soiled face. "Not yet—"

Rasping, drowning in her spittle, the old Queen

breathed . . . and breathed.

"Will it hurt her?"

Percy thought for a moment, remembering. What was it like, she thought, in each of those moments as the death-shadow entered the body? Could she recall any pain, any wrongness in those instants of mutual connection? But no, it had all been empty serenity, nothing more.

"No," she replied gently to the Prince. "It will take the pain away."

He nodded then, quieting, squeezing his mother's cold fingers that barely flexed in return. Did she blink at him in those moments? Was she even aware any longer, or was it a trick of the firelight?

Percy approached the bedside. She gathered her breath with each step, her mind filling with turbulent darkness that was *power*. It filled her, the power, filled the bottomless well of her, resounding in her lungs and gut and skull, and the cathedral bells came to life, tolling with bass bone-rumbling echoes, filling her, flooding. . . .

One instant, and Percy held her grandmother's hand again. Only, no—this time, it was the grandmother of a nation. And this time the death-shadow came to her on its own—bowing before her as though *she* were the queen—and was pulled within, with a rush of seraph wings.

Percy Ayren, Death's Champion and now Kingmaker, watched the old Queen Andrelise Osenni of Lethe sink into oblivion.

When it was over, for the first time in days, the new King of Lethe heard only the crackle of the fireplace, and the perfect relief of winter silence.

Chapter 9

The bells rang all over Letheburg, echoing and reverberating in the cold somnolence of the morning and then day. They had started ringing early, just a few hours after dawn, the majestic sound coming from every church and cathedral, in the solemn bittersweet tradition of the passing of kings.

Queen Andrelise was dead.

The Kingdom of Lethe now had a new King and Queen.

"The Queen is dead, long live the King!" spoke the courtiers solemnly all over the Winter Palace. And those who bore witness to the passing in the Queen's quarters spoke the ancient words while bowing before the former Crown Prince of Lethe.

In the dark royal boudoir that was now a funereal wake, Percy received curt but sincere words of gratitude from both Their Majesties. After he was done speaking, King Roland Osenni again wept, with his whole body shaking, at the bedside of his mother's blessedly lifeless, frail corpse.

"You have done a true and loyal service to your Queen and country, child," Queen Lucia whispered. "You will be rewarded. But for now, you must wait outside, and come when called only. And you too, Grial." The Queen motioned to servants hovering nearby, continuing to speak in a soft voice so as not to impose upon the grief of the King. "Take them back, provide refreshments, rooms, give them whatever they like. Have them wait. Meanwhile, bring the Archbishop and—ring the bells."

And thus, Grial took the somewhat stunned Percy by the arm, and led her quickly out of the chamber of death, while Percy's head continued to be thick with residual power and darkness, and the cathedral tolling that she heard was now both inside her mind and all around the Palace and the city of Letheburg.

"Well done, pumpkin, well done!" said Grial as they walked, squeezing her hand, and glancing at her warmly.

"Grial . . ." Percy said tiredly. "Do you know what it is that I do? Am I a monster? How is it that I do this thing?"

"Come now, dearie, do you really think a monster would grant much needed relief to those in mortal pain?"

"No. . . ."

"Then you've answered your own ridiculous question. Death gave you a *gift*. But it's not the silly kind of gift you put on a shelf to admire, or box it up and take out once a year on holidays. No, what you have here is a gift of *action*. So, use it! But do it wisely, girlie, because now that more and more people learn that you have this gift, they will want to use *you*."

Percy nodded. "I have a feeling," she said, lowering her voice so that the servants walking before them in the corridor would not hear, "that now that the King and Queen have me here, they might—they might not want to let me go."

Grial, pacing at her side, lowered her face to her ear. "Smart girl! Your feeling is exactly right!"

A few paces later, Grial whispered again. "Now that the deed is done—mind you, it was a very important and necessary deed, and Her Majesty is at peace, and the power of the land has been transferred properly—now we need to get you out of here, and back on your way. But for now—hush!"

Moments later they were led into a mid-sized parlor which was not the same chamber where they had met the Royals earlier. It was decorated with gilded wallpaper and cornices, and there were several divans and sofas and settees, covered in pale chartreuse brocade, and lacquered side-tables along the walls underneath chandelier sconces. Upon one sofa sat the Infanta, ivory hands folded in her lap. Her dark grey death-shadow billowed at her side and immediately regarded Percy.

Percy tried very hard *not* to look at it.

The Marquis Fiomarre stood a few steps away, with his back turned, gazing into the bright window and the pallid winter city beyond.

Lord Beltain Chidair paced the length of the chamber, his chain mail ringing softly.

As soon as they entered, everyone turned to Percy. Beltain immediately approached her with a sharp movement and, glancing from her to Grial with unusual intensity, said: "So, it is done. . . . The bells started tolling a few minutes ago."

"Yes," said Grial, "as you can hear, Her Majesty has been laid to rest, all thanks to our Percy."

Percy stood saying nothing, her hands at her sides, clenching the rough burlap fabric of her skirt.

"What now?" the Infanta looked up at Grial.

Grial turned to the impassive servant who brought them here and still lingered in the room. "Would you be a dear man and bring us some tea? Oh, and a bit of pastries and rose petal jam would be lovely too, if that's not too much trouble."

The servant bowed and exited. As soon as the door closed behind him, Grial spoke in an excited whisper: "What comes next is, you all must go! And quickly!"

"What do you mean?"

"What Grial means," Percy said, her hands still gripping the fabric at her sides, "is that because of me, you may all be held here. Or at least, delayed—Your Imperial Highness."

"Why so?" It was Vlau Fiomarre speaking now, looking with concern.

"I see. . . ." The black knight regarded Percy with an unblinking gaze of his slate-blue eyes. "Having control of Death's Champion is a high-level military advantage for the new King, in these complicated times. To have her at his disposal could mean a great deal. And to keep Her Imperial Highness here a bit longer, no matter how briefly, would provide additional grounding in his newly acquired power."

"But—" said Claere Liguon. "How is it that you come to this mistrustful conclusion? The Crown Prince, who is now King of Lethe, is an honorable man of his word and a loyal vassal of my father. And he has just promised to support me and to do whatever he must to aid me, and help me return home! Are you saying he will go back on his word?"

"Your Imperial Highness," said the knight. "When a Prince becomes King, he becomes someone else. It is a necessary evil, and no, I do not presume to say he is forsworn, merely that now things have *changed*."

"It is so," Percy said. And at the sound of her voice everyone again turned to her. *They all look at me so closely now,* she thought. *Every time I open my mouth, they expect something impossible, some new strangeness. . . .*

However Beltain just as quickly looked away from Percy, seeming, in that quick movement, to dismiss her. He again addressed the Infanta, with a tone of courtly responsibility. "Regretfully it has been my own mistake to bring Your Imperial Highness here to the Palace, even though this entire consequence having to do with the Queen was unprecedented. I did not think it through. But I intend to remedy it."

Percy glanced at him, frowning without knowing why. There was something in his superior tone, in the subtle way he assumed control of the situation—even though he had every right—that grated at her. She knew there was no good reason for it, but it did. "What else did My Lord think would happen?" she said with a slight edge, wanting to add: *You had to know the*

King would want me to attend his dying mother.

Beltain turned again to look at her, and this time his glance was searing, in the probing way he seemed to *see* her, almost see right through her to her insecurity. "Whatever I'd thought, Percy, I should have taken into account—*you.*"

"What exactly happened in there?" Vlau Fiomarre asked in turn, his own dark gaze piercing her with worry.

"Nothing. Same thing you've seen before. I put the dead to rest," Percy replied grimly. "The only difference is, this time I also made a King. And he will not let me go, I could see it in the new Queen's eyes, and in his own, in that first instant, right after. . . ."

She had been clenching her skirts so hard, she could no longer feel her knuckles. Percy let go, then smoothed her palms against the front of her poor dress, and said: "But I am Death's Champion, not the King's Champion. And there is something I promised to do. I've yet to find the Cobweb Bride. So I may not stay."

"And you shall not," the Infanta said. "No one will stop you from leaving, for I will insist that you come with me. And no mere vassal king may stop *me.*"

"Ah, Your Imperial Highness," Grial said. "Your confidence is commendable, and in any better days it would be a thing without dispute. However, my dearie, things are about to get very difficult indeed, for so many of us—listen!"

Grial raised her finger up, and in that moment of silence they could hear the bells outside still tolling in grand harmonies. Only—there was something different now. Their rhythm and cadence had changed.

"Can you hear that?" Grial spoke again. "It's no longer bah-dah-DUM-bah-bah! It is now Bah-DUM! Bah-DUM! Bah-DUM!"

"Yes," the black knight said. "The cadence has switched from funeral to military."

And Vlau Fiomare nodded grimly. "Yes! How well I know that sound, from the Styx and Balmue border! Those are the bells of war!"

In the bleak mid-afternoon sunshine, under a white winter sky streaked with charcoal and silver, Duke Hoarfrost sat atop his great warhorse before the walls and closed gates of Letheburg.

Around him was a sea of moving pole-arms—pikes, peasant billhooks, axe-headed halberds—among them ragged pennants held aloft, and cavalrymen of Chidair and others, plus innumerable infantry, men on foot bearing whatever weapons they could hold in their damaged limbs.

This was not an army of living men but the dead. . . . For hours they had marched, streaming along the wide road leading south, in a thick flow of cold broken bodies—human meat frozen to ice and clad in remnants of armor, bound with rigor mortis and then beyond it, bound with freezing temperatures and yet in motion somehow, cumbersome yet relentless. As they approached the capital city of Lethe, their ranks swelled, as more and more undead joined them from all across the countryside, while the living cringed and fled their relentless approach.

By the time they reached Letheburg, they were in the thousands. . . .

Hoarfrost had received his marching orders in the early evening of the previous day. In the twilight, a messenger of the Domain was delivered the news by carrier bird, and had come before the Duke, bearing the missive from the Sovereign. The slip of parchment said simply: "Proceed to Letheburg. Then wait for me."

Lady Ignacia Chitain came along with the messenger to interpret the directive. Slightly shivering despite being wrapped in her new, warm, fur-lined cape that the Duke had gifted her from his long-dead wife's own wardrobe, saying that it was "far more effective here in the cold north than any flimsy bit of nonsense from the Silver Court," she entered his freezing quarters. Because of the broken expensive glass of the "newfangled window" through which he had put his fist earlier, the snow was beginning to pile up on the floor just underneath the opening, and the evening wind came in gusts. And he did not mind it at all, preferred it, in fact. The cold, he claimed, kept him from "rotting sooner" than if it had been spring or warm weather.

The messenger, a nondescript, wiry boy, delivered the note, then waited, holding a candle, the only illumination in the dark room.

Hoarfrost unfolded the bit of parchment, raised it close to his hairy, frightful face, grabbed the candle from the boy and drew it near. He then barked an exclamation. Ingacia could not be sure if it was a sound of acquiescence or protest, but took no chances.

"It is time, Your Grace," she said confidently. "Gather your men and proceed. All your future success—and ours—depends upon your actions now."

"Harrumph!" But the Duke did not appear displeased. Instead he turned full-body to face her, towering over the delicate lady like the side of a mountain.

"By Jove and the Devil, let's do it!" he exclaimed, his voice powered by grand bellows.

There was a pause. . . .

His eyes—Lady Ignacia noticed—oh, in those moments, his eyes started *bulging* with effort, then slowly rolling in their frozen sockets, as he forcefully regained their motion for the first time since he'd died.

"It's time! But first," Duke Hoarfrost added, "first, I need to head out to the stables and personally see to my horse. . . ."

That was the previous evening. Since then, the Duke had ordered the Chidair undead to get ready to advance within the hour, regardless of time of day or night, and so they gathered by midnight, just as light snow started to fall, then spent the night on the march.

But first, as promised, Hoarfrost had gone to the stables where he took out his dagger and killed his great loyal warhorse—with a swift, neat stroke to the neck and a minimum of flesh damage. Supposedly, the beast was already very close to expiring as it was, from all the endless patrolling without rest or respite, for days on end, and living on inadequate, rationed grain. While the horse stood patiently dying, being slowly emptied of its lifeblood, the Duke patted it along the flanks, crooned in its ears, and swore to the frightened groomsmen who stood witness, with torches, that he was doing his old friend a kindness. Now the stallion would be able to "march to war properly, and match his master in every tireless stride."

Lady Ignacia, having attached herself to this entire endeavor, was given use of a small Chidair "carriage"—indeed, a glorified covered wagon cart—and thus rode with the army, all through the night, dozing fitfully and afraid to miss a moment of import.

They had been on the move all night and all through this morning. The southern road emptied of all other traffic as rumors of their approach spread swiftly ahead like freezing vanguard gusts of wind. At the great walls of the capital city—which they approached and then surrounded not long after noon—the main gates and each of the lesser entry gates around the perimeter were drawn shut and every portcullis raised. Meanwhile, at least fifty feet above, on the battlements, bowmen and arquebus marksmen were positioned at each snow-capped crenel and merlon, and their various firearm muzzles and projectiles bristled from each embrasure slit in the parapet wall.

Duke Hoarfrost was pointed out the enemy archers and marksmen by one of his men-at-arms, and his mechanical voice bellowed in raucous disdain. "What do they think they can *do* to us with those puny shafts? Make pincushions out of dead men?

Hah-hah-hah!" And he brandished his huge gauntleted fist and taunted the marksmen and archers of Letheburg. "Come, boys! Let us have some of your pellets or your arrows, arse-headed fools! Right here! Put one right here, directly in my stilled heart! Let your best shot make me a pincushion for your granny! Don't worry, I'll be over your walls soon enough, and you'll have your arrows and your balls back!"

Lady Ignacia, having availed herself now of a horse, and fully aware that this was the second stage of the endeavor, approached the Blue Duke's position, unceremoniously scattering his dead men-at-arms out of her way with the end of a mid-length lightweight pike that she'd borrowed from some poor infantry fellow. The thing was still infernally heavy, and she had to hold it with both hands, but it served its purpose to clear her way.

"Your Grace!" she cried. "We have arrived at Letheburg, precisely as Her Brilliance the Sovereign has instructed. But now, we must make no hasty action—we must wait."

"Ah, it's you, my pretty bird!" Hoarfrost turned his barrel body slightly in her direction. "Waiting is not a thing a man does willingly—not even a dead one, with all the time on his hands. Nor is it a prudent thing under the circumstances. Look, the place is ripe for the picking! We go in, and we take it all! All of it is ours!"

"Your Grace, there is wisdom in waiting, especially since you are not yet informed of the whole plan of the campaign. As soon as Her Brilliance arrives, you will be informed as to its entirety. But for now, as a man of your word, I would remind you to heed your promise."

"Aye, I shall wait, little bird. But only for a short while. Tell your Sovereign I am not a patient man. I give her—what? A day? Two? No more. Then, I go forth and take Letheburg for myself."

Listening to the non-stop tolling of the bells for over an hour, Percy grew uncomfortably aware of a new sense of which she yet had no clear grasp or explanation. It was a strange flimsy tug, a pull at her innards, coupled with a crawling sensation, as though she was being *watched.*

Who or what was watching her?

They were all still gathered in the same fine parlor with the chartreuse brocade decorations. Eventually an exquisite tea service was delivered, with fine baked goods, and a servant stayed to pour the rich amber tea into fragile bone china cups. This was no ordinary tea, but a royal blend prepared for Court. Percy watched the perfectly brewed treasure-drink cascade in swirling ribbons of liquid into each cup, wafting forth a complex aroma of the highest premium tea leaves from the Orient.

The servant attempted to present the first cup to Her Imperial Highness, but Vlau Fiomarre stepped forward and intercepted it with a gesture of one hand.

"I thank you, but I am not thirsty," the Infanta added politely.

"Everyone else, eat and drink up!" Grial wiped her hands with determined enthusiasm against the front of her dress, finding no apron and apparently not caring in the least. "Be sure to have plenty, because you never know when the next opportunity to gobble will come along!"

And saying that, Grial winked at Percy.

Moments later the doors to the chamber opened unexpectedly, and two Chamberlains stepped forward to announce the King.

Roland Osenni did not look much different from earlier that morning, except his countenance was now settled into a blank tired mask, and he had put on an over-jacket of complete black without any decoration, to indicate extreme mourning, and a black unpowdered wig to cover his short graying hair in proper courtly fashion. He was followed by a minor retinue of courtiers, advisors, and royal bodyguards—who all crowded into the room a few discreet steps behind him.

Beltain and the others, except for the Infanta, rose from their seats, clattering teacups against serving tables, and bowed or curtsied before the new King.

"Lord Beltain," he said, addressing the black knight with no preamble. "Are you aware that your insubordinate Duke father has camped outside the city gates, together with an army of dead men? Apparently he has gathered hundreds upon hundreds of rabble from all around my Kingdom, not only Chidair. This is an outrage! And even more so, it is insupportable that it has happened on the day of Her Majesty's passing!"

"What? My father has gone mad! I know he has been obsessed with the hunt for the Cobweb Bride, but I know of no reason for him to rise up against his liege directly!"

"Well, whatever it is that has incited him to rebellion," said the King, "matters little. What matters is the consequence. Because now we are in a siege, in the middle of a rather brutal winter, with no preparation and no means of proper engagement, and only a meager selection of troops and militia stationed inside these walls of the city. Lord knows what prompts you northern brutes to fight during the cold months unlike other civilized men! Furthermore, even if we *had* a full, properly outfitted military force here in Letheburg, there is no conceivable method at our garrison's disposal to fight or even resist the dead in such numbers!"

"There is Goraque," Beltain began. "I bear witness to the fact that after the battle of Lake Merlait, the Red Duke had forged a truce with Chidair. But this is no longer a territorial dispute, Chidair against Goraque—this is war amongst the living and the dead, and the truce is justly nullified. As the dead continue to desert from all sides and flock to my mad father's banner, I venture that the living, such as myself, will do a similar thing and pledge themselves to the nearest living commander, such as the Red Duke. Even now, Goraque might be counted on to rally troops still loyal to Your Majesty and to the Liguon Emperor, and come to the defense of Letheburg."

"Goraque is an option, but not a long-term solution," mused the King of Lethe. "What I require now is the Emperor's significant forces at my back, and something even more effective against the dead—indeed, by all that I hear and have observed for myself, something that's indeed *proven* to be effective." He turned around and pointed at Percy with one finger. "You!"

Percy, discreetly finishing up chewing a piece of flaky tart pastry, started to choke.

"Tell me honestly, girl," King Roland spoke, perusing Percy closely as she turned red, coughing and swallowing to clear her throat and dearly wishing she could take a gulp of tea. "How many dead men are you able to put to rest at once? How close do you need to be? Can you do a long-range propelling strike—"

"Your Majesty," said Beltain. "As the girl herself had said to me just the other day, she is not a musket. Nor is she an artillery cannon."

Roland Osenni raised one brow, but was not in the least bit amused. "My question is serious," he pronounced. "This girl, this so-called 'Death's Champion,' as I am told she is called in the countryside—she just might be our only means of loading the odds in our favor. We cannot carry on a normal war against men who cannot be killed—especially considering that as our own living soldier ranks dwindle, they will cross sides to increase the enemy forces the moment they are 'slain' in battle."

"That is indeed a regrettable likelihood." Beltain nodded.

"What about fire?" It was the Marquis Fiomarre speaking.

The King glanced at him with a brief frown. "What manner of advice should I consider from a traitor and murderer?"

Vlau's dark expression flared with leashed intensity. "I

might no longer have any right to speak as a Peer of the Realm, it is true. However I speak as a soldier—as someone who has served in battle. In my better days, I was briefly employed in a military capacity at the border with Balmue and my native Fiomarre lands, in Styx. We have used fire and gunpowder to great effect, and I myself have seen it burn through literally unbreachable defenses, and have grown rather skilled at packaging and doling out various intricate weapons of flames. And now I pose before Your Majesty this question: do the dead not burn?"

"You tell me!" said the King.

"To be honest, I am not sure what happens to them in fire," Beltain interrupted. "We have not observed anything particular during the battle of Merlait—at least not in any extraordinary detail that I can recall of that hellish day."

"Fire might be one deterrent," King Roland continued. "But it still brings me back to you, girl—Percy, is it?"

"Yes, Your Majesty." She curtsied, still flushed red, and with her gaze to the floor, while her mind raced. . . .

"Answer me now, Percy, how much can you do? How many dead men can you strike down?"

"I—I am not sure." Percy realized that her travel companions were watching her silently—the knight, and the marquis, and the Infanta, all who witnessed her in action, all reluctant to give away her ability. And Grial was looking at her with her steady dark eyes.

But she could not very well lie to the King. And besides, there was something that made her *want* to admit it.

"I touched three, one after another," she said. "And they were *gone*. Afterwards, I was very dizzy and weak."

The King nodded in satisfaction. "Excellent! Just the thing we need to know! Now, how long did it take you to recover?"

"Majesty . . . I am not very certain, but maybe a few hours."

"Very well. Now tell me this—does it have to involve

touch? Or can you look at a man and make it happen?"

"I have only done it by touching someone. I am not sure how else to do it—because I must hold the *shadow* and direct it into the body, or at least it's what it feels like, a kind of pull—"

It occurred to Percy, as she was speaking, that the pull she was describing was the same peculiar sensation she'd had for the past hour. It was as though an invisible death *presence* was just out of reach, powerful and plural, and it pressed upon her from every direction, no matter where she turned. Just beyond reach, she could feel it surrounding her, calling her, a billowing ocean of death shadows. . . .

It was the dead army surrounding Letheburg.

And as this realization entered her, Percy felt a snapping moment of vertigo, of being stifled on the metaphysical plane—simultaneously suffocated by a lack of air and the pressure upon her mind, and yet torn apart by the demanding need she could feel, the hungry terrible *need.*

The dead needed her.

The King was speaking something, saying things to her, and Percy could not hear him. She struggled to focus her awareness upon the present location and not the many leagues beyond in a perfect circle of all directions, as the dead stood beyond the walls, waiting.

Dear Lord in Heaven, were they waiting for *her?*

"—so that at first light tomorrow you will go and stand on the battlements and try to exercise this ability of yours remotely," the King was saying. "You will make as many attempts as necessary to manipulate the dead, cast your full strength into the act of sending their—shadows, as you call them—into final oblivion. I want you to enact death upon as many of their men at once as possible. You will do whatever it takes to make it work."

"Yes, Your Majesty," she replied, knowing in those furious seconds of racing thoughts that instead she would leave tonight—she would have to, for to obey the King and attempt what he asked of her was an impossibility. Furthermore, she would not be allowed to fail, nor would she be allowed to leave.

"Very good, then, girl." King Roland Osseni concluded in a satisfied tone. "You already served us well earlier, and will receive a worthy reward for this and future services to Lethe, in addition to our continued gratitude. I expect you to rest well and early, in case something happens overnight and you are needed—though I doubt they will attack so soon—and be ready tomorrow, for we will test your abilities. Let us hope you prove yourself as skillful as one could hope."

"Yes, Your Majesty." She curtsied again, never looking up.

"And now, I too am weary and would like to rest," said the Infanta. Her travel companions found her words curious, considering that now that she was dead, the Infanta had always underscored her lack of need for rest. She had often told them she no longer knew weariness, or pain, or any bodily discomfort.

The King turned to the seated Grand Princess with a benevolent and sympathetic look. "Of course, my dear, Your Imperial Highness will be well accommodated." And then, as servants were dispatched on many errands, he added: "Naturally, because of the unfortunate circumstances at our door, Your Imperial Highness will have to be our guest a while longer— indeed, I would even say, indefinitely."

The rest of the afternoon was a blur of hectic activity in the Palace, and non-stop tolling of bells all over Letheburg.

Percy was given a small but comfortable chamber suitable for a high-ranking servant, and told to "rest by orders of the King," even though it was not even suppertime. Her room was directly adjacent to the splendid guest suite allocated to Her Imperial Highness, who had insisted she wanted Percy nearby. And for that matter the Grand Princess required that the Marquis Fiomarre and Lord Beltain Chidair were also to be housed in nearby quarters.

For the first half hour, left alone in a room so fine that she had no notion how to touch anything for fear of ruining the brocade or dirtying the embroidered bed coverlet, Percy stood near the amazingly fashioned, tall windows of perfectly transparent glass and watched the hive of activity in the Palace square outside. She was on an upper story, high above ground level, so the snow-covered square appeared to teem with tiny ant figures of men in deep cobalt-blue military colors of Lethe.

They were moving at times in chaotic disarray, at other times, perfect order. Pikemen infantry columns marching in tight formation were interspersed with cavalry knights in full steel-plate armor flanked by their arquebus marksmen intended to penetrate enemy armor plate. The specially trained heavy musketeers followed the lighter arquebusiers. Next came small dispatches of running long-bowmen and sword-and-buckler light infantry. They in turn were followed by supply wagons loaded with cannonballs and barrels of gunpowder from the city arsenals, and immense rolling cannons, all in the process of being carted to the city wall embattlements.

In addition, civilian carriages of every size rolled up and down the approach way to and from the metal gates of the Palace grounds. Servants scuttled about, all of them cumulatively pounding down the old snow into a dirty mixture of slush.

The longer Percy watched, the more mesmerized she became, listening to the harsh orders and the shouts, trumpet blasts, the neighing of the armored cavalry horses and the rattle of carriage wheels. And far out there, where the distant walls of Letheburg stretched all around the great perimeter, she could feel the ever-present massive *pull* of the dead. . . .

Another half an hour later, a young servant her own age came by with a heavily loaded supper tray, and curtsied before Percy after depositing the tray on a table.

Percy bit her lip, feeling awkward indeed. She curtsied back at the maid, exactly the same way, so that the poor servant got flustered, did not know how to respond, and simply hurried out of the room.

At first Percy did not bother to eat. She was still full from the tea and pastries (an extravagant meal which would have lasted her and her family for the entire day at home), and besides, her stomach was queasy with nerves. But then she remembered Grial's good advice about "gobbling."

And so she approached the food, and nibbled a bit of whatever looked most edible, carefully avoiding what appeared to be suspiciously fresh, *live* meat forced into a baked pastry crust and furtively drowned in cream sauce by some desperate royal cook who was hoping to disguise its undead nature.

At some point, as Percy moved a dish aside, she noticed a corner of folded parchment lying underneath. She unfolded it with a sudden excited pang in her stomach. It was a note from none other than Grial.

I know you can read this, dumpling, the note said. *Eat well, rest well, sleep early, then wake by midnight and wait. Be ready to go with someone who will come for you in the witching hour. —G.*

A new pang of terror mixed with relief struck her directly in the gut. Then came pins and needles and leeches of nerves. Percy stopped eating and had to bend over and hold her midriff from the sharp bolts of worry-induced pain that shot through her, tearing at her insides as though she was having indigestion.

She was terrified, and for the first time in her life she was on the verge of panic. Meeting Death in his unreal Keep seemed a mild grey dream in comparison. Percy stood up, started to pace, in an attempt to make the rending feeling dissipate. She reminded herself it was Grial who sent the note, so everything was going to turn out well, or as reasonably well as could be expected under the circumstances. . . .

"Eat," Grial had told her, and so Percy once again turned to the tray and put foodstuff in her mouth and chewed without tasting, then drank it down with cooling tea. She took the parchment note and folded it very, very small and stuck it in her pocket.

Eventually another servant came by to remove the tray, and Percy thanked her and again forgot and curtseyed deeply as though the other were royalty. This was an older woman and did not get flustered at all. Instead, the maid smiled and said, "Would you like me to light the fireplace, Miss?"

"Oh, if it's not too much trouble," Percy replied, flushing. She had made a discovery that servants who served *her* made her very uncomfortable.

But the maid smiled again, adjusted her lace-trimmed bonnet (which Percy noted was fancier than any of her mother's old lace in her dowry treasure trunk at home), and soon had a fire burning golden-orange in the hearth. The crackling radiance brought instant cheer, and when the maid took the tray and left, Percy felt a powerful feeling of peace come over her.

She sat down in a tall-backed wing chair, forgetting that her grimy old burlap and wool dress might stain the fancy upholstery, and stared at the moving firelight, her eyelids grown heavy, with her back to the window. Beyond it, the sounds of preparation for war and the tolling of the bells were still audible, even through the closed window-glass. Soon, the window turned indigo with twilight, and the fireplace stood out even more with its aura of warmth.

Somewhere the Palace clocks struck seven.

Percy came to, stiff and groggy, and forced herself to rise and get into bed. She took off her soggy footwear and old socks, and her outer dress, setting it all out to dry, and remained in her old cotton shift that she had on underneath for warmth, day and night. Oh, what a soft marvel the bed was! It smelled of a perfumed garden on a warm day, a whole field of flowers put together, and it was impossible to tell which flower scents combined to make the bouquet.

The pillow was like a cloud, thought Percy, and closed her eyes. Everything all around her was ethereal cloud softness. . . . No twisted death, no war—no dead pulling at her mind from leagues all around—nothing of the sort. There were no other thoughts to plague her; she shut them all out with a lingering vision of dancing orange firelight standing up before her eyelids to overpower all with its warm serenity, letting in only the softness and the delicate scent of those unknown mixed flowers. . . . And then she sank into warm peace and slept.

The next time she awoke was to near darkness and clocks striking the midnight hour all around the Palace. Awareness of the present moment came to her with the sickening pang of immediacy, and Percy sat up sharply. Her movement sent lurching shadows dancing against the walls in the low illumination of the fireplace that had burned down to a few last sparks and golden embers, leaving only glowing deep red coals to cast a demonic faint glow in the room.

The witching hour!

Percy was out of bed like a coiled spring and then looked under the bed for a chamberpot. She answered the call of nature, washed her sleep-puffed face from the pitcher and basin in the corner, and set about pulling on her socks and other clothing that had had time to dry before the fire.

Any moment now, someone was coming! And then they would run!

Percy was dressed and done with tying her laces at her neck and sleeves and round her socks and thick woven winter shoes, in a few breathless instants. She then grabbed her woolen shawl and clutched it in a bundle in her arms. She was ready.

The midnight clocks had stopped striking several long minutes ago, and in the profound silence she sat, listening to her own heartbeat and waiting.

At last there was a soft knock on her door.

She had heard no footfalls, so whomever Grial had sent must have been silent in their approach. Percy went to the door, opening it carefully, and peeked outside into the dark Palace hallway.

Whoever stood there suddenly took her hand above the wrist in a light grip of a much larger hand. Percy stifled an exclamation and then saw a tall black shape of a man, which in a moment resolved itself when the glow from her fireplace cast its last illumination upon his face. It was Lord Beltain Chidair.

He remained in the hallway, put his other hand up with a finger raised to his lips. His eyes glittered black and liquid in the near-darkness.

Percy had time to notice he was fully dressed, covered in a long midnight cloak, and underneath it, wearing most of his black armor, missing only a few plates and the helm. And belted at his waist was his long sword which she did not remember seeing him bring into the Palace, as it was inappropriate for anyone but Royal guards to bear arms indoors before the King. When and how did he procure his sword?

"Come . . . quietly." He barely mouthed the words. Feeling her heartbeat lurching, Percy nodded and stepped forth into the hallway, shutting the door behind her.

He continued holding her arm above the wrist, pulling her—or better said, maneuvering her—after him, and he walked with amazing swiftness yet without making any sound. Percy realized he had strategically placed pieces of cloth between the largest armor plates so that there was no clanging of metal, and his fine mesh of chain mail was worn over a soft additional undershirt in a silencing layer.

In order to keep up with this long stride, Percy had to nearly run behind him, feeling meanwhile his grip through her sleeve like a warm vice, which for some reason burned.

They passed through what seemed like a myriad corridors,

most in darkness and a few with low-burning lit candles in sconces that had been left unattended by some servant who forgot to snuff them in his rounds. Several times they had to drop back and walk in a different direction to avoid Palace guards on night patrol, or occasional servants going about urgent night tasks. At the end of one narrow hallway in a remote portion of the Palace, there was a small spiral stairwell leading down. They took the stairs with care, hurrying down and yet treading softly upon freezing stone to cause no echoes.

At last, they emerged in the darkness on the ground floor near the kitchens, where the air was warmer from the constantly burning ovens, and furnaces—for despite the implications of the siege outside the walls the Palace staff was working non-stop in preparation for the Royal Funeral and Interment the next night and then Coronation feasts in the coming days. While the old deceased Queen lay in state upstairs, while the new King and Queen slept or sat keeping wake at her side, here was plenty of servant traffic. Cooks and assistants scurried about from kitchen to pantry, carrying bunches of onions, dried marjoram and thyme, sacks of old harvest grains, rounds of cheese, and other foodstuffs unaffected by the stopping of death. No one paid particular attention to a cloaked knight and a mousy servant girl in their midst. Before proceeding, the knight let go of her arm, adjusted the folds of his cloak to cover his sword, and Percy fell in line behind him, walking with her head lowered and holding her shawl as a bundle. Moving with casual confidence past the kitchen servants, Beltain eventually located an unguarded hallway and a scullery door to the outside.

The black knight opened the door a crack, and immediately a blast of icy night air came at them. Outside, the sky was pitch-black in spots but mostly colored by cotton-shapes of grey storm clouds that filtered the faintest shadow of the moon.

Making certain there was no one outside, he then pulled Percy after him into the winter night.

Chapter 10

They exited the main building of the Winter Palace on the side closest the filigree metal fence, and from the back, where it was darkest. However there was no other gated entrance here, and short of having to climb the fence, it was hard to imagine another way out of the Palace grounds except through the guarded front parade gates at the far end of the long driveway approach.

It occurred to Percy suddenly that the bells that had been tolling all day had stopped.

Their constant echoes were replaced with wind and silence.

Percy shivered from the freezing cold that struck her, and realized she had forgotten her outer coat somewhere. . . . Her burlap and wool dress was hardly adequate. She thought she might have removed the coat in the servants' quarters when they first arrived at the Palace that morning. At least her shawl was in her hands.

Beltain released his relentless grip on her arm as they paused just outside the door, letting her wrap herself up the best she could in the thick quality wool, and pull the shawl over her head.

"Ready?" he asked, and pulled up his own tight coif hood over his head that was part of his woven chain mail hauberk. He still spoke softly but not so much as before, since the wind came in frequent moaning gusts around them and created sufficient noise cover. "First, we will be walking for a little while."

"What about the others?" Percy stared at him in new discomfort that was caused by his presence, without anyone else being there to dilute the sense of overwhelming intimacy. "Her Highness . . . and Grial, and—"

"They are not coming," he replied, with a blank, unreadable expression. "I am here, because it is the will of the Grand Princess that I take you away from the Palace."

"So you're not here because of Grial?"

"Grial has something to do with it, yes, and she has indeed orchestrated your escape—but it is not her will that I serve."

"But why, My Lord? Why are *you* doing this, and not someone else?"

In the faint illumination of the night, she could see a light come to his face, breaking for a moment its gravity with a flicker of energy for which there were no proper words.

"Because Her Imperial Highness has instructed me. She believes I can protect you better than anyone. And it is her will entirely that you continue your—*journey* on behalf of Death."

"I am—honored . . ." Percy's words came in a whisper.

"You ought to be. Her Imperial Highness has taken it upon herself to remain in the custody of the King of Lethe in order to facilitate your escape, and to dispel any blame on your behalf. That is how important she believes you to be. Meanwhile, I leave behind my men, and we travel lightly, you and I. As only two people, we can go in the most inconspicuous manner possible."

"What about Grial? And how do we get out past the city walls? And beyond—"

But he took her hand again, this time pressing it lightly with his larger one, so that she felt the blessed flow of his warmth envelop her icy fingers, and with it a strange comfort. . . .

"For now, stay silent and ask me later." He started walking, his long cloak whipping about him in the wind, pulling her firmly along. "No more time to waste in talk."

"Where are we going?" she persisted, moving rapidly at his side, her feet periodically slipping on the hard ground that was once snow slush, now frozen to dangerous ice in the night.

"Right here." They had approached the metal fence in the darkest spot, and Percy saw with amazement that a whole section of the fence, at least five feet across, was simply *missing*. In its place was an opening, a narrow gap through which two or more persons could easily pass.

"Grial told me about this spot," said the black knight under his breath. "It disappears in the twilight, then comes back with the dawn. No one knows or has noticed it yet."

"Just like those missing streets!" Percy exclaimed.

"Yes, hush!" He squeezed her hand to emphasize, and Percy felt his warmth course through her like a scalding thing of fire. She was holding hands with fire. . . .

Stop thinking this, foolish girl! she told herself in the frantic instants as they passed through the gap made by the shadow-stolen missing portion of fence. In an instant they emerged outside in the greater square, unguarded in this spot.

Beltain walked with determination, moving forward into the open square, with Percy clutching his hand. A hundred feet away, several military companies passed in loose formation, crunching on snow, and suddenly there were foot-soldiers everywhere, sword-and-buckler corps, and the two of them were now walking as part of the hive of humanity, ignored by the soldiers.

His grip on her arm was like iron, until they passed through the surging military crowd, then emerged on the other end of the square closer to the outside, where the many twisting streets began, all leading variously to the outer gates of Letheburg.

"Where do we go now?" Percy whispered, struggling to catch her breath and inhaling the scalding cold air. Despite the heat generated by having almost run for many paces, her teeth were starting to chatter.

He paused only for a moment; noticed her shivering condition. "Grial is meeting us a few streets down, at a crossroads. She will tell you more. Come, before you freeze!"

And nodding, Percy resumed her running after him, as they entered the streets of the city.

It was strange to be walking after midnight through silent sleepy streets of Letheburg, with its twisting alleys and balcony overhangs that put the portions of the streets closest to the buildings to permanent shadow even in full moonlight.

Snow had blanketed the city a few days ago, but there had not been a new snowfall since, and thus everything on the ground and cobblestones was frozen slush, while the roofs and tops of lampposts were capped with crystalline whiteness.

The moon rode mostly behind a thick cloud mass, but occasionally it would show itself and paint the snow with iridescent sparks, casting blue shadows.

Whenever it happened, it seemed to Percy that some buildings around her started to take on a peculiar transparent nature. It was a pale, otherworldly winter ice-mirage, and the air itself shimmered—but only for as long as there was moonglow. The moment the moon hid again behind the cloud haze, and shadows rushed in, the buildings took on normal solidity. . . .

Percy blinked, clearing her vision, as though casting away a veil similar to the death shadow illusion. Yet it was something *else*.

"Only another street more," Beltain said, walking ahead relentlessly, and Percy ran along, unused to such a pace. "There. . . ." He motioned before them, as they followed the curving narrow street onto a crossing where it connected to a much larger boulevard.

They had been walking for half an hour, keeping to the

smaller streets, in order to avoid the passing troops that continued to make their way to the walls. The subdued noise of their passing, the orders shouted by commanders, the clatter of heavy cavalry, made it easy to avoid the larger thoroughfares and move in the shadows. Very few civilians were out on the streets in this cold, and the lonely figures they did encounter mostly kept out of the way of the large armored knight and his small companion, and quickly hid in doorways. An old dead woman sitting stiffly, half-buried in the snow before the wall of a house gifted Percy with a watery gaze of eternally fixed eyes, appearing phosphorescent in the flickering glow of the nearby streetlamp. . . .

A few city militia guard patrols moved past with lanterns. In order to avoid those encounters, Beltain in turn would push Percy ahead of himself into the shadows of the nearest alley to wait until they passed.

And now here they were, at the crossroads of two streets, as described by Grial.

At the corner house, parked in the shadow of an overhang, was the familiar cart with Betsy, and next to her, Jack, the huge warhorse belonging to the black knight. Grial, wearing a wide brimmed winter hat with scarf flaps, sat in the driver's seat and waived merrily to them as soon as they appeared in view.

Letting go of the knight's hand, Percy ran forward, feeling an immense sense of relief. "Grial! You're here! Oh, thank the Lord—"

"You mean, thank Betsy! Because she's the one who got us here right on time, and we've only been waiting for a quarter of an hour! Hah! But oh, you made it, dearie! So good to see you! I'll be sure to tell Lizabette and Niosta and Marie that you are safely out of the Palace—Did I mention, the girls will be staying with me while this military mess is going on and Letheburg is on lockdown—" The older woman spoke in a torrent of familiar mannerisms, pitching her usually ringing voice in a loud whisper. In the cold, her breath escaped in puffs of vapor. She leaned forward and took Percy in a partial hug with one hand while with the other she held on to Betsy's reins. Her dark eyes glittered with intensity in the faint filtered moonglow. "And very fine to see you too, Lordship!" she added, smiling at both of them.

"So you managed to bring my Jack," said the knight, coming up to his warhorse immediately and testing his saddle, blanket, and bridle ties. "An impressive feat, Mistress Grial. Did you inform my men, as we agreed?"

"Jacques showed himself a true equine gentleman, so leading him was a pleasure, Your Lordship. As for your fine soldier fellows, yes, yes, of course, they know exactly how to behave and what to do while you are gone. Keeping guard for Her Imperial Highness is an admirable assignment!"

"Good." Beltain paused his examination of Jack to glance inside the cart. "My helmet, shield, gauntlets, and the rest of my plate armor?"

"All accounted for!" Grial pointed to several bundles. "And also a nicely hefty money-purse, with some additional coin from her Imperial Highness, unbeknownst to His Majesty who naturally granted it to her."

He reached into the cart and lifted out a long plain soldier's battle shield of beaten iron over wood, with no insignias. "It will do," he said, after a brief examination. "My own shield has been left behind at Chidair Keep, since I don't bother taking it on a patrol, only to battle. Unfortunately I will have need of a shield tonight."

"What is happening, Grial? How do we get out of the city?" Percy asked nervously, feeling a surge of excitement rising in her like a tidal wave. While she spoke, she watched Lord Beltain Chidair remove his long cloak and fold it in a bundle, attaching it to the back of the saddle. Next, she watched him pull the rag stuffing from underneath some of his armor plates that he had worn in the Palace for silence of movement, and toss the rags in the cart. He tightened his armor pieces around his body, and put on additional ones round his sides and legs, and tied several pieces around Jack's flanks.

"Well, pumpkin, the way you'll be going is rather simple actually. A few more pesky streets between here and there have disappeared, clearing the road for you. So what you're left with is this—" And Grial named half a dozen street names, making Percy repeat them twice, to make sure she remembered. "And then, even if you forget Goldiere and Admiralty and Rowers Row, you will still know to keep heading *thataway*—" Grial pointed in the general direction of the southern walls.

"But how do we get out of the city? It is fortified on the inside, and outside, the dead wait—"

"Hah!" Grial exclaimed. "It's the same way you escaped the Palace grounds. Even now, the insurmountable Letheburg walls have acquired a number of very unfortunate breeches and gaps that appeared when twilight came and stole away portions of stone upper parapet on the battlements, and quite a few support boulders of granite below at ground level. You can thank the shadows for it! You can also bet that neither the dead on the outside nor the living on the inside have noticed these anomalies just yet, else the city would be crawling with the enemy by now."

"Oh, no!" Percy whispered. "Then Letheburg might fall overnight!"

"Well, we'll see about that!" Grial announced cheerfully. "Now, put on this coat, which I've brought for you, dumpling, else you'll freeze off your behind—and then be on your way south, both of you!"

"My coat!" Percy grabbed her familiar old straw-lined wool coat and pulled it on, then replaced her shawl over the whole affair, feeling much warmer immediately.

"And your mittens!" Grial handed her the woolen pair.

"Oh, bless you, Grial!"

"And bless you, child! Remember, once you move forward from this crossroads, you will only have your own clever mind and heart to guide you. The roads all go on forever, but you must make the effort to follow the right ones, especially on *this* night!"

"Then," Percy said, "we will walk with great care!"

"No." Beltain led Jack forward. Setting one metal-booted foot up in the stirrup, he mounted the saddle of his warhorse with one easy powerful motion. "We will not be walking. We ride!"

And before Percy could say a word, the black knight and his great warhorse were before her, and he reached down with one gauntlet and took hold of her by the scruff of her coat, like a kitten. With the other gauntlet he grabbed her round the waist, and she was lifted up and deposited sideways before him in the roomy saddle, with her back next to the fastened shield.

Percy made a small stifled sound, then pushed with both hands against what turned out to be his metal breastplate. She remembered the last time the world tilted in such an exact same way, and how she had been lifted by him—

Apparently he harbored the same thought.

"This time," he leaned forward to whisper in her ear, his warm breath on her cheek, "no skillet. . . ."

They started out at a measured walking pace, riding slowly down the street in order not to draw attention to their movement.

Percy, sitting sideways in the saddle before the knight, pressed against his cold iron breastplate, watched Grial waving farewell to them, until the shadows and the curve of the street took them beyond sight.

Underneath them, Jack's monstrous great body was a moving mountain, and she could feel the swaying power of his muscles with each measured step, and the soft jangle of metal plate on the flanks.

The moon appeared and slid away again into the clouds. Percy watched the streets and alleys recede on both sides, and tried with all her being not to think, not to sense the iron-clad body of the man pressing against her. . . .

The black knight's upper arms, clad in armor rerebraces, then vambraces on the lower parts, ending in great gauntlets, surrounded her, because in order to manage the reins he had to keep her in a kind of metal embrace which did not constrict but created a strange illusion of being pressed in on all sides. Beltain wore his helmet but his visor was up, and when she briefly looked at his face, she could see the angled shadows of his cheekbones and stubble-covered jaw and the liquid sparkle of the moon's glow reflect coldly in his eyes.

They were so black, his eyes . . . so strangely black in the night, with not a trace of the blue that was their real color.

"Watch the streets," he said suddenly, speaking so close to her ear that Percy could hear the baritone of his voice reverberate in her bones.

"I am," she retorted, looking pointedly away from his face. "There is Cane Street, there, right past that alley, see the shingle sign, we turn to the right—"

In answer, he snapped the reins and Jack responded with a sharp lunge forward.

And in the next breath, they were flying. . . .

Percy stifled a small sound, as the world tilted suddenly, fell away from her in a burst of vertigo. Then the shadows sped on both sides, while underneath, the horse that was a mountain sank and rose like a tall ship on monster swells of a black ocean with each great leap and bound. . . .

She had no idea that the heavy charger could move so fast!

Letheburg, with its streets and snow-clad rooftops, was a blur of buildings and alleys, occasional bright golden dots of lampposts, corners and crossroads.

Somewhere out there, getting closer with each galloping stride they made, was the overwhelming *pull* of the thousands of the dead. . . .

Percy held on with her mittened fingers gone numb, one hand on the saddlehorn, the other, she realized, was clutching the knight's iron vambrace on his lower arm. "We're going too fast," she whispered through gritted teeth, the side of her shawl-wrapped face pressed hard against the metal of his chest, while the preternatural *sense* of the infinite dead pushed upon her mind. "I can't see the streets! Was that Rowers Row?"

"It doesn't matter, we're nearly there. . . ." His voice in her ear mingled with the ice wind. "Look! The walls are just ahead. . . ."

In the dark of the moon, they had come out to the final section of buildings that ended before a wide strip of pomoerium, the clearing turned into a roadway that lay parallel to the great outer walls and circled the city like an inner moat. Here, there were no gates, and the walls themselves rose massive and fifty-foot tall all the way to the battlements. A few soldiers with pikes and muskets patrolled the battlements overhead. More pikemen paced on the roadway below, while a slow overloaded cart with lanterns attached in the front on both sides of the driver to illuminate the way was moving along the rutted snowy ground, carrying munitions to the walls closest the gates.

They burst into the roadway and Beltain made Jack take a left turn, and ride swiftly past the company of pikemen alongside the walls. The soldiers gave them casual glances, but did not hail yet another knight on horseback.

"What now?" Percy asked, turning her face away from the sudden wind that blew freely in the open here, and still clutching his arm.

"We look for gaps in the wall. . . ."

And they did not have to search for long. A few hundred

feet later they came into a ghostly place, where the shadows from turrets and parapets above created a zone of darkness below. It was hard to tell what lay before them, but in the next breath, the moon shone silver through the overcast, and they could see it, a place of pure vacant darkness where there should be massive stone, a spectral gap of *nothing*.

"There!" Beltain uttered, his breath coming in a burst of warmth against her right cheek. He pulled up Jack just before the opening, and the warhorse almost reared with an angry snarl, but paused obediently. "Now, I will need the use of my arm, so put this hand on my waist instead, hold on by the faulds, yes, the iron rings here next to the belt." And with those words he gently disengaged her hand in its mitten from his vambrace-clad arm and she instead took hold of the ringed armor pieces at the side of his belt.

As she did thus, Beltain gathered the reins in one hand and reached to the side with his free right hand and drew forth his long sword. It glinted once in the moon pallor of the night.

Percy felt her breath catching in her throat. And now, oh how the *pull* was building in her mind, calling her. . . .

"Are you ready?"

Percy nodded wordlessly.

"Hold on tight!"

Some instinct made her draw even closer against him— press against his metal breastplate until it pushed painfully against her cheeks, shoulder, and ribs—and close her eyes.

Because she could really feel *them* now. Just out of reach. Just beyond the wall, on all sides, an infinite sea of the dead, stretching out for leagues in all directions.

"Oh, God in Heaven . . ." Percy barely mouthed the words on her breath, as they plunged forward into the dark place of nothing, and she squeezed her eyelids shut in sudden overwhelming terror.

They were out through the ghostly breach in the walls of Letheburg and emerged outside the city.

The moon cast its pallor upon a wide snow-covered plain with remote settlements and sparsely forested hillocks in the distance. However, in the closest vicinity there was nothing but thick churning darkness of human shapes—some upright, others hunched over, many of them swaying like ebony stalks of wheat to maintain a strange mechanical balance and remain standing. They were unnaturally quiet; not a human word, not a breath, only the constant creaking of stiff limbs, the clanging of metal and striking of wooden parts like grotesque wind chimes.

And their death shadows—oh, they were a quavering boundless sea, filling the plain to the horizon. . . .

The moment Percy and Beltain emerged through the opening, she felt them blast at her mind with their *need.* And in the same instant, they felt *her.*

Percy whimpered, unable to hold back the sound, stunned by the sheer force of the onslaught of so much negative power, an *anti-force* that sucked at her, pulled, clawed at her.

"Don't be afraid, girl . . ." the black knight's baritone sounded in her ear, close and hard and ringing, and it momentarily distracted her enough to clear her mind.

"Not afraid . . ." she said, opening her eyes. "It's just too many—too much!"

But she was lying. The panic and terror redoubled, coming at her from all directions, because the dead had seen her and they all turned to her, like one.

A wail arose, low and humming on the wind.

Beltain raised his sword arm before him at chest level, blade pointed to the side, ready to sweep. With his other hand he unfastened the long shield, and placed his gauntlet through the grip, holding it in a protective position at Percy's back.

The dead were coming. . . .

The closest ones to them were only a few feet away—close

enough to reveal their broken shapes and frozen eyes, sunken and fixed in their sockets. Faces stilled in a rictus grin of death, gaping wounds, flesh revealing pale bone, gleaming ivory in the moonlight. They all started moving, a wave of swaying limbs, holding upright halberds and pikes, brandishing wicked spiked morning stars and studded maces, their own bodies bristling with lengths of metal permanently lodged in torsos. Everywhere one looked there was something stained with black dried blood— blood, frozen and frosted over at the ragged edges of wounds with a perverse beauty of crystalline symmetry made iridescent by the moon. . . . Meanwhile, on the metaphysical plane, their death shadows rose in smoke-stacks, writhing, spiraling in a morass of darkness throughout the plain. . . .

"Go!" Percy exclaimed in mindless panic.

And the black knight spurred his charger, bursting forward.

Thus again they flew.

It was different, this time. Beltain had to cut a path before them, and he swung his great sword widely, putting his immense force into each sweep, and letting forth a battle roar, while using the shield to punch and block.

In that instant that his berserker voice sounded, many feet behind them now, on top of the city battlements, someone must have heard him. Percy saw, in a hasty backward glance, that torches started to flicker on top of the walls, and there was the sound of soldiers on alert running, and barked command yells. What did they think was happening outside Letheburg walls, just below? No doubt they assumed the enemy was on the move. . . . Or have they discovered the gap in the wall?

But, it occurred to her, it did not matter what the city soldiers thought. They were too far back to offer proper assistance, even if they understood what was going on below.

Percy held on for dear life, cringing away, wanting to make herself small. . . . Oh, how she wanted to squeeze her eyes shut and hide her face in his chest! But there was only the cold hard armor, and she felt the endless *pull, pull, pull* tearing apart her mind.

Meanwhile, the physical world was in chaos. . . .

Shapes of once-living men fell upon them, hands clawing at the sides, crawling up at the flanks of the warhorse, for they had massed in numbers and grown thick like an ocean. Thus, inevitably the charger had to slow down, for it was impossible to move any faster through an endless thicket of human walls wrought of the dead.

The warhorse advanced, moving through churning black molasses, screaming in fury.

Beltain swung his blade like a scythe through the limbs, blocking their deadly bludgeoning strikes with his shield, hacking and cutting off arms, fingers, kicking away others that had reached for them—reached for *her*.

And then the *thing* that was building, the pressure, the pull—something burst inside Percy.

A dead man touched her by the knee, grabbing her in an attempt to pull her down, and it acted as a catalyst inside her mind.

The black churning power rose up in an avalanche, and her head rang with it. A thousand cathedral bells were insufficient to fill her with their rumbling force to match what was inside her, and what exploded forth at one dead man's touch.

Beltain cried out, because even he could feel it, something happening all around them. . . .

Percy opened her eyes wide, and she reached out to the death-shadows—all the infinity of them—like a great spider casting forth a web of *self*, feeling in one fractured moment the unique *death* of every man for leagues around.

And each death she felt, she *took* with her mind, handled it with a myriad fingers of power, and she *held* them all, like marionettes on infinite strings in the palm of her hand. In the holding, she could tell apart each entity from the other—delicate individual threads of gossamer death, each one a billowing shadow on the other end, connected to her through the invisible string of her churning force. . . .

Some of them had been lonely, immediately clinging to her metaphysical lifeline with bottomless hunger. Others struggled like flies in her arachnid grasp. A few regarded her in slavish resignation.

All she had to do was *pull*, and they would all come to her, or come to do whatever was her bidding.

One of the death shadows in the distance she recognized somehow, as belonging to the man called Ian Chidair, Duke Hoarfrost. How she knew, she was uncertain—maybe because he was Beltain's father and she could feel the common signature of their blood—but he was the strongest one among them. Like a great stinging wasp caught in her net, he struggled wildly, enraged by her control over him.

With a mere flick of my mind, I can take them all unto me. . . .

And yet, Percy paused, seared into a moment of timeless impossibility.

A choice to wield infinite power was before her.

Was it hers to take?

Take us all!

The temptation was before her, sweet, thick darkness—oh, to take it all unto her, to take their ghosts and suspended soul sparks, their very oblivion and make it *hers*, and together with it all to gently sink. . . .

Dissolution of will.

To do that would require *all of her*.

And Percy exhaled suddenly, while a strange deafening serenity came to her. She loosened the web of power with her mind, so that the outer edges of her touch, the pulsing threads of connection near the horizon were gently released, while the ones closest to her she still held, like a weaver differentiating the colors of string, based on their proximity.

And calling upon the weaver, she became Arachne, and she pulled subtle individual puppet strings unto herself and into their personal final silence.

In a radius of about twenty feet in their immediate surroundings, she *took* each dead man and his death-shadow, and she pulled them together without any physical contact, except for the one dead man still clutching at her knee. She glanced at each one and touched them with her thought; guided each one of the individual billowing essences of death into their own physical vessels, forcing them down and inward. The dead men she chose collapsed in a small perimeter around them, mannequin bodies piling like logs and growing still and inanimate.

The anonymous dead soldier at her knee let go and immediately slipped away underneath the feet of the warhorse.

"Dear God! Are you doing this?" Beltain exclaimed, breathing hard, pausing his sword strikes, for the way before them was suddenly clear—a narrow path just enough for a horse to advance.

"Yes!" cried Percy, and her vision swam with the intensity of her focus, and the inexplicable welling of tears. "Ride!"

"Well done, girl!" Beltain's hoarse-voiced response was filled with grim exuberance, and he spurred Jack onward.

They picked up the pace once more and started to move forward over piling bodies, faster and faster, until they were again in a gallop. Percy cut a swathe before them, clearing the way, making each man connect with his death in a split-second embrace as soon as she glanced at him.

Her head was growing heavier and heavier, becoming an anvil of power, and she had the strange sensation that she could barely maintain it on her shoulders. She was stuck in a loop, performing a *function*—her eyes did not stop to blink, but instantaneously fixed the details of each man-shape coming toward them in the field, and her mind methodically executed the final act.

Barreling forward, they thus advanced several hundred feet, and the pressing onslaught of dead men around them rarified. It was apparent they had at last passed the bulk of the dead army and emerged on the other side into the empty snow-covered fields around Letheburg.

Bodies rendered suddenly lifeless continued to fall on both sides of the warhorse, but there were fewer and fewer of them, and they no longer held an immediate threat of physical contact. A small number of dead stragglers continued to turn their way, but now Percy did not bother to reach for them with her killing *thought*. She swayed, having fallen against the iron breastplate of the knight, and the dark ocean of power in her mind was clouding her vision. . . .

She blinked, letting go of the infernal focus, allowing her eyelids to relax at last, feeling nausea rising in her gut. Her extremities had gone numb, while her limbs felt leaden with weakness. She slipped forward, to the side—she no longer knew—and again the world was tilting while the moon overhead slipped forth from the clouds yet again, filling her vision with soothing silver, while all the world's cathedral bells tolled in her mind.

"It's over. . . ." The black knight's deep voice sounded in her ear. "You did it, Percy, you kept us alive, as I knew you would. . . ."

"How—" she began, but her lips were dry and lacking sensation, like cotton. "How did you . . . know?"

"Hush now," he replied, and she felt an iron gauntlet holding her up, then gently repositioning her against his armored chest.

"South . . ." whispered Percy with her last strength. "Please . . . keep going south!"

And then she sank into unconsciousness.

B eltain watched with rising concern the very pale, sickly face of the girl lying back against his chest, her head wrapped in her familiar woolen shawl lolling against his plate armor. She had slipped away in a peculiar faint, moments after what must have been a feat of impossible power, because her normally rounded, puffy cheeks and reddened nose appeared grey and lifeless somehow, as though she had been sapped of all energy.

They now rode hard through the open field, headed in the vague direction where, he knew, lay the main road leading south. But Beltain was not sure if to proceed forward this night was a rational choice under the circumstances.

The wind was picking up around them, biting in fierce icy gusts, and the overcast thickened, while the moon started to sink lower on the black horizon. Snowfall was expected, and soon the flakes would start coming down, amid dropping temperatures.

He was afraid she might not make it through such a night— not like this, open to the elements, and not in such a weakened state. In truth he barely understood what was wrong with her, why she had lost consciousness, except that on some level in his gut he knew it had to do with the unnatural power.

His plan had been headstrong and, in hindsight, part-insanity. The Infanta had agreed and given him her honorable orders to take the girl onward against the will of the King of Lethe, and Grial had figured out the clever details of removing her from the Palace, and a way out of Letheburg.

The rest of it—the part that consisted of getting her past the dead army—was entirely his. And Beltain, the madman, had thought his berserker prowess would be enough to cut through their ranks and to deliver her safely back on the road. However, the moment they came out through the breach in the missing section of wall, and he actually saw the extent of the enemy army, their sheer numbers, a cold grim feeling came to settle upon him.

No, he was not afraid—fear had never been his weakness. But he was on some level a realist, and guilt at his own hubris manifested itself. What he saw before them was a hopeless thing.

Still, he had spurred Jack forward, taking all of them into certain death—rather, there would be no death, only mortal damage to their bodies, and ultimately pain and horror of becoming undead. Was it his pride alone that allowed him to take such a terrible risk? Or had he known on some level that Percy, this strange girl with her fat cheeks and pensive eyes and nondescript peasant looks, would manage to do something miraculous?

Beltain frowned, angry at himself, at his own willingness to take that risk. And as the devious moon once again disappeared in the haze overhead, he made a firm decision. They would stop for the night, and he would seek them shelter.

Because he could not bear to have her die in the storm. . . .

And thus, Beltain strained his gaze in all directions about them, and not too far away he noted the dark specks of possible settlements against the white snow.

There, he directed Jack, and they flew onward, riding on their last reserves, a solitary moving object in the plain. They had left all the dead behind them, and Letheburg also.

As they approached the outlying buildings, the structures resolved themselves into a medium sized farmhouse with several lesser buildings, sheds and barns. The houses were half-buried in snow, thatched roofs gleaming pristine white, and there was no smoke in the chimney, and no watchdogs to bark at their approach.

Beltain guessed that the place was abandoned, most likely recently, since every living soul in the neighborhood for leagues around had fled from the onslaught of the dead converging upon Letheburg—either the residents of this homestead were safely ensconced inside the city walls, or they had fled as far away as possible.

The black knight stopped his warhorse before the farmhouse. He dismounted, then carefully took hold of the limp girl and lifted her from the saddle. He carried her in his arms with ease, kicking in the front door open with his metal boot. Fortunately it was not latched. Inside was icy cold and dark—but at least there was no wind here, and no snow would fall. . . .

He took care not to stumble against pieces of furniture in the room, and then found, mostly by touch, a flat piece that was either a cot or a bench, and gently lowered Percy to lie upon it.

Percy was still unconscious. He threw off his gauntlets, and it was freezing cold. First he located the fireplace, added a log, and by touch managed to find flints and start a fire in the hearth. The small feeble fire blazed forth in an angry hiss and immediately illuminated a simple peasant living room, furnished with a wooden table and two long benches on either side—one of which was where he had deposited Percy. In the corner was a low-to-the-ground wooden plank bed covered by a thick straw-filled mattress and faded quilt blanket. A few pantry shelves lined up against one wall, and a tiny dark icon of the Mother of God sat mournfully on a corner shelf.

"Girl! Percy . . ." he whispered, leaning over her, and touched her very cool forehead.

She did not respond. Frowning, he watched the shallow rise and fall of her chest. At least she breathed. . . .

Outside, his warhorse whinnied and made troubled noises, but Beltain steadily ignored him. Normally his horse would have been his first concern, but now, it was slipping to the back of his mind. Everything was slipping to the back. . . . He was suddenly numb, useless somehow, having grown abysmally still, mesmerized, looking down at Percy, plagued with indecision.

A few breaths later, with utmost gentleness he again took hold of her, and carried her bodily, this time to the low bed in the corner, and deposited her on top of the quilt-covered mattress. Her head lolled to the side, and he adjusted her loosened shawl around her, again placing his fingers, then large palm, against her icy forehead and cheeks.

Jack was still snorting outside, accompanied by the whistling wind, so Beltain went back out and quickly led Jack to the nearest barn building. There, he found a dry stall and plenty of hay. As quickly as possible he had the stallion free of saddle and harness, surrounded by clean hay, covered by a warm blanket, and settled for the night.

And then Beltain took out his folded cloak from the saddlebag, locked the barn and ran back to the main house.

Percy lay on the bed, breathing faintly, and her forehead and fingers were cold to the touch. The fire in the hearth had barely begun to warm the room, and the air was still permeated with chill.

Beltain took his long cloak, thick black velvet, and covered Percy with it. Then he quickly started removing his suit of armor, stacking the plates one by one on the floor next to his sword and helmet. Next off came his chain mail hauberk. Straining to raise his arms in the process, he winced at the dull pain from some of his slow-healing bruises near the ribs, having taken on additional new trauma from the battle effort less than an hour earlier. His thick woolen gambeson undershirt came off last and Beltain was naked to the waist, his powerful well-muscled upper body warm and exuding energy despite the residual bruising.

"Percy . . ." He took the few steps to the bed, then lowered himself before her, and placed one arm under her waist to slide her closer to the wall, to make room. Then he lay down on the outside, gingerly pausing for one instant only, to consider what it was he was doing. And then he lifted the cloak covering her and pulled her limp form against him, taking her in a strange embrace, feeling her slightly chubby body through her endless layers of stuffed outer coat, skirt, burlap and wool, and probably cotton underneath.

No, this was not going to work.

He rose up on his elbow and started removing her clothing. The shawl was simplest; he simply unwrapped her and set it aside to be used as an additional blanket. The bulky coat came off with moderate hassle—he pulled it off by the sleeves while carefully raising her up and turning her to the side. Then he took off her frozen wraparound shoes and socks and long stockings, feeling her ice-cold shock of bare feet underneath. He wrapped his palms around her feet and ankles, warming them for a few seconds. She had a coarse burlap dress laced up on top around her neck, and he untied the front and back laces at her throat, gently rolling her to her side to reach around. Her neck was barely warm, and the pulse at her throat fluttered.

As he was fiddling with her ties, Percy inhaled a deep breath and suddenly came to.

She mumbled something, and her eyelids were still closed, but a fierce joy came to him, together with a flood of relief.

"You're back, girl!"

In reply she mumbled again, and moved her arms, weakly resisting him.

"Come, girl, fear not . . ." he spoke softly, rolling her back closer toward him. "This is to make you warm, for your own good!"

Her eyelids barely flickered, and he watched her lashes tremble and rest against her plump cheeks, observed her well-defined dark brows.

And suddenly a heat came to his cheeks.

Beltain quickly looked away from her face, and put one muscular arm under her back to raise her, in order to pull the outer dress off her shoulders. Slowly he shifted down the fabric, leaving her cotton undershirt in place; freed one nearly limp hand from the sleeve, then the other, and then let her lie back while he pulled the burlap dress down to her waist. Here, her wide hips were in the way, and he handled her plump sides while his jaw and forehead and entire neck burned with something for which he had no words. At last he found an additional tie around her waist, loosened it, and then pulled the whole dress down past her hips, holding her briefly underneath the buttocks, then letting go, in order to catch breath. . . .

His head, brow, neck, everything was scalding-hot, flaming under the skin, as the strange flush spread throughout him. . . .

Gruffly he tugged the dress off her completely, crumpled it and pushed the bundle aside. She lay in her old cotton nightshirt, barefoot. Her ash-brown hair, fine and soft like baby's breath, came undone and scattered in waves upon the quilt-blanket. With a trembling hand he tested the coolness of her fingers and toes, and her extremities were still cold.

Beltain steeled himself and then lay down alongside her once more, in a state of hyperawareness, sensing with his bare flesh through her thin nightshirt how her skin was lukewarm. His arms came around her, drawing her close and tight against him—very tight, so that she came to again, and drew a deep breath and parted her lips in an attempt to say something. Her eyes flickered open and she saw the bronzed skin of his shoulder, felt its scalding fire against her cheek, then squirmed against him.

Her nightshirt slid partway down her own shoulders, revealing the tops of her rounded arms . . . and his unshaven jaw was suddenly pressed against plump softness, lying in the hollow of her neck and shoulder.

He stilled completely, hardly breathing, enveloping her. She too, after moving initially, seemed to grow still, and he could feel her chest rising with each slow breath. She was warming up by the second, and for some reason she was trembling.

Warmth was rising between them, resonating. It was an impossible fierce sense of one mutual skin between them, for despite the barrier of her cotton shirt their skins had become permeable, and his vigorous heat radiated at her and was returned to him. Indeed, he no longer felt the slight chill of the room on his bare skin because she had become his inner center, an extension of him, and now it was *she* who warmed him, down to the bones.

"Percy . . ." he whispered in a thick strange voice.

"I am warm now . . ." she replied unexpectedly. And then she shifted in his embrace. Her hands lightly pushed back against his bare chest, and where her fingers and palms touched him, tentative and fragile, he felt searing awareness. "It is all right now, I thank you . . . My Lord."

But he could not let her go. He was molten and stilled with intensity, fixed within the moment. The strange debilitating warmth continued to course through him, turning his limbs into lead and iron, and his breathing ragged.

The girl was a witch and she had taken his mind.

Chapter 11

Rumanar Avalais, Sovereign of the Domain, stood on the balcony of the Palace of the Sun, watching the grand square below. The balcony of heavy ornamental marble—warm cream in hue, with dark veins running in exquisite hairline cracks along each squat curving slit-column that fenced it—was the spot from which Sovereigns appeared before the populace on parade. It faced directly east, hovering a hundred feet above the façade of the Palace, before the square paved with mauve stones.

The square that formally bore the name of Trova, an ancient regal edifice that had once stood in place of the present Palace, was now commonly called the Square of Sunrise. It was at such times as the sun rose that the Sovereigns throughout the ages made important proclamations.

This sunrise was no different.

Rumanar Avalais wore a dress the color of deep ripe pomegranates. It was slim, long and flowing in the old-fashioned style of the former century before the crinoline skirt came to prominence in the royal courts. The fabric of the dress fit her hourglass shape like skin, and it cascaded below her thighs into fullness, ending in a flare at her feet. Her sleeves were bells gathered at the wrists with lace and pearls. Her hair of auburn flames was hidden entirely by a headdress of black and gold, thickly garlanded with pearls from brow to her neckline.

It was the traditional costume of war, worn by historical queens, taken out of treasury storage where it had been on courtly display for generations.

The sun rose over the gilded rooftops of the Sapphire Court, into a cloudless sky of crisp morning and its rays were cast at a right angle directly upon the balcony, so that where the Sovereign stood was only searing light.

Below, the entirety of Trova Square was filled with army formations of every scope and rank, regiments and battalions, cavalry and infantry, all of them clad in the colors of dark red and burgundy, colors of the pomegranate. The military forces that served the Sovereign and the Domain lined up always first in this square, before marching on any campaign, and were thus known as the Trovadii.

Overhead, the pale blue sky was boundless. There was never snow at the Sapphire Court; winter was mild and impotent here, with only a fresh cool edge to the wind and a sun that took a season to turn remote and disinterested, casting no true warmth, only incandescence.

With such indifferent sun in her eyes, Rumanar Avalais stood watching the square below.

At her side, only a few steps back, were three of her Field Marshals, all three decorated veteran generals. They were going to lead the Trovadii on this new immense campaign. Field Marshal Claude Maetra, an imposing stone-faced soldier in his late middle years, hailing from the austere nobility of Tanathe, was swarthy, with leathery olive skin, black hair and eyes, and the posture and demeanor of a dragon leashed in human skin. He did not take his eyes off the armies below, nor bothered to acknowledge the two other men present.

Next to him stood a much shorter man, Field Marshal Matteas Quara, of quasi-noble blood in Balmue, round and red-faced, covered with wrinkles, with fair skin and thinning hair, and a prominent gut. His expression however was satirical, with one heavy-lidded eye set in a permanent aspect of mockery overlaying sharp intelligence, and the other an eye-patch covering a hollow socket. The third Field Marshal, Edmunde Vaccio, was the youngest, energetic and brown-skinned—for he was of Moorish blood with family roots in Solemnis and adjacent Spain—handsome, slender yet muscular, and the tallest of the three.

"Your Brilliance, they are ready for your words," spoke Field Marshal Maetra in an abbreviated dry voice used to command.

With her back to him, Rumanar Avalais said softly: "Yes, they are. But are you? All three of you?"

"We are ready, with every fiber of our being," Maetra responded.

"Aye, we have sworn our all to Your Brilliance," one-eyed Quara echoed him.

"We are yours," said Vaccio simply in a soft bass.

A pause.

The Sovereign lifted her hands high. The thousands gathered in the square below immediately heeded her gesture and faded into absolute silence.

"Trovadii!" she exclaimed in a ringing voice of power that carried all through the square. "Brave and loyal Trovadii! You are unparalleled among warriors! Your valor and deeds are legend. There is no enemy that can face you and remain standing. You have protected our blessed Domain and served me thus for as long as I remember! Will you serve me thus again, this day?"

A roar answered her, as many thousand fists clad in gauntlets pointed to the sky, swords bared, and pikes were brandished.

"Trovadii!" The Sovereign continued holding her hands above her head, stretching out to them like a bird in flames, her shape blazing red in the sun, the color of ripe pomegranates burning. "Will you serve me?"

"*Yes!*" They cried in a million voices, and followed with another roar.

"Then serve me! I take you as mine, on this day and always!"

The roar was deafening.

"And now," she said, and her voice was a sonorous wonder. "Now you will wait for me. Wait, and I will come to you within the hour. Wait, and together we shall march!"

She lowered her hands and turned away, while Trova Square rang with roaring voices, stomping feet, and clanging metal armor brandished in salute, until the very ground around the Palace shook.

"Come, My Lords," she spoke to the Field Marshals. "It begins."

As the Sovereign and her generals exited the balcony, flanked immediately by a company of guards, they were met by a spry young man who bowed before her, delivering a message of some import. Quentin Loirre had received urgent communication from Letheburg.

"Well, what is it, Loirre?" she spoke, continuing to walk swiftly, so that the messenger had to hurry alongside her.

"Your Brilliance," he reported, "Letheburg is besieged as promised, and Hoarfrost waits for your arrival. However, there is one unexpected complication—or possibly, two—"

"What complication?"

"First, as of yesterday morning, Her Majesty Queen Andrelise Osenni is deceased. I do not mean dead and still present among us, but dead in the old way, so that her spirit has fled the body and she is going to be interred tonight. It is rumored that a young woman is responsible for putting her thus to rest. This young woman or girl had been in attendance at Her Majesty's bedside by order of the Prince—who is now King of Lethe."

The Sovereign stopped walking. "I see. However, a king or queen makes little difference at this point."

"Yes, Your Brilliance. Only, there is the other incident—"

"What else?"

"If I understand correctly, Your Brilliance, Hoarfrost claims that there was someone who broke through the siege last night— someone from the city. And in the process, this *someone* killed several hundred of his dead men in passing. And when I say killed, I am referring to the final real manner of death, where the body collapses and the spirit is banished permanently—"

"Yes, enough—it is quite clear what you mean. Now, tell me exactly what happened."

"The same young girl. *She* is responsible. There is a knight accompanying her, and they are both unaccounted for. They rode out of the city—how, the details are unclear—but they are on the move."

"Where are they now?"

"Hoarfrost—that is, the Lady writing on his behalf—did not say, Your Brilliance."

"And what do *you* think?"

Quentin Loirre furrowed his brow in effort. "It is my general suspicion, from all that has been known of this girl, that she is traveling to the Imperial Silver Court."

For several long moments, the Sovereign did not speak. Her generals regarded her. "With Your permission," said Field Marshal Claude Maetra. "It is no longer a question. This girl must be apprehended and brought before Your Brilliance."

"Yes," Rumanar Avalais said. "She is going to be brought before me . . . soon."

"I suggest that Your Brilliance does not send a dead man to perform this task," added swarthy Edmunde Vaccio in his velvet bass. "Since any dead man sent to confront her would end up permanently *dead*. Instead, send the living." And his rich dark brown eyes gazed at her meaningfully. Was there a flicker of hope in that look?

"Are you volunteering, My Lord Vaccio?" Her voice was suddenly like pouring honey.

"I am—with all my heart."

"Ah-h-h. But I need you here, commanding a third of my army, Lord Vaccio. There is no man who can replace you."

The light faded from his eyes. "I understand. And I obey."

"With all your heart?" Her eyes were blue like heaven, laughing at him.

"With that and more. . . ."

"Then stay and serve me, dear Edmunde. I meanwhile, will send another man to do this grim but necessary task."

"As Your Brilliance will have it." And Vaccio gave a curt military bow.

Rumanar Avalais turned to the nearest guard. "Go," she said, "fetch me Ebrai Fiomarre."

He was being summoned by her, now, before the march. What significance did it entail?

Ebrai Fiomarre, raven-haired, with a darkly handsome aquiline profile, walked the Palace corridor in haste to attend the Sovereign's summons.

He emerged in the front chambers, one of the main galleries facing east, close to the location of the parade balcony where he knew she was "performing" before the masses.

And what a performance! She was sublime, persuasive, the perfect symbol of divinely appointed imperial rule. He could imagine her speaking in that compelling siren voice, and the roars of the army crowd, mesmerized by its timbre alone, much less the impossible beauty of her. . . . It was infernally difficult to stay focused on anything else when in her presence. And she knew it well.

Ebrai strode along the marble floor of the gallery and was met by the Sovereign and her retinue, as they were leaving the parade balcony chamber.

As always, the sight of her struck him painfully, so that it was almost a physical sensation, an impact of tangible *presence* upon his senses, a displacement of the ether. Ebrai forced himself into the "casual yet humble yet despair-ridden" complex mask that he cultivated in her company.

In a few long strides he stopped before her, then bowed deeply yet with a twinge of pride—it was in the controlled movement of his head, the aloof clarity of his blank gaze. It was required that he show it, together with the rest of his mask "ensemble," else there would be insufficient dignity and reserve left in him to retain her interest. She would see it and interpret as she saw fit.

"Your Brilliance, I am here."

"My dear Ebrai," she said, and her sky-blue eyes were upon him, full force, devastating in their clarity. "I have a task for you."

"I am a humble servant of Your Brilliance."

"You will prepare yourself to travel. You will take whatever you need."

He wondered then, seeing the Field Marshals' steady watchful eyes, as each one looked at him with an unreadable expression.

"Am I to take it that I will not be traveling with Your Brilliance upon this campaign?"

"No. You will be heading north on your own, into the Realm—where you are a hunted man and must take every precaution, since regrettably you will not have my forces at your side—and your one task of paramount importance is to locate one somewhat extraordinary young girl."

"I see," he said, indeed not seeing at all, and for that reason thoughts were racing madly in his mind. "And who is this young girl?"

"We do not have her name, only that she is from some

remote northern village in Lethe. She is young, hardly a woman, and she has the ability to *kill* the dead."

Ebrai's mind was churning, clicking into place. "Ah, I do recall now. The so-called Death's Champion. She is the one who is rumored to have put to rest her own grandmother."

"Yes, and now she has done the same thing for the old Queen of Lethe. And a few hundred of Duke Ian Chidair's very much *dead* men."

"Ah. . . ."

"We cannot have her continue in this manner. Your task, therefore, is to locate her, discreetly, and bring her to me, unharmed. She must remain living, for I have need of her. And you—you too must stay *alive* in the process, for as a dead man you will be vulnerable to her."

Ebrai bowed deeply. "It is done. Where does Your Brilliance want her delivered?"

The Sovereign's soft laughter followed.

"I can see, Ebrai, that you are eager to demonstrate both your loyalty and your ability. Well then, we shall see how good you really are! Bring the girl to me wherever I might be at that moment—The Silver Court, Letheburg, or even farther north. Find me!"

And Ebrai Fiomarre met her gaze with his own very direct, slightly-mocking-yet-humble perverse combination of looks that kept her engaged in him every moment he spent before her. "It will be done precisely as Your Brilliance desires."

"I know," she said, the gaze of her blue eyes caressing him. "Now, go, and leave within the hour, no later than our armies begin the march."

With a swift bow, he was gone.

The Sovereign watched his receding elegant shape, a raven gone to hunt, and then she resumed walking swiftly, followed by her retinue, on her way out of the Palace.

Rumanar Avalais had changed from the ceremonial war dress of ancient queens to a modern riding habit. Only the color remained, rich pomegranate, the formal military hue of the Domain. Her headdress was replaced by a small platinum powdered wig designed to support a hat of sable fur trimmed with gold, suitable for the northern climes, which was to be worn later. An ermine lined hooded cloak would also later be fastened at her neck once the temperature called for it. For the moment, the cloak and hat were borne behind her by a maidservant who would be traveling with her for the duration of the campaign— the only other woman beside herself, on this campaign.

The Sovereign walked from the Palace and into the square, where an open parade curricle was awaiting her. She was assisted into the gilded seat upholstered in burgundy velvet by two Ladies-in-Attendance who then immediately curtsied and retreated, while her tiny maidservant, named Graccia perched in the back of the equipage with the essentials for the trip. The rest of the trunks and supplies would follow separately in carts, wagons, and sleeping carriages, together with the army supplies and heavy artillery.

"Proceed!" Rumanar raised one fine, sable-gloved hand, and the curricle, driven by a liveried officer and a pair of brilliant white geldings, burst forward, making a round at the Palace driveway to approach the heart of the square.

Here, the Sovereign told the driver to stop.

The Trovadii army stood before her at attention. An ocean of steel-wielding pikemen infantry in endless formations, at least a hundred separate companies of plated cavalry knights from all the four Kingdoms of the Domain, and flanks of heavy musketeers interspersed with light arquebusiers and long-bowmen.

The Field Marshals were already in the square, mounted on their chargers and in full armored uniform except for the battle breastplates, with distinctive epaulets and crest markings over surcoats. If she glanced closely, she could see each of the three men watching her, wise astute eyes, brilliant and clear in determination, exquisitely perfect in their loyalty. Three hero veterans, each in charge of one portion of the Trovadii.

In the center, grim Field Marshal Claude Maetra was in charge of the First Army under the banner of the Spiked Sun, the bulk and heart of the heavy pike infantry and cavalry forces. To the right, Field Marshal Matteas Quara with his distinctive eye-patch, was to lead the Second Army under the banner of a bristling Coiled Serpent, including the bulk of musketeers and artillery. To the left, Field Marshal Edmunde Vaccio, the handsome Moor, headed the Third Army under the banner of a Black Rose that had most of the bowmen and sword-and-buckler corps.

The Sovereign raised one gloved hand, and each man of the many thousands, from the lowest infantry soldier to the highest knight, attended her in rapt immediate silence.

"Trovadii!" she cried. "My Trovadii! Are you ready to fight?"

The square shook with the roar of their reply.

"Trovadii! Are you ready to die for me?"

They roared as one man, and the remote sun, rising higher now, set their metal to a sea of cold liquid fire.

"Then *die* for me!" cried the Sovereign. "Each one among you, take up your sword or dagger! Lift your armor upon your breast and find your heart! Strike your own beating heart, or your throat!"

There was one impossible pause of silence.

The wind blew audibly in the square, so silent it had become.

And in the next instant, three loud, booming masculine voices were heard. Field Marshal Claude Maetra roared a command in an icy voice of precision, and many feet away to his left and right, the same command issued from the mouths of

Field Marshal Quara and Field Marshal Vaccio. Each general had his sword out and reversed, pointing at their own bodies, and their chests were free of chainmail or breastplate—now the reasons became clear. . . .

"Remove sword! *Strike!*"

And each general demonstrated by example, by plunging their swords directly into their own hearts.

They made brief grunts, but remained standing, while red blood surged out of their chests, same color as their pomegranate uniforms.

As their hearts stilled, there was but a moment to transition to the *undeath*, no time to get accustomed, no time to acknowledge agony and that inevitable moment of blackout, and immediate weakness, and spiraling distance, and. . . .

No time.

"Remove . . . sword! Strike!"

Field Marshal Maetra was the first to regain his voice, and it sounded broken at first, as his mechanical gears slipped into place and his lungs billowed like dragging sails.

Knights all across the ranks started moving, reacting. Breastplates were moved aside whenever possible, or helms shifted and throats exposed. Swords and daggers were plunged into healthy living flesh, leathered and weatherbeaten, smooth and virile, white or olive or black as ebony. One after another they moved, striking with all their force, filled with sudden focus born of realization—born of madness—taking last breaths, crying out, or fading in silence.

"Remove . . . sword!"

Some of them hesitated. In quite a few spots, sudden skirmishes took place, quickly quelled by others around them. As men staggered, stood or sat on their horses, bleeding, they turned to those neighbors who hesitated, and daggers or sharp pike ends were plunged into chests and exposed throats.

"Strike!"

One by one, lesser commanding officers picked up the call, as sergeants-at-arms commanded their companies. Some soldiers had to be held down by their fellow members of battalions and troops while they wept and prayed.

Blood rained down upon Trova Square. It had turned pomegranate, cobblestones soggy with dark red juices of once living men.

Horses staggered and slipped. They were slain also, carefully so as not to damage fine limbs or muscles that might interfere with the march. A few of the knights wept then, not for themselves or the men around them, but in the moments they realized they had to take the lives of their own loyal beasts.

"Strike!"

Field Marshal Edmunde Vaccio heard the sound around him as though through ears plugged with cotton, while the last of his pomegranate blood trickled out of his wound in the chest, mingling with his crisp uniform surcoat, staining his gambeson and undershirt below. For the first time in his memory he heard no reliable drumbeat pulse in his temples, and thought of his young wife in Solemnis, imagining her lithe soft body gently swollen with their first child that will be their last.

"Strike!"

In the back of the square, soldiers stationed at the most outlying positions, hearing the orders, looked at each other in suspended disbelief, forced into moments of utmost choice. Others prayed in silence before removing their steel and performing their final living act. "Help me!" a few of them mouthed.

Help me. . . .

In the middle of the First Army, a formation of pikemen had come down on their knees, each one down to a man, refusing to take their own life. Heads bowed, they knelt in silence, mouthing prayers to God in Heaven, while their sergeants-at-arms came around striking them in the chests and throats, followed by benedictions from hooded priests who had emerged in many places around the square, to deliver Last Rites to the most faithful among them.

"Strike!"

Many of the musketeers corps, unable to turn the muskets upon themselves due to length of nozzle, discharged their long weapons into each other, and gunfire came in slow grim bursts, measured like pops, as they received the steel balls into their chests.

"Fire!"

Mother of God, help us all.

It took no more than a quarter of an hour to accomplish the deed.

The Sovereign sat watching them, motionless and serene. Behind her, little Graccia cowered, trembling, holding her white-knuckled hands against her mouth, silent tears streaming down her face.

At last, Trova Square contained only an army of the dead.

Rumanar Avalais, Sovereign of the Domain, lifted her gloved hand and spoke in her ringing voice, painted with pomegranate tongues of invisible fire, which was now all in the mind.

"Trovadii! You are mine now, unto Eternity! And now we march! Our way lies north!"

A blast of trumpets sounded, chill and pristine, powered by no living breath. Everywhere around the square it was picked up by echoes and amplified by powerful acoustics, and new trumpet blasts flared from the remote flanks. Next came the beat of drums, the only heartbeat to serve them all. And then, like a giant beast awaking, a creaking arose . . . the sound of metal striking metal . . . the soft squish of thick pomegranate-hued liquid upon the once-mauve cobblestones. . . .

There was no other sound.

Trovadii were on the move.

Chapter 12

Percy trembled in the embrace of a man whom she knew as the black knight, a man whose nude upper body surrounded her in a blanket of fiery warmth. He was crushing her between his muscular arms and his scalding chest, bronze and copper skin, smooth to the touch and hard underneath, covered with a bristling of fine hairs.

Percy could not breathe. She was constricted, but not enough to be so breathless. Rather, it was the reality of his *presence*, the strange proximity, the overwhelming warmth of him, pressed full body against all parts of her, that made her want to jump out of her own skin and at the same time to stay in place and just *dissolve*.

And then, his voice. . . .

"Percy . . ." he had spoken harshly, strangely, while pressed so hard and warm against her, his jaw prickling her neck.

"I am warm now," she told him in a soft voice, as if it made any sense, then remembered that yes, it was supposed to make sense; that she had been cold as ice, emptied of reason, falling in and out of consciousness as they rode, not even remotely clear on where they were now—and her mind had been tolling with all the bells in the world after the dark killing power had receded—

And yet, all she could think *now* was that she was warm— so warm! And he was all around her, and he was burning her—

or she was melting, soft and malleable and non-existent in the circle of his body.

However, the next instant, before she could squirm or press her hands against his chest yet again because *she did not know what to do with herself,* with her body or with her hands, and where to place them—the next instant Beltain suddenly released her.

With a strange grunting sound he sharply moved away, making the straw mattress buckle underneath his greater weight. And he lay on his back momentarily, then with a sharp movement got up and backed away from her, wearing only his lower body woolens.

Still trembling, this time with some confusion, she was suddenly presented with the sight of his beautifully shaped upper body—torso bruised in places, but muscular and overwhelming with its comely proportions. Comely, yes—because the few times that she had seen a man's bare chest in Oarclaven during summer fieldwork, and could compare, she knew *this* one was the most well-fashioned. He stood before the bed, silhouetted in part against the ruddy light of the fireplace that played along the masculine planes and concavities of his chest and abdomen.

"Forgive me, Persephone . . ." he said in a newly remote and very cold voice. His expression was equally cold and indeed blank, as he then leaned forward again, and took hold of the black velvet cloak that had served as a blanket for them, and pulled it back up and around Percy, adjusting it with his large capable hands around her neck, and pulling the fabric over her still somewhat cool bare feet.

"You are indeed better now," he added. "I was unsure what was to be done, and I am sorry if I had imposed—upon you. But now, I will find us something to drink."

"Thank you . . ." she said again, not knowing what else to say, and holding the velvet folds of the cloak around her to cover her ugly old cotton nightshirt.

As if he hadn't seen it already.

"Rest now," he added. "And I will find water to heat. A kettle maybe—" And he turned and went to look around the room near the pantry. There was indeed a small pot of sorts, and he took it up and then headed directly for the door.

"Don't be afraid," he said, pausing just for a moment. "I will be just outside. Now, rest!"

And she watched him, her pulse still racing in her temples, her body entirely warm—more warm that she had any right to be—and yet groggy now, and filled with something that was either a general ache or the remainder of churning power. And it occurred to Percy that, as he exited outside, he wore no shirt on his upper body—nothing at all—and yet he did not appear to feel the blast of cold that came at him as he opened the door to the winter night.

Beltain returned shortly, carrying a pot filled with snow. It had started to snow outside, coming down thick and fast, and the wind turned the flurries into spinning funnels. Snowflakes had sprinkled with whiteness the tops of his shoulders and the dark brown, lightly curling hair on his head, and some had caught lightly against his fine chest hairs in crystalline points that started to melt immediately in the warmth inside.

He shook his head of hair off lightly, swept hands against his chest with absentminded motions, not appearing to be bothered by the cold, and put the pot on the fire to melt and boil. Then he found his linen undershirt and put it on, no doubt covering himself against her gaze.

Percy continued to stare at him.

"Well," he said. "It is a good thing I found this house to shelter for the night. We could not have ridden through this snow. How do you feel?"

"I am fine, thank you, My Lord."

He turned away and for the next few moments fumbled looking around at the pantry shelves. "Nothing to eat here. No tea, not even bark scrapings. Just a couple of rotten potatoes and turnips on the bottom of the sack, unfit for the pig trough."

"I am not hungry."

He looked around at her, scraped the stubble of his jaw with his hand. "After what you went through, you need to eat, and drink well."

"Hot water is plenty."

He shook his head.

"Truly, My Lord," she said. "Whatever has happened since I made the dead fall, I am well now. It has passed."

It occurred to her that indeed her recovery this time had been much faster than the previous time—when she put to rest only three soldiers on the road and nearly fainted.

"So, Percy, Death's Champion, what exactly can you do?" He stood, looking at her with very serious eyes, having forgotten for the moment the search for something edible. "You managed to take out dozens, nay, at least a hundred men as we rode, and you did not touch *any* of them!"

"I did touch one," she corrected. "He tried to pull me down, and his touch awakened the power. I could then feel them all. . . ."

"Hm-m-m. . . . Then why did you not put the whole battlefield to rest?" he asked musingly.

"I—" She was somewhat taken aback by the audacity of his question.

"Well, *could* you have?" he persisted. "Could you have slain them all?"

"Yes . . . I think. Only, it would have been—"

She did not know how to answer. She could not tell him she was afraid of losing herself entirely to the power, of dissolving into the dark storm. . . .

Most of all, she could not tell him that she did not know if it would destroy her.

"Next time," he said with a ruthless chuckle, "don't bother sparing anyone. They are gone already, might as well send them along to the next world where they belong. Just think, you could have single-handedly taken care of the siege of Letheburg."

"I felt—your father," she said suddenly. "Your father, the Duke, his death. I touched it—him."

Beltain stopped laughing.

"You should have taken them all," he said in a voice hard as flint. And turning his back to her, he returned to the fire to stare at the boiling water.

"Next time . . ." she whispered in his wake. "Next time, I will."

The water boiled and they drank it plain from two wooden cups he found in the corner. They could hear the wind howling outside, a fierce storm. The fire in the hearth blazed higher after he added another log and twigs. The air in the room was almost pleasantly warm.

"I am sorry, but I need to use the chamberpot," she said awkwardly, seated on the bed, with her feet under his velvet cloak.

"Call me when you are done." Without looking at her, he got up from the bench where he had been sitting and immediately headed outside in only his shirt.

"My Lord! Will you not freeze?"

"Not unless you take too long." His answer came in a voice ruefully edged with humor. Not since she had mentioned his father had he smiled. Now was the first time.

Feeling only slightly dizzy as she got up, and remarkably well recovered, all things considered, Percy rushed to take care of nature's business. She hid away the chamberpot again, arose and stood very still for a moment to let a minor headrush pass, then went barefoot to the door and opened it to the storm and called out for him.

Beltain returned immediately, blowing snow flurries and wind in with him.

"Get into bed," he said, glancing only once at her, his gaze purposefully averted from her shape.

Percy stared at him, shivering in her nightshirt.

"Will you not take the bed, My Lord?" she said. "Where will you sleep? You are larger than me."

"No," he said.

"Don't be a ninny, Sir Kni—My Lord," she began speaking, then put the back of her hand against her mouth.

"Did you just call me a ninny, girl?"

Percy stared at him, with very wide eyes.

"That's it, get into bed this instant! Or I will thrash you as I once promised!"

"Hah! You can *try!*" And suddenly she squealed, and panicked, and rushed like a big terrified horse, and threw herself on the mattress, while gulping for air with nervous giggles. She clutched the black cloak and dragged it against herself and cowered in the corner, still giggling and gasping helplessly in what was obviously a crazed fit—similar to the times when she had played with her two sisters upon occasion and they squealed and got out of control—except that now she was terrified, acutely self-aware, and shocked at her own ridiculous response.

"Holy Lord in Heaven!" he said, and stood over her, shaking his head. A smile hovered around the corners of his mouth. He stilled momentarily, and his slate-blue eyes glittered black in the red firelight. They were so intense suddenly, so focused, as he looked at her.

"What a strange little wench you are, Percy Ayren," he said after a long pause, and looked away. "Enough of this maudlin nonsense, you need to get some sleep. And I do, too. We have a long road ahead of us tomorrow."

"What about the bed?" she whispered.

"Don't worry about the bed," he replied. "I've slept outside under the trees and worse."

"But there is plenty of room for both of us! Whole village families could fit in this one bed, and probably have!" she insisted.

"But we are not a family. . . ." His voice came softly. With his back to her he proceeded to arrange his armor and clothing on the beaten floor, then pulled on his thick woolen gambeson back over his undershirt, and easily lay down on the floor, with a small sack under his head for a pillow.

And then he turned away from her, lying on his side to face the fire.

"Good night, Percy."

"Good night, My Lord," she whispered, her mind in a strange soft turmoil.

For long moments she watched his reposing silhouette against the flames.

And then she slept.

Percy awoke at dawn to a profound silence. The pallor seeping from the cracks in the shutters and under the door was a harbinger of a white winter world. The storm had passed and left in its wake a rare serenity.

The knight was awake, and was quietly adding new logs to the fire in the hearth, and indeed its gentle rising crackle was the only sound to intrude upon the silence.

She noticed he was fully dressed already, with his boots and leg pieces on, and the chain mail hauberk in place. He must have made trips outside without her knowing it, because there were a few more logs near the hearth than before.

She shuddered, because despite the relative warmth in the room, she was chilled, and his fine black cloak she had been using as a blanket was hardly adequate protection over a nightshirt alone. Her dress, winter shoes, socks and stockings were drying near the fire, for which she was grateful. But it was awfully embarrassing to consider that he had to handle them on her behalf—the whole poor threadbare smelly lot of them. The realization of it made Percy's cheeks flame.

"Good morning . . ." she muttered, scrambling out of bed, and heading straight for her clothing, while trying not to meet his gaze directly.

"Good morning to you, girl," he replied in a calm voice. "Hope you are well rested. There is snow in the pot ready to heat up, together with some bark I managed to procure. Nothing edible unfortunately, so it will have to wait once we get on the road."

"How bad is it out there?" she whispered, thinking of the usual knee-deep drifts against the door back at home in Oarclaven, and the blanketed roads on the days after heavy snowstorms.

"Bad enough," he retorted. "But none of it matters. We are going forward today, no time to waste."

He finished stirring the kindling and then straightened. "I'll wait for you outside while you dress."

"Thank you, My Lord," she replied hurriedly, clutching her clothing. "I will be quick!" Her entire face was flaming now.

"Take your time." And he went outside.

They had the hot tea to warm them up, finished dressing, and were outside on horseback within the half hour.

The snow had fallen at least two feet deep all around, and once they came out of the house, there was no frame of reference except for the occasional shrubbery and trees and the rising winter sun which cast its impotent light from a washed out blue sky, free of overcast. Percy had to wade through knee-deep whiteness to get just a few paces past the front door, holding her skirts up in order to take each step, while Beltain's much taller metal-booted legs left deep imprints. He had brought out Jack from the barn, and even the great warhorse took each step with massive legs sinking, shook its tail and mane in displeasure and snorted every few breaths.

The black knight lifted her up in the saddle with an effortless hold of his metal-clad arms, so that Percy did not even know it was coming. Then, just as quickly he was up in the stirrups and seated behind her on the saddle. He wore his black cloak, and its folds separated Percy from the icy cold metal plates of his armor.

She once again rested sideways against him, but there was something inexplicably different about his manner—a new subtle reserve and stillness. Beltain made a point of barely making bodily contact with her, held himself stiffly, and his metal vambrace-clad arms on both sides of her took care to encircle without touching her, while his gauntlets kept the reins. As for his face, he kept his head turned directly ahead, eyes upon the way before them, and what she could see of his lean unshaved jaw and lines of mouth was expressionless stone.

"Where will we go?" Percy asked, as they moved slowly through the open field.

"In general, south," he replied, looking ahead. His baritone sounded close against her ear, and again it seemed to go all through her to the bones. She was so acutely aware of every point on her body, the feel of the saddle underneath, every spot where his cold hard armor pressed against her. . . .

Stop thinking, do not think. . . .

"We need to find a road," she remarked. "So much snow!"

"The road is there, just beyond those fields and the shrubbery. The hedge growth defines it. See how it curves along."

And indeed, as she allowed her eyes to take in the general linear pattern of the growth, it seemed to flow in the outline of a roadway. And then, in the hazy distance there were dark shapes it the form of remote settlements.

"Oh, I think that must be Fioren town, just there, far along the way."

"Very likely so," he replied. "Fioren is the next town south of Letheburg."

"I have an uncle in Fioren!" exclaimed Percy. "It's my father's older brother, Uncle Guel. I met him only once when he came to visit. He and his wife have an apple orchard in town. I've never been to Fioren before—"

"We have no time for detours, but if your uncle lives on the way and does not mind visitors, we can stop for a quick meal."

"Oh . . ." Percy hesitated. "I don't know. He was very nice when he came, but he is a bit fancy, and, well—his wife Carlinne and their boy, my cousin, Martin are a little stuck up—I don't want to impose."

"Then we won't. An inn would do, and I have coins enough to pay. But we need to find food eventually."

A lone hawk circled overhead. Percy's gaze swept up to take in the washed-out blue sky of morning, and suddenly, it was as if heaven itself pressed down on her with all its infinite layers, and she had a choking sensation of vertigo. An otherworldly wind swept inside her mind and pulled at her. . . .

Percy gasped and went very still.

The black knight noticed her strange reaction and turned his head to glance at her. "What is it?"

"Oh! So many *dead!*" she replied in stunned wonder.

"What?"

"I am not sure—suddenly I feel something new in the distant south, a whole great overwhelming number of death shadows! They came into being just now, in the last few minutes, so many of them, thousands! And all in one place, it's why I can feel them!"

"Dear Lord, I did not know," he said, looking at her intensely. "I had no notion you could feel the dead all around us so much. Even when they are out of sight?"

"Oh, yes. I always feel them a little bit, since the world is filled with mortals, after all. There are dead things everywhere around us, little dead things. Even now, under the snow. . . . It's like a prickling in the back of my head. It is how I feel *her* out there, the Cobweb Bride. I know her in particular, for she has been singled out to me by Death Himself. But—"

And she turned her face to him, her eyes dilated with intensity. "But this is different. So many have died just now, that it's as if a whole lake of death has flooded, nay, an ocean, and all in one place."

"And is it where we are heading?" he asked. "Must we?"

"I—I think so. . . ."

"In that case, Percy Ayren," he said in a grim voice, "you'll need to make ready."

Chapter 13

I t was time to send the birds.

Ebrai Fiomarre moved silently through the remote north wing corridors of the Palace of the Sun. It was only half an hour since the entirety of Trova Square became a field of slaughter for an army of thousands upon thousands. And with some deadened part of himself he still heard their voices and ringing tandem strikes, the hum of strange butchery filling the expanse with reverberating acoustics. And then they had marched. . . .

The onlookers from the Palace, the myriad windows and balconies, and all around the edifices of the square, were suspended in a strange impossibility, a kind of psychic stillness. They had mostly fallen silent—first in disbelief, then in horror— a few were shaking, some weeping, holding their mouths and faces, others praying. They were witnessing a unique moment in history. Never before had it known and never again would Trova Square know such methodical mass atrocity enacted upon a friendly army by their own, of their own free will.

Yet, was it indeed free will that moved them to this act? Or was it *her* influence upon them, taking away all truth of will and choice, all rational awareness of what was real, of what was duty and what was madness, and binding their mind to her own?

Ebrai walked with a blank demeanor, encountering almost no one in the corridors.

Rumors had spread all over, and the Sapphire Court was stunned, broken, impossibly empty. They hid all over the Palace and in houses overlooking the square and outlying streets. Soft muted weeping came from shuttered windows. Many of the Trovadii had come from remote parts of the Domain, each of the four Kingdoms having sacrificed their best and brightest sons to the highest honor of Sovereign's brilliant military service. But even more of them had been local—sons and brothers and husbands.

They who witnessed the slaughter this sunrise, were seeing their own loved ones fall before their eyes.

Ebrai himself had not expected this; had not had any warning. He was present for each of the preliminary war councils, watched the Field Marshals discuss strategy with the Sovereign over great maps. Watched them place tiny painted figures of tin and pewter soldiers to mark battle movements and formations. And not once had he heard this part of the plan, the part where the orders were given to take their own lives.

No wonder the three distinguished generals had looks of such desperate intensity, such impossible poised calm when he last saw them alive in the Palace at *her* side.

What had she done?

Ebrai turned a few more corridors along an older terrace, and found himself ascending a stair of old marble, well polished by generations of feet, up to the uppermost level of the Palace, almost near the roof. Here, perched in a remote forgotten spot were the small apartments allocated by the Sovereign to Micul Fiomarre, his father.

Micul Fiomarre had been living here for months now, in the subtle role of a man touched by tragic fate and diminished in his senses. After being marked as a traitor by the Emperor of the Realm, he had thrown himself at the mercy of the House of Avalais.

The Sovereign took him in out of amusement, and Fiomarre

the Elder expected no true trust from her, only an opportunity to remain and fix himself firmly in this position. He immediately demonstrated that he was not quite in his right mind—but not so much that he was perceived as an outright madman, merely enough to be considered an eccentric given to periodic fits and turgid moods in-between relative clarity. And as such he took it upon himself to show an obsession with cultivating flowers in his apartment near the attic and upon the small rooftop terrace given him.

"As long as he does not decide to cast himself off the roof, he may do as he please," the Sovereign had announced casually. But there was not a moment of doubt that Micul Fiomarre was continuously under surveillance, or that the Sovereign ever underestimated him. Thus, Fiomarre the Elder had to play a very subtle game of real quasi-insanity, and took his horticultural pursuits very seriously. His terrace roof and greenhouse was soon overflowing with plants and flowers of all hues and varieties. In addition, he made a point of requesting strange varieties of seeds and grain of every sort, attempting to plant and nurture new hybrids, and scattering more than half of what was brought to him underfoot and all over the rooftop garden, so that soon flocks of birds came to roost nearby. Thus, under the guise of eccentricity, he somehow managed to acquire and keep a number of carrier pigeons and other winged messengers that pecked alongside the wild birds of the Sapphire Court.

Ebrai Fiomarre reached his father's apartments and knocked softly on the door in the designated manner. Moments later, the door was opened by a tall dark-haired man in his late middle years, bearing a strong family resemblance but with heavier brows, graying temples, and a receding hairline.

He did not look well at all.

Ebrai was particularly concerned, knowing how soon this came in the wake of the recent hard news of his younger brother Vlau having committed that unfortunate atrocity at Silver Court, taking the life of the Emperor's daughter—all because of a mistaken impression, all because he could never be told the honorable truth of their spy status and their true loyalty to the Imperial Realm. When their father learned the news of his second son's murderous act, he was taken genuinely ill for a day, despite putting on his usual mask of composure. And now, for the first time he was showing signs of a real decline in his focus, health, and faculties.

"Good morning, father," Ebrai said, and entered, closing the door behind them then locking it from the inside. But even here, in the relative privacy of confined quarters, there was the possibility of surveillance—for the walls of the Palace had ears; political factions always vying for advantage, each with their own agenda and various degrees of loyalty to the Sovereign—and thus they had to continue in their act, even between themselves, speaking half in code and half in bitter jest.

On this day, even Micul Fiomarre was shaken, having just observed the slaughter in Trova Square from his rooftop terrace, and his grim pallor and lines of exhaustion went deeper than usual.

"Not a good morning, my boy," he replied, taking one second too long to decide what kind of mood to portray on this occasion. And then he settled into his character. "The rain was a strange color today, Ebrai, my boy. Looking outside, it painted the cobblestones red. Come with me up to the garden, and I can show you. At least my flowers were untouched, thank heaven."

"There was no rain this morning, father," said Ebrai in a calm voice, but looking at him with eyes that were wrung of all life.

"No rain? How strange, then. I could've sworn I saw droplets of red flying every which direction. They made rosy rainbows in the sun, for it rose quickly, just now, and it shone so very brightly through the downpour."

"Let's go up on the roof, father and see your garden." Ebrai then picked up a few pieces of parchment lying in the corner and a quill and inkwell. "Here, let me carry your drawing pages with you, and you can sit and sketch your flowers in the sun."

"Very thoughtful of you, dear boy. And how have you been, son? I don't see you much these days, what with you having to attend the lovely young woman who rules this country. Where is she, by the way? All in good health?"

And they went through the dark small apartment into an even lesser cell, then up a narrow spiral staircase of iron and wood planks, emerging on top of the world.

All around them, slanting gilded rooftops and ornate cornices. Only here, in this tiny spot under heaven was a green niche open to the sun and partially enclosed from the elements with a retractable translucent awning of fine fabric that kept moisture away but allowed most of the sunlight through like a fine sieve.

Under the protection of the awning stood pots of roses, irises, gardenias, fuchsias, trellises with climbing vines, and blossoms of every shape and color, blooming year-round and emanating heady fragrances upon the cool morning breeze. A few loud cooing pigeons flapped wings and scattered from underfoot, flapping up and away into the pale blue winter skies.

"Her Brilliance is quite well, father, in perfect health as always, and has today embarked upon a new campaign. And she has instructed me to travel on an errand for her, which shall take me away from the Palace for some time. Since I will not be able to visit you again for many days, I thought I might sit with you now, before I depart. Now, come, sit down and sketch something for me."

"Very well! Would you like a rose or maybe a narcissus? An orchid!"

"You know I am not so expert in all the different blooms you keep so well. Their names escape me for the most part. Why not make a few sketches and I will tell you which I like best.

Make sure they are all the best and prettiest ones, large and fully open."

"Of course," Micul replied, and grabbed a small pinch of seeds from a little pot nearby, tossing it on the floor, at which point a small grey pigeon hopped dutifully forward and started to peck at his feet.

"Now, first, my father, I would like to see an open rose, the greatest and most fair one of all."

"How about this one?" And Micul Fiomarre pointed to a nearby rose of the deepest musk burgundy, the color of blood, wafting forth a powerful perfume.

"Yes, this one is beautiful," his son replied. "And the color is *precisely* right."

I t was time to send the birds.
The Royal study was crowded. King Roland Osenni of Lethe sat behind his large mahogany desk strewn with parchment and abandoned vellum-bound tomes from his library. Next to him, at an upright standing podium desk perched his secretary, with a number of quills and inkwells ready.

All around had gathered courtiers, military officers, and high-ranking advisors, pressed closely around His Majesty's desk—several rows thick—each one straining to find a place nearer the King.

A few steps away, in a deep wing chair, sat the Grand Princess Claere Liguon, with her back perfectly aligned with the straight back of the chair, wood to upholstered wood. Next to her, like her invisible sentinel death shadow, stood Vlau Fiomarre, grave-faced as always.

The King cleared his throat. "First, Your Imperial Highness, be so kind as to dictate a letter to His Imperial Majesty, Your Father. Inform him of your health—that is—"

"I am well aware how to proceed with a letter, Your Majesty," interrupted the Infanta's measured, bellows-driven, mechanical voice. Every advisor and military man in the room turned to stare her way.

The King cleared his throat again, in a combination of chagrin at his *faux pas* comment regarding her "health" and in his general frustration with *her*.

Claere was strongly aware of this frustration and displeasure, and had been in fact expecting it as soon as she had discreetly given her order to Lord Beltain Chidair the night before, to remove Percy from Letheburg. The knight had complied and disappeared, together with the village girl. And Claere spent the dark hours of her sleepless night not in mere contemplation of her personal eternity—as had been her pastime every night since her life had been taken away from her together with any other human function such as sleep—but also in the visualization of the highly unpleasant consequences that would manifest the next morning. She had expected the King to send for her in anger as soon as he awoke, but instead there was noisy action in the Palace, and a constant hive of activity in the square below, illuminated by golden street lanterns and occasional torches carried by running convoys of soldiers on their way to the city walls. From what she could gather by inquiring from a harried servant, there had been a breech in the wall, or possibly the walls had merely manifested the strange disappearing act that Grial had talked about. Whatever it was, new defenses and barricades were hastily being erected in the vulnerable spots along the walls. There was also mention of someone who had ridden outside, and was seen from the battlements. . . . And, rumor had it, there were many fallen dead, each one a true corpse, gone in the same permanent way as had the old Queen.

Claere could only suppose it was Percy's handiwork.

In the pre-dawn twilight, with only a candle and a useless warm fireplace illuminating the fine boudoir allocated to her, Claere paced, moving her desensitized limbs like clockwork. At some point a soft knock came, and she uttered: "Come in." She expected a Royal summons, but instead it was the tall slim figure of a familiar dark man. Vlau Fiomarre entered her bedchamber and stood at the door, columnlike and peculiar.

"You," she said. It simply came out of her, unexpected. And because she did not make the conscious effort to draw in the breath needed to inflate her lungs for speech, the utterance was a silently mouthed whisper.

"Forgive the intrusion," he said. "But I thought you might want company, before the King's inevitable summons came."

"Marquis," she said. "My thanks. Though I am not sure what is to be said now. I am not afraid of Lethe, merely resigned to an unpleasant exchange. There is nothing he can do to hurt or punish me."

"He can lock you up and forget where he keeps the key. That would be the worst indeed," Fiomarre said, taking the steps to approach her. "However, you can be sure he will have far better use for you. You are his leverage with the Emperor."

"My father will not stand for blackmail."

"Ah," said Fiomarre, and the firelight cast moving shadows along his austere face and its sardonic expression. "But it is not blackmail he will wield, Your Imperial Highness."

"What then?"

"Love," replied the dark man simply. And his absolutely black eyes were full of demonic liquid flames, barely contained shadow-fire.

And as she stared up at him, her great haunting eyes in their sunken hollows watching him with their soft, tragic intensity, he continued: "Love is the force with which he will manipulate the Liguon, and it will be a subtle, legal manipulation, quite within what is permitted a loyal vassal king merely asking for his liege's aid. Osenni will ask the Emperor to come to the rescue of his own beloved daughter who happens to be safely ensconced at Letheburg. 'The King of Lethe is merely acting as your protector now,' he will insist, 'with the forces of the city and the entire

Kingdom at your disposal.' 'This siege must be broken on your behalf,' he will inform the Emperor."

"And my father of course will come." She nodded, her delicate cold neck moving stiffly to indicate her understanding.

"So you see," Vlau continued, "there will be no need to hide you away or do anything that might appear punitive. So, be not afraid for the dawn to arrive. . . ."

"Thank you. . . ." She continued to look at him, at the strange, unblinking, boundless depths of his gaze. "As I said, I am not afraid. But—had I been—your words offer comfort indeed."

"I regret . . . I can offer little more."

And he stood then, at her side, silently, with infinite patience, while the windows slowly filled with a pale bluish glimmer of dawn. It was infinite patience and possibly more, to thus attend the dead.

Soon afterwards, the summons had indeed come. The Infanta and Vlau Fiomarre were brought before the King of Lethe in this same study. And here, in snatches, the variously upset and discombobulated King poured forth his grievances. "How could Her Imperial Highness let the girl go? At such a precarious time as now! How, in all Heaven, with the dead rebels surrounding the city, about to storm us at any moment, and *that peasant* being the only known and effective means of stopping them?"

But Clare found herself more artful and resourceful than she imagined. "Your Majesty," she retorted, with just the right expression of innocent surprise. "Surely you realize that I have sent the girl out of the city on purpose—with my loyal knight to back her—on my precise orders to find my father and beseech him for aid on behalf of Letheburg. As Your Majesty clearly understands, no one else is as qualified to pass safely and travel the countryside in such turbulent times. My knight will protect her against any threat from the living, while she will take care of the hostile dead. Together they will arrive safely and relay the message to the Emperor."

The King was somewhat mollified, absentmindedly scratching the top of his head and skewing his fastened wig in the process. "My dear child," he said, in a much milder voice. "It is a good and noble and caring thing you have done, on behalf of all of us in this wretched, besieged city. But, have you any notion how much we lose now, in our defense capabilities? Could we not have just as well sent messenger birds?"

"Birds may be easily intercepted," she replied, getting into her role. "A bird can be taken out with one well-placed shot of a marksman, or slain by a hunting hawk. And now that death has stopped, a bird may be damaged enough to prevent its flight or simply lose its living desire to return home to feed. But my Percy Ayren will be unstoppable."

"Well, it *is* a clever decision on Your Imperial Highness's part, I must admit. But, we will send birds nevertheless—must send them in fact, with more details than merely a request for aid. Details of all things must be urgently conveyed to His Imperial Majesty and others."

Musing thus, King Roland Osenni called for a secretary and all his advisor corps, until in the next hour the room had filled with every courtier imaginable, and several aviary cages were brought in.

And now, here they were.

Claere Liguon was given first courtesy to dictate her formal letter to her Imperial Father. She did so, in a calm voice, powered by her soft bellows of lungs. It was brief and to the point, easy enough to fit in a tiny square of parchment to be attached to the leg of a small carrier pigeon. She was "not a Cobweb Bride, but as well as can be," and "merely asked for assistance on behalf of Letheburg and herself."

After she was done, the secretary brought the parchment bit up to her on a tray, and she signed her name with awkward clenched fingers. The King nodded with an approving smile to her and ordered the letter sealed and attached to the most reliable carrier bird in the Imperial cage.

Next, the Infanta was courteously ignored as the King dictated several more missives. The first was to the Emperor, directly from the King of Lethe. "Your Imperial Majesty, your loyal vassal Lethe begs for urgent aid, ere we fall. Your Daughter and Letheburg are besieged by a dead army of Chidair, and supplies are limited."

The second letter was to Duke Vitalio Goraque. "Gather all your military forces immediately and come to the aid of Letheburg and Your King," it said, and was signed, sealed and attached to a bird from another, lesser cage, this one of locally bred birds native to Goraque's holdings and keep.

The next two letters were intended for the neighbors—Morphaea and Styx. Neither of the two Kingdoms were on particularly warm terms with Lethe, or were expected to respond in time, but it was an automatic gesture invoking the bonds of common solidarity to the Realm. "Your Neighbor and Friend, the King of Lethe, begs your swift aid, at a time of siege and despair, on behalf of the Emperor's Daughter and Lethe," it said, in duplicate. The mention of the Infanta was intentional—if either Styx or Morphaea needed a stronger reason for action. The young King Augustus Ixion of Styx in particular might want to garner favor with the Emperor by assisting his daughter in her plight. And Morphaea's King Orphe Geroard would come eventually, out of a sense of general duty to the Realm.

With the birds from the appropriate cages selected, and letters attached, the King sat back in his chair while the bird trainers took up all the cages including the special one with the outgoing missives, where all the selected birds were placed together with their tiny loads. This cage would be taken up to the rooftops and the pigeons released into the fair weather sky of morning.

"Now, we pray and wait," His Majesty announced to the room.

"If I may point out, Your Majesty," said one military man of high command wearing the cobalt blue colors of Lethe. "We have been rather fortunate so far. The enemy outside the gates has not yet given the orders to attack. Hoarfrost appears to be waiting for something."

"Or someone," said the King. "Yes, it troubles me, this calm before the storm. Why has he not attacked? Why not, especially, take the opportunity this past night when the breach occurred and that peasant girl and his own son plowed through their ranks so easily?"

"Could it be he *knew* it was his son?"

"Knowing Hoarfrost, that would hardly make a difference. Indeed, he would be likely to capture and thoroughly punish his boy in a protracted execution."

"Then, Your Majesty," ventured another advisor, this one a civilian diplomat, "we can only hope and pray that His Imperial Majesty sends reinforcements before this mystery of Hoarfrost's motivation need be solved."

"I will be praying," the King said, "at Her Majesty's funeral tonight. That my late Mother might be laid to her final rest tonight, in blessed peace, before any blood is spilled."

It was time to send the birds.

Lady Ignacia Chitain of Balmue sat in a small tent erected on her behalf by the orders of Duke Hoarfrost, right next to his own greater one. They were situated on a small rise, just outside the range of Letheburg marksmen. The snow had started falling a few hours after midnight, and overnight had piled on heavily all around, so that the canvas roofs of both tents sagged mightily under the load.

It was serene and yet utterly grotesque to be surrounded by the walking dead in all directions, Ignacia thought—all of them remote and no longer human, and only she and the Domain messenger boy being of the living. She *should* have been afraid, and yet somehow she had no fear—confident in herself and her effect upon the Duke, she had no true fear of Hoarfrost, and he ruled them all.

The incident with the knight breaching the city siege and blasting through the thicket of the dead army was a thought-provoking thing. Ignacia did not know what to make of it. She had awoken from yet another brief and troubled sleep among a crude pile of furs to the distant sounds of a peculiar commotion. It came, not among the besieging army ranks—for the dead generally remained impassive to all stimuli except direct commands from their newly appointed lord—but far ahead, up on the actual battlements of the city. She had emerged from her tent and only then observed that someone was riding hard from the direction of Letheburg and directly into the army, and making a significant headway. Apparently the dead were *falling*.

What occurred next was unclear. Hoarfrost had come outside also from his tent where he'd been brooding like a stump, and he himself had gone very still at one point, together with the entirety of the dead around him. And then, it was as though a single metaphysical breath had been expelled, and they were all released by an invisible hand. . . . Hoarfrost's roar of fury and impotence was enough to make her put her hands up to her ears, and she prudently decided against approaching him in that moment. Now he stood staring as though he were a boulder rising from the earth, a barrel-chested monstrous figure that had once been a man. There was something peculiar in the obsessive way he watched the receding figure of whoever was on horseback, cutting through the army like butter and then receding into the night darkness of the plain, moving south.

Soon afterwards, the snowfall started.

Ignacia went back inside, huddled in her fine ermine cloak, and slept once more, until dawn. And the young spy from the

Domain slept a few feet away, next to the warmly covered and well-coddled cage containing his precious carrier pigeons.

When next the lady awoke, it was to white morning light outside, and tall snowdrifts. After a few brief morning ablutions, she headed directly into Hoarfrost's tent.

"My Lord," she inquired, with no preamble. "Did I hear something happen last night?"

The dead man turned to her, creaking his rime-frosted limbs. Then the bellows of his lungs came to life. "You heard indeed. Someone has made a fool of me, pretty bird. Indeed, as I speak of birds, one such bird has flown the Letheburg coop. A very strange feathered thing, I must say."

"What coop?" said Lady Ignacia bluntly, because she knew it was the best manner to take with this man. "Please be simple with me, Your Grace, for I have no notion of what you speak."

"This one is a very special bird," he said, fixing his grotesque marbles of eyes upon her. "For she could get into my mind, and I could *feel* her—feel her pulling me like a fish on the end of a line. One pull and I would be no more. And yet, somehow she let me go."

"Birds, now fish, Your Grace? And who is this *she* of whom you speak?"

With a creak and then a shaking rattle sound, Duke Hoarfrost started to laugh. "You really don't know, do you?"

For the first time, Ignacia had a moment of doubt, and with it a twinge of fear. This was not planned ahead, none of this. This was an unknown factor.

Seeing her suddenly thoughtful face, Duke Hoarfrost laughed even harder, a pumping bellows mechanism sprung into full motion. "You need to tell your Sovereign," he said in-between guffaws, "that a Cobweb Bride is the least of her problems! Death, the gallows bastard, has another Champion!"

And then he laughed again, seeming to no longer be aware of her presence, and would not stop.

Moments later, Ignacia quietly left the Duke's tent. She went inside her own, and hurriedly wrote on a tiny piece of parchment, then prodded the messenger boy awake. He took her rolled-up note and selected a plump grey pigeon with white-tipped feathers, trained specifically to fly to his native coop in the Sapphire Court.

"No," said Ignacia. "This one is too late. The Sovereign and her armies are already on the move and the message will never reach her. Use a pigeon that returns to Balmue."

The boy nodded, and took out another creature, this one of a darker coloration. "This one, My Lady. It will fly directly to His Majesty Clavian Sestial's personal coop in Ulpheo."

"Perfect! Ulpheo will be directly on the way, and there Her Brilliance will likely add to her Trovadii the Balmue battalions, so it will involve a sufficient delay. Now, attach the message and let the bird fly."

The boy nodded, and in minutes he had released the pigeon into the clear winter sky.

Ignacia stood looking up at it. She thought about the contents of the note that said simply, "Hoarfrost is no longer entirely ours. He is likely to take Letheburg within a day, for himself. How shall I proceed?"

It was time to send the birds.

The Emperor Josephuste Liguon II of the Realm stopped briefly on his walk along the highest terrace of the Imperial Palace. It was his favorite haunt, meticulously kept free of the fresh powder of snow that had fallen overnight, by servants who had swept the marble floor and filigree gilded iron railings hours earlier.

Here, hundreds of feet above ground level, he could see the variegated hues of whiteness in a panoramic sweep of rooftops and cathedral spires, with the immense gilded dome of the Basilica Dei Coello to his right, wearing an ermine hat of snowfall, and everywhere distant rooftops and balconies of the outlying buildings and lyceums. Far beyond to the north lay Lethe, with its wintry forest wilderness. To the west, stretched Styx, bordering with verdant temperate France. And directly southeast was warm, fertile Morphaea, touching with its lower southern borders the foreign Domain Kingdom of Balmue, and with its upper eastern side the lofty ridge of the Aepienne Mountains and beyond it, the Domain Kingdom of Solemnis.

Here in this spot on top all things, was the heart of the Empire. The rest of the world radiated in all directions around him.

The Emperor was a slight man of less-than average height, so that his thin figure was often elevated with curving heels in the French fashion, and attired in resplendent finery of high Court, while rouge and powder were applied to his face to disguise the washed out, sallow quality of aging skin.

Today was not such an occasion.

The Emperor wore an ordinary tailored jacket and trousers, drab mourning colors, an overcoat and sensible winter shoes. His graying head and bald spot was covered with a plain unpowdered black wig, and his face, untouched by artifice, was clearly that of a grieving old man. He walked slowly, leaning on a polished walking cane, and took frequent stops to admire the view. A few discreet feet behind him walked two of his personal attendants and, farther back, the Imperial guards.

It had been several days now since the loss of his daughter. After the Infanta was assassinated on the fateful day of the Event when death stopped and *everything* began, the Emperor had grown apathetic, finding it harder and harder to focus on the daily routine, or to make the simplest of decisions. And now, with news of all manner of unrest, conflict, and general misfortune coming to barrage him every waking hour, he found it more and more difficult to face the duties of each day.

They told him the foodstuffs were hardly in sufficient

supply to last a month at most. And then, there was expected to be widespread hunger all over the Realm and beyond. No fruits or vegetables reaped or grown after the Event could be consumed by the mortal body in order to gain nourishment, no livestock slaughtered. It was as if all living energy itself was suspended, and would not be released into the chain of life. Only old harvest grains, fruits, and other aged food kept the hunger at bay.

His dead daughter had gone north to the wilds of Lethe to offer herself as a Cobweb Bride, and nothing was heard of her since. The Emperor tried not to think, tried instead to look at the clear morning sky of pale blue, with not a cloud in sight.

They told him that something was happening in the north country, a massing of the dead under the banner of the Chidair Duke who himself was one of them. Again, the Emperor tried not to think, not to imagine, for it all made so little sense.

The Empress spent her time mostly in her own quarters, working on endless, useless needlework or making charitable visits. Again he tried not to think of his wife's white face purged of all animation, carved by grief into a shrunken elderly doll. Indeed, the two of them now made a fine pair.

And the bizarre, unsettling news continued. More recently, within the last two days, there were such inexplicable events reported that the Emperor could not even grasp the meaning of what was being suggested. According to so-called reliable witnesses, various landmarks were *disappearing* from all around the Realm. Sections of the land gone—forests, entire portions of towns, remote settlements missing, roads abbreviated, hills misplaced. Utter nonsense, he thought, and chose to think of it as a mere sign of the troubled times—an escalated state of frenzy in the impressionable minds of everyone made vulnerable by the cessation of death to the barest hint of the metaphysical in all things. God had abandoned them, and so did reason.

One other superstitious rumor that particularly infuriated

him had to do with a supposed young girl from a distant northern village in Lethe who had the miraculous ability to lay the dead to rest. Death's Champion, they called her. She traveled the countryside and performed miracles on old women and pigs. Or maybe she was but an angel sent from Heaven, a precursor of the Last Judgment. Upon hearing of this "Death's Champion," he had gone into a quiet rage and forbade any more mention of it.

But there were other things, undeniable and real.

They told him there were new stirrings beyond the foreign border of the Domain. Something on a very large scale was taking place. . . . Balmue had grown so quiet it was surely a calm before the storm. Clandestine chatter was at a minimum, and all his own sources had gone extraordinarily silent. Oh, how he tried not to think on that!

The Emperor took a turn about the terrace, reaching its eastern end. It was here that Andre Eldon, the dashing and dandified Duke of Plaimes, and Claude Rovait, the bearded and distinguished Duke of Rovait, caught up with him. Both men were Peers of the Realm from Morphaea, consummate diplomats, and his finest Imperial advisors. Both also supervised a wide network of clandestine operations, with ties all over the Domain and the outlying foreign territories.

The men walked swiftly and bowed before the Emperor.

"Your Imperial Majesty," spoke the younger man, the Duke of Plaimes, who held the secret distinction of handling the deep cover spy network based in the Domain. "If we might have a moment of your privacy—some news."

The Emperor grimly acknowledged them; motioned with a tired gesture for the assistants trailing him to walk further back. The Imperial guards fell back also.

"Bad news, I surmise?" the Emperor said as soon as they were out of hearing range of anyone else.

"I am afraid so," replied Plaimes. "Today I received a series of flower code messages from Micul Fiomarre. The first bird brought a carefully drawn likeness of the dreaded red rose, which means the Sovereign armies are on the march against us, blossom opened wide, which indicates the entire Trovadii force. Immediately after, a second bird arrived, also with an open rose, but this one black—a somewhat cryptic message, since black indicates death, and also a black rose is the symbol of one of the Trovadii generals. Later, two more pigeons came in, one with a blue fleur-de-lis which means Solemnis is on the move in the west, and the other bearing the likeness of a green leaf, which indicates that the Balmue border is on high alert."

The Emperor sighed. "So, it begins. . . ."

"Fortunately, in this we have advance notice." This time it was the ever-tactful and levelheaded Duke Claude Rovait who spoke. "I suggest Your Imperial Majesty puts the Imperial Forces on alert within the hour. And by the end of the day we will have the entire military of the Realm ready to counter the threat."

"Good, yes, let us proceed thus," muttered the Emperor. His eyes continued taking in the wide expanse of sky, serene and fathomless. A crisp late afternoon wind swept in sudden biting gusts along the terrace.

"With your permission," continued Rovait, "We will alert Morphaea."

"Yes, yes. . . ."

"One bird to His Majesty at Duorma, immediately," said the Duke of Plaimes—for it was within his Dukedom that the capital city lay, and his prime responsibility was for the defense of the Morphaea-Balmue border.

"Another to my own Dukedom," Rovait said.

"One to Styx, to alert the young Augustus," said the Emperor thoughtfully.

"Styx has very few resources at the moment, Your Majesty," Plaimes mused. "If I recall, a single battalion is all he can manage at such short notice. It will have to remain as part of his own garrison, to counter Solemnis, and none to lend to the Imperial army."

"Poor boy." The Emperor continued to stare at the rooftops, the distant haze of the outlying edifices, swept with snow. "He will have to manage on his own for quite a while. I have no expectations on his part. Now, what of Lethe?"

"Lethe," Rovait said, "might be problematic. They are dealing with the civil uprising—"

"Ah, yes," the Emperor mused. "The eternal cesspit of discord that is Lethe."

"The Red and Blue Dukes have made things very difficult indeed, and now the alliances along the lines of the living and the dead are stretching things further. . . . There has been no word yet as to the developments in the north, but I do expect something shortly."

"Well then, wait on Lethe until more is known."

"Your Imperial Majesty, one more suggestion, if I might make it," spoke Claude Rovait, in his rational, calming manner. "It might be prudent to send something beyond the Domain. The Sun King of France is not likely to respond, but it would be worth trying to fortify a solid rear front against the Domain there. The House of Bourbon has fickle and complex loyalties, especially on the side of Marie-Thérèse, the Infanta of Spain. As for Spain itself, feeble and starving, especially at such times as these, Carlos the Second is of little use to us."

"Then send a bird to France, and tell them of our plight."

"It shall be done, Your Imperial Majesty." Rovait's wise, comfortable gaze offered the Emperor a soothing moment of emotional balm.

"What a mess. . . ." Josephuste Liguon II muttered. "How long? How long do you think we have until the Sovereign reaches the Balmue border?"

"Even is she arrives tomorrow morning, we will be ready, Your Imperial Majesty," the Duke of Plaimes spoke with utter confidence.

"And what if—what if she comes . . . tonight?" The fears arose, starting to gnaw at him full force, and the Emperor looked away from the false serenity of the panorama and focused at last upon his two advisors.

"Highly unlikely," Rovait's expression was mild, and a steady smile of reassurance played on his lips, partially obscured by his well-trimmed beard.

"Regardless, our battalions will stand ready." Plaimes spoke reassuringly to his Imperial liege.

"Then go! Make it happen! Call the generals to war!"

They bowed, and hurried away, two of his favorite, most reliable men.

It was time to send the birds.

Chapter 14

Percy sat before him in the saddle and listened to the black knight's steady breathing as he guided the warhorse forward on the roadway.

There was no one else on the road this morning. The road itself was almost invisible, an abstraction barely defined by the subtle hedge growth on both sides. After such a heavy snowfall, few bothered to make a trip of even a mile. And thus, the way was pristine, untouched by ruts of cart or wagon wheels or footfalls of man or beast.

Only a few birds sped overhead, and the occasional roadside trees shook off the crystalline burden from their branches.

Another half an hour of steady walking on the part of Jack, and they had ridden close to the outlying settlements of the town ahead. Here, the first cross-traffic of the day greeted them, as a few carts and warmly-dressed working class pedestrians approached and passed them.

"There it is," said Percy in curiosity, turning her head from one side of the road to another, to stare at roadside establishments, as they grew thicker and thicker together. "I didn't think it would be so big. . . . Not compared to Letheburg of course, but Fioren is a big place!"

"Hm-m-m," the knight retorted. His steel eyes were on the

road and he did not look at her, but she noted a slight tensing in his brows. "There is something—I cannot place what it is, but something is off," he said. "For one thing, Fioren has no walls that I know off." And he pointed with one gauntleted finger at the distant rising short walls of stone, directly in their path. They were nothing in comparison with the great parapets of Letheburg, but there was a definite enclosure, and a gate up ahead.

"What in Heaven's name?" Beltain muttered. "This is not Fioren! This is Duarden!"

Percy stared in confusion. "What do you mean?"

"I mean, this is *not* the town of Fioren."

"How can that be? Did we somehow miss it on the way back there?"

Beltain did not reply, but hailed the next passerby. "What town is this?"

"Duarden, My Lord," the bearded peasant replied.

"What of Fioren? Is it not supposed to be here?"

"Aye, My Lord, it is. I am from Fioren, but a miracle has come, and it's gone!" The peasant spoke, gesticulating with his mittened hands for emphasis. "I just spent the night here, out of noplace else to go! My horse an' I here, we were out deliverin' and now I got nowhere to return to. What with the snow an' all, had to stay overnight."

"So you say that Fioren has disappeared. . . . You're sure of it?" Beltain persisted.

"Not sure of nuthin' much these days, Lordship," the man replied. "But if it is there, I'll be looking for it, since my wife and the boys are there, and my home. Maybe it'll come back? They say some places that disappear like that come back—"

"So this is not the only place that's disappeared?" Percy asked.

The peasant looked up at her, rubbed the bridge of his nose with the back of his mitten. "Oh, no, girlie. They say, a few miles off, a whole field and forest are all gone. People woke up a day ago, and there was just nothing there. And up in the tavern back there in Duarden, they tell me half the streets are missing. And worse!"

"What's worse?"

"It's the dead, girlie. They're everywhere. Not afraid of the cold they are. Hardly any place left for an honest livin' man. Not much food left, either."

He shook his head wearily, raised his hat up to the knight in politeness, and then was on his way.

"Will that be a problem for you?" Beltain asked. "The dead?"

"Not any more so than usual. . . ."

"Good. Then we proceed onward."

But Percy's mind was reeling. "My Uncle Guel is in Fioren. . . . *Was* in Fioren!" she marveled, as the knight again directed the charger to walk forward.

"Wherever your Uncle and his family are now, say a prayer for them," Beltain replied grimly.

They approached and passed the gates into Duarden, a mid-sized affluent town just a stone's throw away from the Silver Court. The streets were snowed-over, with light traffic, and the buildings stood close to each other, with many overhangs and quite a few expensive shingles indicating various high-end establishments.

A few odd looking figures were indeed seen about, some sitting calmly right in the snow before buildings, others standing upright, like statues. A mother and child of no more than five, both deceased, lay dejectedly in a bundle before the wall of a bakery storefront, looking with apathetic glassy eyes at the passerby. Their faces were greyish-blue from the cold, and white powder covered the tops of their bare heads. Each one had a billowing death-shadow at their side, noted Percy. None were particularly threatening, and were left well enough alone by the living. But their presence was a strange psychic burden upon the place. . . .

As the knight and Percy rode by, she could see the dead slowly sensing her, turning their fixed stares upon her, and following all her movements with their eyes. None of them made any move to approach, and she took a deep breath and steadily looked away from them.

The sun rose higher, signaling near mid-morning, and Percy's stomach was rumbling. She flushed again, knowing Beltain could hear it, while the knight simply said, "Time to get a meal. Lord knows, I could use a tankard of a real brew about now."

They found a tavern and eatery within a few minutes, and right next to it, a bakery with a tantalizing storefront displaying apple tarts and great round loafs of golden-browned bread and long braided baguettes. The mouthwatering aroma of rising yeast and flour was devastating.

While Percy stood staring at the breads, Beltain took Jack around the back where quite a few empty stalls were available in a small stable structure adjacent to the tavern. He spent some time there taking care of the great warhorse himself without allowing either of the two tavern stable boys to come near. And so, by the time he came around to the front, Percy was ready to start gnawing her own knuckles in hunger.

They entered the eatery, a dark parlor with a wooden beam ceiling, furnished simply with a long, narrow table with benches. Two or three men in plain or dingy clothes were eating, hunched over soup bowls. A plump country-faced woman greeted them with a curtsy and a slightly nervous smile, and told the knight to sit anywhere he liked. "We don't have much today, Your Lordship, but there is fresh barley and turnip soup and a whole lot of good bread from next door. For you, I might be able to also cut up a bit of pepper liverwurst sausage that's blessedly old and decidedly edible. None of that horrible newly butchered stuff that's indigestible, as you know—"

"Yes, I know," said Beltain, seating himself at the table and removing his gauntlets. "Bring it out. And have you any decent beer or ale in the house, good woman?"

"By all means, Your Lordship, we have a wonderful brew that my husband made himself a while ago, and it's aged well, and will refresh you!"

Percy paused before sitting down, considering, then took a spot for herself across the bench from him, so that they faced each other across the short width of table. She took off her mittens and placed them in her lap. It was all so strange—well, just a little strange, or maybe a whole lot of strange—to be sitting thus in a distant tavern, directly across the table from the black knight, facing him, as though they were equals, having an ordinary mid-day meal. What a notion indeed, it suddenly struck Percy. How impossibly strange this whole thing was!

"And what would you have, dear?" the proprietress asked Percy gently, seeing that the girl was with the knight—in whatever capacity, was unclear.

How in Heaven's name did a person ask for a meal at a public tavern? Percy had never been at an eatery before, not with Pa and Ma, not with anyone.

"Whatever's not too much trouble, Ma'am," Percy replied, wondering suddenly if it was right for her to go and help with the dishes in the back. "Maybe some soup and bread would be all right?" And she looked up at Beltain with a questioning expression.

He was looking at her very closely, and did not say a word. Oh, but his eyes! Up close like this, they were so clear, so rational, so impossible to look at. . . .

Percy again felt the familiar flush-heat rising in her cheeks that seemed to come at her out of nowhere. And so, she looked down instead of looking directly across at him. And she considered her present situation.

A few minutes later, the plump woman brought out a pitcher of warm water and a small copper basin with a towel for the knight to wash his hands. Then she returned with a tray with two large bowls of steaming soup and a tall tankard of frothing beer. Next to her came a small boy, of no more than seven, with sweet light curls and a pale serious face, and he carried a large basket of fresh bread loaves and a trestle cutting board.

"Right here, André, put the bread right there before His Lordship, and set out the basket near the board. That's right!" The woman directed him while unloading the contents of her tray. The boy nodded and set down his burden, then bowed lightly and very properly before the knight.

Beltain's mouth started to turn up in a smile at the sight of the boy's diligence.

"Good, now run along and bring the rest of it, and be careful not to spill!" the woman instructed him.

"A smart boy," the knight commented, taking a loaf of bread and cutting into it with the knife.

The proprietress, apparently the boy's mother, broke out into another proud but nervous smile, and curtsied. "Why, thank you, Your Lordship, yes he is, my André!"

Percy watched the boy walk very carefully to the back, and with a sorrowful pull at her gut she eventually saw the slight little billowing sentinel shadow follow the child closely.

Little André was dead. And it was unclear whether his mother knew it or not.

The chunk of bread that Percy had started hungrily chewing a few seconds ago suddenly lost its flavor, replaced by a lump in the throat.

Soon the boy came back out, carefully carrying a plate of liverwurst sausages. His little white hands held the sides of the plate precisely right, and when he came back up to their table, he again bowed, moving so effortlessly for a dead one that it was no wonder he was not immediately apparent as such. Even his face,

Percy noticed, seemed to have a residual glow around his cheeks, and there was not a sign of blemish or lifeless fixation in his limbs.

"Put it down, André, right there—now, serve His Lordship."

"Yes, Ma." Even his voice seemed at first glance that of a normal healthy seven-year-old. It was only the slight delay before inhaling, and then the overly even speech, that hinted at something not exactly normal. . . .

Percy looked at him, stunned. And the boy and his little shadow, also seemed to sense her. As all the dead did in her presence, he eventually turned to her, and looked up in her eyes with his earnest green-blue ones.

"Say hello, André!" said his proud mother, wiping her round pudgy hands against the front of her apron. "There, speak to His Lordship first."

"Hello, Your Lordship," the boy said, looking away from Percy momentarily, and again bowing before Beltain.

"How old are you, André?" Beltain asked kindly.

"Will be seven in three weeks, Lordship." And the boy, having unburdened himself from all the plates, now dug his hand into his breeches pocket and took hold of something.

"What's that you have there in your hands, little man?" While taking a deep draught of his beer, Beltain had noticed his movements.

"My horse and cavalry man." And the boy turned out his pocket and pulled out a small, carved wooden figurine of a horse and rider, with the rider holding a tiny little shield and pike.

"I see. That's a very handsome soldier. Well armed too."

"Yes, Lordship."

"Oh, now, don't bother His Lordship at his meal, André," his mother spoke hurriedly, suddenly looking in the direction of the outside door and unshuttered front windows showing the street. "You run along now! Go in the back and wait for me!"

"Yes, Ma." And the boy ran slowly, holding the wooden toy soldier in his hand.

The next moment, the outside door opened, and two very large men came in, moving stiffly with the telltale awkwardness of the dead. They had grim cynical faces, the look of mercenaries, and a shabby quality to their clothes. Percy noticed a few belted weapons on at least one of them. Their death shadows moved alongside, large and menacing, she saw.

Beltain sat with his side partly turned from the entrance, but there was not a moment of doubt he saw everything, including the new arrivals, with his sharp peripheral vision. He was dipping bread in the barley soup and bringing the ladle up to his mouth, but for some reason she noticed a subtle quality of relaxation in his muscles, like a coil loosening, ready to spring.

She redoubled her efforts to slurp her own soup and stuff her cheeks with the bread, keeping her head down over her bowl, even though now the flavor was gone, and her pulse was in her throat.

The proprietress of the tavern however, did not waste any time. The woman took a few steps, putting her hands on hips, and said loudly to the dead man who entered first. "What do you want, Jared? What now?"

"And a good day to you, Mistress Saronne," spoke the dead man, dark haired and bearded, with heavy overhanging brows and a deeply rutted pale face. The act of ballooning his lungs caused a crackle of breaking ice on the inside of his chest cavity, which indicated that he'd been out in the cold without speaking for some time. "Need a man have a reason to come inside a public establishment?"

Percy heard that crackle, and continued staring into her bowl. Everyone else in the room heard it too, as a few of the townsmen paused eating and glanced warily at the newcomers.

"You're no longer welcome here," Mistress Saronne replied in a firm voice. "I've asked you before not to come in any longer, and now I ask you kindly to leave, both of you."

The two dead men slowly looked at each other, and their fixed eyes did not change but the mouths shaped themselves into grotesque versions of smiles.

"Why so uncharitable to an honest dead man?" said the second man, leaner and also dark, with a long gash scar running up his neck and jaw, its wound edges frosted over and crystallized with pallor.

"Because, Hendrick, you are *dead*, and a rude villain to boot. You were a right horror when you were alive, and I can just about tolerate that kind of thing if you're living flesh and blood and can pay me with coins for your supper. But no longer! You don't belong here, where honest folk are trying to have a meal. You are scaring the customers!"

"Come now, why so mean, Mistress Saronne? No one here is scared." The first man slowly walked into the room, stiff-limbed yet managing to saunter insolently. He walked up to the table edge and stopped next to a man having a bowl of soup. "Well, am I a bother to you, good fellow?" he asked.

The man shook his head silently, but his eyes were troubled, and he'd stopped eating and put down his ladle.

"Jared Gaisse, begone!" Mistress Saronne exclaimed, in a rising voice.

"See, there, he ain't bothered." And the dead man called Jared moved away from the eating customer and sauntered over along the table, moving deeper into the room.

Meanwhile, the other dead man also began edging into the room from the other side of the long table. Slowly they were moving nearer to Percy and Beltain who were close to the middle of the long table, across from each other.

The black knight calmly chewed bread and sausage, picking up the next slice with the end of his knife, then taking a long pull of the beer. He did not even look up or around.

Percy gave him a series of hard looks, widening her eyes,

then raising her one brow meaningfully, and then the other. He did not seem to notice her antics at all, and was completely engrossed with his meal.

The dead man called Hendrick stopped on the side near Percy and leaned to stare at a small balding townsman who was timidly eating right next to her. "What's that you have there, my friend?" he drawled, ice crackling in lungs. "Any good, this swill? Wish I could taste some, but I don't remember how that works any more. How does eating and drinking, and pissing work?"

Percy glared at Beltain . . . who pointedly ignored her. And when she finally caught his eye, she could have sworn there was a bare shadow of a smile around his eyes and near his lips—that is, if they would only stop moving long enough between chews and swallows.

"Ah! And, look here, we've got us a comely little thing, with a fat little arse! Stuffing those fat round cheeks, are yah?" Hendrick had stopped behind Percy. Had he been alive he would have been breathing down her neck. Instead, there was only crackle in the inside of him and creaks of settling limbs.

"You ought to leave now," said the black knight softly. He wiped his mouth and jaw with its newly sprouted growth of beard with the back of his hand and put down his tankard of beer.

"What's this?" Hendrick looked past Percy's back and at her dining companion. "Is this a mighty knight I see? Your Lordship, what, with your fancy mail and a sword belted on, are yah?"

"You are a dead idiot," said Beltain, looking up at Hendrick with his very clear slate-blue eyes. "I will overlook your insolence, your crude words to the girl, even your lack of courtesy to the good woman whose establishment this is. Simply turn around and go."

"Or you'll do what, Lordship?"

"*He* is not going to do anything," Percy said suddenly. And without getting up, she turned around and took the dead man's ice-cold hand.

It was as if out of nowhere a windstorm moved inside her, entering with a hard snap, filling her, swelling, rising, rising. . . .

And suddenly the entire tavern *rang*.

Percy felt it with her mind, the homogeneous blanketing pressure of raw power, resonating among the rafters of the high wooden ceiling, and echoing to the beaten rush-swept floor and the winter-hardened earth below. And it made her cold and hard and full of knife-edge clarity. She held the animated corpse by the hand and saw his death-shadow, long and billowing like a torn sail, come to attention before her as she took it by its gossamer filaments into a chokehold.

The dead man called Hendrick went perfectly still before her, immobilized by her touch.

"*This*," Percy said. "This is what *I* am going to do."

Everyone in the tavern was also taken by a stillness—by something they had no words for, even though they could not feel the electric coursing of power all along the room.

"And you—" Percy said to the other dead man across the room, reaching out through empty mind-space and taking his death shadow's thread of energy into a similar hold. He froze also, completely immobile, watching her with suddenly obedient fixed eyes. "—You can feel it also. I hold you both now."

"What . . . are you?" Hendrick's voice creaked.

"I am your *end*," she replied. "Would you like to know it now? Or would you like to stay in this world a while longer?"

"Please . . ." the dead man called Jared croaked, "I want to stay . . . here . . . in this world."

"Then get the hell out of this tavern, and let us eat in peace!" Percy said, releasing the two death-shadows with a hard snap of her mind, so that they flickered like blown candle flames before resuming their pitiful vigilance next to the dead men's bodies. She then turned her back to Hendrick and picked up a large chunk of bread, dipped it in the barley and stuffed it in her mouth.

In the sudden perfect silence of the tavern, the two dead men turned around, and walked out of the tavern, moving as fast as their frozen log-limbs would allow.

"Fat arse, indeed. . . ." Percy mumbled incomprehensibly with her mouth full. The ringing power was gone and she was suddenly ravenously hungry, even more so than she had been before she started eating.

The tavern came back to life. Customers took in big breaths, resumed their meals and conversation, and cast a few curious glances her way. But none of them of course had any idea what had just passed on the level of the mind, the kind of exchange of power that took place before their noses. All they saw was that a young peasant girl had just told off a pair of big dead ruffians and somehow sent them running.

The knight regarded her with a half-amazed, half-amused gaze. He parted his lips to speak.

But the proprietress, Mistress Saronne, came rushing up to Percy, and waved her hands about in joyful gesticulation. "Oh, my dearie! Oh, bless you, sweet girl! Whatever you've done or told them, oh, thank you! You have no notion how rough it's been, with 'em coming by every day it seems, harassing the good folk here! I fear they even robbed some folk just outside the door! Now why would a dead man need to be robbin' anyone, I don't know! That Jared Gaisse was no good, even back when he was living, and when he got in a fight a few days ago, and got himself cut up for dead, what with the death stopping and all, now he's been a rotten nuisance around town! And that Hendrick too! Cutpurses, both—"

Percy watched the woman speak, passionately waving her hands around. "I don't think they'll be back to bother you any more, Ma'am," she said.

"Oh, bless you! I have no notion of what you said to frighten them off, and I don't want to know, but it was sweet magic! Now, what else can I get you, dearie? Something sweet indeed! How about some tea and tarts? Would you like that? And it's on the house, I'll have you know!"

"Oh . . ." Percy said, with a smile. "Yes, please!" And then she snuck a glance at Beltain who was struggling to hold back his lips from sliding into a grin, and instead busied himself again with chewing.

Mistress Saronne hurried away to deliver Percy's tarts, and was back soon, with little André trailing her, carrying a round-bellied pot of tea and cups on a tray. With an almost apologetic curtsy to the knight, she served the girl first, and Percy found a large fragrant apple and pear tart swimming in honey syrup, on a saucer before her.

While André stood by dutifully, holding the tray, his mother poured two steaming cups of the amber liquid and set them down before Percy and then Beltain.

"No tart for you, little man?" the black knight said, turning to the boy once again. The child stood looking very intently, his pale blue eyes never blinking, so it was easy to mistake his manner for interest in the sweet course.

"No, Sir."

"Want a bite of mine?"

"No, thank you, Sir."

Mistress Saronne seemed to become flustered. "Oh, no, Lordship, don't you be worried about my André, he has plenty to eat whenever he likes!"

"I'm not hungry," the boy said simply.

Percy bit her lip.

"Go on, child, take the tray back now," his mother said, starting to pile the empty dishes on the main tray in her hands, after putting just a few lighter ones on the boy's.

When André moved away, Percy said very softly to his

mother. "Begging pardon, Ma'am, but your little boy—he is—well, you do know what he is?"

The woman's smile was instantly gone, and an expression of anxiety came to her rounded features, and the loaded dish tray in her hands clattered precariously. "Oh!" she said. "Goodness! Why, what is he? What do you mean, dear?"

In that moment Beltain looked up at them both sharply, ignoring his platter. By the serious gravity in his expression, Percy knew that at last he understood.

"Let me help you with the tray, Ma'am," Percy said, rising from her seat. She then took the tray from the startled Mistress Saronne and went with her to the back of the tavern, walking past the table and benches.

When they came to the back room and kitchen door, there was little André, just standing there at attention, his back straight, and arms at his sides. The firelight from the large oven illuminated his porcelain delicate beauty of suspended childhood.

Percy put down the tray on a table then turned to the older woman. But before she could speak, Mistress Saronne exclaimed to André, "Now go upstairs, boy, right now, you hear, child? Go up there and wait for me! Hurry, now! Scoot, scoot!"

And as the boy obeyed, and moved away in his little measured paces, his feet making small creaks on the stair, the woman turned to Percy. "Oh, for the love of God, I beg you not to say anything to anyone, my dear!"

"So you do know that he is not *alive*—"

"Yes, yes, oh, I beg you to hush!" And the poor woman wrung her hands and then took Percy's with her own, clutching them in a moist trembling hold. "However did you know, girl? Oh, I know not how you discovered it, but please don't say anything! Yes, my poor little André fell down a few days ago, and hit his head against a railing. There was only a little blood, and I cleaned him all up, right there at the back of his curly sweet little hair, and after the washing it was all covered up, just as well as you please! And he looked all fine and rosy, just a little bit pale, and he went to lie down for a bit, and then he was up and wouldn't lie back down ever again. I had no idea about death stopping yet, so at first I wanted to take him to the apothecary, and then of course we all learned the truth of the world. . . ."

Mistress Saronne started to tremble, and Percy looked at her with compassion.

"And now," the mother continued, "he does not sleep. He never sleeps. He sits or stands all night, and plays with that wooden toy of his. And he does not know. *He* doesn't know!"

"Oh, I am so very sorry. . . ."

"Never you fear, my girl, I am glad I have him now, and it doesn't matter in the least what he is. He is a precious good boy. He listens to me, and helps around the tavern, and serves the customers, and he never says an unkind word to his old mother or to anyone. It is God's blessing that I have him with me for as long as I do—however long that may be."

The woman let go of Percy's hands and again clutched her apron. "So you see, it is so important that no one knows! Not so much the customers, or the neighbors, but I don't want *him* to know! Oh, he mustn't!"

"But," Percy said gently, "will he not find out eventually? And once he does, he will be faced with the truth no matter now much it may hurt or scare him. He does have the right to know. . . ."

"But he's so young! He's but a baby! He can't know about death yet! No, not yet, please!" And Mistress Saronne broke out into deep heartrending sobs, with snot and tears distorting her face into a mask of grief, while she bit her knuckles. "And as for his father, he is gone out of town, and when he comes back, oh Lord Almighty, at least he will be able to speak to the boy! It is a miracle, this whole thing is, to have him with us! But oh—I just cannot tell him—either one of them!"

"Would you like me to speak to André on your behalf?" asked Percy. "Also, it is a hard thing to say, but now that no one can die, there is yet a way for the dead to be put to rest. I am able to do that for André, if you like. . . ."

"Oh, God, no! Oh, no, no, please, don't take him away!" There was panic in the face of the woman.

"I will not take him away without your or his consent," Percy replied. "But it may be the right thing to do, to ask him what he wants. It is not a happy thing for him to be as he is, neither properly alive nor dead. This is not *real*, none of it. He will never grow, you know, never get older—"

Mistress Saronne began to sob once more, and in that moment, there was again a creaking on the stair. And then André's little shape came down, and he stood before his mother and Percy, looking at them both with very intent clear eyes.

"Oh, what are you doing here, André? I told you to stay upstairs!"

"Why are you crying, Ma?"

"It's nothing, child, I am—I got onions in my eye, you know how I cry from all them awful peeled onions!"

"Where are the onions, Ma? I don't see any."

Percy watched their exchange, and then she turned to the boy very gently and asked: "André, you don't want to go upstairs and sleep, do you?"

"I am not sleepy."

"Would you like to sleep?"

He paused, looking at her, with that same soft watery intensity that was caused by the connection with her for which neither she nor the dead had any words.

"Would you like to lie down and go to sleep at last, André?"

The boy was silent, regarding her. And his mother, no longer hiding her state, burst into hard weeping again.

"I can help you go to sleep, André, but only if you want."

"Can I have dreams?" he said. "I haven't had dreams, not yesterday, not before that."

"Can you promise him dreams?" the mother exclaimed in a wild voice, then added, "You're the one they speak of, aren't you? I know you! Oh, I know who you *are!*"

Percy felt her throat closing up, and she said, "I cannot promise dreams. I—I can only give you rest."

The boy nodded then, never taking his eyes off her, and not once looking at his broken hysterical mother. "Yes," he whispered. "Then, yes, I want to go to sleep. And I will dream on my own, all by myself. Help me go to sleep. . . ."

"No!" Mistress Saronne slowly slid down on the floor, holding herself with her arms wrapped around her middle. "No, please! Oh, God, no. . . ." Her words trailed off into incoherent sobs.

"André," Percy said. "Go and kiss your mother before you sleep."

The boy obeyed, and turned, then slowly lowered himself on his knees before his mother. "I love you, Ma," he said. "Good night."

Mistress Saronne grabbed him in a big messy embrace, and held him, stroking his curling baby hair, his cool ivory forehead, his round cheeks with their faint shadow of a wilted rose. She released him at last, and said, "Go on, now, go. . . !"

Thus, Percy Ayren took the little boy by the hand, and together they went upstairs. There she turned down the quilt of his small bed and helped him crawl inside, and then tucked the blanket covers around him. His small feeble shadow sentinel streamed at the side of the bed, delicate like vapor over a warm milky bowl—waiting.

"Where's your cavalry man and his horse?"

And when the boy dug in his pocket and offered the wooden toy to her, Percy held his fingers briefly, and then put the soldier figurine up to his chin and along the boy's chest, where she lifted it up and down, saying, "see, how he rides!"

A smile came to André, and he watched the moving soldier and his horse, as they navigated the hills and valleys of his chest and blanket.

"Where does the cavalry man ride?" he asked, settling back against the pillow.

"Oh, he rides on an Adventure! I'll tell you a story, André, a story about this very special brave Cavalry Man and his Horse, as they gallop!"

"What's the Horse's name?"

"Well, you'll have to ask the Horse himself, but he's a fine and wondrous Horse, faster than the wind, and I think he'll show you his name, once you close your eyes. . . ."

"I can see it!" André smiled, as his eyelids came down, with soft pale lashes brushing against his cheeks.

And Percy continued the story.

When she came downstairs, the mother sat like a stone on a bench in the kitchen. Percy's face was immobile, leached of all energy and her eyes were red-rimmed.

"Is he—"

"He's gone," Percy said. "Peace be with you."

And as Mistress Saronne rushed upstairs with a hoarse, rending, guttural sound, Percy came out into the common room of the tavern, mostly emptied of customers, where the knight had long since finished eating and was waiting for her, his face locked in a sober expression. He had left a generous pile of coins up on the counter.

"My Lord," Percy said, looking at him and yet past him. "We need to go now."

Beltain nodded, rising.

And there was no need to say another word.

Chapter 15

Lady Amaryllis Roulle and Lord Nathan Woult waited for what must have been at least a whole day and most of the night before the urchin Catrine returned for them again with a plan for escaping Chidair Keep.

It was long past evening twilight, and an anxious-faced servant girl had come with their poor meals of whatever turnip-and-carrot swill concoction the kitchen made that day, together with a new pitcher of water. And then another servant came to empty their chamberpot.

Amaryllis, still miraculously elegant despite her many days without proper ablutions, used a bit of the fresh water to sprinkle her hands, in an illusion of washing before a meal, then stirred the fearsome lukewarm gruel in her bowl with one slim finger and tasted the mushy carrot stew with a grimace.

"I am afraid they are feeding us whatever they must feed the pigs," she observed. "Has it gotten even more foul, or am I mistaken?"

Nathan dipped his chunk of bread into his own dish, and then scooped up a large glob and popped it into his mouth. "Really, my dear, you are far too fastidious. Think not of what it is, but what it could be! This stuff is not half so bad now, though it could use a bit of salt and pepper, and—oh, all right, it could use gravy and wine and the entire contents of a proper pantry."

Unlike the lady, Lord Woult looked very unkempt, with his tussled hair, several days' growth of black beard, and circles under his eyes. In the near-darkness of their chamber, he could very well have been taken for a monstrosity.

Amaryllis looked up, barely registering the sight of him— untrimmed beard and whiskers and his hair standing up wildly— and shook her head in piteous disdain.

"What?" Nathan said, pausing with his mouth stuffed full of bread and stew.

"Dear Heaven, but have you looked at yourself, my dear boy? You appear perfectly horrendous. It's a good thing I know there is a handsome man underneath that apish Caliban. It is also a good thing the moon is not out yet, to illuminate our woe, or I would be forced to look at you."

"Hah!" he said, and continued chewing. "It is not to be helped now, is it? Not all of us can maintain esthetic decorum while locked up and denied toiletry and cosmetics."

"Tis too true," she replied, then sat back on her cot with resignation and dipped the tip of her finger again in her stew, scooped up something unspeakable, and brought it up to her mouth.

"I, for one," continued Nathan, stuffing his face, "can certainly use a barber's blade and comb, and a nice soak in a rosewater bath, followed by an application of emollient and powder, all while listening to a dulcet melody played on the harp and viol. However it is but a cruel poet's fancy. And to be honest, I would gladly sport a beard worthy of Bacchus for a fortnight, all in exchange for a well-done ragout, a platter of *escargots de Bourgogne*, and a large plump *coq au vin*."

"The poets always do languish so prettily," mused Amaryllis. "Always a drafty attic and sallow cheeks, and never a stench-filled privy and boils."

"Dear God, My Lady, let us not speak of boils! We are quite far removed from boils, just yet. I choose to hope that we shall never achieve that blessed state wherein one exudes pus."

"Oh! Oh! Oh, fie!" Amaryllis uttered a sound very close to an undignified squeal while her gentleman cellmate burst out in an ungentlemanly laugh. He then used his last chunk of bread to wipe the bowl clean and landed the bread in his mouth.

"How can you eat and speak thus in the same breath?"

"A man learns to make do, my dearest Amaryllis," he replied, wiping his mustache with the back of his hand, then dropped his empty bowl, letting it clatter on the stone floor. And then he belched.

"Ah! Ah! Lord, but I don't think I can endure another moment of this Tartarus!" the lady cried, and turned away from him, setting aside her own barely touched bowl. "You are turning insufferable!"

"Oh, come now, do learn to suffer me, sweets," he retorted, lying back down on his cot and putting his hands under his unruly head of hair. "After all, m'dear, you are the one who brought up *boils*. . . . Incidentally, do you intend to eat the rest of that?"

In silent indignation, Amaryllis handed him her portion.

A quarter of an hour later, the servant returned, together with the usual guard, to take away their finished dishes. And just moments after their footfalls receded in the corridor, a soft scratching knock sounded on their door.

Nathan perked up, and Amaryllis turned her head in apathetic despair. They watched the door and its noises, until it opened, and there again was the freckled girl by the name of Catrine.

"Good evening, Your Lordships!" she said, slipping inside and shutting the door behind her.

"It is a horrid evening," said Amaryllis, "but I expect you will make it all better, now that you are here." And she rolled her eyes in disdain.

"Really now, girl, we did not think you'd return," Nathan

said, sitting up. "All hope was dashed and I grew another
fingertip's width of mustache. It's been what, a day?"

"Begging all pardon, but I'm so very sorry, but they put me
to work an' I couldn't get away, even a minnut. Had to make
ready, Lordships, gathered us a bit of supplies." Catrine pulled
out a satchel that she had hidden among the folds of her skirt.
Inside was a ball of twine, some needles, a few other small
blades and hand tools, several tallow candle fragments, a flask of
oil, and a small lantern.

"Now, here we go, Lordships!" Catrine exclaimed. "Today
the Keep is nearly empty, since the Duke an' his dead army had
gone off to war—"

"What war, by Jove?" Nathan said.

"Dunno, Lordship, the kitchen staff say they had gone to
take Letheburg, and that the crazy Duke has made a high and
mighty 'Liance—"

"Ignacia!" Amaryllis said. "That is surely her work!
Remember, Nathan, what she said to him, something about an
alliance with the Sovereign. I was so stunned that I paid little
heed to the details of her treachery."

"Well, well . . ." Lord Woult mused.

"And anyways," Catrine continued, "as I say, the Keep is
almost empty an' lightly guarded. They'd gone off yesterday,
but I waited long enough to make sure, and now is the best
moment to run!"

"Must we really follow your harebrained scheme to go
down into the dungeons and follow some kind of subterranean
hell-maze?" Amaryllis interrupted again. "If you say the Keep is
so lightly guarded now, why not chance an escape past the
walls? I am certainly willing to brave the difficulties of the
forest—"

"There's been a snowstorm, Your Ladyship," Catrine said,
scratching her brows with her dirty knuckles. "So much snow,
buckets an' buckets. The forest is very deep now, waist-high in

some places, and I wouldn't wanna wade through it if I were you, or to get lost in all that wilderness."

"Ah, a pity. . . . In that case, what are we waiting for? Let us instead descend into your delightful hell." And Amaryllis stood up.

Half an hour later, after walking in silence along abandoned unlit corridors of a very unsightly old portion of the Keep, with Catrine ahead, shushing them every few paces whenever Nathan made too much noise, they arrived at a stairwell.

The stairs went down, and they could see it twisting into a distant well of darkness below. The moon came out, shining in a clear night sky, and casting even pleats of light through the narrow slit windows of the outside walls.

"The dungeons are way down there!" Catrine spoke in a high whisper. "And then, right next to them is where we get out! It's a great big—oh, well, you'll see!"

"I still don't understand, is there a tunnel of some sort?" Nathan began.

But Catrine said, "Shush!"

And Lady Amaryllis shook her head in disgust and simply began walking down each stair, carefully placing each delicate booted foot forward, and holding on to the walls. She was still favoring one foot a tiny bit, because of her sprained ankle, but it had healed enough so that she could keep up a steady pace.

They went down and down, with just a few landings to mark lower floors, and eventually the well of darkness had grown so complete that they could only see a bleak bluish spot of moonlight if they looked up. After half a dozen floors, they were now moving entirely by feel, carefully testing each step down.

"When can we get some light?" Amaryllis whispered tiredly. "Surely a candle would not kill you, nor would anyone really see us down here in this abysmal cellar."

"If your Ladyship insists. . . ." There was a sound of striking of flints, and a tiny candle flame bloomed in the darkness. It threw wild jerking shadows along the circular stone stairwell and illuminated Catrine's grubby face, and Nathan's fierce bearded visage.

"Much better," Amayllis said and proceeded walking down.

"We could still be seen, 'tis true," Catrine mumbled. "But it is not as likely now, Ladyship. Besides, we are almost there."

"No doubt," muttered Nathan. "I can just about hear devils stirring their coals."

"Oh, no, Lordship!" Catrine said. "Nuttin' of the kind, don't you be afeared."

They reached the next landing, and it was blessedly the last. It had gotten significantly colder too, if that was possible, considering the chilly draftiness of the upper floors. By the light of Catrine's candle they saw a wide tunnel, and on both sides, rows of ancient cell doors of partly rotten wood planks and reinforced iron castings. Some had tiny slits with vertical bars set in place. Beyond the bars was absolute darkness.

"What a horrible place!" Amaryllis whispered, her breath curling in vapor from the cold air. "Are there any prisoners languishing in those cells?"

"Goodness, no, Ladyship, those are not the dungeons," Catrine cheerfully reassured. "That is, they are some kind of very old an' rotted leftover dungeons, but they don't use 'em these days. The new dungeon's up ahead."

And indeed, a few turns of the dismal corridor later, they came upon an opening and beyond it a twilit great chamber, filled with a remote soft sound. A strong draft came blowing at them at the entrance.

"Just a minnut." And Catrine paused right at the entrance to the chamber and blew out her candle.

"Now why in Heaven's name did you do that?" Nathan grumbled.

In the new dismal twilight, Catrine turned to him, her eyes glittering, and said, "Oh, but we have to do that, before we go inside! You see, Lordships, there are three very important rules to going inside the dungeons. The first rule is, we cannot bring any new light beyond what's already in there. Not even a single candle, else real bad things will come to pass!"

And Catrine walked ahead of them into the dim chamber.

Nathan and Amaryllis found themselves in a huge cavern. No, this was not a mere cave-like chamber of stone, something wrought by man, but a genuine subterranean formation, a pocket of air within the earth, grander than the tallest hall, with smooth dripstone rocks coming down from the remote ceiling in long stalactite icicles and rising up in stalagmite columns.

On the side nearest the entrance to the cavern, there was a long iron-barred enclosure, indeed a cage, with many divisions, and it was filled with prisoners. Young girls and maidens, most of them peasants—although there were quite a few well-dressed maidens among them—were on the other side of the bars, locked inside, huddled in bundles and shivering from the relentless cold, and there was no one guarding them.

"Here are the other girls, Lordships!" Catrine said, blowing on her fingers for warmth.

But Amaryllis and Nathan were not paying attention. Instead, they both stared in amazement at the opposite side of the cavern, where, beyond shallow banks, a dark silvery river flowed, with slow-moving waters and no apparent bottom. It was the source of that strange whispering sound that they had first heard upon entering the cavern. Overhead, the stalactites dripped softly—must have been dripping for centuries—casting droplets of water onto the river below, and it resonated in delicate tinkling echoes along the current and the cavern walls.

On a distant wall near the bank of the river, mounted in a rusted sconce, was a solitary oil-burning lantern. It was the only source of light, casting a warm golden halo of steady radiance upon the whole cavern, reaching far and wide, and giving the ivory stone a delicate blue-green quality of subtle iridescence.

"Heaven! What an amazing sight!" whispered Nathan. "How high that cavern ceiling must go!" And he turned to Catrine. "Give me a candle, girl, I am dying to see the extent of this place!"

"Oh, no!" Catrine exclaimed and almost jumped back away from him. "You mustn't light another light in here!"

"Say what?"

"Rule two," sounded a girl's voice from fifty feet away, from inside the iron cage enclosure. "You must never let the lantern light go out, and you must never light an additional one for as long as *that* one burns. Or at least that's what they keep telling us."

They turned to see the speaker, and there were at least five girls, who had gotten up to stand, hands holding the bars. "Enough dawdling, Catrine! Let us out of here already, before someone comes!" said the one who had just spoken, and Amaryllis vaguely recognized another girl from the incident on the road a few days ago.

"Sorry, Sybil, took us a while to get here. And don't worry, no one's coming for hours!" And Catrine ran over to the great cage and started fiddling with the lock.

"Good Heavens," Amaryllis said to Nathan softly, "how many of them are there? Will they all be going with us?"

The lock was finally picked, and the door of the cage opened, releasing the girls. Sybil, a freckled redhead wearing a well cut hooded coat of royal blue, with a nice mulberry wool scarf tied around her neck, was out first, stomping her feet and straightening her skirts. After her came another familiar girl, by the name of Regata, also better dressed than the majority, in a warm green coat and a fur-trimmed cape-hoodlet.

As Catrine came around with her skillful lock-picking, the rest of the girls, at least two dozen, started coming out of the other partitioned enclosures, some looking frightened, others mostly dazed. A few remained seated in the cage and shook their heads indifferently when prompted by the others to follow.

"So, a whole warren-full of Cobweb Brides!" Nathan remarked. "Whatever shall we do?"

"Don't worry, Lordships," Catrine said, approaching once again, followed by three others. "They are not all going with us, just Regata and Sybil here, whom you've met, and Faeline, who's a local. Some of the girls just wanna hide in different spots around the Keep and bide their time for later, you know, sneakin' out. They're far too afeared of the river."

"Rule three," said the girl called Faeline, a slim tiny blonde in a grimy tattered dress, and then awkwardly curtsied before Lady Amaryllis and Lord Nathan. "You must never drink from the river, nor touch its waters. Everyone else is afraid to come near it. But me, I don't really care all that much, Your Lordship, Ladyship, I just really want to get out of here."

"I see," said Amaryllis, pulling her warm burgundy cape closer about her in the cold. "So what exactly is wrong with that river? And do you mean to tell me we will be going near it? Dear Heaven, you don't expect me to *swim?*"

"Oh, no, we'll be taking the boat."

"What boat? I don't see—"

But Catrine pointed across the cavern, and said, "That one!"

Nathan and Amaryllis saw that at the farthest end of the cavern, past the watery expanse, the opposite shore was visible. On the bank, sat a long wooden boat of bright yellow oak, pulled out of the water and resting on its side against a stalagmite. Two oars were lying on the floor of the cave alongside it.

"Let me see if I understand correctly now," Nathan reasoned. "We will all of us get inside the boat—after by some divine miracle it floats across the river and comes to us of its own volition—and then we set sail along this possibly poisonous river that mustn't be touched, into a dark unlit series of abysmal caves and tunnels that go lord knows where for lord knows how many leagues under the earth. And *that* is your idea of an escape? Are you *addled*, girl?" Nathan folded his arms and exhaled in anger. "Take us back upstairs; at least there are cots and swill waiting for us."

"Pardon, Lordship, but the boat will get us out of here, it is as sure as I got me a nose on ma' face." Catrine fiddled with her satchel, digging around for something. "The whole reason I had your Lordships come down is 'cause the boat needs you to operate it."

"What she's saying is, the boat may not be used by anyone but a lord of noble blood, they tell us here," added Regata.

"And who are 'they' who tell you all this nonsense?" Amaryllis trained her cold withering gaze upon the girl. "Who came up with these three idiot rules? The guards? The local servants? You seriously believe they would tell you things that are designed to be anything other than a way to keep you here?"

"Indeed!" Nathan began to pace. "If they tell you not to touch the river, then it may very well be a real way out of here! As for the extra lights, it's certainly a way of keeping you from seeing possibly another exit or some other useful things to help you escape."

"That's sort of what I believe too," Sybil said. "Been sitting in that stupid cold cage for days now, with nothing to do but think. I bet if we light up another candle or two, it might scare some bats up in the ceiling, no worse. And if that lantern goes out, well, that's just giving us an easy way for us girls to sneak out of here!"

"Well, let's see indeed what happens if we take a better look!" Nathan reached for the satchel, pulling it out of Catrine's hands, and took out the short tallow candles and the lantern with the oil flask.

"Oh, Lordship, no, no! You mustn't! What if some terrible monstrous thing comes out of the river?" Catrine put her hands up to her mouth. The other girls who had been wandering around the cave and heard this pronouncement, squealed, and a few of them started running for the corridor exit.

"Frankly, I don't care if a three-headed behemoth emerges," said Amaryllis curtly. "He is welcome to eat me whole, for I am cold and hungry and weary to death of this—all of this! Proceed, Nathan, do light up this place!"

And Nathan took two flints and struck them together, while Catrine covered her eyes in fear. He lit the first bit of candle and gave it to Regata to hold, then another, and handed it to Amaryllis who took it carefully between two fingers and held it as far away from herself as possible, so as not to drip the melting tallow upon her cape. Sybil took the last candle, and then, with the tip of her candle flame, she lit the wick dipped in the oil flask, and stuck it inside the lantern which Nathan held.

With their small individual flames sending up grotesque shadows in the cavern, they all turned about, looking in every direction, and then—because the constant gentle sound in the cavern suddenly started to fade—one by one they all glanced at the river. . . .

It was *gone*.

In place of the deep slow-churning waters with their silvery reflection on the surface, there was absolutely nothing—empty space beyond the bank.

Catrine, who had been cringing, lowered her hands from her eyes and gasped.

"The river!" she said. "Holy Lord!"

Nathan frowned, then holding the lantern walked up to the edge of the bank and looked down.

He saw that the bank fell away into a ravine only about eight feet deep, and there was a rocky floor below, perfectly flat and dry. The entirety of the riverbed was fashioned in a similar manner, a reasonably flat floor that could easily be walked across, and then on the other end the bank rose up again and tapered against the walls of the cavern. There sat the boat in the same place they could see it—all he had to do was march across the bottom of the riverbed and climb up a few rocks to get to it.

"What is it, Nathan?" Amaryllis asked, without approaching. "What's down there? A precipice?"

"No, my dear," he drawled, and started to climb down in easy leaps. "There is nothing but a few rocks on the floor, and I believe I have our solution." His voice resounded in louder echoes, now that there was no water in the cavern and more empty space, as he quickly made his way across the hundred feet of riverbed. "Just keep shining those candles, and do not let any of them go out! Not until I tell you to!"

Within minutes, Lord Woult had reached the opposite shore, clambered up easily and stood next to the wooden boat. He looked inside, examined it for defect, and then pulled it a few feet, dragging it so see if it was at least superficially free of breaches to be seaworthy.

"Now," he said loudly, and his voice echoed across the expanse of the cavern. "Blow out all your candles!" And in the same moment he blew out the lantern held in his hands.

The girls all complied, and the moment the light faded to the level of dim twilight of the single lantern in the wall sconce, the sound returned, and with it the silvery river—it was flowing as though nothing had happened, in the same channels where it was before.

"What manner of magical river is this?" whispered Catrine.

They watched Nathan pull the boat and attach the oars, then splash it into the silvery waters. He climbed inside with a minor grunt of satisfaction, then gripped the oars and started rowing with powerful easy pulls against the slight force of the current.

In a few breaths he had crossed the river and was climbing on the bank on their side, then pulled up the boat after himself. His hands were slightly wet and he examined them after releasing the oars and said, "No, nothing is damaged, I see. No caustic burn, no poison leaching my flesh off the bones. I touched the river and I am still decidedly myself. No behemoth either, you will be glad to note, Amaryllis, dearest."

"The girls were staring at the river in wonder. Those of the remaining potential Cobweb Brides who had not scampered off, stood timidly, whispering amongst themselves.

"I think I know why they say a lord has to be the one to operate the boat," Catrine said. "Who else would have the insolence to break the rules?"

"There is a difference between insolence and a gentleman's proper education," said Nathan.

"Or, a lady's," added Amaryllis coolly. "I would have done the same thing."

"Yes! For one must always cultivate skepticism against abysmal superstition and other common idiocy," Lord Woult continued. "Natural philosophy, my dear! Nature and reason, observation and experimentation can explain everything in this our Age of Enlightenment."

"Yes, well," said Amaryllis. "Except for the disappearing river. And the cessation of death. And—"

"All right, by Jove! If I cannot have my vanity and fashion, give me at least my moment of scholarly triumph, will you now?"

"Since we are experimenting," Amaryllis said, "the next step would be to attempt removing all sources of light. I suggest someone go over to that lamp on the wall and snuff it out."

"A solid notion!" Nathan stepped up to the riverbank, crouched down, and placed his hand into the running current.

Regata nodded, and then ran to the wall and stood up on her tiptoes to remove the reservoir of lit oil in the lantern. She brought it to her face and blew on the flame but it was too large to be extinguished with a mere breath. So then she spat on her fingertips then quickly pinched the wick.

The lantern smoked and then the cavern was plunged into

absolute darkness ... and again came the silence born of receding waters.

There were a few terrified squeals.

And then Nathan's calm voice echoed. "Yes, just as I thought, no water once again. My hand is submerged but suddenly feels no liquid. This river is a marvel. It seems to dislike the darkness as much as it does excessive light."

In the next second a small flame bloomed again as Nathan re-lit his own lantern. With it, the river came back into being, with its soft sound and running waters.

"What a clever river you are," he said, addressing the swirling currents. "I wonder who fashioned you, what deity's caprice? A river that lives only in twilight!"

"So, dearest Nathan," Amaryllis said, looking out over the cavern's expanse. "Shall we brave the current and see where it takes us?"

"The trick to traveling this river would be to keep the twilight alive . . ." he mused.

"In that case, we take a single lantern in the boat with us and keep it lit." Amaryllis turned and looked directly at him with a challenge and a smile.

"Oh, Lordy, Lord!" Faeline said. "What if it goes out in the middle of the river, and everything goes dark? Won't we and the boat plunge goodness knows how far down to our deaths?"

"Very likely," said Nathan, looking back at Amaryllis with a smile of his own. "All the more reason not to let the lantern go out!" he added cheerfully.

"I dunno . . ." Catrine muttered, "sounds awful risky to me!"

"It sounds delightful!" Amaryllis exclaimed. "Oh, I was so deathly bored! And now, Heaven knows, I find a reason to live, at least for the next half hour. . . . Let's go! This very moment!"

"Your wish is my command, sweet Amaryllis!" spoke the gentleman, adding: "Everyone, on board!"

Chapter 16

The day advanced into soft evening as the black knight and Percy rode along the snowed-over road past Duarden, steadily moving south.

There were more travelers on this portion of the road with them, pedestrian and wagon traffic in both directions, and the pristine thickness of snow was soon mashed and beaten down into brown slush, which made each pace slippery and dangerous.

Percy was unusually quiet. Resting sideways against the now familiar solidity of the knight's ebony breastplate, encircled by his metal-clad arms, she gazed ahead of her, hardly bothering to turn at the various sounds around them on the road—carts creaking, the squeaky turning of badly oiled wheels, the crunch and squish of crudely-booted peasant feet.

Beltain was mostly silent also, fixed in his imposing posture, and lightly guiding Jack's reins.

A number of times, companies of fast riders passed them in the opposite direction, holding banners aloft. Among them were liveried Imperial Heralds, racing swiftly north and away from the Silver Court, bearing news and Proclamations into the depths of the Realm and the Kingdom of Lethe. At other times, the Heralds were Ducal, wearing the colors of the Duke Vitalio Goraque and not the Emperor, and they rode in the same direction as Beltain and Percy, south and into the Court.

"Make way!"

"Stand aside!"

The outcries came so often and had grown so familiar, that it made good sense to keep to the side of the road rather than get plowed over and splattered by slush from their horses' hooves—though, the latter was unavoidable.

It was also fortunate that Lord Beltain Chidair wore his long black cloak to cover himself instead of the ice-blue Chidair surcoat that he'd removed and folded away in the travel bag. To sport Chidair colors at this point deep in Goraque territory would have been imprudent.

The closer they approached the heart of the Imperial Realm, the more traffic there was, and the thoroughfare eventually widened. Gone were the unrelenting snow-plain and fields, and instead wooden settlements revealed themselves on all sides of the road, alongside orchards and roadhouses and smithies. In the twilight of the coming evening, torches and lanterns came to life and burned orange-gold against the darkening sky. Vendors with supper stalls were common, and the noise and smell of bread, onion, charred sausage, and burning wood smoke rose up from many chimneys. It was as though they were moving through a center of a sparse but sprawling town.

Urchins ran about, their yells and breath rising in the chill air. Interspersed with the vivacious children were human shapes grown remarkably still, seated in pitiful lumps along the hedges or aimlessly moving along the road in the telltale manner of the dead. Upon occasion, some passerby stopped and divested the indifferent dead of their clothing, leaving their cold pale limbs exposed to the elements. Percy watched from the corner of her eye as three older boys surrounded a gaunt old man with a frosted beard and crystalline sheen of snow on his face, and stripped his jacket, britches and belt, leaving him in threadbare woolens. They guffawed and ran off with his belongings, and the dead man watched them helplessly with fixed marbles of eyes, turning his head slightly in their wake.

"For shame!" cried an old woman draped in a thick shawl, gesticulating at the young robbers. She paused momentarily before the seated dead man to offer him words of kindness, even though he seemed not to hear her, then shook her head, crossed herself, and was again on her way.

In the near distance before them rose walls of darkness, punctuated, up in the lofty heights, with moving and stationary lights signaling the upper edges of battlements. During day, the walls would have gleamed silver-white with mortar-bound granite, their angular elegant bulwarks jutting out in regular intervals along the perimeter. But at night, the defensive walls of the citadel that was the Silver Court were shapeless black giants, with only necklaces of distant lights to mark edges and openings.

"Behold—we have arrived at the Silver Court," the knight remarked. "The Kingdom of Lethe ends at these walls. And just beyond these great outer walls lies the greatest jewel of the Realm."

Percy, groggy from the sway and movement of the horse underneath them, nodded wearily. Her face, in the flickering torchlight all around them, appeared leached of color. Her round cheeks were paler than usual, despite the regular chill of frost that had reddened the tip of her nose and chapped her lips.

Beltain looked down at her, and saw her drooping eyelids and lethargy.

"I'll find an inn for us, so we can stop for the night." And he added: "Now that we are here, can you sense if the *thing* you seek is here, or nearby?"

He was referring to the Cobweb Bride—the one distinct death-shadow that Percy was following, on her quest on behalf of Death.

Percy turned her face toward him . . . then looked partly away.

She appeared abstracted, trained inward with an unfocused

gaze. After a few moments she shook her head negatively. "No, it is not here. *She* is not here. She is further that way—south." And she pointed at the walls of the Silver Court and beyond, toward the Kingdom of Morphaea.

Beltain sighed.

"Well then, we still need to rest overnight, so we are going inside."

"Must you not, in any case, seek audience with the Emperor to give him news of his daughter?"

"No. . . . Her Imperial Highness had instructed me not to bother. I am solely intended to accompany you."

"Oh. . . ." Percy nodded again.

They rode to the massive metal and oak gates, pausing with other traffic to be allowed to pass and enter the grounds of the citadel. It was chaos of men and beasts and wheeled wagons. At the gates they had to wait for a troop of infantrymen in formation, and then watch the pikemen on the march followed by their arquebusier rear columns.

Finally they moved past the gates and entered the citadel.

Percy opened her tired eyes in slow growing wonder, for it was akin to discovering a single blooming rose amid a wall of ivy. Beyond the crude outer walls, the inside of the citadel was an artful marvel—an intricate series of structures of mathematical symmetry, illuminated on the inside by glittering light, each structure a delicate core around a disembodied source of illumination—or so it seemed, through laceworks of glass windows. Domes and columns, arches and friezes—these were not mere palatial buildings but temples to beauty. At night lines were sharp and silhouettes prominent; streets went on, broken by perfect right angles, creating parallel lines of perspective upon rounds of winter gardens and fountains that were snowed over. Fresh fallen powder dusted the domes and cornices of marble, while icicles decorated ironworks and each upright streetlight wore a cap of snow.

Somewhere in the center of this clockwork jewel, lay the Imperial Palace. If Percy trained her gaze in the distance, she could just make out the sharp spires of the cathedrals and the dome roof of the Basilica Dei Coello, illuminated from the ground up and fading overhead . . . dissolving into the blue twilight sky cast in the shadows of early evening.

It had grown dark enough now that the stars had come forth like shards of ice. But the moon was not out yet, and it had suddenly gotten to be very cold.

"I cannot even comprehend this place. . . . It is not real, not like anything I've seen or imagined," whispered Percy, waking up with all her senses. "Letheburg and its Winter Palace are small, so small compared to this—all this."

"Yes," Beltain replied, glancing at her with bemusement. "On my first visit to the Silver Court, when I was a lad of twelve, I remember hiding behind my father's back and gawking at everything, even though he'd warned me not to show any reaction or, Heaven forbid, undermine our family honor by revealing ourselves as distant country bumpkins. It mattered not; my fool mouth remained open and I think I caught more flies than a pot of honey that day."

A faint smile came to Percy's lips. "I cannot imagine you, My Lord, as a lad of twelve. Or, on second thought, maybe I can. . . ."

He did not reply, merely continued riding along an open plaza immaculately cleared of snow, then turned past rows of lovely curving lanterns with fleur-de-lis frames into a side street of stone houses, each one more impressive than any single building in Letheburg short of the Winter Palace. Expensive carriages were parked in even rows along the street, and pedestrian walkways marked by more streetlights separated the roadway from the houses.

The buildings here, Percy noticed, all had proper façades, with moldings near the roofs and beautiful framing overhangs above raised doorways, which were in turn preceded by at least three stairs over ground level.

Here too, carriages moved along the street and well dressed ladies and gentlemen were seen along the sidewalks together with the more ordinary working class.

Beltain approached one such fine building, bearing an elegant sign of an inn, and dismounted, then lifted Percy down. Two liveried footmen approached immediately, and bowed before him, and he conveyed Jack wordlessly into their care, together with some coins. "Come along, girl," he said, walking up the stairs to the door, which was opened by another bowing servant before him. Percy wordlessly followed, with a sudden pang of discomfort of the same sort that she'd felt when entering Lethe's Winter Palace.

They were trailing filthy wet snow inside, she thought, probably about to damage fine Persian carpet and leave mud stains on polished marble. . . .

Well, it turned out, they were, and they did.

The bewigged and liveried butler gave a single look of distaste at the condition of their travel clothes, and especially Percy's "rags," but quickly averted his gaze and bowed in perfect decorum, while His Lordship asked for rooms for himself and "the young lady," plus two suppers and baths to be carried up immediately.

Next, they were taken up a flight of stairs along more fine Persian carpet, and shown within a suite that rivaled the Winter Palace, with brocade upholstered sofas on curving legs of polished wood, fancy chintz curtains and embroidered silk throw pillows. There were two boudoirs, decorated in tertiary tones of delicate silver-threaded lavender brocade and pale green. Both were connected through a small interior dressing room parlor, and each one, in addition to all the other furnishings, sported a massive canopied bed, a carved marble fireplace, and great windows of glass, revealing a picturesque view of the street scene below and the magnificent rooftops of the Silver Court.

"Oh, this is too much!" Percy whispered, holding her hands over her mouth, for these accommodations were worthy of a Royal.

But Beltain ignored her, and informed the valet and maid assigned to them that they required laundering services and a change of clothing for the night.

Within a half hour, two exquisite porcelain claw-foot tubs were carried into each boudoir, along with endless basins of hot water. Then a row of maids arrived with towels and robes.

The black knight disappeared into one of the boudoirs where his valet assisted him with the divesting of his armor and under-layers. While he was being stripped, Percy was taken by a maid and wordlessly assisted out of her own rough wool and burlap dress, stockings, socks, and crude shoes. "I shall turn around, Miss, while you take off your shift and drop it here, and enter the bathtub."

"Oh!" Percy was blushing all shades of pink, mostly from mortification. What will the maid think, seeing all such horrible filthy underclothing? As soon as the maid turned her back discreetly, Percy stepped out of her dirty threadbare nightshirt and hurriedly entered the steaming hot water. She had never had such a luxury bath in her life. Indeed, a large wooden barrel filled with boiled water in their barn was all that she had known at Oarclaven of bathing.

As soon as Percy was submerged up to her chin, the maid curtsied again, picked up the strewn clothing without any comment, and left the room while holding it in a pile. Moments later another maid came in, bearing a silver tray of soaps and fragrant oils.

"Allow me to scrub your back and help with your hair, Miss."

"Oh, no, thank you . . . oh, goodness!" Percy's muttering however was tactfully ignored, while the servant went to work, pouring basins of water over her hair, and massaging her scalp with some kind of sudsy soap that had the extraordinary consistency of cream and smelled of sweet alyssum, orchids, and lily-of-the-valley. She then dutifully scrubbed Percy's back and other parts with a sponge, periodically pushing the girl underwater to wash off the residue. At last, when the rising steam began to cool, the maid held up a fine soft robe and Percy was told to rise and wrap herself in the fabric.

As soon as Percy pulled the robe around herself and settled in a chair before the fire, the bath was taken away, and her maid stayed to brush her hair with infinite gentle strokes, and tell her what a sweet and pretty head of hair she had.

Percy thanked her in some confusion, since her mousy hair had never received a compliment from anyone. But she was feeling so warm and languid after the wondrous bath, her skin all flushed and rosy, and her cheeks touched with a healthy glow they rarely displayed, that she did not protest the kind words.

Percy's hair, fine and listless, usually wrapped around her head or braided and tucked out of the way, had seemed to take on a strange new life and sheen from the creamy soap. As it dried, it sparked with electricity under each brush stroke, and spread in large waves upon her back.

"What an unusual color your hair, is, Miss," said the maid. "It is nether dark nor light, neither fair nor raven, but almost like a warm breath of shadows. . . ."

"Thank you kindly," Percy said, "but I believe that color is called 'ratty poop.'"

But although the maid, being quite her age, giggled, she also shyly protested, "Oh, no, Miss, it is so very beautiful! I do think many Court ladies would love to have this shade in their wig!"

Percy decided to imagine she was stolen away into faerie paradise. And thus she sat with a softened countenance, dry and warm and perfectly relaxed before the fire, and as squeaky-clean as she hadn't been in weeks.

Very soon afterwards, as the sky outside the great glass windows went perfectly dark while the citadel lights cast a golden radiance upon the snowed rooftops, supper was served.

A small mobile table cart was rolled in, on Beltain's side of the suite, and then the knight's valet knocked on Percy's parlor interior door from the dressing room separating them and invited her to dine with His Lordship next door.

Percy arose, wrapped herself closer in the fine lady's robe of the faintest shade of mauve, and then put her feet into a pair of embroidered slippers that had been brought for her.

While the valet bowed before her, she shyly walked through the small middle parlor and emerged in Beltain's boudoir, feeling like a crown princess of an imaginary kingdom that took up exactly three rooms.

But a shock greeted her on the other side—something for which she had no warning, no means to prepare herself.

Lord Beltain Chidair—newly bathed, clean-shaven by the valet, clad in a plum velvet robe, his softly curling brown hair groomed in High Courtly fashion, and the skin of his face polished and glowing from the warmth of the bath—was seated in a tall-backed chair near the fireplace.

He was a man of devastating beauty.

And Percy stopped at the entrance, because her breath had been taken from her.

She stilled with all her being, looking at him. And then, very slowly, she curtsied deeply. Never again would she casually meet the look of his clear pale blue eyes, for now it was denied her. Always, from that point onward, must she steel herself into a blank artful semblance of composure, and put on, like a mask, an abstract shallow gaze that did not register the full *depth* of him.

After a strange pause that she did not particularly notice—for she was submerged inward, thinking all this—he spoke to her.

"Come, Percy, our excellent supper is here, and I am starved. . . . Sit down."

Beltain watched the girl enter his quarters, and the sight of her caused an unexpected jolt in his gut. It was followed by an effusion of sudden warmth flooding his chest, or maybe a constriction within his solar plexus. It was impossible to describe the series of sometimes painful, sometimes joyful sensations of turmoil that came to him. . . .

Gone were her colorless rags and her many layers of peasant winter clothing. Her hair, a strange, soft intermediate hue, fell long and loose around her shoulders like that of a wild maiden nymph from a ancient woodland portrait.

Her form was Venus on a shell riding the foam, as painted by the Florentine over a century earlier, only richer, fuller, and as sweet as churned cream—even though it was now hidden so well by the voluminous folds of her lady's robe.

Her face—its childish roundness, and its unconscious emergence of womanly lines—was averted, as she curtsied so deeply before him—so well and with such genuine intent.

"Come, Percy," he had told her, saying he was starved. And she obeyed, sitting down at the short table across from him, her hands in her lap, and her gaze still lowered.

He watched her with pleasure, sitting thus before him, as he took the bread and the ripe fruits on his plate, and cut into the well-aged smoked meat and cheese, taking up pieces on the end of his knife and tasting the juices that ran down his fingers and glistened on his lips.

But she remained motionless, even as the valet poured red wine into silver goblets and stood aside discreetly.

"Are you not hungry, girl? Or thirsty?"

She did not reply, simply took up a chunk of bread, some cheese, and placed it in her mouth, then chewed without appearing to savor.

"What's wrong, now?" Beltain sensed that something was amiss, something new. Could it be she was rendered shy by their fine new circumstances, the exquisite fabrics and clothes, the palatial surroundings? He realized she was immensely weary, drained by the events of the day.

"I . . . I am so very tired, My Lord," she said, looking at her bread.

"I know. But you need to eat before you rest."

She nodded, took another bite, then picked up the goblet, swallowed and grimaced. "What is this?"

"Wine. Have you never had wine?"

"No. . . . It is so bitter."

Beltain turned to the valet and asked for tea to be brought for the lady.

"Thank you," Percy whispered.

They ate thus, she nibbling at her food, he eating ravenously, sensuously, watching her as he consumed the flesh and the fruit and the generous chunks of bread.

When the tea came, she drank a cup gratefully, along with a slice of flaky pastry followed with a small dish of crème brûlée.

He watched her rounded cheeks and the innocent movement of her lips, soft and puffy from the warmth and comfort of the tea.

At last they were done eating, and she simply got up, and once again curtsied, and then backed out of his room and fled into her own boudoir.

Beltain was left alone with the mostly consumed supper service and the courteous valet.

Beltain was awakened in the night by the soft sounds of weeping coming from the other boudoir. He rose, casting off his silken sheets and bedspread, and stood listening, his silhouette bathed in the moonlight. He knew her voice, heard the soft repressed sounds of despair. . . .

Taking up his robe to cover himself, he did not pause for a second, but went to her, through the small parlor dividing their suite.

Her room was a temple of the moon.

Bright as day, the light came through the open windows, as the full moon rode high over the Silver Court, eclipsing the myriad tiny golden lights of the city with its immortal glamour. It filled the bedchamber, and illuminated Percy, sitting on the bed, her hair strewn about her like translucent cobwebs, her face half-turned to the window, shining with streaks of bright liquid.

She looked impossible for a moment, impossible and not of this world. . . .

He had made no sound, but she sensed him enter, and gave a small start, turning her face with her haunted liquid eyes to him. Her fine new nightshirt slipped low over her shoulders, and they gleamed alabaster white.

"Percy . . ." he said in a voice belonging to someone else. "What is it?"

She took in a shuddering breath.

He took the few steps toward her, then sank down on the bed at her side, never touching her, only so very close. . . .

"Forgive me for waking you," she replied in a faint whisper that was leached of strength. "I could not sleep."

"Is there something wrong? Something that pains you?"

"The . . . little boy," she said. "André . . . I think of him."

He watched her eyes—colorless irises, widened pupils, a welling of waters to mark their fathomless opacity. There was so much in her eyes, the faint edge of the universe, with dark starlit expanses on the other side, with no end. . . .

"I am sorry. That was a truly tragic one—of all the ones you had to lay to rest. . . ."

She looked away from him, as though recalling something, and not wanting to bear his gaze. "I . . . could not give him dreams. He . . . had wanted to dream. And I took him away from his mother. He could have spent more time with her, untold moments more—being. . . . Not living, but simply *being*."

"Is merely being the same as being alive?" Beltain spoke gently, still motionless, seated at her side.

"I should have left him be. . . ."

"Maybe," he replied. "But maybe you gave him a rare gift, one that few of us ever dream of possessing—a choice."

"But was it his choice, truly? Did he, a small child hardly able to recognize his self, his existence, the nature of what he was—did he and *could* he make the right choice? How much did he really understand of sleep and death and endings? What have I *done?* He had only asked for dreams!"

And Percy broke into shuddering weeping, hiding her contorted face against her sleeve, wiping the side of her face, her nose, cheeks, all of her, swollen with hopeless grief.

Beltain had grown so still, he could feel no motion in his own lungs. And then he forced himself to move, to reach for her. He took one of her trembling, tear-smeared, clammy hands, and he held it feather-lightly.

"Come," he said. "Let me tell you of Queen Mab. . . ."

And as Percy again turned her receptive face to him and softly quieted, he pulled back the deep piles of bed coverings, like a warm silken ocean, and he moved it aside gently. He placed both hands along her upper arms, his large warm palms encompassing her smooth resilient softness, and he slowly guided her backwards into bed, until she rested her head against the pillows. He held her thus, for a few seconds longer, his hands upon the sides of her arms, warming her—himself—with the gentle pressure of steady contact. And then he drew the covers up over her.

"Queen Mab," he spoke, leaning lightly over her, his voice entering into a soft cadence, "is the one who brings the world its dreams. She is a tiny little thing, a fairy that could fit on the end of a pin, they say—or at least my mother used to say—and she drives a coach fashioned of grasshopper wings, with wheel spokes made of spiders' legs, and other parts of her coach are gnats and worms and cricket bones and moonbeams. In short, she is an unspeakable fairy creature, possibly ridiculous, possibly sublime. When we lie down to sleep . . . she drives her chariot up your nostril, wagon and all, and then she fills your head with the stuff of your desire. . . ."

Percy lay watching him in amazement, her eyes great and liquid in the moonlight. Her cheeks still glistened with tears, but a peace had come to her features, and she breathed evenly, without shudders, her chest rising lightly.

"And so," he continued, "Queen Mab is the midwife of dreams. She helps each one of us give birth to our own airy infants, those very reveries that fill the hungry recesses of the mind. And none other can take that function away from her—not even you. The little boy who asked for dreams—in that same breath he called upon *her*, upon Queen Mab and her power."

"I could not give him dreams . . ." Percy whispered.

"Of course not!" And Beltain smiled, his lips curving gently, and his eyes filled with something that was also light as air and warm . . . yet fey and vulnerable, and so very peculiar. "But Queen Mab very likely did. Such is her unearthly power!"

"Do you think it is so, My Lord?"

He placed his fingertips upon the pillow, near the edges of her hair that fanned around her.

"I know the power that comes from our . . . desire."

And as she watched him unblinkingly, he said in a more steady voice, "The best way to answer your own questions, Percy, is for you to go to sleep. Sleep, now, and make the decision to dream by calling upon Queen Mab herself. Ask her anything you like!"

"Will she come to me?"

"By Heaven and all sweet angels, she will! But only if you

close your eyes. There, your lids must be shut tight, so as not to allow a peek. . . . But you must keep your nostrils open—at least one of them, else the fairy might decide to drive her wagon through your mouth, or worse, one of your ears!"

Percy chortled and smiled, and her eyelids, fluttering, had indeed closed.

"Now, start imagining the kind of dream you would want," he said. "And I will sit here with you until you sleep. I promise, I will not leave you until you dream. . . ."

"How will you know. . . ?"

"Oh, I will know." And he adjusted the bed coverings at her chin, his fingers suddenly making contact with her smooth shoulder, feeling a pang of warmth followed by a spread of languor in that one single point on his flesh . . . pausing just one instant, before moving his hand away.

The moon spilled its endless immortal light upon them as he sat thus, for long unmarked moments that were also like the blink of an eye, watching her breathe, watching the peace descend upon her as she quieted and eased into slumber at last.

Her lips had grown full with relaxation, and he gazed like a man drunk with the moon, seeing the nimbus of ethereal light around the edges of her hair, the dark brows that gave such a strong cast to her face, her lashes resting upon her cheeks. . . .

At last, when he no longer had a sense of self left to him, having dissolved entirely into the moonlight, he was compelled. . . . He leaned forward, his face over her, closer and closer until only breath was between them. He stilled again, trembled, drinking her breath. Just beyond him, her parted lips.

And he lowered his own mouth over hers, feather-light, pressing lips against lips, in a kiss that was so soft that he almost did not think it happened.

One pause, just long enough to feel it—as shock traveled throughout him—a touch that pierced and caused a resonance throughout all things. . . . The shock held him suspended, then left him through the pores of his skin, entering the air beyond, where it fed the now-electric moonlight. . . .

He drew away. He stood up silently, and backed away from her sleeping form.

And then he retreated into the night.

Percy was sinking in the many layers of approaching sleep and receding moonlight, falling lower and softer, lulled into sweetness of peace by the soothing cadence of the baritone voice. The voice was like ermine encasing her in safe warmth. . . .

At some point, it too receded, dissolved into moon silver and an outpouring of steady, perfectly comforting silence.

And then, just before she fell away entirely, she felt a touch upon her lips—a strange unfamiliar pressure.

She knew *him*.

Through all the subtle layers of unconsciousness—of somnolent dissolution of the self, that came to claim her just before the instant of submersion into sleep—she could sense him, pulling her upward out of the morass of jumbled thoughts and images, into perfect waking clarity . . . into awareness.

His *lips* were upon hers. Had been.

And then the moment was gone.

His touch—an impossibility. Such utter sweet softness!

She felt it bloom forth into her, a current of expanding wonder, spreading in a languid, honeyed flow. . . .

Then it was over.

She dared not move, nor respond, nor react, and held her breath until she could no longer, slowly letting herself exhale and inhale in tiny shallow movements of her chest.

At last, when she could not stand it any more, she opened her eyes.

In the moonglow and silence of the winter night, there was no one there.

He had gone. . . . Or had he even been there in the first place? Queen Mab indeed! Had *he* been a dream?

Percy lay with her pulse racing, for an untold length of time past midnight, her eyes opened wide to the night.

Eventually she slept.

Chapter 17

In the morning, Percy woke late with the sun in her eyes. She had missed the dawn by an hour, and now the brightness was overwhelming, and the reality of where she was came to her, with all the brocade furnishings and fine chintz curtains and the gold trim around the boudoir.

The Silver Court shone in the winter morning sunlight like a fluted sculpture of ice. And as Percy sprang out of bed, and went looking under the bed for a chamberpot, it occurred to her suddenly that she had had a very strange dream.

No, it was not the kiss. (Somehow she was quite certain that *it*, the *kiss*, had been real. And yet, any further thoughts in that direction were unthinkable, to be hidden away in a deep little memory trunk within her consciousness underneath all the mad fancies, to be analyzed and comprehended later.)

The dream she recalled suddenly, as she was finishing up her morning ablutions, was that of a very strange golden figure in the shape of a woman—indeed, a golden goddess, seated with one leg folded underneath her, and wearing nothing but a headdress and garlands of jewels. . . .

She was considering the meaning of this dream, when a maid came in, carrying her pile of laundered clothing. The servant made a little sound of surprise seeing that Percy was up and about—unlike the young ladies she was used to waiting on who all slept past noon—and the curtains had been left open all night.

"Oh dear, Miss, I am sorry! Would you like something brought up immediately?"

Before Percy could reply, the interior dressing room partition was opened and Beltain entered the room, fully dressed in his own freshly clean clothing, and wearing most of his armor that had been polished overnight. His head with its soft waves of hair was bare of helm or coif hood, and his countenance was absolutely composed as he glanced once at Percy, still in her nightshirt, and his steady grey-blue eyes seemed cool and matter-of-fact.

"Good morning. Get dressed, girl," he said. "We need to head out as soon as possible. It was good you had the rest, and so did I, but unless we hurry, we may not be able to leave at all. Rumor has it, the Silver Court is about to close its gates, except for limited entry and exit for the military. War has been announced."

"What?" Percy said. Even the maid, pretending not to listen, seemed to pause momentarily.

"Yes, war," he said, "but it is not what you think. It has little to do with Letheburg being under siege by the dead. It is something far more serious—a foreign war with the Domain. The news is, we are under attack by the enemy at the border with Balmue. And Morphaea may not be able to hold them."

Percy took her fresh clothing—her cheeks flaming with color once again as she had to unravel it, in all its poor threadbare glory, before the knight—and started dressing herself. He gave her some privacy by turning his back, and with the help of the maid she was dressed in half the time.

They were outside the inn within a half hour, after Beltain generously settled his bill with the proprietor. Outside, Jack was waiting for them, held by two grooms and a footman, having weathered a fine night in a warm stall with regal grooming and premium hay.

Percy was lifted up into the saddle, and she cleaved to the knight's chest armor in a mixture of reserve and newfound intimacy.

The street was busy with carriages and much foot traffic, and everywhere she looked, gold gleamed underneath ice and snow, as the splendor of the Court was revealed.

They rode through streets straight as arrows, directly through the heart of the Silver Court, past the Imperial Palace and all its adjacent buildings, for they had to cross the citadel in order to reach the opposite gate, the one that opened south into the Kingdom of Morphaea.

In-between the many sights and wonders of the Imperial city, it occurred to Percy that the dead here either kept out of the way or were very well hidden. Not once did the sight of a dead man on the street made her pause and engage her sixth sense. . . .

As they passed yet another tree-lined boulevard, with snow-laden or bare branches amid upright lampposts, a small garden park opened to view. A clearing and a fountain blanketed by snow presented itself, and Percy made a small gasp because the statue that presided over the fountain was the golden goddess of her dream.

"Wait! Stop, My Lord, I beg you, please!"

"What is it?" But he drew the reigns nevertheless, and Jack stopped, neighing in frustration.

Percy stared. "Who is . . . she?"

Beltain considered the direction where she pointed, furrowing his brow.

"I . . . had a very strange dream last night."

The instant she spoke it, a flush of color overpowered him. Heat rose up to flood his neck and jaw and cheeks, his entire head. It was fortunate she was not looking at him in that moment.

"I believe," she continued, "just as you said, Queen Mab

had visited me in my sleep."

He remained silent, unable to respond just yet, then managed at last: "What—what was your dream? What did you . . . see?"

"That statue!" said Percy, pointing again at an upright form of a lithe golden female, nude except for a covering of snow and garlands of jewels in a collar around her neck, and a headdress over her braided crown of hair. "The same golden woman, except in my dream she was seated with one leg folded under and the other raised and bent at the knee, and her hands were folded. Who is she, what does she represent?"

At her unexpectedly safe line of questioning, Beltain felt his high color drain away and a cool relief to replace it. "Oh," he said. "She is an antique. I believe she is the Goddess of Tradition. I forget her name now, but she was worshipped by Ancient Rome and before that, the Greeks."

"Why would Queen Mab send me a dream of her?"

Beltain smiled. He was charmed somehow that she would remember his words and a childish tale. "So, you paid attention to my story."

"Of course!" Percy continued looking at the statue in her little garden spot amid the frozen fountain. "I remember all the kind things you said to me—*everything.*"

And like a damned fool, Beltain blushed again.

He recovered well by giving a light snap to Jack's reins, and the warhorse was gladly moving again.

In minutes they had reached the opposite end of the citadel and approached the lofty inner walls of white granite and the great gates of the Silver Court.

Here, the circumstances that Beltain had been worried about, confronted them. A company of military guard stood at the open gates, blocking the general free exit and entry, and evaluated all prospective traffic in both directions.

They waited for long moments while a few carriages and

riders before them were stopped and examined and questioned.

When their turn came, an officer of the guard in Imperial colors of black and silver with a fine trim of gold and red over his chain mail drew a polished iron lance to block the way and inquired about the black knight's business.

"I am Lord Beltain Chidair of Lethe and my business is my own, in Morphaea."

The mail-clad officer paused, looking sharply at him, and then noticed the girl seated in the saddle before him. Truly, it was something out of the ordinary, since the girl looked to be a peasant. "Chidair?" the guard considered, and a frown grew on his face.

"Yes, *Chidair*," Beltain retorted, and his low voice resonated well enough so that a few other heads turned in their direction. "Is that a problem?"

Before the guard could respond, an energetic voice sounded a few steps away among the back of the guard company. Their ranks parted and a high-ranking youthful officer with an air of undeniable authority approached the black knight.

"Chidair! Lord Beltain, is that you? I'd recognize your accursed black armor anywhere! And that monster beast of yours!"

The words were spoken with deep laughter, and immediately Beltain showed recognition on his face in turn. He turned to the man, acknowledging him with a respectful nod of his head. "Your Grace! Duke Andre Eldon! It is good to see you! How fare you? How long has it been?"

"Well, let me think—since you unhorsed me at that tourney in Duorma, and then trounced me so soundly that I could not sit on my arse for days—what, two years ago?—I've fared quite well indeed!"

Beltain grinned. "As usual, Your Grace, you exaggerate."

But the Duke of Plaimes laughed again, slapped him on the armored leg and then waived the guard away, so that Beltain rode a few steps from the main roadway and they could talk without blocking traffic. The moment his back was turned to the Imperial guard, the Duke's grinning handsome countenance became serious.

"Now then," he said in a much lower voice. "What in Tartarus are you doing here, Beltain, and what must I tell these men to let you pass? You know, my friend, that the name Chidair does not evoke particular love these days. We've just had word of the siege at Letheburg. Ugly news, first thing in the morning. Your father has crossed each and every line."

"I know," the black knight said, his expression also becoming grave. "I am come from Letheburg, but from within the city, not from the occupier side. I can tell you only that my father is dead and has gone insane. As of last week, I am forsworn to him, and serve the Emperor directly. To be precise, I serve Her Imperial Highness, Claere Liguon. It is on her orders that I travel."

The Duke's expression grew alert. "What do you know of the Infanta?"

And Beltain told him. "She is reasonably safe for the moment, under the protection of the new King of Lethe. You've had news, I assume, of Her Majesty's passing?"

"Oh yes. Something having to do with a mysterious girl from one of your northern villages—"

And in that moment as he spoke, the Duke seemed to have noticed Percy. He threw her one astute stare, then looked up again at his friend. "This is *she*, the very girl who is responsible for—?"

"Yes."

"So it's true then. She really can perform the deadly miracles?"

"I have witnessed it myself. And—they are not miracles so much as—"

"Please . . ." Percy said suddenly. "Your Grace must let us

go."

The Duke of Plaimes watched her, narrowing his eyes, thinking.

"What exactly are you, girl?" he said softly. I have heard the term 'Death's Champion' used by men I usually consider fools. So, what is it, really?"

"I've been to Death's Keep," Percy admitted, knowing somehow it was not a bad thing to speak the truth now, before this man. "And there I have been given this ability and a purpose. Now I seek the Cobweb Bride, for I have the means to know where she is and to recognize her. I must bring her back to Death, in order to stop all this—this broken world."

"Ah, yes, we live in a broken world indeed . . . now, especially. So, where is she, this Cobweb Bride who is the cause of all our earthly despair?"

"There!" And Percy pointed in the direction of the open gates.

The Duke raised one brow in surprise. "What, in Morphaea?"

Percy shrugged. "She is south of here, is all I know. I *feel* her."

"You mean, like a bloodhound?" And the Duke's serious face momentarily eased into a smile. "Can you sense her with your nose, you're telling me?"

Beltain intervened. "That's about as much as I understand it too," he said. "She can somehow feel the dead, sniff out each individual death shadow, if you will."

"You know," the Duke mused, "this ability of yours can come in very handy." He folded his arms, lingered, then ran one hand through the back of his stylishly trimmed dark hair.

Beltain and Percy both regarded him with the beginnings of worry.

"In fact," Duke Andre Eldon said, "I will be heading in the exact same direction as you . . . so I think having your miracle girl along for the ride will be an excellent thing indeed. And no, fear not, I will not hold you back on your quest. In fact, I condone this mission of yours with all my reason, and will support you—discreetly—in any way I can. However, let us ride together, at least as far as the common direction takes us."

Beltain nodded with some relief. "Yes, that will work out well."

"Indeed it shall!" The Duke brightened again, and once more slapped Beltain's armored thigh, making the metal plates ring at the minor impact. "It's settled then, we ride! My way, incidentally, lies all the way to the Balmue border, which right now is a sorry mess. There's been fighting, since before dawn, if not earlier, we have learned—possibly through the night. According to the latest reports, they are barely holding the lines. And so, I do believe your presence—both of yours, the girl and your own damn self and your force of arms—will be a boon. What's your name, by the way, girl?"

"Percy Ayren, Your Grace."

"Well met, Percy Ayren! Now, both of you give me a few moments to prepare my horse. I thought I'd be riding with only a single man-at-arms to have at my back—since, by my own orders, no more men can be spared from the citadel's Imperial defenses—and instead I get the blessed unholy likes of you, Chidair! Hah! Fortune has smiled on me!"

And the Duke went off in a hurry to make himself ready for the journey.

As soon as the Duke of Plaimes joined them, armored and astride a blood bay charger, they rode through the southern gates of the Silver Court and into the Kingdom of Morphaea.

Percy gazed before them in relentless wonder, for until last night she had never stepped foot outside the Kingdom of Lethe, and the Silver Court was such a world unto itself that it had not really sunk in that she was away from her native land—not until now.

Ahead of them was a snow-covered plain. Nothing too drastically different from the basic landscape of Lethe. That is, until she cast her eyes upon the distant horizon.

There, among the white pallor, was a faint shadow of green and earth-brown, as the distant and verdant rolling hills of Morphaea revealed themselves through the haze of morning mist.

Eventually, winter would come to an end. Morphaea was a land of temperate transition, from a mixed weather clime on the northern tip near the Silver Court—where they were now—to the southern border with the Domain Kingdom of Balmue where began endless summer. At the lower bottom end of Morphaea was the capital city Duorma, just a little away from the foreign border.

However, that warm portion of the Kingdom was many, many leagues away. First, they had to ride through snow along a familiar winding road that looked very much like Lethe.

"So, tell me," Lord Beltain Chidair said to the Duke, "what is really going on in the Imperial Realm? What is this sudden great war that comes to us?"

"Not sudden at all, but the culmination of oh-so-many things," replied the slightly older man.

And for the next hour, the Duke of Plaimes spoke of things that made very little sense to Percy, as she listened, while leaning drowsily against Beltain's chest. There were intricate army movements and details of chain of command, and talk of Kings and generals, and something about the one referred to as the Sovereign—an all-powerful woman who was the supreme ruler of the Domain, and the equivalent of the Realm's own Emperor. They called her Rumanar Avalais, and the Duke's voice dipped into a half-conscious whisper every time he mentioned her.

"Who is she, this Sovereign?" Percy suddenly asked. "And

why does she want to invade us?"

"A fine question," retorted the Duke, without being the least bit patronizing—which Percy appreciated. "We have all asked this question for years, as we bade our time and continued to send our skilled agents into our hostile neighbor's house. And we discovered no easy answer—for indeed, it turns out that despite all our watching and careful investigating, no one truly knows *who* the Sovereign is, or the full extent of her motives for conquest. And thus, an even better question arises: why *now?* Why attack the Realm during a time of common crisis? Death's cessation affects the Domain and the rest of the world as much as it affects us."

"Maybe," ventured Percy, "Death's stopping is somehow related to this—this war."

"What a smart girl you are, Percy Ayren." The Duke looked at her with a sharp look of appraisal, and then glanced back at the black knight. "I see now why you have undertaken to look after her, Beltain. She is no mere country wench."

"I have been instructed to see her through till the end of her quest, and assist in any manner possible," Beltain replied in an even voice, looking directly ahead at the road, and his expression remained entirely impassive.

So impassive it was, that His Grace the Duke of Plaimes took careful note.

A t around noon, as they continued following the road, among occasional cart and pedestrian traffic, there came a strange sense of unrest.

It was nearly impossible to pinpoint, and the only comparison Percy could make was the time at Letheburg when she recognized the heavy sensation of the many dead.

This time the uncanny sensation had a different quality— not a tightly enclosing fist or circular vise, coming to choke her from all directions, but a general loose oppression, approaching like a wide sweeping wave from the south, and behind it an ocean of immense power rising, looming at the edges of the horizon.

"There is something coming. . . ." whispered Percy, straining her face into the oncoming cold wind.

"What is it?" said Beltain.

"What? What can you see?" Duke Andre Eldon asked, with an expression of immediate concern.

"I can tell that the Cobweb Bride is still far beyond, in that direction. But, she is no longer as far away as she was only moments ago. . . ."

The Duke frowned. "I am not sure I understand."

Percy strained to see, hear, look, into the south. She reached out with all of her being, willing herself to take flight like a hawk into the noonday winter sky. With a tingling at the back of her head, with tiny hairs rising along her skin, she could just about feel it, the sense of aerial *lift*, the soaring.

She imagined what was before her. Death, through its infinite shadow manifestations, was present all throughout the fabric of the mortal world, permeating it. By seeing death's many locus points of entity-shadows, like dots on a map, she could *see* the geography of the land itself. Yet in that boundless panorama of her inner vision, the many leagues of the world spreading out before her had suddenly lost cohesion, became malleable—rising like bubbles on the surface of a boiling liquid, then popping out of existence. As a result, the surface area of the entire land became *abbreviated*, then came together at the newly formed seams, only now it was shorter. . . . In each spot the land was pulled, compressed, then shrunken down upon itself, as though a pocket had been taken out of the fabric of the world.

And putting all the missing land pockets together, it amounted to an area the size of more than half a Kingdom.

Percy comprehended it, and in the same instant she put her hands up to her mouth.

"Percy!" Beltain was speaking to her, his gauntlet lightly shaking her shoulder.

"I actually felt it . . . just now, I felt another portion of the world fade," she replied. "Like those disappearing streets in Letheburg, like Fioren town. . . . And because it is a portion that lies directly before us, somewhere past that green haze, the distances within it have been shortened. . . . Now that everything is closer, I can feel so many dead approaching our way!—as though swept here by a great divine hand, narrowing the distance in the blink of an eye. A great scattered army, from horizon to horizon! The Cobweb Bride is out there, yes, but first, these endless hordes of the dead will come. Oh, Lord in Heaven! The siege around Letheburg is a small platoon compared to their numbers!"

"An army of the *dead?*" the Duke mused, his face paling. "No! Impossible! And you say they breached our borders already? So, *that* is what was meant by a black rose. . . ."

"How close are they?" Beltain did not blink, merely reached back with his right gauntlet, resting it on the pommel of his sword.

"I believe . . . they will be upon us within the hour."

Chapter 18

Lady Amaryllis Roulle, with the help of Lord Nathan Woult, was the first to step into the boat. It rocked lightly under her delicate step, and with a small cry Amaryllis grabbed Nathan's outstretched gentlemanly hand for balance.

Such strange, sweet, breathtaking, treacle-sugary terror! To know that the silver-spun black waters underneath her—underneath the floor of faded wood slats of this rickety boat—were nothing but a flimsy bit of illusion born of twilight!

As soon as Amaryllis settled on the narrow middle bench, gathering her fine burgundy skirts about her, Nathan proffered her their precious burning lantern.

"Here, dearest, hold this thing, for it feeds our means of transport and in that sense our entire journey! Now, be careful not too breathe too much upon it, nor let the oil slosh around within the reservoir flask, else we extinguish the light and with it the river. Also, do keep it upright and raised just so, else the light will not properly reach the waters—"

"Not another word, Nathan, really, I am not a half-wit. I am quite aware of the magnitude of this lantern and all its philosophical implications. Now, please hurry and board, before we lose any more time and, Heaven forbid, someone comes to check on the prisoners!"

With His Lordship's continued gentlemanly assistance, the remaining girls climbed on board. First came Regata, slim and careful, and she took a seat in the front, closer to the bow. Then, little blond and fair Faeline came on, and she clambered lightly to sit behind Regata. Sybil was next, and she lingered in uncertainty, unwilling to take even a few extra steps deeper than necessary into this questionable vessel. At last, very slowly and awkwardly she climbed in behind Amaryllis and sat in the boat's rear portion at the stern.

Finally, Catrine made a grimace, glaring with distrust at the fey running waters on both sides of the boat that Nathan held with one hand, keeping it momentarily anchored close to shore. And then she muttered a prayer, said a hearty curse, and climbed in, finding a spot next to Sybil and behind Amaryllis.

Lord Nathan Woult was the last one on shore. He threw one look back at the cavernous dungeon chamber where a few of the freed girls wandered, most of them staring with cautious curiosity at the progress of the brave escapees in the boat.

"Ahoy, there!" he said to the girls left behind. "As soon as we float away, I strongly suggest one of you run along immediately and light that lantern on the wall, else there will be no river and many highly unpleasant questions. Besides, you do want light for yourself in this cave, do you not? Just in case there are behemoths—"

"Enough, Nathan!" Amaryllis tugged the filthy remnants of lace at his sleeve, and he went quiet with a light wicked smile on his face. He then took the oars and stepped into the boat, claiming a bench seat in the middle, just in front of Amaryllis, where the rowlocks were attached.

As soon as the boat was released from shore, it started to float gently on the current in the direction of the distant cavernous tunnels at the farthest end of the cave. Nathan fiddled with the oars at the rowlocks, making sure they were held in place as properly as he imagined they ought to be. And in the meantime the boat simply drifted slowly like a swan until it had gone away far enough from shore that their solitary light started to diminish, if viewed from the banks.

"Oh! It's fading now! The river near here is gone!" a girl's voice spoke from the shore, her voice carrying in echoes. "It is getting dark too, should I light the lantern on the wall?"

"Not just yet!" Nathan responded from the boat. "Wait till we are completely out of sight. If you light another one too soon, remember, it will be too much illumination! The river will disappear likewise, and we shall plummet down very unpleasantly!" His voice also echoed and reverberated from the growing distance.

"All right then, Lordship!" spoke another girl on the shore. "Fare well!"

"You too!" cried Catrine from the boat, waving. "Please be prayin' for us!"

And in another few breaths they had reached the end of the cavern and the opening of a tunnel.

"Oh dear . . ." said Amaryllis. "I just had a very dire thought."

"You, a dire thought? So, what is it now, Amaryllis, sweet?"

But Amaryllis frowned, clutching the lantern frame with her still hand. "The tunnel is going to *narrow*, my dear boy. You—clever scholar of nature that you are—you do know the implications of this, for our lamp?"

"What implications?" Nathan spoke, knowing he was not going to like the answer one little bit.

"Why, only that in a smaller enclosed space the light will appear *brighter* than in the middle of a grand cavern! It will *reflect* off the nearby walls of the tunnel, and dispel the twilight to a degree that will make our river fade!"

"But it is the same light, is it not?" asked Faeline.

"Sure it is," Catrine responded. "But a candle at open sea has nuttin' but open spaces 'round it, so there's nuttin' to shine off, an' so it looks teeny tiny! I know, 'cause my Pa's been on a sea-boat way down south, after they been out robbin'—beggin' pardon! But once you stick a candle in a closet, the whole closet goes all bright! I get it!"

"Well, well . . ." Nathan went so still he nearly released his grip on the oars.

"Ladyship," Sybil said politely. "If the light starts being too much, try putting the palm of your hand around the lamp, maybe?"

"By Leonardo and his nonpareil genius! By his bright Italian soul that even now rests with the angels and no doubt observes our curious plight!" Nathan exclaimed, with an excited glance at Sybil. "Girl, this is a thought invention worthy of Da Vinci himself!"

"In other words, you suggest, my sweet boy," Amaryllis said, "that I treat the lantern as if it were a mechanical device, or better yet, an instrument of dulcet music, and *play* it with my fingers to increase or decrease the amount of light?"

"Not I, but this fine girl with very red hair and a marvelous philosophical grasp!"

"Well, I am afraid, such a virtuoso shadowbox performance might be too much even for me." And Amaryllis offered the lantern to Sybil. "It is all yours, my dear. You've conceived it, now you must call upon your own technique and bring it to fruition. Quickly now, tell your nimble fingers to start playing!"

And in the next moment they entered the narrow tunnel.

Sybil grabbed the lantern, but then handed it right back to Amaryllis the next second, for their boat sharply dipped, and was sinking downward—while some of the girls let out shrieks, "Less light! Less light!"—and the river started to fade, quite in proportion to how much the stone walls of the tunnel lit up in sudden pallor and iridescence. "I have an even better idea, Ladyship," she cried, "you hold it, and I will cover it up!"

Amaryllis received the lantern back, and Sybil loosely closed her hands around it, so that the somewhat diminished light streamed between her trembling fingers. It took her just a few heartbeats to get the amount of light necessary to keep the twilight at a sufficient level that it maintained the river.

"Well, that was rather exciting," Nathan muttered, gripping the oars with white knuckled hands. "Indeed, are you pleased now, Amaryllis? Are things entertaining enough now, or has the ennui returned to plague you?"

"Oh, sweet Mother o' God an' the angels . . ." Catrine muttered under her breath. "I just about crapped my guts!"

But the lady had no time to answer, since the walls of the tunnel widened around them, and they were now passing through another cavern-like bubble formation underground, with a lofty fathomless ceiling and endless dripstone rocks rising and falling from the sky in icicles.

Once more the river started to fade, and this time everyone cried, "More light!"

Sybil took her fingers away and the lantern shone its full light upon the wide lake-like expanse of the water around them.

"Another thing occurs to me," Amaryllis said. "We have no notion where this river goes, or how far. We are merely floating aimlessly along, in hopes of coming upon something, an opening above ground, or any blessed way out. But—what if there are none? What if, indeed, this strange magical river floats downward into the depths of the earth, straight to hell itself?"

"Then, my sweet, we are going to be visiting the devil very soon."

"Fie, Nathan!"

"Well, what did you think might happen when we embarked on this mad adventure?"

"Honestly, Nathan, I only try to think a quarter of an hour ahead. Anything longer and things are always unpleasant."

"Sailing into the Underworld, and here we are, bickering as always."

They passed the widest place of the underground formation and again a series of tunnels lay before them, of varied width, with layers of rock upon rock, like stone collar pleats folded into a royal fan. There was no other light than the solitary lantern in Amaryllis's hand, and yet there seemed to be a radiance, a soft, silver phosphorescent light coming up from the waters and reflecting off the cave walls.

"How fortunate that this river flows so slowly, almost like a dream. Here, hold the lamp a while." And Amaryllis handed the lantern over to Sybil. The lady then placed her fingers into the water over the side of the boat and drew the tips lightly against the current, watching the tiny metallic sparks and spray.

"Oh," she said. "It is not at all cold as I expected. Rather lukewarm actually, strangely so. Or maybe, neither cool nor warm, but indifferent, like a shadow. . . ."

"Well, I thought it was cold at first," Nathan remarked. "But you are right; it was not the ice cold of the winter outside, despite the cold of the dungeon chamber."

"Look in your bag of tricks, Catrine, and hand me that other empty flask," Amaryllis said.

Catrine fumbled in the satchel and pulled out a small glass vial, then gave it to Lady Amaryllis.

"What are you going to do?" Nathan regarded her with a moment of suspicion.

"I want to capture some of this water," Amaryllis replied. "Its impossible twilight nature bothers me, and I must investigate it under better circumstances, once we get out of here—for yes, for the next few moments I firmly choose to believe we shall escape." And saying this she unstoppered the flask and dipped it in the current, then brought it up full of the same clear silvery liquid.

Indeed, it was surprisingly clear in the bottle, almost like normal water, Nathan thought. None of that dark inky hue, or the metallic surface tint—that too had been illusion also, born of play of light and depth and darkness.

However, as soon as the filled flask was brought near the

burning lantern, the water inside it *faded* and the bottle appeared empty. Amaryllis exhaled an "Ah" of delight, then replaced the stopper, and put the flask into an inner pocket of her cloak, watching the water bloom back into being as it was moved away from the light.

Just in time—for they had entered another narrow tunnel and the use of four hands was required to "play" the lantern and keep the river in the physical plane.

A t least two hours passed, of dreamlike sailing through soft currents all around, and constantly changing caves and niches and tunnels of variegated stone.

The girls spent the first hour staring at all things around them in constant heightened wonder. But by the second hour, everyone started nodding off.

Eventually, maybe it was but another illusion, but indeed the stately current grew even more slow and sluggish. Nathan barely had to row, only moved the oars gently to keep them away from the rocks on the sides, mostly letting the river carry them along.

They emerged from yet another narrow tunnel into a larger cavern hall. Here, Sybil took her fingers off the lantern to give twilight its full power, and then they were all faced with the strange sight of a panoramic shore up to which the river waters lapped and then simply *ended*.

It was the effect of having the river pour into a great round basin of a shallow lake.

They gazed ahead, and as the boat moved closer to that final shore, with nowhere else to float, they noticed that the bank before them was smooth, polished, granite rock, or maybe alabaster.

The boat arrived, and then gently bumped the rock of the shore's edge. There was no place to anchor it, and indeed there was no need. So clear, so silver-shadowed was the river here at the edges, that when they looked down over the boat's sides, they could see the transparent bottom through the still water, hewn like a stone bowl, curving up to rise toward them at the very lip of the shoreline.

And now that here they were, at the end of the river, they looked beyond at the shore and saw that it was the beginning of a great shadowed hall—not a natural cavern but an artificial structure—and it was formed of perfectly dull grey stone. Instead of walls, there were endless evenly spaced columns and arches, monumental and gothic, and they were lined in rows all the way to the distant horizon where they simply ended in a haze of remote darkness.

"Where in Heaven's name are we?" Nathan stood up in the boat, then balanced his way to the front at the bow past the seated girls, and leaped onto shore.

One by one the occupants of the boat followed him, stepping carefully on the dull granite floor. When everyone was out, Nathan pulled up the boat and dragged it a few feet unto the bank, even though there was no danger of it floating off anywhere. He placed the long oars inside, and then stood up and stretched, stiff from sitting for so long.

"Curious—there appears to be no end to this hall," Amaryllis remarked, looking about them.

"Oh, look!" Regata pointed up at the ceiling, and when they all glanced up, there appeared to be a night sky above, littered with pinpoints of stars. But it was so dreamlike, so unreal, that it truly made no sense.

"There's stars, but I don't think we're outside," said Faeline. "It's not at all cold!"

"Indeed," Nathan flexed his fingers. "I no longer see my breath, and the air has grown so still, with not even a gust of wind. We are definitely indoors, likely in the bowels of the earth."

"So quiet here . . ." Sybil stood holding the lantern. "Where are we?"

"Do you notice, Nathan, that there is a very peculiar general illumination here, coming from everywhere? I don't think we require this lamp." And Amaryllis took the lantern from Sybil and quickly snuffed the wick out with her fingers.

The light winked out and the lamp smoked, but surprisingly there was no sudden onset of darkness. The hall remained the same, grey and shadowed and distinctly visible in the vicinity. Only when they strained to look far into the distance did the shadows seem to come together into a thick vaporous haze. Everything was smooth and soft, with no sharp edges, as though seen through an ethereal gauze veil.

"Behold, a soft landscape rendered in *sfumato!* I have seen its like on cathedral altarpieces and usually renderings of the afterlife and angelic visitations." Nathan spoke in appreciation, while pacing around the shore.

Amaryllis threw one glance behind them at the softly lapping river. How was it that the waters flowed in, entered this round pool basin, and then had nowhere else to go . . . and yet did not flood and rise above the banks? There was no visible outlet underneath, no precipice to plunge downward and into the underworld. Everything here was transparent, and the bottom of the basin was smooth pale stone.

"I think we ought to go forward into this hall," said Faeline. "There has got to be a way outside, somewhere up ahead."

"Agreed," said Lord Woult, shaking off his unkempt clothing and running a hand through his tousled hair and growth of beard. "Nowhere but forward lies our way—it is surely destiny. So then, dearest Amaryllis, shall we?"

"By all means." And Lady Amaryllis simply started walking.

They paced for about fifty feet forward, moving past a dozen arches and columns, and then, as some of them looked back, they were presented with a physical impossibility.

Behind them, the river was gone. Not simply the supernatural water born of twilight, but the basin that held it!

Gone too were the cavernous entrance at the shore before the hall began, the round basin with the smooth granite shoreline, the boat they had left behind, and the distant stone tunnel that had brought them floating here.

In their stead, the same hall with its arches and columns stretched unto infinity behind them. Indeed, they were now in the middle of a hall with no walls, no end, and no beginning.

"Oh, Lordy, Lord!" cried Catrine.

"Stop!" Nathan stopped walking and stood very still, looking behind them with a furrowing of his brow and utter disbelief.

"We couldn't have gone all that far . . ." whispered Sybil. "How did we get here?"

"I dare say, we must be either in hell or in purgatory, at the very least," Amaryllis pronounced in a cool voice that had in it just a remote tinge of disturbance. "So, where is your devil, Nathan? I expect he is up ahead, waiting for us."

"Oh, no! No!" Both Catrine and Faeline whimpered. Regata put one hand up to her mouth, while Sybil just stood motionless.

"Maybe this is indeed the Underworld," Nathan reasoned. "Or maybe—since we are so far north, and the infernal river has likely taken us into a deep wilderness somewhere underneath the forests—could it be we have arrived at Death's own realm? His so-called Keep?"

"An interesting notion, my boy. . . ." Amaryllis breathed deeply, tasting the air in her lungs, bland and flavorless, with neither scent nor temperature. "It truly is so *dead* here. And yet, it is also very peaceful. . . . Somehow I do not sense infernal flames, or foul pitch smoke, or cries of pitiful charred sinners receiving eternal punishments on the ends of pitchforks. Do you?"

"No, not at all. Not even a tiny little scream to properly set the atmosphere."

"So, then. If this is Death's own palace and domain, let us go forth and seek the Skeleton himself. Heaven knows, what if I am the Cobweb Bride? Or possibly, one of these girls is the Cobweb Bride? Wouldn't it be a wonder?"

Nathan turned to stare at her with a very intense gaze of his dark eyes. "Honestly, Amaryllis, do you still *aspire* to be that doomed creature? I thought we'd gone on an adventure, not a funeral march!"

"I think it's stopped being merely an adventure as soon as we were detained by the mad Duke and Ignacia turned out to be a treacherous harridan. Now, I rather think it a quest on our part. If one of us is the Cobweb Bride, then, my dear, we might have it in our power to save the entire mortal world."

"And that would be indeed commendable," Nathan said. "Only, why must it be *us?* All I ever wanted was to have my well-done roast! A bit of steak, that's all! Nothing too outlandish, is it? Must I be a hero in order to eat beef?"

Amaryllis smiled, turning her exquisite yet weary and dirt-stained face to him, and gazed at Nathan with a countenance full of faerie mischief. "Let us find out!"

And then the lady cried out in a loud petulant voice: "Lord Death! If you can hear me, make yourself known!"

There was a pause. The ringing echoes of her voice rebounded lightly in the immense hall, and then softly faded into nothing.

Perfect silence.

And then, a masculine voice sounded, remote and disembodied, coming from every direction in the hall, even from the starlit ceiling and the granite floor. . . .

"Come to me."

And then, came rushing wind.

Chapter 19

The vanguard of the dead army came upon them softly.

Beltain, with Percy in the saddle before him, and next to him the Duke of Plaimes, had been making their way along the main road leading past occasional settlements and mostly cropland blanketed by snow. As they were further removed from the Silver Court, traffic became somewhat sparse in their direction, with only an occasional peasant cart clattering south, while many more were headed north toward the Silver Court. Bundled pedestrians on foot—usually entire households, by the looks of their large packs of belongings—moved past them rapidly, giving the two great knights and their warhorses a wide berth. More than a few swift carriages flew by, carrying frightened Morphaea aristocrat families toward the relative safety of the Silver Court's massive walls.

News of the war was spreading like a flame.

At one point, the noise of clanging metal came up ahead, and the length of the road about a mile in the distance shone bright with bristling long steel in the sun. Pikemen were coming in columns, followed by arquebusiers and musketeers, all infantry ranks moving at a running trot march, and judging by their tan and teal uniform coats and their banners they were soldiers of Morphaea.

As soon as the Duke of Plaimes noted their approach, he

spurred his stallion forward and rode toward them, then raised his gauntlet in a greeting.

"Formation, halt!" cried the officer in the front, seeing the Duke approach, and apparently recognizing him immediately. "Formation, salute your Field Marshal, His Grace, the Duke of Plaimes!"

And the soldiers came to order, infantry columns stopping one after another along the road.

"Commander, your report!" said Duke Andre Eldon. "What is happening? Have I been misinformed, and has the border been breached?"

"It is indeed so, Your Grace! Regretfully! We are in retreat from the enemy who is in pursuit!"

"Retreat? By Heaven! On whose orders?"

"By orders of His Majesty King Orphe Geroard!"

"Tell me what happened," said the Duke. "Where were you stationed?"

And the commanding officer told him. Apparently these troops were not from the Balmue border, but were part of the city garrison of Duorma, the capital of Morphaea. About three hours ago, Duorma was attacked from the south by an immense unspeakable horde of entirely dead men. "Not a living man among them! All ranks in normal formations, all bearing the various identifying banners of the Domain elite forces of the Sovereign—the ones known as the Trovadii!"

"The Trovadii are *dead?* All of them, you say?"

"Yes, Your Grace."

"But—how can that be? An entire army! *Why?*"

"We have cause to believe their condition is self-inflicted. . . . As for reasons, that we do not know."

The Duke listened with a grave face. "So what has come to pass since the attack? How fares Duorma?"

There was a slight horrible pause as the officer gathered himself before speaking. "Your Grace, there *is* no Duorma."

"What does that mean? Was it a complete rout? How bad are the casualties?"

The commanding officer paused again, looking down before speaking. "With apologies to Your Grace, but—worse than a rout. The city was in fact never breached nor overrun. It has *disappeared*."

"What?"

"We were out in full force, outside the walls in the pomoerium, readying the line of defense, and the perimeter. His Majesty was with us also—was about to lead the charge. We saw the enemy approach on the horizon, and as they came closer, we realized suddenly that behind us, instead of the city walls and tall battlements with friendly marksmen and bastions of cannon artillery at our backs, there was *nothing*. The walls and bulwarks had disappeared, and so had the entirety of the area on which Duorma stood, with all that it contained—buildings, men, and beasts."

"But—how on earth can that be?"

"No notion, Your Grace. Some of us had assumed it was sorcery or ungodly magic! Our formations were thrown into confusion, and while we tried to maintain order with nothing at our backs, the enemy attacked."

"What of the King?"

"His Majesty was last seen in the heat of battle, with a cavalry brigade fighting to protect him. As soon as the retreat order was given, we have lost track—"

"Dear Heaven. . . ." The Duke of Plaimes sat upon his charger, plunged in thought, considering and weighing impossibilities.

Beltain, with Percy, rode up to him and stopped, observing.

"This is damned unprecedented," the Duke turned and muttered to Beltain. "I must think, and quickly!"

The Duke then turned back to the men before him. "You say the enemy is in pursuit now—how close behind you are they? How much of their main force?"

"Your Grace," replied the commander. "If we continue standing here, they will be upon us within a half hour! As for how many, we do not know! During the melee there was much confusion. And as for those of our men who have been slain—in truth, I may not be able to vouch for them or their continued loyalty to the Realm. The dead army may have swallowed them and taken their allegiance—"

"I refuse to believe that!" exclaimed the Duke, speaking in a manner intended to rally the troops. "They may no longer be as sharp or as willing—or even able—to follow orders, but a man's soul remains the same, no matter what. A loyal soldier will be loyal for as long as he understands what he is fighting for. I don't expect that even death will twist that!"

"God willing, Your Grace is right. What are your present orders?"

Duke Andre Eldon paused only for a moment. "My orders are, continue your retreat, and make haste. Go and join the garrison at Silver Court. Tell them to prepare for siege! And tell the Emperor that I will return as swiftly as I may, after ascertaining our present situation. Now, proceed, and Godspeed!" And he rode to the side of the thoroughfare, with Beltain following, to allow the formations to pass.

As the pikemen and marksmen saluted, then broke into their ordered trot, the Duke stood at the sidelines watching, his brows drawn in a frown.

"What will you do now?" Beltain asked.

"I have no blasted idea!" Plaimes replied in a frustrated whisper. "You know, I had been on my way to assume command of the border defense. . . . But now—everything has changed. How do you fight a war when the battlefield itself has just shifted under your feet? We had a front, we had a border; by God, we even had a viable fortress in Duorma! And now, what? Where do I return to assess the situation? What lines do I draw?

How can I plan strategy when the very map of the military theatre is redrawn?"

"Not to mention, the enemy is a dead army, and invulnerable to the usual methods one might use in war," Beltain observed. "How do we fight the dead? The question came up at Letheburg and someone mentioned fire—and this girl here."

"Oh, blasted hell, yes, the dead that keep coming—don't even begin to explain that impossibility! Any of it!" The Duke's ringing baritone voice rose enough that the columns of passing soldiers likely heard his ranting as they quickly jogged past.

"For the short term, Your Grace, what will you do? Continue forward with us, south, and hope we do not run into the enemy head on?"

"Oh, but we *will* run into them head on, there is no doubt. My question is, how will you proceed then? Can this girl strike the dead down as you ride?"

"She has done so before. It's how we broke out of Letheburg."

The Duke looked at Percy appraisingly. "Ah-h-h, now I am sorely tempted to hold you, girl, and confiscate you on behalf of the Imperial Crown as an asset, and take you back to Court. . . ."

And as Beltain's expression began to darken, the Duke shook his head and said, "Fortunately, I pride myself for always thinking long-term. Your immediate value may be a temptation, but your ability to bring this whole no-death situation to an end is the priority. Worry not, you are free to continue your quest—on behalf of Her Imperial Highness, naturally." And he winked at Beltain.

Beltain and Percy both exhaled in relief. "I thank you for your understanding, Your Grace," she said softly, while Beltain nodded.

"Never let it be said that I am not a reasonable man," the Duke replied. "And now, what is there to do, but proceed onward? So much needs be done—the stunning things I've been told about the manner of fighting at the border! A handful of my men have ridden hard all night to make reports, as early as this morning, even before the enemy breached our lines—as I am only *now* being told of this latest calamity. Apparently, the more limbs the dead lose, the more of their humanity goes with it, and they become rather single-minded in their few remaining options—the options being, to just lie there like a wine sack or to fight with every fiber of their being, with every spark of what's left. And yes, just as this unit commander here has mentioned, often they simply go on fighting regardless of allegiance, striking out at anyone whom they might perceive as being in their way, once they lose enough of their spirit and perspective. Or so I am told, for I am yet to see such a melee in person. Indeed, what fine fortune awaits me, eh, Chidair?" And the Duke gave a sardonic laugh.

Beltain shook his head grimly. "Oh yes, it's a rare delight, Your Grace."

"It is said, war is our purgatory on earth, and as such, it calls upon us," the Duke concluded. "So, let us not waste a moment!"

They had to wait only a few minutes longer while the remainder of the retreating army passed, and the road was clear. And then they resumed their journey, moving south.

"I shall ride along with you for the moment, as I think on what to do," admitted the Duke. "For in truth, I am at a loss. I might as well turn around and return back to the Imperial citadel and assume command of these same poor fellows as they arrive. The Silver Court was to have the Field Marshal services of the Duke Claude Rovait in command of the Rovait portion of the Morphaea military, stationed there in defense of the Emperor— while I was to handle the southern front, out here. And now that my own portion of the forces at the border and Duorma are amassing back at Court, I will be needed there likewise. However, we must know more, infinitely more, in order to gauge the extent of the damage done already. . . . I must find my King at least, and I refuse to concede that we have lost all of southern Mophaea!"

"What is that?" said Percy suddenly, pointing ahead of them at the road and the surrounding fields on both sides. "I believe, it's *them*. I can now sense their death shadows."

"Where?" Beltain cast his gaze at the white panorama ahead.

The Duke lifted his gauntlet to shield his eyes and looked also. Neither of the men was able to see any approaching army movement, however.

"Percy, there's nothing there," Beltain said. "Are you certain?"

Percy nodded.

"They're there. They're—"

And Beltain understood at last. "They're *underneath* the snow!"

It was then that the white-blanketed plain in the visible distance all around them began to bubble and churn, as the surface of the land itself acquired impossible motion.

The dead, those without sufficient limbs to remain upright, *crawled* upon the earth. . . . They plowed directly forward, regardless of terrain or road, and many of them dug themselves into deep snowdrifts, and yet continued forward relentlessly, unable to feel need or pain or weariness—only a single-minded *purpose*.

"Surely, these are not Trovadii . . ." the Duke thought out loud. "No, I think these must be the dead who had fallen along the border earlier this morning or last night, possibly Balmue occupying forces, possibly some of our own boys, the poor bastards, trying to return home. They've had a head start and are thus arriving first. . . ."

"How can you tell?" Beltain said. "They are still too far to observe."

"An assumption." The Duke gave him a hard thoughtful look. "Men crawling will be swiftly outdistanced by men on foot or astride, unless they've had a long head start. Their less damaged fellows were probably given new orders, or told to wait and be absorbed by the bulk of the arriving Trovadii. These, meanwhile, are likely of no use to anyone, pitiful carcasses with hacked off limbs . . . so they simply continue waging war on their own, following their last recognizable orders, bent on their one and only final purpose—"

"Has anyone told Your Grace you're a gruesome bastard?"

The Duke laughed and tapped Beltain along his rerebrace armor on the upper arm, with the back of his gauntlet. But his eyes remained bleak.

They had stopped riding forward meanwhile, halting their warhorses that neighed and spat in anger at being reined in. And the two knights stared at the bizarre soft approach of the confusing enemy, slow and yet inevitable, along the width of the plain.

"I believe they are not a sufficient threat to us if we ride hard forward," said Beltain, narrowing his eyes.

"Agreed," replied the Duke. "Shall we?"

They spurred their horses onward. Beltain lifted his long shield in position so that once again it was protecting Percy's back. And both men drew their swords.

The powerful muscles of the ebony warhorse contracted underneath them, as the world went into motion. And alongside Jack, like molten deep red fire, galloped the blood bay. . . . Percy held on to the saddle and to the black knight's ring armor near his belt, giving him free use of both his hands. The churning field on both sides of the road became a blur.

She could *feel* them, hundreds of death shadows, billowing softly, while the broken amputated bodies of the men to whom they belonged, crawled relentlessly upon the earth.

Many of them had moved onto the road, and were crawling

directly in their way, underfoot. Stumps of arms and occasional hands reached up, a few attached fingers still clawing. . . .

And the two great warhorses plowed right *on top* of them.

The snow-covered, vaguely human lumps revealed themselves upon occasion and it was possible to catch glimpses of torn shreds of uniforms—mostly sienna brown trimmed with silver, the colors of Balmue, and occasionally the tan and teal of Morphaea. Among snowdrifts, misshapen heads breached the layers of snow, with faces stilled in their last fixed expressions before the freezing cold made them permanent; torsos moved, limbs shifted slowly like snakes. . . .

"I was correct, these abominations are not Trovadii," cried the Duke, riding hard at the side of the black knight.

"No, they are not . . ." Beltain retorted, leaning forward into the saddle and holding Percy tight in his armored embrace. "But, look ahead!"

And as they all stared, in the distance, among the hazy whiteness and beginnings of green and brown at the horizon to mark the changing nature of the terrain, there was a hint of red in motion—blood and pomegranate.

"And so . . . it begins," mused the Duke in snatches.

"Percy!" Beltain whispered close to her ear. "Will you be ready?"

But she heard him only with one half of her awareness. The rest was consumed by the pressure of an approaching tidal wave of death—a hundred thousand death shadows upon her mind.

So thick they came!

Blood and pomegranate.

Percy closed her eyes. "Yes," she said, "I am ready."

But once again she lied.

Nothing could have prepared her for the onslaught. *Something* infinitely complex and yet misshapen, something the size of a mountain, was coming down upon her mind, blasting and pounding at her with the anvil weight of darkness and unrelieved hungry *need*.

The void itself had arrived—an empty place that needed to be filled . . . with the rest of the world.

The Trovadii came.

But first, came their drums. The dead had no heartbeat, but it was provided for them by the rhythmic pulse of wood against taut animal skins. The drums gave their movement structure and cohesion and a marching rhythm. And since they had no blood, they were clad in it—pomegranate uniforms of the color that was closest to the thing that once flowed in their veins. And now these were also stained with the juices of themselves and others.

The horizon became a red line. In the winter sun the red was a fiery shade against the predominant whiteness of the landscape, and as the formations and squares and columns came closer, the immortal symmetry of their motion was a thing of beauty.

Infantry was displaced by ranks of cavalry, then repeating, again and again. Formations advanced in a sea of pikes held with points forward in the charge position, with unwavering hands that felt no weariness and could thus maintain the position indefinitely.

But not all of them came in ordered units. Some cavalry companies rode haphazardly, dead men mounted upon dead lumbering beasts that could not move with the grace of the living no matter how they tried. They scattered over the fields unevenly like approaching wild herds, moving in bright red flashes of metal and color.

"May God give us strength!" exclaimed the Duke of Plaimes, and raised his sword. Within moments, they would clash head on with the first of the enemy, a sparse line of runners and mounted cavalrymen.

"Hold on tight, Percy!" Beltain said through his teeth, and drew her even closer in the metal embrace of his immense arms and shield. . . .

The Trovadii were upon them.

Beltain held his sword at the ready and in seconds the first rider passed him, while the next clashed against his sword. Beltain's arm held, and the rider was pulled down halfway out of his saddle by the impact with the black knight's unshakable force. There was but an instant to see the dead man's pale bloodless face, and then they were past him and riding onward. . . .

Percy heard the Duke striking another approaching rider, and the clash of his sword against the other's, and then the dead man's severed arm came flying down, under the feet of the horses.

Percy took a deep breath and allowed herself to exhale softly in order to gain a steady focus. She then reached out with her death *sense* to a perimeter of about thirty feet around them, casting a bubble of awareness, and taking hold of whatever came within that sphere, picking up the closest energy threads, and then *snapping* them.

The dead around them—those within the short perimeter—started to fall.

"Is she doing this?" the Duke cried, riding slightly ahead of them and turning around to glance momentarily at Beltain and Percy.

"Yes!" Beltain glanced at Percy's strangely blank face, inches away from his own. "Now, simply look ahead and treat the oncoming as obstacles. Anything that falls, ride around them! Do not bother to engage!"

"Understood!" And the Duke leaned forward into the saddle and flew like the wind, meandering out of the way when necessary, as great oncoming warhorses and cavarlymen slid off their saddles like limp sacks and occasionally fell down directly in his path.

Percy's head was ringing.

Soon, all the dead became aware of her, and they came like

bees at honey. She could feel them turning inward from all directions, breaking ranks, and simply approaching their moving position.

"This is not good," the Duke gasped, again readying his sword.

"No, it is not—but nothing is to be done," replied Beltain. "She can only do so much before she collapses."

It seemed they were now swimming through a sparse forest of the pomegranate uniforms.

At one point, Percy saw a large column of pikemen directly in their way, and she cast her mental net wider, so that the entire formation collapsed before they even reached the first bristling row of pole weapons directed at them.

The Duke and Beltain both pulled up their horses sharply, since it was unsafe to ride through the bristling mountain of the piled dead and their sharp weapons. And so they rode around, warhorses carefully stepping over steel poles and corpses. . . .

"How much longer is this infernal army?" Beltain muttered.

"Indeed!" the Duke threw back at him. "We are making rather better progress than I dreamed, but I think we have quite a ways to go—"

And as Percy heard their exchange, in that same moment, she felt *something* ahead, just half a mile in the distance. It was something out of the ordinary, something new.

Not more of the dead, but a *living entity* approaching.

This entity was a fixed point.

A perfectly opaque mental wall arose, between Percy and this *other*. It grew softly and then, like an outreaching finger of energy, Percy felt the exploratory *touch* upon her mind, and with a snap, there was made a *connection*.

It was as if someone on the other end had reached out to *her* in the same manner she reached out to the dead. And this someone now gently caught and held her own thread of living energy, tugging it expertly, feeling its reach and resonance . . .

Percy gasped. And then she let go of the dead and their shadows in their vicinity.

"Percy! What happened?" Beltain exclaimed, and in the same instant he had to engage his sword and shield and to deflect the very real and deadly attack of an animated dead knight who did not simply fall before him but swung a sharp-ended morning star and flail. There was a resounding crash. . . .

"*Merde!*" the Duke of Plaimes cried, and swung his sword also, barely missing being skewered in the neck by a short lance in the hands of a mounted Trovadii knight.

"I am sorry!" Percy cried, "I don't know what's happening! There is someone out there, someone *living!* And this person has just touched me in the same manner that I touch the dead!"

"What?"

"I don't know! Let me try again!" And Percy cast her mind forward fiercely, and pulled herself back and out of the mental *grasp* of the other, letting her thoughts move like slippery fish past the ethereal net of this new unknown force. In the span of a breath she was free, feeling the unknown entity's hold upon her loosen, and then she reached around and struck back, sending her own thoughts like arrows in the direction of the entity.

And in the doing so, Percy suddenly felt and saw *her.*

Across half a mile, within her mind's eye, Percy saw the *woman*, dressed in the same color as her army, seated within a gilded carriage, swiftly moving with the Trovadii forces all around her.

The woman was a stately swan, beautiful in the same unearthly way that beauty can be attributed to seasons, or the wind, or the dream fabric of the starless night.

And she was cruel and cold and devastating.

Her face, an exquisite perfection, her hair, the auburn dawn.

Her eyes, bright vivid blue, with the sharp ethereal clarity of the same winter sky that now rose up above them. These eyes were now trained upon Percy, their gaze piercing her in her own vision, following her.

"I just saw her . . . it is the *Sovereign!*" Percy whispered in disbelief. "I don't know how I know who she is, but it is *she* who had touched me, and she knows me now. She is coming!"

And as Percy continued thus, watching in a strange dream state of double vision, the woman in her mind's eye also continued looking at her.

And then she smiled.

Percy drew back into her own body with a snap, and vaguely heard—as from a distance, or through thick layers of cotton in her ears—the harsh sounds of Beltain and the Duke fighting the attacking dead all around them. She had lost her grasp upon the dead . . . and the three of them were now surrounded by a thicket of soldiers in pomegranate red.

Percy shuddered, feeling abysmal weakness, feeling her extremities burning with debilitating cold, a precursor to shock. Despite this, she again cast forth her killing force, and started gathering the threads of the billowing death shadows around them.

The dead started to collapse once more. Their way was clear.

"Ride!" cried the Duke. "Ride, and do not stop for anything!"

And Beltain squeezed Percy in the protective metal cradle of his arms, and burst forward.

They flew straight ahead through the uneven snow terrain of the field, dodging oncoming enemy figures. They had lost the road some time ago, and it did not matter.

At some point, as Percy allowed her concentration to slip for one second, she turned her head to the right and saw, on a distant road to her right, the actual golden regal carriage from her vision of just moments ago, driven by a team of flesh-and-blood living horses and surrounded by an honor guard of the dead, in blood colors.

They came together in two parallel lines, then passed in opposite directions. . . . And it seemed for an instant that the occupant of the carriage turned her head and gazed out of the window at Percy riding hard past her.

"Yes, that was indeed the accursed Sovereign of the Domain," cried the Duke. "She is known to ride on campaigns behind her military. And it is a minor blessing! For it means that most of the Trovadii army is beyond us now, and headed north toward the Silver Court."

His words proved accurate. The numbers of the dead in their path were now sparse, and Percy found it easier to pull their threads and cast them into their own bodies. The sound of the marching drums too had receded.

They could at last slow down. Jack and the great blood bay charger were foaming at the mouth from the gallop. And thus the knights allowed them to walk at an even pace through the trampled empty fields before them. Here the land was a mixture of black frozen dirt and patches of snow.

Breathing hard in exhaustion, they looked at the line of the horizon ahead of them. The greens and the browns were much closer now. In the hazy distance, the snow was slowly leached from the land, fading into intermediate terrain.

The Duke of Plaimes frowned, narrowing his eyes, and stared for a long time before speaking. "This cannot be," he said. "This land, all of it—it is not Morphaea! There, those distinctive hills curving to the left, and then the forestland to the right— those are landmarks I've seen in Balmue!"

And as they gazed, in a mixture of confusion and doubt, Duke Andre Eldon wiped his dusty forehead with his gauntlet. "This world of ours—I no longer know what is happening. Neither this war nor the world makes any sense. It's true, wars make little sense in general—except for a handful of fools—but they at least require a theater of military action that is fixed geographically. Here, we have a phenomenon without explanation that is negating everything."

"You think, Your Grace, this is what happened to Duorma? Since your soldiers say it was—displaced?"

"I assume so. This is all rather unspeakable. Because it means we are now at the border with the Domain and most of Morphaea is gone from the face of the earth. How? Where? My family, my *son* was in that city!"

Beltain glanced at Percy lying against his breastplate, her eyelids fluttering closed, and her face had a greenish unhealthy tint. "Girl," he said gently. "Are you with us?"

Percy mumbled something.

"She appears ill," the Duke noted, taking his gaze off the horizon for a moment.

And in the next moment both the men glanced to the remote left and saw dark specks of movement in the distance.

"Not more of the dead, I pray?" Beltain's eyes hardened with renewed energy, as he prepared again for combat.

But the Duke shrugged, then narrowed his eyes again, resigned to anything.

Meanwhile Percy again muttered, this time recognizable words. "No. . . . Not these, not the dead."

"A small relief, then," said Beltain.

Some time later, as they rode gently forward, they were met by a small, severely battered brigade of living soldiers of various ranks. They came both on foot and riding dejected horses, and they moved beyond any semblance of orderly formation, wearing the tan and teal colors of Morphaea.

Among them, flew the solitary banner of the King.

The Duke of Plaimes turned to Beltain and said in a low voice: "We shall speak nothing of the girl—nothing about what she can do. That way you will be able to proceed discreetly on your way."

"But, wouldn't there be questions?" Beltain wondered.

"How will we explain having survived the onslaught of the entire Trovadii army?"

"Hah!" said the Duke with a bitter smile. "Leave that to me. The simplest explanations are always best. I will inform His Majesty that because we are so few in number, we've had extraordinary luck and were mostly unseen and unengaged by the enemy as we rode through their most outlying, remote, and sparse flanks. Apparently, the Trovadii—whose one entrenched purpose has always been to obey without question the Sovereign's grand orders of conquest—have better things to do than occupy themselves with two mounted knights and a young peasant girl. And now that they are *dead*, they are possibly even more single-minded in their purpose than usual. Who knew that death could bring such sharp focus?"

And then the Duke was moving away, riding through the ranks toward the pennant of Morphaea held aloft by the bearer next to the King himself.

King Orphe Geroard of Morphaea was a man in his late middle years. His deeply tanned gaunt face with its neatly trimmed silver beard and grizzled temples was all that could be seen, for he wore a chain mail coif and helmet, and was clad in a full suit of armor plate, finely embossed with intricate designs upon metal. Astride his large chestnut warhorse, he was an imposing sight, despite the dirtied condition of his armor and the minor gashes upon his face. And yet he had fared better than many others in the battle, for most of his knights showed wounds, many of them serious, and some were barely keeping themselves upright in their saddles.

The Duke saluted his liege and then they conversed for several long minutes while Beltain, with Percy, kept wisely several paces away. At some point the King turned to stare in their direction, but was apparently convinced by the Duke of Plaimes that they were of insufficient consequence.

Eventually the Duke turned and rode back to them. Beltain

regarded his approach with a grave expression.

But the Duke, his back turned to the others, winked discreetly, then said in a calm voice that was carried back to the others: "And so we part ways, my friend. I have found His Majesty alive and well—reasonably so—and we must now proceed to rally the best we can, to bring together our remaining forces. At the same time, we attempt to make sense of this defeat and the circumstances of Duorma."

"What does His Majesty intend to do?"

The Duke took a deep breath, exhaled a weary sigh. "We will try to make our way west, then north, to Styx. It might be our best course of action since the Silver Court is now cut off from us and we from it. Instead of a solid deep front with the Imperial forces at our back, and a protracted successful line of defense and maneuverability—as we had fully intended, before the earth itself decided to relocate underneath us—we are isolated without a base of operations. Meanwhile, the young King of Styx will appreciate our allied support, now that he is being attacked by Solemnis from the south. And thus, we go to Styx. I only hope we'll make it. By Heaven, I hope Styx still stands in its proper place when we arrive!" He paused. "As for you—Godspeed, and proceed, and may you do what must be done, on Her Imperial Highness's orders. I have faith in you, my Lord Beltain, and in your brave little Percy—who looks like she is about to fall off your saddle, by the way."

Beltain gently shifted half-conscious Percy in his hold, and she raised a very pale grey-green-tinted face to barely glance at him, before closing her eyes once again.

"Go, now!" The Duke nodded to him with a grim smile. "Till we meet again!"

"Farewell, Your Grace!" And the black knight inclined his head in a bow, then turned Jack about, and rode past the soldiers of Morphaea and their King.

The way, as always, lay south.

Chapter 20

The day was closing upon evening, and the country they entered beyond the last of the snow-swept fields was a strange, intermediate, temperate zone. The earth here was mostly naked soil, with rock formations and sparse forests and a few rolling hills that began as sienna brown earthen clay and slowly revealed shrubs and some hardy greenery.

According to the Duke of Plaimes, this was Balmue. Thus, they were no longer within their native Realm but had entered the territory of the Domain.

Betlain had no doubt. Even though he had never set foot beyond the Morphaea border, the predominant reddish brown color of the land around them—sienna brown, the native color of Balmue, renowned for its unusual deposits of clay soil—spoke loudly for itself. Balmue wore this shade upon the majority of its land, in an intricate rich palette.

It was still cold, but no longer the same biting, overwhelming chill of snowy winter that had come with them on the majority of the trip from Lethe and then northern Morphaea. Even the sky was a warmer hue of blue, and hinted of autumn or spring.

Percy slept for the past hour on Beltain's chest. There had been no good place to stop for rest, only an exposed plain, and thus no way to assure safety for them.

But at last, the plain ended and a mixed terrain brought the hills and the forestland closer.

Beltain rode with a seemingly impassive set to his features, but concealing a deep worry on behalf of the girl. She looked far more ill than she had ever been before under similar circumstances. True, she had not lost consciousness entirely as she did after taking on hundreds of the dead at the siege of Letheburg. However, her condition was more perilous now, even though she was partially awake, because her lethargy was overwhelming while her skin was very cold to the touch, and a sheen of cold sweat beaded on her brow.

"Percy . . ." he whispered. "How do you feel?"

"I am . . . alive," she replied. For some reason he noticed the very light trembling smile on her lips. Then her eyes opened wide, clear and aware, yet unearthly, and full of that strange intermediate color of grey-blue-swamp-green.

And with those eyes she gazed at him.

Beltain felt a painful constriction in his chest, followed by a stab of intensity. He had to look away, unable to meet her gaze for longer than a moment, saying instead, "We will stop to rest shortly. Just a little more until I find a good place, safe and out of view, and then—then you will rest."

She continued to watch him thus, occasionally closing her eyes and falling again into a peculiar unhealthy sleep that was close to a swoon. And he meanwhile stared like a hawk at their surroundings, watching out for landmarks, for moving enemy figures, for anything that might be of use or of harm.

As the sun started to slant at his back and his right, painting the western sky with plum fire, Beltain finally rounded a hill then went up an incline and into a small valley that was mostly green, with spots of the ever-present sienna. Jack was now stepping over clumps of earth and rock and grass underfoot, and like a miracle the snow was almost entirely gone.

In the middle of the valley, among a small woodland

clearing, stood a structure.

Beltain raised his gauntlet to stare, because the glare of the setting sun sent horizontal rays over the top of the hills to reflect off something golden and bright amid that structure. It was as if another small captured sun had been brought to ground and placed inside a terrestrial cage.

As they drew closer, with the knight carefully looking out for any signs of life or sudden enemy movement, Percy sighed, coming awake, then opened her eyes again.

She blinked at the golden reflected radiance. "What is it?"

"I am not sure yet," he replied. "I don't know if we should approach. There may be people there. And frankly, I am too weary myself to welcome another protracted fight."

"There are no dead there," she announced. "That's good, at least."

Beltain made his decision and decided to approach the structure.

As they moved in to narrow the distance, the sun sank over the hills, and the painful radiance no longer made it impossible to look directly at the thing down there.

It was a temple.

An ancient, overgrown one.

There were fluted columns of white marble, wrought in the classical Greek Ionic order of architecture, their capitals ornamented with spiral volutes up on top, surrounding an interior wall with a central gate.

The surrounding trees had sprawled around the temple perimeter, eclipsing a portion of the roof, and old thick vines climbed up, bare of leaves in the winter chill. Had this been summer, the greenery of the tree leaves would have hidden the structure completely, but now the bare branches revealed the gilded frieze and the cornices, which were reflecting the last rays of the sun moments ago and now had softened in the last light of sunset to a warm buttery haze. However the marble bore many cracks, and the golden sheets were peeling in places.

"This place is very old, and apparently neglected," Beltain remarked, as they rode up close, and saw the external details of disrepair. "As such, it will serve us as shelter against the unknown night."

The black knight dismounted, then led Jack up to the nearest colonnade, and took Percy in his arms, carrying her down from the saddle. He put her down softly to sit on the third stone stair, and she reeled slightly, then put her hands down to steady herself upright.

"Can you manage to sit for a few moments, girl?"

"Yes, My Lord."

"Good. Let me deal with Jack, and then we'll go inside."

And he brought the warhorse up a few more stairs and into the colonnade overhang, out of the wind, and where the shadows would keep the great beast out of sight. He did not bother removing the bridle or harness, since they might have to ride on a moment's notice. Instead, he took out a small feedbag from the back of the saddle, and hung it around Jack's neck, after giving him some melted snow from the water sack. After the warhorse was settled, Beltain took with him a water flask and the small satchel of food that he'd had the good sense to request from the inn at Silver Court when they left that morning.

With it, he approached Percy, just as the sunset began to fade into twilight.

The girl could barely stand up on her own. Beltain drew his arms around her waist and shoulder, holding her around her thick old coat, and they entered the temple through the doors that were left unfastened years ago.

Inside was near darkness.

Beltain was alert for any sign of movement, but they were completely alone. A large hall awaited them, dust-filled and at the same time smelling faintly of mildew and forest, with similar rows of Ionic colonnades around its rectangle perimeter, and a lofty angled roof held up by horizontal beams and columns. The roof was broken in places, admitting an open vision of indigo sky and thus allowing in the elements—which accounted for the moisture and the hint of rot.

In the back of the temple before the sanctum stood a great statue of a goddess, gilded and crowned with a headdress of stalks of wheat, and seated upon a throne. Garlands of embossed moldings in the shape of jewels appeared to cascade from her braided curving crown of hair and her earlobes, and her wrists and arms were braced with wide ornate bands. She was not nude but wore a noble chiton that came down in marble folds to her sandaled feet.

And although this attire was more ceremonial and formal, Percy immediately recognized the Goddess of Tradition.

It was like coming home.

A strange peaceful sense of rightness immediately settled around Percy's heart. The expanse of the hall was no longer an unknown void of dust, cracked marble, and menacing shadows but a familiar welcome sphere of comfort. Each column breathed solidity, familiarity, and the remote ceiling overhead was like a bower of wild roses woven together to create a shelter from the sky.

Percy stared at the great ancient goddess before her, with her smooth serene features and her wheat crown. "Who are you?" she whispered, through her debilitating weakness. "Why do I know you so well?"

Beltain, still assisting her to stand, with his one powerful arm around her, heard her speak and replied. "Strange serendipity, that we come upon her now, the same goddess of your dream. The Goddess of Tradition must be watching over you, out of her golden antiquity."

"What are . . . gods?" Percy whispered. "There is God who watches over us and yet there are these others."

Beltain shrugged, his lips curving in a smile that she could not see in the twilight. "Priests would tell you such things are old pagan blasphemies. It may well be so. And yet, in this gentle light, the ancient one looks down at us, and she is soft and harmless and fair. . . . If mortal men have an order to them, why not gods? Let there be One who presides over the others. Perhaps they take turns—just like men—and choose one of their own to be God supreme throughout the ages, until another one is chosen to lead a new Age. Or—maybe there is always the same One God, and simply an ever-changing pantheon of the lesser ones who march in varied prominence through time alongside us mortals, fading in and out of favor and worship, powered by our own desires and dreams."

And while Percy continued to stare at the goddess in a dreamlike daze, Beltain gently pressed her shoulder and guided her deeper into the temple.

The black knight found a sheltered spot in the back of the sanctum itself, that alcove behind the statue where the ancient priests met in secret and performed their most sacred rituals. Here, in the shadowed niche mostly free of nature's debris and dust, he spread out his cloak on cold marble and set down his pack. With gentle care he helped Percy sit then lie down, resting her head on a small bundle that was his folded blue Chidair surcoat. While she lay down thus, closing her eyes, he quickly removed his gauntlets and the most cumbersome portions of his plate armor so that he could flex his body and sleep. The chain mail hauberk remained for both protection and warmth. But he unbelted his sword in its steel and leather sheath and set it down at his side.

It was so quiet in the temple. . . . As the evening deepened, the wind increased outside. It whistled through the fine cracks in stone, giving chase to itself, with occasional gusts entering through the parted doors and from the missing portions of the damaged roof above. In the openings was dark velvet sky, with a cold sprinkling of stars.

"I dare not build a fire for us, girl, not here," Beltain said after a few minutes. "But now you must drink and eat, to regain your strength and warmth. Food is fuel when there can be no fire. . . ."

Percy weakly opened her eyes and watched the black knight as he took out a loaf of bread and cheese from the satchel. Again she smiled faintly, and Beltain could have sworn she was *bemused* with him, with his very motions—the practiced way he broke apart the loaf with his large capable hands, and then used his knife to carve out a piece of hard cheese for her.

He took out the water flask, and drew near her, and put his hand gently underneath her head wrapped in its woolen shawl to lift her up enough so she could drink. Percy received the water from him and swallowed, with difficulty at first, so that rivulets flowed past her cracked lips and down her pale cold chin which he wiped with his warm fingers, making her tremble slightly. He was uncertain why she trembled, but somehow it made him very aware of the contact . . . and now his fingers trembled also.

After she had drunk a few swallows and took a deep breath, he helped her sit up again, and she rested the palms of her hands down on the cloak to balance herself.

Next, he made sure she chewed the bread and the cheese, and watched her grow steadier as she consumed a small amount.

She ate and breathed gently, bundled in her coat, her legs folded primly to the side and under her, keeping the folds of her skirt around them for warmth. Soft wisps of hair had come loose from her shawl as it slid back from her forehead.

"How do you feel?" he asked again.

"Better—thank you." She chewed another piece of bread and cheese absentmindedly, and some of it ended up on her round cheeks and the rest crumbled down her chin and the front of her coat.

He reached out without thinking and swept the crumbs away from her chin with his fingers, then realized what he had done and moved his hand away. . . .

"You've recovered well, this time," he said, keeping his voice matter-of-fact. "There had been so many more dead that you put to rest this time, compared to Letheburg. I marvel how you do this thing."

Percy looked up to meet his gaze tiredly. "I don't really know how I do it. It must be done, that is all."

Overhead, the moon appeared. Beams of soft light fell in dappled spots from the holes in the roof.

"Will you not eat also?" she asked, and then handed him the remaining bread and cheese.

His fingers touched hers, in a warm instant of contact, and he took the food, then ate, remembering that he was ravenous also. After he was done, he put the leftover portion of the loaf and cheese away, and drank the water from the flask, wiping his lips with the back of his hand.

She watched his every movement.

"Time to rest now," he said.

"I'm sorry, but first, I need to go outside and—"

He smiled. "Yes, unfortunately there's no chamberpot here. Can you manage on your own?"

"Yes!" she exclaimed, and even in the faint moonglow he could see her blush.

"Good. Then go slowly and take your time, and call for me if you need help. I'll take my turn afterward."

Later, they both returned to the sheltered niche and their makeshift campsite consisting of spread cloak, two small bundles, and piled armor plates.

In truth, Percy had barely managed to answer the call of nature on her own, and dizziness nearly overpowered her upon getting up and on her way back. Now she moved slowly, holding on to some of the columns for balance, and took each shaky step inside the temple until she could gratefully lower herself back down on the cloak.

Beltain took his own turn and was back shortly, after also checking up on Jack. He carried with him his long shield that he'd removed from the warhorse's saddle to lighten Jack's load a bit more, overnight. The shield was placed with the armor, and Percy stared at it briefly, seeing the frightful evidence of impact damage it had suffered in the last few hours during their insane ride through the Trovadii army.

It struck her then, the realization of the horror that they avoided, and what might have been had they not. . . .

"Thank you, My Lord . . ." she whispered. "For all that you've done for me, in the course of your own duty. For being so kind to me. . . ."

Beltain, seated down on the cloak beside her, turned his face to her in three-quarter profile, washed by the silver glow of the moon. His eyes were liquid and dark, and he spoke nothing, only looked at her.

"No need to thank me," he said at last. "I would do the same for anyone in my care. It is my responsibility."

"I know . . ." she whispered. "I know you are only following the instructions of Her Imperial Highness, Claere. But—I still thank you with all my . . . heart."

At this, he smiled. It was a smile that touched his eyes.

"I should be the one thanking you," he said. "You are the one who has saved us, many times over, Percy Ayren."

But she was not done. "I also want to ask your forgiveness—for—for hitting you with that skillet. . . . And for tying you up. . . . And for dragging you inside the cart—"

He started laughing. And then said, "To be honest, I am glad you did. For none of us would be here now, if it had been otherwise." And then he added, "Now, enough! Get some sleep."

She nodded, then lay down, resting her head on the small bundle. Seconds later, she felt him lie down also, directly behind her. And then his arm came down and around her waist, drawing her closer to him, so that she was cradled in his full-body embrace.

"I'll keep you warm . . ." he whispered in her ear, and his baritone was a sweet rumble down to her bones.

Percy felt a flush of overwhelming heat rise up in her cheeks, spreading out to the rest of her, and she was suddenly warm indeed, from head to toe, as she felt his powerful muscular body behind her, like a wall of strength, through all the thick layers of their clothing.

She went limp and motionless, and simply remained thus, afraid to breathe from the wonder of it. He too seemed to feel some kind of effect, for inexplicably he became as still as herself. And then slowly, he pressed himself even closer against her, nearly crushing her with his embrace against the length of him.

She could feel his heartbeat. Or maybe it was her own, pulsing in her temples. It was no longer possible to differentiate where her own body began and his ended. . . .

They had become one strange bound thing. A single entity of living warmth, cleaving together in the pale night that had no temperature, no wind, no sound.

"Percy . . ." he whispered suddenly. "I am not . . . *kind*."

And while she was still considering the strange deep thickness of his voice, his mouth came down, hard and impossible, upon the hollow of her throat. . . . And his other hand was now digging into her hair, pulling her clumsily up to his face, while he was wallowing against her throat, her cheeks, and at last her lips. . . .

Maybe she had died, and this was a fever dream of the underworld. Percy was a thing of liquid clay, and her single shuddering breath had come and gone—was *taken* by him—and he was now above her and she was under him, and his mouth was against hers, and it was not comprehensible, not possible, to be so much a *nothing,* to be rendered into weightless air and pouring amber, and at the same time to be molten warm honey and malleable sun.

He moaned hoarsely, coming up for air, and then his mouth kissed her again—for yes, this is what it was, a *kiss*—and then suddenly with a cry he let her go.

"No!" he cried, "forgive me!"

And she was released and lay back, in a shock of loss, of sudden cold . . . separated from him while he backed away from her, taking deep panting breaths, and his eyes were opened wide and dark with repressed desire.

"Oh, God, what have I done . . ." he whispered, quieting, staring at her, in horror of himself, then sat back at the end of the cloak.

Percy lay, taking deep breaths also, in a vain attempt to still her racing pulse. Her limbs refused to obey her, in a strange debilitating languor that continued to make her into formless water. . . .

"Why?" she uttered with the last strength of her breath.

"Because I am—" He strove to speak but could not finish.

"What, My Lord?"

"Because I am a liar," he concluded.

She listened, barely breathing. "What . . . do you mean?"

And he again neared her, coming down on his elbows, leaning over her face, and he remained thus, looking down at her.

"I lied to you," he said in a hard voice of barely repressed emotion. "I told you that I am here merely on the orders of Her Imperial Highness. . . . But in truth, I had *begged* her to let me go with you as much as she had insisted that I accompany you."

"But why?" asked Percy, gazing up at him in amazement.

"Because," he said, "I love you."

Percy was in shock. It was as if something had struck her, a hard blunt object, and made her powerless with an infinite impossible joy.

Beltain was looking down at her, his eyes glittering with the moon, an indescribable expression on his face.

"You . . . *love* me?" she whispered like a broken fool.

"I had not realized it then," he said. "Not at first. At first, I simply knew you were the most inexplicable being in the world and I had to *understand* you, and also to make sure that you were not harmed by anyone—ever."

"But—how can you love *me?*"

"How can I *not?*"

A lump was building in her throat. She lay shuddering, her breaths coming quick and agonized, and at last her eyes were completely flooded, and she could no longer see the moon or *him* through the tears. They ran down her fat puffy cheeks, and her nose was suddenly swollen full and she could not breathe.

"You . . . are like the sun to me," she managed to speak through the morass of tears. "And I am like . . . *dirt.*"

"What?" he cried. And then he lowered his lips gently on her forehead and then put both hands at either side of her face, pressing his large warm palms against her cheeks, and wiped away her tears with his strong fingers.

"Never say such a thing again!" he exclaimed, his warm breath bathing her face.

"I—" And indeed she could hardly speak.

And then he spoke instead. "I must further admit, I have taken advantage of you. And I am sorry to have placed you in such an uncomfortable position, Percy. I never intended to do anything more than be near you, for as long as I could— especially considering that all this time, up to a few moments ago, I thought you could not stand the sight of me."

"What?" It was now her turn to be shocked. "My Lord, I am a clumsy mannerless oaf and idiot. I had never seen or met anyone like you before, and I was terrified of your grace and beauty. At first, 'tis true, when we first met, I had not formed a

fair opinion of the fearsome Black Knight. But now—I *love* you with all my being. And I had expected to go to my grave with that secret."

"If I die now . . ." he whispered. "If I were to die, it would be like this, with you. . . ."

In that very moment Percy lifted her arms about his neck. And with all the love her heart could hold, she kissed him.

They did not say another word for a long time, simply lay in a quiet, chaste embrace, separated by so many layers of clothing between the two of them, and yet infinitely warm.

At some point, Percy whispered against his neck, "I am dreaming . . . are you really here? Is this real? Is any of this a dream?"

"I am here!" he replied. And his arms moved hard around her, pressing her to him until she almost could not breathe, while she heard his own ragged, shuddering intakes of air, as he trembled, and his eyes were vulnerable with desire. . . .

At last, as the moon disappeared from the exposed openings in the roof above, they slept and did not wake till morning.

However, soon after dawn, from outside came the sound of neighing horses.

Beltain was awake in an instant, like a coiled spring, and he went for his sword.

Percy opened her eyes, blinking, but his finger was placed softly upon her lips. And then he was up and gone, moving through the dappled morning sunlight in the shadows of the temple.

The additional sounds outside resolved themselves into voices. A man and a woman were speaking in subdued tones. And then, footfalls sounded upon the marble stairs leading up to the front colonnade.

The black knight froze in the shadows on one side of the doorway, his blade bared. Another moment, and someone entered the interior hall, a man in dark somber clothing and a heavy winter cape. Before he could walk more than a step, Beltain's sword was held at his throat.

The man, a middle aged nobleman, made a short exclamation, then froze in place, putting his hands up in resignation.

"Halt!" said the black knight softly. "I can take your life in a blink and make you a walking dead man. What is your business?"

"Please, no . . ." the man responded in an accent of Balmue. And in the next instant, behind him appeared a woman, dressed in dark travel clothing. She looked inside and barely stifled an exclamation of fear, while her eyes widened in her thin pinched face.

Beltain assessed the situation immediately and slowly lowered his sword.

"I mean you no harm," he said. "If you in turn feel the same way."

"Oh, Lord!" the woman exhaled with a shudder, and the man also let out his breath in relief.

"You—you are not a cutpurse?" the man said.

Beltain examined him with a gaze of thorough appraisal. "Is there anyone else with you outside?"

"Oh, no!" exclaimed the lady. "It is only the two of us! But I'm sure many more will be coming soon!"

The gentleman meanwhile gave her a warning glance, but it was too late.

"Not a cutpurse, but a careful traveler," Beltain replied.

The man considered for a moment then decided that the danger had passed. "We are travelers also, here to visit the Temple Thesmophoros, to honor the one who is Thesmos divine and—and to pray on behalf of Ulpheo. Not many remember her or honor her, these days. Now, of course, it will all change—"

"Is that the name of the Goddess?" Percy had come forth

quietly from her hiding place in the alcove of the sanctum.

The man started slightly at the sound of her voice, but seeing that it was only a young girl, eased again.

"Yes," replied the woman in his stead. "It is but one of her many names."

"We have taken shelter here for the night," the black knight said, "and did not expect any other visitors."

"We do not begrudge your presence here," replied the man in a polite and gentle voice. "But we have come to pray. And thus, I hope you allow us the freedom to do so. Indeed, it appears we are the first to arrive, for soon many others will come also. . . . But please, put away your steel, sir. This is a sacred place, and Thesmos does not permit violence."

"Gladly," said Beltain. He then turned his back on them calmly in a show of peaceful intentions and returned back to their sleeping spot and started to pack away the items and put on his plate armor pieces.

Percy lingered for a moment, watching the man and woman as they in turn ignored her and Beltain and gazed up at the face of the golden Goddess.

"I have dreamt of this Goddess," she said suddenly. "Only, in my dream she was clad in nothing but golden jewels, a collar, and a headdress, and she was seated with one leg folded, and the other upraised at the knee."

The man and woman turned to regard her. Then they exchanged curious glances. "How exactly did you see the Goddess Thesmos?" the woman asked. "Was there anything else? Anything—did she *speak* to you?"

"It was a gentle dream," Percy replied. "There were no words I could recall, only her small golden shape."

Again the woman and man exchanged glances.

"There is only one such likeness of the Goddess," the man uttered thoughtfully. "And it is found in the Hall of the Sun beside the Sapphire Throne. . . ."

Beltain stopped what he was doing and returned to listen to their exchange.

And then the noblewoman raised her earnest face to glance from Percy to Beltain, and to her companion. "There may be some significance to this—to our very meeting here," she admitted with weariness and inexplicable vulnerability. "I am the Countess Arabella D'Arvu, and this is my husband, Count Lecrant D'Arvu of Balmue. I know not who you are, kind travelers, but my heart tells me we are all brought here for a reason. I, too, have had *dreams. . . .*"

"Arabella, please, caution!" said her spouse, throwing another glance at the black knight and his newly attached imposing plate armor.

But the Countess did not heed him. She abruptly stepped forward and crossed the remainder of the distance between herself and Percy. She took the girl by her hands, her own fine jeweled fingers shaking, and she looked into her eyes with a desperate expression. The fine velvet hood slid off her head and her black wig had been dislodged slightly, revealing the edges of graying hair at her temples. "Please . . ." she said, "tell me what you saw of the Goddess! Anything! For it might mean the world for the life of my daughter! I have—I have lost my daughter, and she is—"

"Arabella!" the Count exclaimed. "Enough! Not before these strangers! We are here to pray for Ulpheo, nothing more! It is bad enough the entire Sapphire Court knows and mocks us in our unfounded grief! We have no concrete proof she was harmed—"

"Oh but we *know!* We know in our heart, in our breast, our very gut, deep here, yes! You see," continued the Countess D'Arvu, staring into Percy's eyes, and pressing her hands with her own, "I've also dreamt the dream of the Goddess—long before her blessed visage appeared before the multitudes of the city!—and it was of her very same aspect that you mention—it is the one rare form of hers, that can only be found in the small statuette placed at the side of the Throne, where the Sovereign sits! She looks upon the Goddess, I am told, and there is something there—"

"I wish I could help," said Percy gently, allowing the woman to continue holding her fingers. "But in my dream the Goddess was silent. All I can imagine is that somehow it is a means to aid me in my quest, for I search for the Cobweb Bride—"

"Percy!" This time it was the black knight who signaled caution.

But Percy did not heed him. There was something important about this thin, pinched, grief-wrung woman before her, something that evoked confidence and trust. "We are traveling south," Percy continued thus. "And we have come from a place that is very far."

"Percy!"

"Ah, you're from the Realm . . ." said the Count. He glanced back at the knight and then the girl. "I know not who you are, My Lord—for yes, I can see as much by your demeanor that you are no common knight—and it does not particularly matter. There is a war being waged, but I want no part of it, nor do I believe in it. . . . Especially not now."

"It seems your Sovereign has started this particular war," said Beltain softly.

Count Lecrant D'Arvu nodded. "Indeed it is so, and I do answer to her in my allegiance. But in the latest series of actions of hers, she has undermined the trust of many of her own, including myself. The Sapphire Court puts on a brave face and the semblance of complicity, but behind closed doors there is weeping and dark words spoken. And Trova Square still stands in a lake of blood, for we have had no rain . . . and no one dares to clean the cobblestones. . . . And now, *Ulpheo!*"

"What of Ulpheo?" Beltain approached even closer,

listening, while Percy stood as she was, mesmerized, a look of intensity coming to her face.

"Ah, you have not heard!" Count D'Arvu said. "For you come from the other direction. Well then, if you travel deeper south, you will come upon it within the hour. . . . Only you will not be able to *enter* it."

Beltain and Percy watched him with growing attention.

"It happened on the night before last . . . early that evening, I am told—for we were not there to witness. Just before sunset, the Sovereign with her *dead* Trovadii army entered our blessed city, in passing. Ulpheo met her with adulation, as she had been expected, and His Majesty, King Clavian Sestial paraded half the forces of Balmue before her, as they readied for the common march on the morrow. Well, as all of this was taking place, unbelievable things were happening outside the walls of Ulpheo. . . . All the land, for leagues around, started to change, to grow thin and *transparent*, and then it all was gone! Only the city remained, in the middle of this unnatural madness, standing hard and solid, and inviolate!"

"We've had similar incidents in the Realm," Beltain said.

"Oh, but no, not like this!" the Count continued. "Now—all those people inside the walls of Ulpheo, none of them knew what was happening all around. Apparently, the strange instability was taking place throughout the night, but only *outside* the walls. . . . Meanwhile, at dawn the city awoke, and the Sovereign with her Trovadii forces continued on their way, followed by the select battalions of Balmue, and they all marched beyond the walls, heading north through the now changed landscape—as though nothing was amiss.

"When the last soldier was out of the city—and here is the part that I still question, for I simply do not understand—it is said the Sovereign turned her head to look back . . . and possibly she spoke words of which we know nothing. . . . And as she did thus, Ulpheo started to *fade*—as though it had been waiting for her to let go, to pass beyond and *abandon* it. Thus, it too grew thin and translucent, and the morning sun shone past layers of vaporous streets and houses, through translucent people and beasts and carriages, through fading walls of stone—and then it stopped. It stopped fading, halfway, and did *not* disappear. And the city *stayed* thus."

Beltain frowned. "How, exactly?"

"It is neither here nor there!" the Countess interjected. "It is fixed within a mirage! No one can enter, and no one may leave! The city with all its people is still among us, yet it is suspended in another place, like a flimsy shadow of itself!"

"How can that be?" Percy whispered. "We've seen shadows fade with twilight, yes, but they can always be entered—"

"Not this one!" the Count continued, wiping his brow where sweat was beginning to sheen. "People gathered and stood at the walls on both sides—stand even now—and it is like glass, an unspeakable veil of some kind of physical *impossibility. . . .* Not even sound can pass; no words can be exchanged. Those inside Ulpheo could be seen crying out, their lips moving, their hands pounding at the empty air at the open gates. . . . And then—as hours passed and the morning sun rose higher, it is when they all saw *her*—they saw the face and form of the Goddess."

"The Goddess Thesmos!" said the Countess. "Those who witnessed it from outside the gates of Ulpheo, claim that her form stood many stories tall, as high as the battlements! And she too was translucent, yet golden, and her face was like the sun. Not many recognized her at once, for she is ancient, mostly forgotten now. . . . But once they did—apparently the people inside Ulpheo could see her also, and they knelt in multitudes, filled with awe, and they prayed to her. And now, those of us on the outside of Ulpheo are convinced the Goddess can help somehow—and everyone is said to be coming here!"

"To this temple?" Beltain frowned.

"Yes!" the Count replied.

"But we have come first, for we were already on our way here," the Countess continued in an urgent voice. "For we must do this thing first, we must pray for—"

"Arabella, no!"

"My *daughter!* My sweet Leonora is missing!" the Countess interrupted. "You've had your say, Lecrant, and Ulpheo still stands at least, but I must tell our own truth now! Just a few months ago she had accepted the honor of entering the service of Her Brilliance, Rumanar Avalais, as her Lady-in-Attendance. It is a rare honor, bestowed only upon a select few, a handful of maidens of noble blood. She has been elevated by the Sovereign, and we as a family have received many worldly rewards, in addition to my husband's enhanced position. But— only a few weeks ago, we've stopped receiving any communications from our child. Not a single letter! We inquired, and indeed she was not seen around Court for at least a month. And when we arrived in person, and begged an Audience, we were told by Her Brilliance herself that Leonora had been indisposed and had simply forgotten to write."

"A minor detail, it would seem," said the Count. "Except, we were then not allowed to see her, under a variety of seemingly minor pretexts—"

"That is when the dreams started! The Goddess, she began appearing to me every night . . . long before Ulpheo!" Countess Arabella exclaimed.

The Count nodded in resignation, then remarked, "What kind of a thing is it, not to allow concerned parents to see their own sickened daughter? Thus, our suspicions grew. Formally, of course, these suspicions were, and still continue to be unfounded. However, upon further inquiry around Court, at my own discretion, I've learned a number of very disturbing things."

Percy and Beltain listened intently.

"We have learned something truly dark and unthinkable

about our Sovereign . . ." the Countess resumed her telling, and her voice became a whisper. "They say—they say that she has a *daughter*. A child of whom no one knows but a tiny few! And that recently she has done something to her, to her *own* flesh and blood, that is a dark and terrible thing of the most profane black sorcery, the like of which is not known. . . . For yes, there *is* an imperial daughter who is kept a secret, and who is rumored to be so sickly that she is never seen outside her own quarters, and has been thus for as long as anyone can remember. And this daughter, it is said, is kept under lock and key, in a hidden place underground. No one is entirely sure where, not even the clandestine 'ghosts' of the various surveillance factions who keep tabs on everything and who know all there is to know about the world and its nether sides."

"In short, this daughter and her mysterious illness is the key," said the Count. "It is related somehow to the disappearance of our own child. And possibly the cessation of death."

"Could she be the Cobweb Bride?" Percy exclaimed.

The Countess gazed into Percy's eyes, and she nodded silently.

"If I am to find the Cobweb Bride," said Percy, "I have it in my means to take her away, to restore the world's death and natural cycle, and possibly to help your daughter, if she is a part of this. I admit, I have no notion how or what it would entail . . . or even whether your daughter might survive or if she is already beyond anyone's reach. But—if you take me to the place where stands the Golden Goddess, maybe, just maybe, we can make things right, together."

"Impossible!" said the Count. "That would mean getting you not only inside the Sapphire Court and the heavily guarded Palace of the Sun, but into the exclusive Hall where the Sapphire Throne stands!"

"Yes," the black knight echoed him. "It's at the very least a mad scheme. Even I am not up to fighting off the entire garrison of the Palace and citadel."

"Not to mention," the Count said, "I will have no part of such overt betrayal of my liege."

"Speak not untruth!" the Countess said passionately. "You were willing to do all manner of disgraceful things on behalf of Leonora—up to and including a coup and an outright imperial revolt—just an hour ago, as we spoke on our way here. If getting these people into the Palace is all that is required to find her, then we shall do it! Indeed, it will be much easier now, since the focus has shifted and everyone is preoccupied with Ulpheo! Once inside, let them ransack and plunder and burn the entire Sapphire Court for all I care!"

And the Countess stood shaking with a strange furious grief.

"I give you my word as knight and Peer of the Realm—for that is who I am—that I will not engage in any hostile action short of defending our lives if we are attacked. Take us inside this Hall, and give us safe passage, and I promise you we will be gone with the Cobweb Bride and nothing more—except possibly your daughter."

"Yes! Oh, yes! Please, do take away our daughter from that evil place! You shall do it! For it is the will of the Goddess! She came into my dreams every night, until I knew I had to come here to her one true temple to find the answer. . . . And the answer was *you!* See, even now Thesmos looks down upon us! She is smiling, can you see—there, just now—" the Countess exclaimed in a voice grown thick with tears, again grabbing Percy's arms, and pointed up at the great gilded statue.

"If there is a way," mused the Count, "it is not a direct way. We will do nothing that is overt. I know of places—passages that comprise a hidden network of the Palace—which allow movement with discretion. We will utilize them."

"Then you agree to this?" Beltain looked at the man,

evaluating him.

After a minor pause, Count D'Arvu nodded. "Yes. We will help you. But only under the condition that once inside you will do whatever it takes to find our daughter."

In that moment, the sound of neighing horses and several new voices came from outside the temple. Indeed, it had grown somewhat loud outside. . . .

Percy looked at Beltain, then at the softly weeping, broken Countess. "Let us hurry! I think someone's coming . . ." she said, for apparently indeed, other pilgrims were arriving.

And suddenly—was it a trick of the chill morning light through the broken sections of the temple roof, the spinning dust motes in the air?—she thought the face of the Goddess statue grew animated, warm, *alive*, and in her stone-and-gold eyes was a blooming maternal smile.

Chapter 21

They rode together, Percy and Beltain, alongside the Count and Countess D'Arvu, away from the ancient overgrown Temple Thesmophoros, and into the heart of Balmue.

The countryside was sienna brown, and sparse forests topped rolling hills. Sunlight filtered through nude branches of the winter-bare trees against a pale blue sky.

Quite a few pilgrims on behalf of Ulpheo were moving in the opposite direction, and initially they passed all manner of mounted travelers and pedestrians entering the valley of the temple. With such busy traffic, no one paid any attention to the black knight or Percy, or their two companions.

At some point they came upon a road, rutted with cart tracks, meandering around the dips of hillsides, and here Percy touched Beltain's arm and said, pointing into the distance, "There. I can feel her. There lies her death—the Cobweb Bride."

"The direction which you indicate is indeed the same direction as the Sapphire Court." The Count mentioned.

"How far is it?" asked the knight.

The Count, riding an elegant Arabian grey stallion, took a while to answer, as he gazed at the close line of the hill-swept horizon. "So much has changed," he said. "Even as short a time ago as yesterday, this land was wider, more sprawling. Again, I have no means of explaining, but—parts of the landscape have been mysteriously disappearing, all around the Domain. Unlike Ulpheo they are gone entirely, without a trace. They tell us that a white-cliffed island has gone missing from the balmy southern sea near Tanathe. And in our own Balmue, the plains and hills upon which we ride are only a small part of what used to be sprawling picturesque countryside. Also, to the east, fair Elysium with its blessed flowering fields is now a wistful memory. . . .”

"In the Realm, we have whole cities and towns gone, as if the earth is shrinking upon itself.”

"It is a curse! A vile misfortune upon mortal kind . . .” the Countess muttered, ending with some other inaudible words that were spoken under her breath. She was seated on an ornate side-saddle fit for an upper class matron, upon a docile white mare. And although the mare paced softly, the Countess held the reins in a trembling fixed grip.

"If nothing else disappears, Ulpheo lies beyond the next two hills. Soon you shall see it. Once we pass around it, we should reach the Sapphire Court before evening.”

"And then?” Beltain persisted.

"Then, I will conduct you to the place you seek,” replied the Count D'Arvu.

"And the Goddess Thesmos shall watch over you!” added Arabella D'Arvu, glancing up at them with a hopeful gaze.

They made good time, and in minutes the hills opened to a strange sight that was indeed like a mirage, impossible for the eye to grasp.

The sun illuminated a dreamlike panorama that at first seemed to be the vision of a distant city witnessed through a milk haze. Except, it was not distant at all, with the walls beginning within a few hundred feet. Once the eye forced itself to accept the impossible, everything indeed was recognized as *translucent*, so that the walls appeared to be made not of stone but of a dark grey-tinted glass. On the inside, streets and houses and figures were visible, moving as if in a dream. . . . And everything was taking place in perfect, abysmal silence.

Overhead, distant clouds sailed in the heavens. A few birds flew near the parapets, but they suddenly struck an invisible wall of air upon approaching the city perimeter and several had fallen upon impact.

There were many people gathered outside the walls, observing, arguing, bewailing, and the living sounds they made was the only noise in the vicinity.

Percy was amazed, for the silence of the city extended into her sixth sense. She could feel no death shadows beyond the translucent walls, as though they had all indeed receded to a distant other place, beyond mortal reach. . . .

"Behold, Ulpheo, the proud capital of Balmue!" said Count Lecrant D'Arvu bitterly. "We shall not linger at this sorry sight, for apparently even Thesmos has gone—for I see no golden Goddess figure rising to the clouds, do you? Indeed, had she even been there in the first place? Or was she but a hallucination?"

"Lecrant!" said the Countess in reproach. "I believe she was there, and it is enough."

Thus, without more argument they rode around the milling crowds near the walls, and past the misfortunate, impossible city itself, following the road south.

From thereon, the morning and afternoon flew by in a monotonous haze of rolling taupe and sienna and sand browns of the countryside. The Count and his wife were gentle company, with the Count D'Arvu speaking for the most part, telling of his views on war and his recent ordeals at the complex Court of the Sovereign.

Beltain mostly listened and remarked occasionally, while Percy reclined against the black knight's chest, cleaving to him softly, all her form exuding such a wordless peace and contentment that even the others noticed. The Count leaned to the Countess with a smile and whispered something about "young lovers" that made her stoic gaze regain a moment of soft clarity.

The road beyond Ulpheo was mostly free of traffic, and a few occasional peasants traveled it. Once again, no one paid a second glance to the knight, for he again chose not to wear his surcoat with the Chidair colors, and such anonymity was prudent. They also noticed no military formations passing, and Beltain wondered about it.

"Since the Trovadii had passed, it is to be expected. They have all gone forward past your border already, or are milling about Ulpheo," the Count said. "I know not what Tanathe and Serenoa will do, and whether or not they will send their forces to supplement the Trovadii, but Solemnis is on the move in the west, and I assume they have advanced already. Thus, nothing more to expect here."

Percy was relieved to know that Beltain would not have to make the choice of engaging in needless combat with anyone on the road.

At some point, Beltain asked about the Trovadii, and how it was that they were all dead, to a man. The Count related, with a grim face, the events of Trova Square.

"That was the moment when the patriots of the Domain felt their faith shaken and in many cases destroyed."

"I am surprised the Sovereign has ordered such an ungodly act of suicide upon her own most loyal of troops," Beltain mused. "Even from pure strategic reasons, what sense is there in a dead army, except for an immediate short-term conquest? They are unreliable, at best. And once death resumes and the natural order is restored—as I firmly believe will happen, since the alternative is unthinkable—then the entire army will be no longer."

"Maybe," the Count responded. "Maybe the Sovereign

knows something we do not, considering what happened at Ulpheo. And maybe her purpose is so far removed from that of a normal ruler that—oh what use is there in speculating? My lady wife here thinks our queen's a witch."

"And what do *you* think?" Beltain watched the older man with an astute gaze.

"I think there are two kinds of kings or queens—those who rule and those who are ruled. History knows both. The former are the tyrants and the benevolent despots who leave a mark, while the latter are the weak nothings who also leave a mark, or rather, a splatter, like squashed flies. Unfortunately both kinds are messy. I think the present Sovereign, Her Brilliance, is both a benevolent tyrant and a madwoman, and possibly something else altogether. In the past, she has done enough for the Domain to be remembered, but due to more recent events, she will be remembered in ways both good and bad."

"You are far too kind, my love," said the Countess D'Arvu. "Rumanar Avalais is neither. I have not yet decided *what* she is. And what she has done to our Leonora—"

And again the Countess went silent, while moisture welled in her eyes.

When the sun slanted toward evening and the heavens turned deep orange and persimmon along the western horizon, they saw before them, upon a hill, the towering golden walls of the Sapphire Court.

No, they were not gilded, merely a bright yellow sandstone color that reflected the light with a warm radiance worthy of the golden citadel it contained.

Even this close to the city, the traffic was not overwhelming on the thoroughfare, and consisted mostly of civilians of the lower and working classes, not much different from the peasantry of Lethe or Morphaea. One detail stood out however—the complete lack of snow. It must have disappeared subtly since morning as they had traveled the countryside. Or, possibly it was gone long before, but the land itself had corrugated together and carried some remnants along into places where they did not belong.

Percy looked around her in curiosity, and also in a constant state of hyper-vigilance, because now a constant blessed silence was in her mind—she could feel only a few dead beyond the city walls before her—indeed they had all gone to war.

But she felt, like a butterfly puling at her, the single death presence of the one she came to regard in her mind as the Cobweb Bride.

"She is nearby!" Percy whispered, looking up at Beltain. "I can feel her, beyond the walls!"

And the black knight merely gazed upon her with a soft-eyed look of undisguised emotion that combined wonder and adoration.

The Count D'Arvu took charge and rode forward with his spouse, moving ahead of them, with Beltain discreetly following on his great charger, keeping his black cloak pulled about him to downplay his suit of armor. At the gates they were examined only cursorily, treated as part of the D'Arvu traveling party.

And then, they rode into the exotic wonder of the Sapphire Court.

Sunset turned the golden roofs to liquid fire. . . . Percy covered her eyes from the overwhelming splendor, a perfect complement to their own Silver Court. Except, the latter was a northern jewel of ice to this southern jewel of flame.

The city perspective here was drawn in the same magnificent arrow-straight design, with streets and boulevards laid out in concentric circles or perfect parallels or perpendiculars, by some ancient genius architect, to be seen as a carpet of intricate symmetry from the tallest vantage points of the citadel, the cathedrals, and the Palace of the Sun.

"Come along, no time to waste . . ." Count D'Arvu told

them, as they rode past one of the many lesser squares, glancing around like countrified tourists at the marvels of architecture.

In a quarter of an hour, just as twilight grew and the street lanterns bloomed forth in rosy gilded points of radiance, lit by diligent evening watchmen, they arrived in the center of the citadel, before a tall, ornate brick house of at least four stories, situated just a few blocks away from Trova Square.

"You will share with us a supper in our home and a brief rest," said the Count, stopping before the front entryway, and observing the footmen of his household approach in haste, bowing, ready to take their horses. "And as soon as darkness falls, we will proceed."

Beltain nodded, though even now he never fully let down his guard, and they were assisted by the diligent footmen to dismount and go inside.

After a nearly silent weary meal of finely prepared yet perfectly tasteless foodstuff, consumed in a beautifully appointed dining room that had a lofty ceiling painted with antique frescoes, the Count asked them to wait.

He was gone then, for at least half an hour, while Beltain and Percy sat on a finely upholstered divan and watched the sky turn dark blue then black outside the arching windows. The Countess had retired to lie down meanwhile, for she was exhausted and rather unwell after their day-long journey. But she insisted she would be going along with them on their final stage to the Palace.

"Do you trust them?" whispered Beltain at some point, looking deeply into Percy's eyes. "Please, be wary, Percy . . . for despite their words we truly know nothing of them or their intent—"

"Yes, I trust them . . ." she responded gently. "The mother's grief is true, and the father shows honor. Everything else matters not."

And to that he nodded, and then took her hands and pressed them between his own warm palms, sending the sun flowing through her veins. . . .

Eventually, the Count returned, accompanied by a nondescript man dressed in working attire, with pockmarked skin and a seedy appearance. The man bowed politely before the knight, appraised him with one sharp look, and then introduced himself as Diril.

"He will guide us through the underground maze," said D'Arvu. "I have worked with this man many times, and will vouch for him."

"Then lead on!" Beltain said, rising from his seat, and Percy got up also.

As they walked down a marble staircase, the Countess D'Arvu was waiting for them below, covered in a dark lace veil and cloak. "You shall not go without me," she insisted. "For I must see my daughter for myself. I must be there when she is found—"

"My dear, I am afraid the way will not be comfortable," her husband protested. "We shall go through filthy dark tunnels, and—"

"I care not for filth or darkness!" the Countess exclaimed. "Let's go!"

And thus, they all followed Diril who took them outside into the street. They made a turn into another street, just before Trova Square, then entered an older venerable building through a small side-door.

Next, there was shadowed darkness and many, many slippery mildewed stairs going down. . . .

Their way lay through a brick-trimmed tunnel space, consisting of a long corridor that stretched underneath the length of the Square itself, with occasional horizontal wooden support beams overhead, garlanded in spider silk and cobwebs. Knife scratches and scrawlings of antique graffiti made by generations of criminal denizens of the city's underbelly, decorated the bricks.

None of it had any detrimental effect on the Countess D'Arvu who walked steadily after her husband, unafraid of the squalor of the tunnel.

Diril walked before them all, carrying a small candle lantern that he had lit only once they were inside. Percy and Beltain came last, and the knight periodically moved his gauntleted arm to the pommel of his sword, ready to act in a split second.

The tunnel turned in different directions a number of times, then widened into a small square room with a stone floor covered in deep dust. There was a door, and Diril opened it with the skill of a lock-pick, then proceeded upwards through the narrowest stairwell imaginable, black and covered with soot.

They followed him silently, and emerged from a doorway behind a wall-hanging inside a dark corridor—elegant, dimly lit, and at least three stories above street level. They were now inside the Palace of the Sun.

The man named Diril extinguished the lantern, motioned for silence, and for them to follow. They moved through the empty corridor for about fifty feet, following its turns and observing a veritable gallery of old paintings in gilded frames and various hangings every few feet on both sides of the corridor.

Diril stopped before one particular floor length tapestry depicting an antique scene of battle. He lifted the corner end of it, and a discreet door was revealed, painted the same color as the walls. He opened it with a skill born of familiarity, and they were again faced with a claustrophobic passage. In they went, without light, and this time walked for interminable minutes in unknown directions, by feel, moving between walls, and taking endless turns past what felt like quite a few other doorways that Diril ignored.

At last he stopped before one, and he opened it a crack. He paused, listening, then moved aside what must have been a large hanging, and in the shadows they could see his hand motioning to follow.

They emerged from a shadowed corner into a grand splendid Hall—possibly the grandest Percy had ever seen. This was the Hall of the Sun. It was perfectly empty and silent, locked from the outside, and no candelabras were lit. But the curtains were not drawn, and thus the moonlight filled the expanse with silver illumination, bright as day, and set the crystal garlands suspended from sconces everywhere to a cold winter sparkle.

The Countess D'Arvu drew her breath in sharply, and put her hands over her own mouth in an emotional reaction at the sight of the Hall and the memory of the last time she stood here.

Diril remained near the secret doorway while the rest of them walked in soft careful steps along the polished parquet floor.

Before them, all the way on the other end of the Hall loomed the Sapphire Throne, a grand single perfect jewel upon a dais. . . . Even from a distance it sparkled fiercely with a cold immortal fire in the moonlight, its smooth sharp facets and cabochon rounded edges capturing the light in their own ways, transforming it in prismatic motion.

Percy went still, her breath catching, and she clutched Beltain's hand. "She is here . . ." she whispered, and pointed at the throne.

Up on a column pedestal on the right of the throne sat a small golden statue of the goddess.

They neared the throne, taking each step in such silence that they could hear their own breath and nothing else.

Before the dais they paused. Percy stood, dumbstruck, and then she reached out with her own death *sense* because the pull of the Cobweb Bride had grown overwhelming. The golden figure of the goddess was before her, and yet, it was not what called her, and thus she glanced at it only momentarily. But the Cobweb Bride—*she* was here too, yes! Only—

Percy turned around slowly, compelled by the pull, the impossible need of the death shadow. And she approached the Sapphire Throne itself.

She did the unthinkable, by climbing the three ceremonial steps directly up to the throne, a place that only the Sovereign had the right to occupy. She stood on the top step, right before the throne—so near, she could sit upon it if she chose— breathing deeply, and sensing the single death billowing, fluttering . . . *under* her feet.

Thus, she pointed down at the throne, and underneath it, and she whispered: "Here . . . *here* lies the Cobweb Bride."

They stood watching her in a mixture of fear, wonder and urgency.

Percy turned her back on the Sapphire Throne and walked back down the stairs of the dais, pausing before the pedestal with the Goddess Thesmos. "Is there something down there?" she whispered, looking at her companions. "Down, underneath the Throne?"

The Count shook his head negatively. "No . . . That is, I don't know."

"Could there be a hidden passage," said Percy. "Similar to the one we just used? Anything?"

"Ask your man," Beltain said softly, pointing to Diril who remained on the other end of the Hall.

The Count raised his hand and beckoned for Diril to approach. The man neared, and they consulted in whispers, and Diril shook his head negatively several times.

It was Countess D'Arvu who interrupted. "We must pray!" she exclaimed in a stifled whisper. "Pray to Thesmos for truth! The answers must lie here, else she would not have called us to her! Pray, child!" and the Countess wrung Percy's hand with her clammy own.

Nodding to her, Percy turned to the Goddess.

The golden shape was smooth and exquisite, a statue formed by a master sculptor. The true brightness of gold was leached by the moonlight into a silvery cream softness. The face of the Goddess has a serene expression, languid half-closed eyes. Her lips were shaped at the corners in the faintest shadow of a smile.

Percy reached out and placed her fingers upon the folded leg of the statue, trembling at the touch of cool metal that was somehow also warm, in an impossible dichotomy of the senses.

"Oh, no! You mustn't touch!" The Countess put her hand to her mouth in worry.

"Why not?" said the Count D'Arvu. "She may be able to call upon Thesmos with her touch. It is said that touching the gods' sacred effigies can heal the sick and bring enlightenment upon those who seek answers—"

Percy let go, then sighed and continued gazing at the divine form before her. Moonlight shone softly from the great windows, and just for an instant a spark glittered on the very top point of the headdress, sliding like a pinpoint star upon the braided wheat of the harvest crown. It beckoned her. . . .

Percy was compelled. She reached out with her fingers and placed them on top of the crown, reaching for the elusive spark of brilliance, moon silver upon tangible gold.

She touched, and then, because it seemed the right thing to do, she extended her palm and rested it fully upon the spot on top, feeling a sudden effusion of warmth coming to her, or maybe leaving her flesh and entering the cool metal.

How strange it was, that she felt the need to press her palm in just such a manner, to give and receive warmth, as though this was the perfect spot, and her hand a source of inner fire. . . .

Long moments passed. Her hand—it was now a part of the goddess, flesh to flesh, and the warmth had become a thing of love.

The spot no longer felt like anything but an extension of her own mortal body. Moved by instinct, Percy pressed down and then caressed it, with a slight turn of her wrist.

As she did thus, the goddess figurine *moved*. It rotated softly, turning on its base, until it reached ninety degrees. At the same time, a grinding noise sounded, coming from the back of the Sapphire Throne.

Several gasps sounded. One of them belonged to Diril, a sound of grim satisfaction. The Countess and her husband were staring, their countenances filled with terror and hope.

"Ah! It is indeed a *key!*" Diril began to speak in an energetic whisper, excitement in his eyes, for the first time showing a living expression behind a mask of impassivity. "All these years, we have suspected! We in intelligence have searched for the meaning behind this effigy! Skilled hands from many factions have touched it, examined it variously for hidden latches, for any signs, and all for nothing—until now! The trick is to hold it down for long moments, then turn! A simple but effective combination!"

They swiftly went to observe what had been revealed behind the throne. "Come!" Diril signaled eagerly. "It's a passage leading down! What a magnificent discovery!"

The parquet floor had been moved aside along interlocking geometric portions of its mosaic pattern, sliding apart to reveal a dark passage.

One by one they entered and descended, with Percy and Beltain walking last, behind the others. The darkness became soft grey in hue, then resolved into a strange illumination that seemed to have no source. A sterile stone chamber was before them, and ahead a passage corridor with arches and light sconces in each niche, their lanterns like disembodied moons behind frosted glass.

They walked, following the corridor, and the Countess

D'Arvu moved unsteadily, held by her husband who gently assisted her.

At last they emerged into an impossible larger chamber, filled with soft overwhelming light, anemic lavender.

Percy felt herself trembling because the pull was so strong now, the Cobweb Bride and her death, were here, were just ahead. . . .

She entered last, after everyone else who had paused at the entrance, stilled in what must have been terrible mind-freezing shock.

The room was filled with people—with *women*. They were motionless and covered in fine, white cobwebs. A sargasso sea of cobwebs.

They seemed to be statues, but somehow Percy knew they were not—because at the side of each was a gentle mournful thing of supernatural smoke, a death shadow, also petrified somehow, suspended into an impossibility—a shadow imprisoned, turned into invisible stone. Stilled in different positions, seated on chairs, standing upright, lying in repose on the smooth stone floor, these women and their shadows were a chilling sight, possibly because of their pristine beauty coupled with mortality. Not even dust here, only clean spun magic of silken strands, like a lace forest. And they were drowned in it. . . .

Percy sensed their different deaths, held, imprisoned, *changed* in nature. And yet, she registered it all with only a periphery of her attention.

Her main intensity was focused upon only *one*.

She lay in the very center of the chamber, upon a long slab of ornate marble, her funereal slab. All in white she was, young and fair and ageless. Not a blemish upon her, only a soft matte sheen of infinite silken threads.

The Cobweb Bride.

Percy moved forward, past Beltain and Diril and the Count

and Countess.

And she entered the cobweb forest.

"Leonora! Oh, *Leonora!*"

Somewhere behind her, Percy heard the Countess cry out in a piteous rending sound of despair. And there was a rush as they moved frantically toward one of the frozen figures, the one seated closest the entrance, right before their eyes—the one whom they recognized at last as their missing daughter.

But Percy did not look around, and continued moving forward. A few more steps, past stilled women-statues whose strangely untouched, open, living eyes seemed to follow her motion.

A few more steps, through a forest of fine spider silk that made her skin crawl and sent shudders of instinctive revulsion throughout her body. Percy used her fingers to move the strands out of her face and hair, closing her eyes when it became unbearable, and persisted forward.

Just another step. . . .

And Percy stood at last before the Cobweb Bride.

The maiden lay before her, fragile and anemic and *perfect*, her eyes opened wide, gazing eternally upward. There was a spot of curious darkness here, surrounding her in a shadow cocoon, for the infinite layers of cobwebs filtered the light down to a faint glow.

Percy stopped and she was now right before the death shadow—a mere breath away. It stood, translucent and petrified, formed of both twilight and pallor, shadow and light, as though the two had become intermingled and thus fixed in place.

Percy put her finger forward and touched it. And it rang! It was like touching impossible immortal glass. At the point of contact, the shadow rang and resounded, singing like crystal, for it was encased in an impenetrable field of energy. It seemed to strain, to want to cleave to Percy, but it could *not*.

Percy frowned. She looked down at the maiden, and

observed her for several long curious moments—hearing meanwhile behind her the sobbing of the Countess and the subdued voices of the men. And then she leaned over the maiden and examined her face even closer, noting the odd pattern of lights reflected in the pupils of her eyes.

Those were the colored stars she had seen in a vision so many days ago it seemed, when she was inside Death's mind at his Keep. She knew them now for distant prismatic reflections from overhead—for directly above in the ceiling was the base of the Sapphire Throne, and it was like a star field, burning with dots of colors, casting a reflection directly down, in a rainbow sieve of pinpoints of light.

The same dots of light sparkled in the whiteness of the maiden's hair, as though she was sprinkled with powdered sugar. Such was the strange optical illusion spun by the cobwebs.

Look closer—through the cobweb filaments of her hair and along each strand shine stars. . . .

And Percy forced herself to look. She made her vision into razors, and she cut through the air and narrowed in a beam of force on the edge of infinite sharpness.

She put her fingertips upon the maiden's white hair, sensing the granules of crystalline energy ring also, in the same manner as the death shadow.

They were both encased in it, death and the maiden.

It was a *veil*, this energy—a veil between life and death. And it was never meant to be.

Percy felt herself shuddering, her mind filling with the tolling of cathedral bells, deep, primeval, bass tones of dark power. She let go of the maiden's cobweb-spun hair, and clenched her hands to herself, until her knuckles were bloodless white—

"Percy!" Somewhere in back she could hear Beltain's familiar voice calling her, but it was coming through many thick layers of cotton. . . .

Percy placed her one hand, cold as ice, upon the delicate doll's hand belonging to the Cobweb Bride, gripping her tight. She then reached out and placed her other hand upon the maiden's death shadow, crystalline and hard and impenetrable.

And then, she reached out in both directions, the maiden and her death, and she pulled with every fiber of her being.

The cobwebs in the room started to vibrate. They floated and shimmered, each tiny strand ringing in an invisible wind. Faster they moved, vibrating, microscopic, razor-fine, infinite. . . .

And Percy's *pull* increased.

There was a sensation of wind gathering in the chamber. And then, something *exploded*, like a world of shattering crystals, and the preternatural veil of force was *gone*.

Percy felt herself lose consciousness for a split second from the impact slamming upon her mind. She had broken through. All along the room, the cobwebs broke apart, the filaments turning into fine grains, shattering the bonds between the smallest parts of themselves, like crumbling formations of salt and sugar, raining down into pale dust.

The maiden lying before Percy shuddered suddenly, her eyes growing wide, and she took in a deep breath of air into long-suspended lungs. She breathed, gasping, and at her side her death shadow billowed at last, released from its impossible crystal prison.

The room suddenly came alive—or rather, the shapes of the women suspended as they were, were freed of their ethereal bonds at last.

They crumpled down where they were—sitting, standing, lying. Each was a lifeless corpse. Percy sensed in horror that their crystalline death shadows—those shadow shapes that she thought were simply imprisoned—were in fact ancient remnants, indeed an illusion. Maybe they *had* been something once, real death energy shadow-forms. But it was oh-so-long ago. Death itself was leached out of existence, softly, delicately, through the strange debilitating magic of the crystal veil that separated death from life.

Because all these other women had died so long ago, they were not even the animated undead. They were now simply *gone*.

All except for two—the maiden who was the Cobweb Bride, and . . . Leonora.

Apparently, while the other women collapsed all around into sad pitiful shapes of true death, Leonora inhaled a deep breath of her own, and sat up in her chair.

"Leonora! Oh, my child! You are alive!" cried the Countess. And the Count rushed forward to support her, for his spouse nearly fainted.

"Mother!" Leonora exclaimed, her voice cracking and weak, and her face pale and sickly, but seeming to regain a little color before their eyes. "Oh, mother! And my father!"

Their reunion was a thing of joy and, for Percy, amazement, because Percy noted that there was no death shadow hovering anywhere near Lady Leonora—which meant that the girl was well and truly *alive*.

But those observations were incidental, to be savored later. Because in this immediate instant, the maiden who was the Cobweb Bride started to rise stiffly from her sepulchral death bed, and the white crystal dust of shattered cobwebs rained from her hair, clothing, and limbs upon the stone. And her white raiment was revealed to be a soft dusky rose, the same shade as her cheeks. She was strangely vibrant and full of life for someone whose death shadow billowed at her side.

It was then that all eyes turned upon the maiden, even Leonora and her parents pausing to stare.

"Who are you, My Lady?" said Percy gently, addressing the Cobweb Bride.

It took the young woman several breaths before she could

form words. "I . . . am . . . Melinoë." Her voice started as a mere whisper, cracking, and there were hints of sonorous tones in it that were yet unrealized.

The Countess D'Arvu spoke up. "Dear child, who is your mother? Is it Her Brilliance, the Sovereign, Rumanar Avalais?"

The maiden who had named herself Melinoë appeared to be recalling something. "Yes," she finally said. "My mother—the Sovereign, she is my mother. Though I hardly know who she is—or who I am. I—hardly remember . . . my name."

"By Heaven! And has she done this to you?" asked the Count.

"My mother has blue eyes," spoke Melinoë, starting to get up from her seated position, and Percy immediately assisted her with her hands under her arm. "My mother is beautiful and bright and she rules the Domain. She used to come and visit me . . . in the room of the sun. In the Palace of the Sun. She used to brush my hair and tell me about the flowers in Elysium. And then she stopped coming, and—and I no longer remember."

"Oh, dear Lord!" The Countess used a handkerchief to wipe her face, while Leonora stared with a dazed and frightened expression around her, at the corpses, suddenly realizing where they were. "What is this place, mother?" she whispered, hugging the Countess in fear. "The last I remember is being in the quarters of the Ladies-in-Attendance, and then—I don't remember!" And Leonora turned to look at the Cobweb Bride who now stood with difficulty, supported by Percy, and she said, "Melinoë? I do not remember you! Have I seen you in Attendance? Oh, I am so frightened, mother!"

"This lady is the daughter of Her Brilliance," said the Count.

"What daughter? I know not of such! This must be a mistake," said Leonora. "I am so confused! What is this terrible place? Why am I here?"

"I think it is time we made our exit," said Diril in that

moment. He had been making rounds of the room, crouching down to examine some of the corpses, and now said to the Count: "This is rather disturbing. I know and recognize some of these young women—they have been fixtures at the Court many years ago—decades. I was a young boy, and I remember one of these at least, when she was a debutante, and another had been deceased and taken, strewn in flowers, in a burial procession along the streets of the citadel. How is it possible they are now here, and even though corpses, they are fresh, and have not aged or deteriorated a moment since? It is definitely a form of sorcery. Thus, we need to leave, *now*, all of us."

"Agreed," said Beltain. And he went forward to help Percy with Lady Melinoë.

"What of all these unfortunates?" the Count asked, pointing to the scattered bodies. Should anything be done, perhaps—"

But Diril shook his head negatively, with a grim demeanor.

"Leonora, can you walk, dear girl?"

Lady Leonora nodded, and with the help of both her parents she was up also.

And then they began their intricate and careful trip back up and out of the horrible secret chamber.

Once they emerged from the underground chamber back inside the Hall of the Sun, gently leading the two revived young ladies, Diril himself went to the golden goddess and he pressed and twisted the statuette until the secret floor passage was again concealed.

Next they crossed the Hall and found the secret passage in the wall, and started moving, with as much speed as possible, while half-carrying Lady Leonora and Lady Melinoë, and passing them from arm to arm.

The passage through the exposed remote corridor was the most harrowing portion of their escape.

"Do not fear," Diril reassured them before they emerged, "The worst is behind us, for the only guard to be expected is in the central potion of the Palace, and their attention has been sorely divided these last few days."

However, moments after they had come forth, a series of servants turned a corner, one after another. Diril immediately lifted his voice and acquired a nasal accent and embarked upon a cultured lecture about the history of the hanging tapestries in this particular wing of the Palace, achieving the perfect illusion of a palatial tour guide. The Count fell in with him adroitly and asked a series of annoying questions about the noble subjects depicted, while the ladies pretended to examine the wall hangings, and the Countess held Leonora and Melinoë suspended on both her arms, and laughed softly, genuinely seeming inebriated. Beltain, wrapped in his black cloak, took up a calm and bored pose near Percy, who in turn simply moved to the wall and pretended to adjust a bit of tapestry, feeling, unlike the others, utterly conspicuous, ridiculous, and terrified.

The servants bowed and curtsied, and were perfunctorily ignored by the aristocrats who were obviously out on a whim, taking a midnight tour of the Palace.

When they had gone, the Countess D'Arvu nearly collapsed, resting against the wall, and for a moment, it was the two young ladies who supported her.

Somehow they managed to miss any more encounters with Palace servants or guards, and finally entered the underground tunnels with their filth and scrawled graffiti, in utmost relief.

A half an hour more and they arrived at the house belonging to the Count D'Arvu.

B ut there was to be no rest.
"We can no longer remain at Court," said the Count to Beltain, once they had come within doors. "I take my family and we leave, with our child Leonora, this very night. There is no knowing how long we have until the Sovereign discovers this, and then—it is unspeakable. The House D'Arvu is done for.

Thus, we must run. You are welcome to come with us."

"I was about to suggest the same to you," replied Beltain softly. "But I am afraid we go back inside the war zone. I am Lord Beltain Chidair of Lethe, and my place is back north. And especially now, we will be going to a place where no mortal will choose to go willingly. Thus, we part, with kindness."

"You and the girl have my eternal gratitude," the Count replied. Where we go, I am not yet certain. But it will be as far away as possible from this evil war . . . and from the monstrous creature who almost destroyed our daughter. I serve the Sovereign no longer."

And thus it was that several riders left the citadel that night. Two riders traveled through the northern gate—Beltain and Percy, riding the great black charger, and on a chestnut mare provided by the D'Arvu, came the Lady Melinoë, bundled in a thick dark coat, hooded, and tied securely to the comfortable side-saddle. Next to her on the saddle, unseen by all except Percy, rode the maiden's death-shadow. Beltain held both the reins of Jack and the mare, and led them past the gates in the wake of several peasant carts and noble carriages.

Thus, the Cobweb Bride left the Sapphire Court.

Chapter 22

No one spoke much until they were well away from the citadel walls and on the road heading north. The moon rode the sky in her full radiance, and was beginning to sink toward the tree-lined horizon, for it was now many hours after midnight, and the world reposed in a contrast of silver, blues, indigoes and shadows.

"My Lady, how are you?" said Percy at some point, watching with concern the nearly limp form of the young woman to whom she was so strangely bound.

"I am well. . . ." Lady Melinoë raised her hooded face and the moonlight illuminated a part of it, in particular her shimmering liquid eyes.

"Apologies that we may not rest just yet," said Beltain. "But we cannot risk stopping until we are well away from—your mother's Court."

"I have no wish to rest," Melinoë said. "I have been resting a very long time."

"Oh, can you remember any of it?"

But the maiden shook her head. "All I remember are . . . endless dreams."

Percy felt a painful constriction in her chest. This girl was young, gentle, beautiful, and seemed in good health—except for the death attached to her. What abomination made her suffer this fate? How had it come to pass?

"So you remember nothing at all, of your mother?"

"I am not sure," the lady replied. "I remember her kindness. Then, nothing."

"What manner of kindness is it, to conceal her own daughter from the world? And then, to perform dark sorcery?" mused Beltain in a hard voice.

Percy said nothing. There was yet the most difficult thing to be said—something that they had not told her yet.

For all appearances, the Cobweb Bride had no notion that she was *dead*. Or that she was intended to meet Death, her Bridegroom.

How was one to even explain such a thing?

And what if—what if after all this time, she learned the truth and then *refused* to comply with her singular and horrible fate? And as a result, the world would have to continue as it was, broken?

Percy took a deep breath and began. "Lady Melinoë, there is something you must know."

Lady Melinoë Avalais, daughter of the Sovereign of the Domain, listened to the grim details of her true nature and her fate explained to her as gently as possible, while they rode underneath the waning moonlight.

Afterwards, she spoke nothing for a long time.

Percy, terrified on her behalf and feeling wrenching guilt—a completely new, unexpected circumstance she had never dreamed she would be subjected to in the course of her fulfillment of Death's quest—glanced at the maiden repeatedly, seeking any kind of reaction in her delicate face painted by the moon. Eventually she noticed the liquid pooling in Melinoë's eyes, and then, as drops coalesced, long streaks appeared, illuminating her cheeks. She cried wordlessly, with her face unmarred by emotion, and it was peculiar indeed to observe a dead one cry. Was it even possible?

At last, the lady wiped her eyes and said: "So. . . . *This* is how much my mother loves me. I thank you for the truth, and for not sparing me. Well then, so be it. If Death is my true Bridegroom, and if the world itself depends upon this one small thing—small, in the greater scheme of things—and needs my compliance, then I agree and go to my fate."

"My Lady . . ." Percy whispered, her own eyes welling with tears. "I am so sorry! Oh, if there was but any other way—"

"It matters not," said the Cobweb Bride. "As you say, I am dead already. And now at least I know that *someone* loves and waits for me. And thus, I go gladly to him. In truth, it was meant to be. Therefore, take me to Death! Take me to him *now!*"

And no longer able to hold her face impassive, Lady Melinoë wept hard, with shuddering sobs, putting her hands up to cover her contorted cheeks.

Beltain and Percy remained in grim silence, watching her.

They rode on, in the deep night darkness, for now the moon had sunk below the close horizon defined by filigree shapes of trees.

The maiden sobbed her heart out, and then eventually quieted. And for an hour, as cold and grave as a tomb, there was perfect silence between them, only the sound of their breathing and the soft snorts of the horses in the chill air.

Half an hour later they had reached Ulpheo. The translucent capital city reposed, like an anemic lotus blossom filled with crawling gnats, in the residual phosphor glow of the night sky bereft of moon and impaled with sharp stars. They circled past its sickly glass walls and continued onward.

Another quarter hour, and the eastern sky at their left started to lighten with the faintest precursor of silver.

The hills ended suddenly, and the last sparse scattering of forest was all that remained between them and the wide open plain that was the approaching Morphaea.

It was then, in this strange in-between time, the delicate slate blue twilight of the dawn, that the form of the landscape before them began to shimmer and *fade*.

Right before them it was happening, a strange surreal mirage of permeable half-solidity, and all things took on smooth edges, all hard delineations softened.

Beltain reined in Jack and pulled back the mare. They stopped sharply, staring, in disbelief, as the unnatural phenomenon that they barely knew about was taking place before their eyes—yet another portion of the land was disappearing—lord knows where.

And then a wild, impossible thought came to Percy. . . .

What if it was Death himself, gradually taking all things to him? And if so, could it be that the place to which all these things went was none other than the underworld, Death's own twilight realm?

"My Lord Beltain!" Percy whispered suddenly looking up into his eyes, while only a few feet before them the ground churned and the air warped in an act of displacement, and a mist arose to cover all things before them in a shimmering ethereal veil. "Do you trust me, my beloved?"

Beltain did not pause for a second. "You know I do! I trust you with my life."

"Then trust me this once, and do what I say, for it will take us directly on our journey to where we need to be. Thus, ride forward, my love! Ride directly into this fading land before us!"

And the black knight nodded, and he gave free rein to both Jack and the chestnut mare. With a snap and pull, the horses went into motion.

"Hold on, My Lady Melinoë!" Percy exclaimed, "Hold on tight!"

And they plunged into the swirling mist.

What happened next was either the blink of an eye or interminable compounding moments of grey eternity. They passed through the mist and emerged on the other side . . . into a now familiar Hall of boundless silence, with arches and columns lining up in rows unto the horizon, no end and no beginning, no walls, only the granite stone slabs under their feet.

Overhead, the distant impossible ceiling that was neither starry sky nor a dream.

The air was neither cold nor warm, but as indifferent as the grey silence of oblivion.

The horses' hooves rang dull upon the stone floor, as they paused, finding themselves displaced and yet exactly where they needed to be.

"Oh, thank Heaven!" Percy muttered. "We are indeed here. . . ."

Beltain's metal-clad arms pressed around her and his baritone sounded soft and amazed. "You were indeed right, we are back in this accursed place! Ah, how well I remember our last time here."

"What is this place? How . . . did we get here?" Lady Melinoë's tremulous voice sounded, and they both glanced to see her dilated frightened eyes. Maybe she was beginning to regret her decision now. . . .

"We are within Death's kingdom, My Lady, and this is his Keep."

"But how? We were just riding—"

And Percy explained the circumstances of twilight and the fading of shadows as it related to entering Death's domain. "If we had not come upon this moment of blending between worlds, we would have had to ride a long way north through the real world. This was a fortunate shortcut given us. I would not be surprised if Death himself had intended it to be. And now, we are here, we have arrived!"

"So where is he?" Melinoë said. "Where is my

Bridegroom?"

"You must call upon him," Percy replied gently. "Speak, and he will listen, for all here is his kingdom, and he hears us even now."

Melinoë raised her lily-smooth hands to the hood of her cloak, and she lowered it, revealing her bright golden hair that did not lose its gleam even here in this place of dull, disembodied half-light.

"Lord Death!" she exclaimed, in a sonorous voice that echoed along the stones. "I am here! I am your Cobweb Bride!"

The echoes ended.

There was only silence.

And then, a remote masculine voice spoke, ringing in the very stone of the Keep, coming from all directions in the Hall.

"Come to me!"

In the wake of the words came a gale of wind.

They followed the wind that served as guide, and rode through the hall, hooves striking stone, past arches and columns in an infinite army of monotonous languor, until the nature of the shadows changed, and cobwebs garlanded the niches, hanging like old funereal lace.

Granite soon became bone. Pale ivory cream, the world transformed around them, and overhead was a softly floating upside-down sea of cobwebs, spun by ancient spiders that had long since gone from this lifeless Hall.

This was Death's grand tomb, a sepulcher of wondrous proportions. The columns were now caverns of bones, wrenched from a giant's ribcage, and it was now impossible to ride through this chaos.

Beltain dismounted, pulling Percy down with him, and then he assisted Lady Melinoë from her chestnut mare. Once on the floor, the lady stood upright with some difficulty, still rather unsteady on her feet shod in fine traveling boots given her by the

Countess D'Arvu, and wearied after the extended ride.

Percy came to take her hand, feeling its coolness. And at the same time the death shadow of the Cobweb Bride responded, compelled to follow and to cleave—it was in fact a difficult urge that Percy had to fight, *not* to pull the two together immediately. . . . But she reminded herself that it was not for *her*, that final sorrowful task, but for Death himself.

The two girls moved together thus, with Beltain walking behind them and leading the two horses carefully over the shards of bones underfoot.

Before them, the cobwebs thickened, and at the same time the Hall widened into an anemic radiance-filled expanse. Up ahead, between two massive bone columns, upraised on a dais amid decadent pallor stood a grandiose ivory throne. Two sharp needle-spires rose from its high back like horns.

And upon this throne sat a man clad in a black doublet and hose. He wore a wide starched collar of faded lace, and he reposed lightly to one side, elegant hand propped underneath a bearded chin trimmed in the angular manner of an antique grim Spaniard.

His face was shadowed and for some reason impossible to look upon directly—as though the focus in one's eye shifted slightly when one tried. . . . As though the face was not there, but a vacant spot of shadow and illusion.

Such was Death.

But the most remarkable thing about him was that he was *not* alone.

At various spots around the throne and at the base of the dais sat a number of somewhat dejected human figures. Indeed, there were six of them. Four were young girls, bundled in warm winter clothing, and sprawled on the floor among fragments of bone and on the dais stairs, sitting cross-legged, or with legs folded, or in one case lying on her back with hands crossed underneath her head in place of a pillow.

Two more were a lady and gentleman, both handsome, both attired in once stylish travel clothing that had undergone quite a bit of combat with dirt and dust and disarray. The raven-haired lady with a face of sharp faerie beauty sat primly upon the top stair just next to Death's elbow, fiddling with her stained and torn gloves, and right next to her, the gentleman lay, resting his equally dark but rather wildly tousled and bearded head in her lap.

As soon as Percy approached, holding Lady Melinoë's hand, followed by Beltain and the horses, everyone turned in their direction.

"Lord Death!" Percy began. . . .

There was a bit of shrieking.

"*Percy!* Oh, Lordy, Lord! Is that you, Percy Ayren?" The girls had gotten up and it was Catrine, and Sybil and Regata, her former original companions from the road to Death's Keep, all of whom Percy recognized immediately.

"Regata! Catrine! And you too, Sybil!" Percy was stunned momentarily out of her somber mood, and let go of Melinoë's hand. "What are you all doing here? How did you get here? I thought you had been captured by the Duke's patrol—"

"Oh, thank Heaven and all blessed saints!" said the gentleman, rising up on his elbows from the lady's lap. "They are indeed here! That is, *someone* is here!"

Percy vaguely recognized both the gentleman and the lady—they were the same haughty and aristocratic travelers whose curricle had broken down on the side of the road when the girls were passing through Chidair lands on the final leg of their journey to the northern forests—possibly there had been another lady with them?

But none of it mattered.

Percy looked at Lord Death, sitting on his throne of bones. His face was in eternal shadow but somehow she knew he was looking at her, and at the maiden at her side.

Percy glanced at Melinoë and noted her strange focused stare as she was gazing onward in the direction of the throne. "My Lady," Percy said gently. "You may not see him, but Death sits there, before you."

"I . . . see him," replied Melinoë, never taking her eyes off the one who was Death.

"Oh, you can actually *see* him?" Percy wondered, recalling that the last time they were all gathered here, no one could see Death's human form until she touched him.

"Of course she can see him!" the lady sitting on the dais stair said in annoyance. "We can all see him, it is all rather tedious."

"On, no! Percy!" cried Regata, suddenly noticing Beltain. "That's the Black Knight! And his fearsome horse! Oh, no! He's here to drag us back to the dungeon!?"

"I assure you, I am not," Beltain replied with a rueful smile.

But Percy paid no attention to anything but Death and his Cobweb Bride.

Melinoë took several slow steps forward, and neared the throne. Her death shadow drifted behind her.

"My Lord . . ." she whispered and her face was exalted. "I am your Bride . . ."

Death moved.

He stood up, a tall, elegant, masculine shape, and then he walked down the stairs of his dais.

In that moment everyone grew silent.

"You are indeed *she*." Death's voice sounded from the depths and within their minds.

"Will you have me, my Bridegroom? Will you take me unto you?"

"I take you," said Death. "As you are mine."

And he reached out his hand, his wrists draped in ivory lace, his elegant fingers with their sharpened claws. This pale great hand he offered to her.

Melinoë did not hesitate. She put her delicate lily-white hand into his, feeling his great ivory fingers close over hers.

With his other hand, Death reached for the shadow that stood behind her, the death shadow of the Cobweb Bride.

"At last. . . ."

His immortal whisper resounded throughout the Hall.

Melinoë trembled and closed her eyes.

Drawing the maiden and her death shadow to him, Death leaned down, towering over them both, and he kissed Melinoë once on the forehead and once on the lips.

And then he *pulled.*

Percy felt the world—the fabric of the world around her— begin to *shift* and rip asunder.

Columns trembled and the floor underneath them shook in a deep rumble of moving bedrock and rustling bones. Stronger and stronger it grew, and a wind arose, becoming gale force, as it rushed through the sea of cobwebs overhead and swept through the Hall, buffeting all of them, swirling vortexes of dust and impossible chaos. . . .

For long interminable moments it raged and then it was over.

Melinoë was standing exactly as she had been, before Death, her hand clutched in his, and her death shadow still at her side.

Nothing had happened.

Everything and everyone had gone terribly silent.

And Lord Death himself, if such a thing were possible, appeared perplexed.

Percy released a held breath and stared in terrible confusion.

"What is the meaning of this?" said he who was Death, holding the hand of his Bride and her shadow. "Why is there no *union?*"

Lady Melinoë opened her eyes and looked up at the one

who held her by the hand. "Am I still . . . dead?" she whispered. "What has come to pass?"

And Death continued looking at her with his shadowed visage invisible to all, and he said, "I do not know."

Then, slowly, he turned to look at Percy. "You, who have been given a fragment of my heart—come to me."

Percy wordlessly obeyed. She climbed the few steps of the dais and stood before her immortal liege.

"Now, *you* must try to do what I have taught you. Take my Bride and her death and unite them!"

"What? *I?*" whispered Percy. "But if *you* yourself, My Lord, cannot—"

"You are mine also, and my power is yours. I must observe what comes to pass when it is exercised."

With her trembling fingers, Percy reached out and received Melinoë's ice-cold hand and then she took hold of the billowing shadow. . . . She felt the immediate gathering of dark roiling power, and the familiar echoing sound descending upon her mind.

Dear Lord in Heaven! She was supposed to do this thing before Death himself, as if she were his young apprenticed pupil!

Percy felt the immediate connection between the maiden and her shadow, and then she drew upon all that was contained within herself and *pulled* the two together—recalling the same thing she had done before in the shadowed chamber underneath the Sapphire Throne—only this time it was not merely to break the bond of the energy veil, but the real thing, to enact the final true death.

She pulled, and the world within her mind fell apart to mirror shards and crumbling pieces then coalesced together again from the effort. She pulled—

And nothing happened.

Percy let go of Melinoë and drew her hands to her mouth in

fear. "My Lady Melinoë," she said, "can you feel me when I attempt to do this thing? Was there anything at all you felt just now?"

"Yes . . . I feel a slight pull, as if my soul is being called forth, and then, nothing."

"Oh, for Heaven's sake! What now?" suddenly said the beautiful, shrewish lady still seated on the dais. "This is simply unbelievable! What on earth is going on?"

The young gentleman meanwhile placed his tousled head between his legs and groaned. "No! Oh, no, no, no! A thousand times, no! This cannot be happening!"

"I do not understand," Death said again. "Why is there no union?"

"Maybe because a *union* requires love, or, at the very least, a bit of affection?—nay, familiarity? An attempt at courtship? Mild flirtation?" exclaimed the lady, while the gentleman hurriedly retorted, "Hush, my dear Amaryllis! By Jove and Tartarus, do hold your delightfully waspish tongue, at least with this particular dark gentleman—"

But Death seemed to attend to her words.

"Love . . ." he uttered. "I know not of it—not as a proper mortal man, for I am not one of you. And yet, I know that when I take your kind upon me, each one of you is more precious and beloved by me in that one moment than the entirety of the world."

"A lovely sentiment, but a bit excessive upon first acquaintance," said Lady Amaryllis. "For indeed, that is all any of us gets with you, Lord Death, is it not? A moment for acquaintance and then—pouf!—and then only Lord knows what happens next. I do suggest you start enriching your time with our mortal kind. Have you considered an extended wooing ritual? Begin with a simple flower folded in a sealed and perfumed note declaring your true affections—it would be a rather fine start. Followed up with, perhaps, a lovely serenade under the balcony of a moonlit boudoir? Or is that too much to expect in exchange for uncharted eternity?"

"Maybe—" Percy meanwhile said gently, with a glance at Beltain who stood behind them all, observing with unbelieving eyes. "Maybe when I freed you, Lady Melinoë, maybe I *broke* something in the process? For, I still don't quite understand the dark sorcery, the nature of that ethereal veil that held you imprisoned and fixed in stasis."

"I know that you set me free," Melinoë replied, looking at her with a lost but sincere expression. "Whatever my previous existence had been, whatever illusion or lies or horror my own mother, the Sovereign had enacted—"

"Wait, her mother is the Sovereign of the Domain? *The* Sovereign?" whispered Catrine, staring at the other girls.

"—Whatever it was," Melinoë continued, "I am grateful to be free of it. If only I knew more, if only I remembered! My own mother did this thing to me! How could she? She who braided my hair and brought me blooming flowers to adorn me and told me wondrous tales? My beloved mother with her kind blue eyes? She is no mother of mine!"

"Perhaps," Death said, musing, "I might try this thing, this mortal courtship. I will try to woo my Cobweb Bride who is no longer bound in Cobwebs. . . ."

"Well, that's just splendid and dandy!" exclaimed the gentleman with the unkempt demeanor and an untrimmed beard. "And while he woos and courts her, what are we to do in the meantime? Eat our knuckles?"

"To be fair, it is all your fault, Nathan," said Lady Amaryllis, "for if you had not made us go sailing on that infernal river, we would not be here in the first place, stuck and unable to depart this excruciating unrelieved hell, next to this mirthless, immortal *antique!*"

"No! No, no!" Nathan moaned again. "This! To be resigned to this eternity in this dank hall surrounded by bones and these poor girls, and now these newly arrived persons, whoever the hell they are—"

"We have been told that a Cobweb Bride is all that is required to set the world aright!"

"—and all I wanted was to have a bit of steak once more, a single decent dinner before I became a stiff and walking corpse myself!" Lord Nathan went on.

"Silence!"

Everyone heeded Death's ringing voice of power.

And the dark Bridegroom turned to Melinoë and again offered her his hand. "My Lady Bride, come to me. Tell me your name, so that I may woo you."

"My Lord, I am . . . Melinoë Avalais," she replied. "At least it is all I can remember of my former life. I remember nothing else but vaporous dreams, and none of them have solid form. Nothing to grasp or recollect. . . . I—I am—"

"Tell me . . ." spoke Lord Death gently, and for the first time his immortal masculine voice took on a strange vulnerable sound, as though a wound had been opened to the air. "Tell me of yourself. . . . All that you can remember."

"But there is so very little!" Lady Melinoë cried. And yet she took his hand.

And leading her thus, Death took the lady to the first stair and helped her step upon the dais and stop before his ivory throne.

"I have no seat to offer you but my own," he said. "Take it, if you choose."

But, "No," said his lady Bride. "Sit in your own place, My Lord. And I will lie by your side. . . ."

And as Death resumed his throne, the maiden came to rest at his feet, beside his throne, lying down softly on the dais of bone, and resting her head against his sculpted legs clad in dark hose, in a gesture of perfect trust.

She remained thus, for long moments, in silence.

"This is all the stuff of poetry and minstrel song," muttered Lord Nathan after a quarter of an hour—or its seeming equivalent in this timeless place—had passed. "But surely something must be done to hurry along this infernal courtship process—by Hades, or Zeus, or Bacchus, just look at them, they aren't even *moving!*"

Percy meanwhile, seated next to Beltain on a pile of crumbling bones, atop their black cloak, looked at the young man with a gaze of wonder. She had forgotten, in this sweet somnolent silence, where exactly it was they were and what was happening. It was as if the world itself was suspended, and just for the instant, nothing mattered. . . . And the black knight took her by the hand and smiled down into her eyes with his own internal fire that filled the air of grey apathy around them with a nimbus of common warmth.

"Percy!" exclaimed Catrine, interrupting their reverie. "Since we're all stuck here, "Tell me about sis! How's Niosta? Where is she?"

"She is at Letheburg, with Grial," Percy said, tearing herself from Beltain. And then she told Catrine the whole story of their adventures—since they apparently had all the time in the world. As she spoke, Beltain listened to her with bemusement.

Many long minutes later, Catrine told her own side of the story.

"—An' after we got off the damn boat on that damn fool river," she concluded, "we ended up here. Only, for some reason, we could all see an' hear Death, and that's because of the dratted river itself, he told us! Because we sailed the river made of twilight, and felt its waters, what with the wet spray and stuff durin' all the rowin', and Their Lordships sticking their fingers in the nasty water, now we are all *marked!* Unless the world is set aright, we cannot leave this hall!"

"What?" Percy shook her head with a frown. "How awful!"

"Awful is right! We'll starve to death!" Catrine said. "An' Death himself will just sit there, do nuttin', and look at us!"

"What a strange river it is that you describe!" Beltain interrupted. "You say it is that same river that is down below in our old Chidair Keep dungeon? I remember it vaguely, for I had gone there maybe a handful of times, if at all, mostly as a young boy, to hide and play with other children of the Keep. In those days, we kept no prisoners in that rotten damp cavern. And, now that I think about it, I vaguely remember those same strange rules and warnings you mention, about not touching the water or drinking from it or extinguishing the lantern—childish games, I thought, told by adults to scare us and keep us away from harm, from possible drowning."

Apparently the Lady Amaryllis heard their discussion. "The river," she said, coming a few steps to join them, "supposedly has a name. Lord Death had told us it is the River Lethe, the most ancient and secret river in all of the Realm, one that no one knows about in truth, except in very old stories."

"The Kingdom of Lethe is named for it," mused Beltain. "I do know this, having somewhat dubiously learned my history lesson years ago."

"My Lord," said Amaryllis, giving him a glance of appraisal. "Are you indeed Lord Beltain Chidair, the son of that insane Duke Hoarfrost? The same man known as the Black Knight?"

"Regretfully, yes," said he.

"Rumors of your prowess have reached the Silver Court." Lady Amaryllis gazed at him with an interested smile. "But in truth you appear neither gruesome nor fierce, and rather a fine sight for a man of your terrifying reputation. It is a pleasure to make your acquaintance now, Lord Beltain, under these impossible circumstances. Indeed, I am suddenly far less bored than I was only moments ago."

"Ah, Chidair! Don't listen to My Lady, for she is always

bored out of her wits, and furthermore, flirts outrageously," said Nathan from where he half reclined on the floor. He threw one sharp glance of his handsome dark eyes in their direction.

"And what does it matter to you, sweetest, that I flirt?" said the lady, with a backward glance. "When one has nothing else to do but flirt and starve, which do you think is the best course of action?"

"The River Lethe," Nathan said, ignoring her. "Supposedly, it has wondrous properties not found in nature. And I refer not only to its impossible existence in the twilight state. Lord Death informs us that if one were to drink from the river once, everything one knows will be forgotten."

"Oh, yes!" exclaimed Catrine. And then she recited: *"Drink once, and you forget everything you know, drink for the second time and you remember everything you knew, drink for the third time and you die!"*

"Lovely and gruesome, is it not?" Nathan said. "At least none of us had the fool notion to drink. It is bad enough we all touched its waters. And darling Amaryllis even bottled some in a flask."

Percy was struck with a sudden thought.

"What if—" she said, turning to Lady Amaryllis. "What if the Lady Melinoë, who can remember nothing of her life, were to be given this water to drink? Your Ladyship has a flask of this water, is that not so? If the magic is true, then if the Cobweb Bride drinks *twice*, she will then remember everything she ever knew!"

And Percy stood up in excitement, and she turned to look at Death on his throne, and his Bride reclining before him at his feet.

"Lord Death! Let your Bride drink the water from the River of Lethe!"

Lady Melinoë stood holding in her trembling hands the flask filled with a strangely swirling liquid that appeared at times dark and yet colored with silver, and at the same time transparent. Since it was permanent twilight here, the water in the flask was visible.

"Will you do this?" Death asked. "This is the most potent water of all the sacred rivers. It is never to be taken lightly, and I may not insist that you drink, only offer you this choice."

But Melinoë looked up at her Bridegroom and she whispered: "I drink gladly, for I must know what kind of mother it is who did this to me. She is no mother of mine! And yet, I must know."

"Then, drink . . ." said Death. "But remember—drink once, then drink again. Two sips. But no more. For such death as will come upon you if you drink for the third time is even beyond my scope. It will take you and cast you out beyond the universe, further destroying this mortal world."

"Then, My Lord," Melinoë said, "stand here beside me and help me drink each time, and hold me up when I forget myself entirely."

"I am here with you, always," he replied, placing his ivory fingers upon her own, and uncorking the flask.

And Melinoë drank. She took one sip, and swallowed, and then set down the flask, into Death's hands.

She stood, her face becoming radiant and her eyes clear, as though the grey world itself was shifting all around her in the Hall, surrounding her with golden light.

"Your remember nothing now, Lady Melinoë," said Death, gentle as the wind. "Now, drink again."

"No," she replied. "Now I—remember *everything*."

And as they all gazed upon her in amazement, noting not only her remarkably clear eyes but also the radiance coming from her, she continued.

"I remember everything now, because I have drunk the

water of Lethe once before. *This* is the second time. And no, she is indeed no mother of mine. For I am *hers*. My true name has never been Melinoë. . . I am not dead, and I can never be."

The light grew around her, golden and radiant, and her visage changed, so that Percy felt a crack in her own heart and with it a flood of recognition.

"You know me. . . ." She who had been Melinoë spoke directly into their minds. "I am the one known as Thesmos. You know me also as the Goddess of Tradition. I am not the Cobweb Bride, for I am Demeter, and I am immortal."

The End of Cobweb Empire, Book Two

The story concludes in . . .
Cobweb Forest, Book Three
Coming Soon!

Author's Note:
Imaginary History, Geography, Weather, and Warfare

If you've made it this far, you are probably wondering about some of the liberties taken with history, in particular the fantasy version of the Renaissance, and the unusual European geography and topology in this alternate universe.

The *Cobweb Bride* trilogy takes place in an imaginary "pocket" of Europe sometime in an alternate version of the 17th century Renaissance. I've modified the continent of Europe by inserting a significant wedge of land between France and Italy, dissolving Austria and Hungary into Germany and pushing the whole thing up north, shifting Spain halfway to the east and lowering the northern shores of the Mediterranean by pushing the southern portion of the continental landmass further down south so that the French Riviera is now where the sea is in our own reality.

Imagine a cross, with Germany up north, Spain to the south, France to the west, and Italy to the East. In the heart of the cross lies the imaginary land that comprises the Realm and the Domain.

The weather is an enchanted microcosm, with a greater range of temperature contained within a smaller area than in its counterpart in our own reality, continental Europe. The Realm is a cold land, especially the Kingdom of Lethe, with harsh winter in the north and a mild summer. The southern portions of Styx and Morphaea are temperate, with milder winters and hot summers. Meanwhile, the Domain is hot and subtropical, with no snowfall except the temperate northern portion of Serenoa and the small northern tip of Balmue that borders with the Aepienne Mountain range.

The Renaissance warfare here portrayed takes full advantage of the complexities of a remarkable transition period between the brute force of the Middle Ages and the more sophisticated mixed warfare that followed, expanding the use of gunpowder and explosives, so that firearms are employed alongside plate armor, swords, and pole weapons, similar to the way it happened in our own reality.

The culture of the Realm and the Domain is an uneven mixture of French, Italian, Spanish, and German influences of the late Middle Ages and early Renaissance. The language spoken is Latin-based "Romance," and the linguistics are also a mixture of the same.

Other minor liberties taken include the referral to some physical parcels of land as "Dukedom" as opposed to the correct term "Duchy." Royal and noble titles, ranks, and their terminology are similar, but not the exact equivalents of our own historical reality.

And now, please see the next page for a list of all the character names with a pronunciation key.

List of Characters
(Dramatis Personae)

With Pronunciation Key

Death, Lord of the Keep of the Northern Forest

Village of Oarclaven (Lethe) (Oh-ahr-CLAY-ven)
Persephone (Per-SEH-phonee) or **Percy** (PUR-see) **Ayren** (EYE-Ren), middle daughter
Parabelle (Pah-rah-BELL) or **Belle** (Bell) **Ayren**, eldest daughter
Patriciana (Pah-tree-see-AHNA) or **Patty** (PEH-dee) **Ayren**, youngest daughter
Niobea (Nee-oh-BEH-ah) **Ayren**, their mother
Alann (Ah-LAHN) **Ayren**, their father
Bethesia (Beth-EH-zee-ah) **Ayren**, their grandmother
Johuan (Joh-HWAN) **Ayren**, their grandfather
Guel (Goo-EHL) **Ayren**, their uncle from Fioren (south of Letheburg)
Jack Rosten (ROS-ten), villager
Jules (JOOL-z), Jack's second son, promised to Jenna Doneil
Father **Dibue** (Dee-B'YOU), village priest
Nicholas (NIH-koh-luss) **Doneil** (Doh-NEYL), village butcher
Marie (Muh-REE) **Doneil**, his wife
Faith Groaden (GROW-den), village girl
Mister **Jaquard** (Zhah-KARD), villager
Uncle **Roald** (ROH-uld), villager, the Ayrens' neighbor across the street.
Bettie (BEH-tee), village girl

Kingdom of Lethe (LEH-thee) *(Realm)*
The Prince Heir **Roland** (Roh-LUND) **Osenni** (Oh-SYEN-nee) of Lethe
The Princess **Lucia** (Liu-SEE-ah) **Osenni** of Lethe
Queen Mother **Andrelise** (Un-dreh-LEEZ) **Osenni**
Prince **John-Meryl** (JON MEH-reel) **Osenni**, son and heir of the Prince.

Dukedom of Chidair (Chee-DEHR) *(Lethe)*
Duke **Hoarfrost, Ian Chidair** of Lethe
Lord **Beltain** (Bell-TEYN) **Chidair** of Lethe, his son, the black knight
Rivour (Ree-VOOR), Beltain's old valet
Father **Orweil** (Or-WAIL), Chidair family chapel priest
Riquar (Reek-WAHR), Beltain's man-a-arms
Laurent (Loh-RENT), pennant bearer of Chidair
Annie, girl in the forest

Dukedom of Goraque (Gor-AH-k) *(Lethe)*
Duke **Vitalio** (Vee-TAH-lee-oh) **Goraque** of Lethe

The Silver Court (Realm)
The Emperor **Josephuste** (Jo-zeh-FOOS-teh) **Liguon** (Lee-G'WON) **II** of the Realm
The Empress **Justinia** (Joo-STEE-nee-ah) **Liguon**
The Infanta **Claere** (KLEH-r) **Liguon,** the Grand Princess
Lady **Milagra** (Mee-LAH-grah) **Rinon** (Ree-NOHN), the Infanta's First Lady-in-Attendance
Marquis **Rinon** of Morphaea, her father
Lady **Selene** (Seh-LEHN) **Jenevais** (Zheh-neh-VAH-is), Lady-in-Attendance, of Lethe
Lady **Floricca** (FLOH-ree-kah) **Grati** (GRAH-tee), Lady-in-Attendance, of Styx
Lady **Liana** (Lee-AH-nah) **Crusait** (Kroo-SAH-eet), Lady-in-Attendance, of Morphaea
Lady **Alis** (Ah-LEE-s) **Denear** (Deh-ne-AHR), Lady-in-Attendance, of Lethe
Baron **Carlo** (KAR-loh) **Irnolas** (Eer-noh-LAH-s), Imperial knight
Lord **Givard** (Ghee-VAHR-d) **Mariseli** (Mah-ree-SEH-lee), Imperial Knight
Doctor **Belquar** (Behl-KWAH-r), head Imperial physician
Doctor **Hartel** (Hahr-TEH-l), Imperial physician

Kingdom of Styx (STEEK-s) *(Realm)*
King **Augustus** (Uh-GUS-tus) **Ixion** (EEK-see-ohn) of Styx
King **Claudeis** (Kloh-DEH-ees) **Ixion** of Styx, deceased
Queen **Rea** (REH-ah) **Ixion** of Styx, deceased
Marquis **Vlau** (V'LAH-oo) **Fiomarre** (F'yoh-MAH-r) of Styx
Micul (Mee-KOOL) **Fiomarre** of Styx, Vlau's father
Ebrai (Eh-BRAH-ee) **Fiomarre**, Vlau's older brother
Celen (Seh-LEH-n) **Fiomarre**, Vlau's younger brother
Marquise **Eloise** (Eh-loh-EEZ) **Fiomarre**, Vlau's mother, deceased
Oleandre (Oh-leh-AHN-dr) **Fiomarre**, Vlau's younger sister
Lady **Ignacia** (Eeg-NAY-shuh) **Chitain** (Chee-TAY-n), of Styx/Balmue

Kingdom of Morphaea (Mohr-FEH-ah) *(Realm)*
King **Orphe** (Or-FEH) **Geroard** (Geh-roh-AHR-d) of Morphaea
Duke **Claude** (KLOH-d) **Rovait** (Roh-VEY-t) of Morphaea
Andre (Ahn-DREH) **Eldon** (Ehl-DOH-n), the Duke of **Plaimes** (PLEY-m's), of Morphaea
Duchess **Christiana** (Khree-stee-AH-nah) **Rovait** of Morphaea
Countess **Jain** (JEY-n) **Lirabeau** (Lee-rah-BOH) of Morphaea
Lady **Amaryllis** (Ah-mah-REE-liss) **Roulle** (ROOL), of Morphaea
Lord **Nathan** (NEY-th'n) **Woult** (WOOL-t), of Morphaea

The Road
Grial (Gree-AHL), witch woman from **Letheburg** (LEH-thee-b'rg)
Ronna (ROHN-nuh) **Liet** (LEE-eh-t), Innkeeper at **Tussecan** (TUSS-see-kahn), Grial's cousin
Mrs. **Beck** (BEH-k), cook at Ronna's Inn
Jenna (JEH-nuh) **Doneil** (Doh-NEY-l), butcher's daughter from Oarclaven
Flor (FLOH-r) **Murel** (M'you-REH-l), baker's daughter from Oarclaven
Gloria (GLOH-ree-ah) **Libbin** (LEE-bin), blacksmith's daughter from Oarclaven
Emilie (Eh-mee-LEE) **Bordon** (Bohr-DOHN), swineherd's daughter from south of Oarclaven
Sibyl (SEE-beel), tailor's daughter from Letheburg
Regata (Reh-GAH-tah), merchant's daughter from Letheburg
Lizabette (Lee-zah-BET) **Crowlé** (Krow-LEH), teacher's daughter from Duarden (Doo-AHR-dehn)
Catrine (Kaht-REEN), sister of Niosta, from south of Letheburg
Niosta (Nee-OHS-tuh), sister of Catrine, from south of Letheburg
Marie (Mah-REE), girl from **Fioren** (F'YOH-rehn), originally from the Kingdom of **Serenoa** (Seh-REH-noh-ah) (Domain)

The Sapphire Court (Domain)
The Sovereign, **Rumanar** (Roo-mah-NAH-r) **Avalais** (Ah-vah-LAH-ees) of the Domain

Kingdom of Balmue (Bahl-MOO) *(Domain)*
King **Clavian** (Klah-vee-AHN) **Sestial** (Ses-tee-AH-l) of Balmue
Marquis **Nuor** (Noo-OHR) **Alfre** (Ahl-FREH), ambassador of Balmue, Peer of the Domain
Viscount **Halronne** (Hal-RONN) **Deupris** (Deh-oo-PREE), Peer of the Domain

New Characters Introduced in Cobweb Empire

Kingdom of Lethe (Realm)
Carlinne (Kahr-LEEN) **Ayren**, wife of Guel, in Fioren
Martin (MAHR-tin) **Ayren**, Percy's cousin in Fioren
Mistress **Saronne** (Sah-RONN), tavern proprietress in Duarden
André (Ahn-DREH) **Saronne**, young boy, her son, dead, in Duarden
Jared (JEH-red) **Gaisse** (Gah-EESS), dead man in Duarden
Hendrick (HEN-drik), dead man in Duarden
Faeline (Fey-LEEN), girl in Chidair Keep
Jacques (ZHAHK) / **Jack**, the black knight's horse

Village of Oarclaven (Lethe)
Martha (MAR-thuh) **Poiron** (Poy-ROHN), old village woman
Rosaide (Ro-ZAH-eed) **Vellerin** (Vel-leh-REEN), village gossip

Kingdom of Tanathe (Tah-nah-theh) *(Domain)*
Flavio (FLAH-vee-oh) **San Quellenne** (SAHN Kweh-LENN), young boy on the beach
Jelavie (Zhe-lah-VEE) San Quellenne, his older sister on the beach

Kingdom of Solemnis (Soh-LEM-niss) *(Domain)*
King **Frederick** (Freh-deh-REEK) **Ourin** (Oo-REEN) of Solemnis
Duke **Raulle** (Rah-UHL) **Deotetti** (Deh-oh-TET-tee) of Solemnis
Duchess **Beatrice** (Beh-ah-TRISS) **Deotetti** (deceased, undead), wife of the Duke Deotetti

Kingdom of Balmue (Domain)
Count **Lecrant** (Leh-CRAH-nt) **D'Arvu** (D'AHR-voo) of Balmue
Countess **Arabella** (Ah-rah-BEL-lah) **D'Arvu** of Balmue
Lady **Leonora** (Leh-oh-NOH-rah) **D'Arvu** of Balmue, their daughter
Lady **Sidonie** (See-doh-NEE), young lady playing in the fields in Elysium
Valentio (Vah-LEN-tee-oh), young gentleman in the fields in Elysium

The Sapphire Court (Domain)
Quentin (KWEN-tin) **Loirre** (Looh-AHR), spy in the service of the Sovereign
Marie-Louise (Mah-REE-Loo-EEZ), maiden in the cobweb chamber
Lily (LEE-lee), maiden in the cobweb chamber
Beatrice (Beh-ah-TRISS), maiden in the cobweb chamber
Lady **Melinoë** (Meh-lee-NOH-eh) **Avalais**, daughter of the Sovereign
Thesmos (THES-moss), the Goddess of Tradition
Trovadii (Troh-VAH-dee-ee), the loyal special army of the Sovereign
Field Marshal **Claude** (CLOD) **Maetra** (Mah-EH-trah) from Tanathe, commanding the First Army of the Trovadii
Field Marshal **Matteas** (Maht-TEH-ahs) **Quara** (Koo-AH-ruh) from Balmue, commanding the Second Army
Field Marshal **Edmunde** (Ehd-MOOND) **Vaccio** (VAH-chee-oh) from Solemnis, commanding the Third Army
Graccia (GRAH-chee-ah), personal maidservant of the Sovereign
Diril (DEE-rihl), secret surveillance agent, of unknown affiliation

About the Author

Vera Nazarian immigrated to the USA from the former USSR as a kid, sold her first story at the age of 17, and since then has published numerous works in anthologies and magazines, and has seen her fiction translated into eight languages.

She made her novelist debut with the critically acclaimed arabesque "collage" novel *Dreams of the Compass Rose*, followed by epic fantasy about a world without color, *Lords of Rainbow*. Her novella *The Clock King and the Queen of the Hourglass* from PS Publishing (UK) with an introduction by **Charles de Lint** made the *Locus* Recommended Reading List for 2005. Her debut short fiction collection *Salt of the Air*, with an introduction by **Gene Wolfe**, contains the 2007 Nebula Award-nominated "The Story of Love." Other work includes the 2008 Nebula Award-nominated, self-illustrated baroque fantasy novella *The Duke in His Castle*, science fiction collection *After the Sundial* (2010), self-illustrated Supernatural **Jane Austen** Series parodies *Mansfield Park and Mummies* (2009), *Northanger Abbey and Angels and Dragons* (2010), *Pride and Platypus: Mr. Darcy's Dreadful Secret* (2012), *The Perpetual Calendar of Inspiration* (2010), and a parody of paranormal love and relationships advice *Vampires are from Venus, Werewolves are from Mars* (2012).

Vera recently relocated from Los Angeles to the East Coast. She lives in a small town in Vermont, and uses her Armenian sense of humor and her Russian sense of suffering to bake conflicted pirozhki and make art.

In addition to being a writer and award-winning artist, she is also the publisher of Norilana Books.

Official website:
www.veranazarian.com

CPSIA information can be obtained at www.ICGtesting.com
Printed in the USA
LVOW08s2050120416

483242LV00008B/1080/P